"THESE BE ALL THE CREW OF OUR PRIZE?" CAPTAIN CORROBOC MADE EYE CONTACT WITH EACH OF HIS OWN CREW IN TURN.

"A brave bunch you are. A bloodthirsty, death-dealing collection . . . of infants!" His tail quivered with anger. "Infants, the lot of you!" The cutthroats were completely cowed by this battered green parrot.

"Four against nearly a hundred, was it? A fine lot you are!" He cocked his head sideways to gaze at the prisoners. "Now then. Where be you four bound?"

"Just a few days out from Tailaroam," Mudge volunteered ingratiatingly. "We were just on a little fishin' trip . . ."

The wooden leg was a blur. It caught the otter between his short legs. Mudge turned green as he grabbed himself and collapsed on the deck. Corroboc eyed him indifferently.

"The Emir of Ezon has a tradition of employing eunuchs to guard his palace. I haven't decided what to do with any of you yet, but one more lie like that and you'll find yourself a candidate for the knife o' the ship's doctor . . ."

ALAN DEAN FOSTER

The Day
of the Dissonance

Spellsinger Volume Three

ORBIT

An *Orbit* Book

Copyright © 1984 by Thranx, Inc.

The moral right of the author has been asserted.

*All characters in this publication are fictitious and
any resemblance to real persons, living or dead,
is purely coincidental.*

First published in the US by Warner Books Inc.

This edition published in 1985 by Futura Publications
Reprinted 1986, 1987, 1988, 1990
Reprinted in Orbit 1992, 1993 (three times), 1994 (twice)

ISBN 1 85723 143 0

Printed in England by Clays Ltd, St Ives plc

Orbit
A Division of
Little, Brown and Company (UK)
Brettenham House
Lancaster Place
London WC2E 7EN

For my cousin Adam Carroll,
An idle evening's read to sandwich in between
Business Week and *Forbes*.
With much affection.

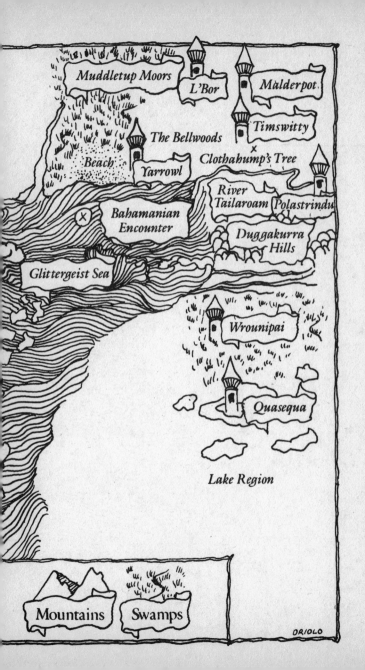

Muddletup Moors

L'Bor

Malderpot

Timswitty

The Bellwoods

x

Clothahump's Tree

Beach

Yarrowl

River
Tailaroam

Polastrindu

x

Bahamanian
Encounter

Duggakurra
Hills

Glittergeist Sea

Wrounipai

Quasequa

Lake Region

Mountains

Swamps

ORIOLO

I

"I'm dying," Clothahump wheezed. The wizard glanced to his left. "I'm dying and you stand there gawking like a virginal adolescent who's just discovered that his blind date is a noted courtesan. With your kind of help I'll never live to see my three-hundredth birthday."

"With your kind of attitude it's a wonder you've managed to live this long." Jon-Tom was more than a little irritated at his mentor. "Listen to yourself: two weeks of nonstop griping and whining. You know what you are, turtle of a wizardly mien? You're a damned hypochondriac."

Clothahump's face did not permit him much of a frown, but he studied the tall young human warily. "What is that? It sounds vaguely like a swear word. Don't toy with me, boy, or it will go hard on you. What is it? Some magic word from your own world?"

"More like a medical word. It's a descriptive term, not a threat. It refers to someone who thinks they're sick all the time, when they're not."

"Oh, so I'm imagining that my head is fragmenting, is that what you're saying?" Jon-Tom resisted the urge to

1

reply, sat his six-feet-plus frame down near the pile of pillows that served the old turtle for a bed.

Not for the first time he wondered at the number of spacious rooms the old oak tree encompassed. There were more alcoves and chambers and tunnels in that single trunk than in a termite's hive.

He had to admit, though, that despite his melodramatic moans and wails, the wizard didn't look like himself. His plastron had lost its normal healthy luster, and the old eyes behind the granny glasses were rheumy with tears from the pain. Perhaps he shouldn't have been so abrupt. If Clothahump couldn't cure himself with his own masterly potions and spells, then he was well and truly ill.

"I know what I am," Clothahump continued, "but what of you? A fine spellsinger you've turned out to be."

"I'm still learning," Jon-Tom replied defensively. He fingered the duar slung over his shoulder. The peculiar instrument enabled him to sing spells, to make magic through the use of song. One might think it a dream come true for a young rock guitarist-cum-law student, save for the fact that he didn't seem to have a great deal of control over the magic he made.

Since the onslaught of Clothahump's pains, Jon-Tom had sung two dozen songs dealing with good health and good feelings. None had produced the slightest effect with the exception of his spirited rendition of the Beach Boys' "Good Vibrations." That bit of spellsinging caused Clothahump to giggle uncontrollably, sending powders and potions flying and cracking his glasses.

Following that ignominious failure, Jon-Tom kept his hands off the duar and made no further attempts to cure the wizard.

"I didn't really mean to imply that you're faking it," he added apologetically. "It's just that I'm as frustrated as you are."

Clothahump nodded, his breath coming in short, labored

gasps. His poor respiration was a reflection of the constant pain he was suffering, as was his general weakness.

"I did the best I could," Jon-Tom murmured.

"I know you did, my boy. I know you did. As you say, there is much yet for you to learn, many skills still to master."

"I'm just bulling my way through. Half the time I pick the wrong song and the other half it has the wrong result. What else can I do?"

Clothahump looked up sharply. "There is one chance for me, lad. There is a medicine which can cure what ails me now. Not a spell, not a magic. A true medicine."

Jon-Tom rose from the edge of the pile of pillows. "I think I'd better be going. I haven't practiced yet today and I need to . . ."

Clothahump moaned in pain and Jon-Tom hesitated, feeling guilty. Maybe it was a genuine moan and maybe it wasn't, but it had the intended effect.

"You *must* obtain this medicine for me, my boy. I can't trust the task to anyone else. Evil forces are afoot."

Jon-Tom sighed deeply, spoke resignedly. "Why is it whenever you want something, whether it's help making it to the bathroom or a snack or someone to go on a dangerous journey for you, that evil forces are always afoot?"

"You ever see an evil force, boy?"

"Not in the flesh, no."

"Evil forces always go afoot. They're lousy fliers."

"That's not what I meant."

"Doesn't matter what you meant, my boy. You have to run this errand for me. That's all it is, a little errand."

"Last time you asked me to help you run an errand we ended up with the fate of civilization at stake."

"Well, this time it's only my fate that hangs in the balance." His voice shrank to a pitiful whisper. "You wouldn't want me to die, would you?"

"No," Jon-Tom admitted. "I wouldn't."

"Of course you wouldn't. Because if I die it means the end of your chances to return to your own world. Because only I know the necessary, complicated, dangerous spell that can send you back. It is in your own interest to see that I remain alive and well."

"I know, I know. Don't rub it in."

"Furthermore," the wizard went on, pressing his advantage, "you are partly to blame for my present discomfort."

"What!" Jon-Tom whirled on the bed. "I don't know what the hell you've got, Clothahump, but I certainly didn't give it to you."

"My illness is compounded of many factors, not the least of which are my current awkward living conditions."

Jon-Tom frowned and leaned on his long ramwood staff. "What are you talking about?"

"Ever since we returned from the great battle at the Jo-Troom Gate my daily life has been one unending litany of misery and frustration. All because you had to go and turn my rude but dutiful famulus Pog into a phoenix. Whereupon he promptly departed my service for the dubious pleasures his falcon ladylove could bestow on him."

"Is it my fault you've had a hard time replacing him? That's hardly a surprise, considering the reputation you got for mistreating Pog."

"I did not mistreat Pog," the wizard insisted. "I treated him exactly as an apprentice should be treated. It's true that I had to discipline him from time to time. That was due to his own laziness and incompetence. All part of the learning process." Clothahump straightened his new glasses.

"Pog spread the details of your teaching methods all over the Bellwoods. But I thought the new famulus you finally settled on was working out okay."

"Ha! It just goes to show what can happen when you don't read the fine print on someone's résumé. It's too late now. I've made him my assistant and am bound to him, as he is to me."

"What's wrong? I thought he was brilliant."

"He can be. He can be studious, efficient, and eager to learn."

"Sounds good to me."

"Unfortunately, he has one little problem."

"What kind of problem?"

Clothahump's reply was interrupted by a loud, slurred curse from the room off to the left. The wizard gestured with his head toward the doorway, looked regretful.

"Go see for yourself, my boy, and understand then what a constant upset my life has become."

Jon-Tom considered, then shrugged and headed under the arched passageway toward the next chamber, bending low to clear the sill. He was so much taller than most of the inhabitants of this world that his height was an ever-present problem.

Something shattered and there was another high-pitched curse. He held his ramwood staff protectively in front of him as he emerged into the storeroom.

It was as spacious as Clothahump's bedroom and the other chambers which somehow managed to coexist within the trunk of the old oak. Pots, tins, crates, and beakers full of noisome brews were carefully arranged on shelves and workbenches. Several bottles lay in pieces on the floor.

Standing, or rather weaving, in the midst of the breakage was Sorbl, Clothahump's new famulus. The young great horned owl stood slightly over three feet tall. He wore a thin vest and a brown and yellow kilt of the Ule Clan.

He spotted Jon-Tom, waved cheerily, and fell over on his beak. As he struggled to raise himself on flexible wingtips, Jon-Tom saw that the vast yellow eyes were exquisitely bloodshot.

"Hello, Sorbl. You know who I am?"

The owl squinted at him as he climbed unsteadily to his feet, staggered to port, and caught himself on the edge of the workbench.

"Shure I remember you," he said thickly. "You...you're that spielsunger...spoilsanger...."

"Spellsinger," Jon-Tom said helpfully.

"Thas what I said. You're that what I said from another world that the master brought through to hulp him against the Pleated Filk."

"The master is not feeling well." He put his staff aside. "And you're not looking too hot either."

"Hooo, me?" The owl looked indignant, walked away from the bench wavering only slightly. "I am perfectly fine, thank you." He glanced back at the bench. "Is just that I was looking for a certain bottle."

"What bottle?"

"Not marked, thish one." Sorbl looked conspiratorial and winked knowingly with one great bloodshot eye. "Medicinal liquid. Not for his ancientness in there. *My* bottle," he finished, suddenly belligerent. "Nectar."

"Nectar? I thought owls liked mice."

"What?" said the outraged famulus. For an instant Jon-Tom had forgotten where he was. The rodents hereabouts were as intelligent and lively as any of the other citizens of this world. "If I tried to take a bite out of a mouse, his relatives would come string me up. I'll stick to small lizards and snakishes. Listen," he continued more softly, "it's hard working for this wizard. I need a lil' lubrication now and then."

"You get any more lubricated," Jon-Tom observed distastefully, "and your brains are going to slide out your ass."

"Nonshensh. I am in complete control of myself." He turned back toward the bench, staggered over to the edge, and commenced a minute inspection of the surface with eyes that should have been capable of spotting an ant from a hundred yards away. At the moment, however, those huge orbs were operating at less than maximum efficiency.

Jon-Tom shook his head in disgust and returned to the wizard's bedside.

"Well," asked Clothahump meaningfully, "what is your opinion of my new famulus?"

"I think I see what you're driving at. I didn't notice any of the qualities you said he possesses. I'm pretty sure he was drunk."

"Really?" said Clothahump dryly. "What a profound observation. We'll make a perceptive spellsinger out of you yet. He is like that too much of the time, my boy. I am blessed with a potentially brilliant famulus, a first-rate, worthy assistant. Sadly, Sorbl is also a lush. Do you know that I have to make him take a cart into town to buy supplies because every time he tries to fly in he ends up by running head-first into a tree and the local farmers have to haul him back to me in a wagon? Do you have any idea how embarrassing that is for the world's greatest wizard?"

"I can imagine. Can't you cure him? I'd think an anti-inebriation spell would be fairly simple and straight-forward."

"It is a vicious circle, my boy. Were I not so sick I could do so, but as it stands I cannot concentrate. Past two hundred the mind loses some of its resilience. I tried just that last week. All those methyl ethyl bethels in the spell are difficult enough to get straight when you're at the top of your form. Sick as I was, I must have transposed an -yl somewhere. Made him throw up for three days. Cured his drinking, but made him so ill the only way he could cure himself was by getting falling-down-drunk again.

"I must have that medicine, lad, so that I can function properly again. Otherwise I'm liable to try some complex spell, slip an incantation, and end up with something dangerous in my pentagram. It's hard enough making sure that idiot in there passes me the proper powders. Once he substituted lettuce for liverwort, and I ended up with a ten-foot-tall saber-toothed rabbit. Took me two hasty re-traction spells to bunny it down."

"Why don't you just conjure the stuff up?"

"I do not possess the necessary ingredients," Clothahump

explained patiently. "If I did, I could just take them, now, couldn't I?"

"Beats me. I've seen you make chocolate out of garbage."

"Medicine is rather more specific in its requirements. Everything must be so precise. You can make milk chocolate, bittersweet chocolate, white chocolate, semisweet chocolate: it's still all chocolate. Alter the composition of a medicinal spell ever so slightly and you might end up with a deadly poison. No, it must be brought whole and ready, and you must bring it to me, my boy." He reached out with a trembling hand. Jon-Tom moved close, sitting down again on the edge of the soft bed.

"I know I did a bad thing when I reached out into the beyond and plucked you hence from your own comfortable world, but the need was great. In the end, you vindicated my judgment, though in a fashion that could not have been foreseen." He adjusted his glasses. "You proved yourself in spite of what everyone thought."

"Mostly by accident." Jon-Tom realized that the wizard was flattering him in order to break down his resistance to making the journey. At the same time he felt himself succumbing to the flattery.

"It need not be by accident any longer. Work at your new profession. Study hard, practice your skills, and heed my advice. You can be more than a man in this world. I don't know what you might have been in your own, but here you have the potential to be a master. *If* you can wrestle your strengths and talent under control."

"With your instruction, of course."

"Why not learn from the best?" said Clothahump with typical immodesty. "In order for me to train you I need many years. One does not master the arcane arts of spellsinging in a day, a week, a year. If you do not fetch this medicine that can cure this bedamned affliction, I will not be around much longer to help you.

"I need only a small quantity. It will fit easily into a

pocket of those garish trousers or that absurd purple shirt that foppish tailor Carlemot fashioned for you."

"It's not purple, it's indigo," Jon-Tom muttered, looking down to where it tucked into the pants. His iridescent green lizard-skin cape hung on a wall hook. "From what I've seen, this qualifies as subdued attire here."

"Go naked if you will, but go you must."

"All right, all right! Haven't you made me feel guilty enough?"

"I sincerely hope so," the wizard murmured.

"I don't know how I let you talk me into these things."

"You have the misfortune to be a decent person, a constant burden in any world. You suffer from knowing right from wrong."

"No I don't. If I knew what was right, I'd be long gone from this tree. But you did take me in, help me out, even if you did use me for your own ends. Not that I feel used. You used everyone for your own ends."

"We saved the world," Clothahump demurred. "Not bad ends."

"You're also right about my being stuck here unless you can work the spell to send me home someday. So I suppose I have no choice but to go after this special medicine. It's not by any chance available from the apothecary in Lynchbany?"

"I fear not."

"What a lucky guess on my part."

"Tch. Sarcasm in one so young is bad for the liver." Clothahump raised himself slowly, turned to the end table that doubled as a bedside desk. He scribbled with a quill pen on a piece of paper. A moment passed, he cursed, put a refill cartridge in the quill, and resumed writing.

When he finished, he rolled the paper tight, inserted it into a small metal tube which hung from a chain, and handed it to Jon-Tom.

"Here is the formula," he said reverently. "She who is to fill it will know its meaning."

Jon-Tom nodded, took the chain, and hung it around his neck. The tube was cool against his chest.

"That is all you need to know."

"Except how to find this magician, or druggist, or whatever she is."

"A store. Nothing more." Clothahump's reassuring tone immediately put Jon-Tom on his guard. "The Shop of the Aether and Neither. It lies in the town of Crancularn."

"I take it this Crancularn isn't a hop, skip, and a jump from Lynchbany?"

"Depends on your method of locomotion, but for most mortals, I would say not. It lies well to the south and west of the Bellwoods."

Jon-Tom made a face. He'd been around enough to have picked up some knowledge of local geography. "There isn't anything well to the southwest of here. The Bellwoods run down to the River Tailaroam which flows into . . ." he stopped. "Crancularn's a village on the shore of the Glittergeist?"

Clothahump looked the other way. "Uh, not exactly, my boy. Actually it lies on the other side."

"The other side of the river?"

"Noooo. The other side of the ocean."

Jon-Tom threw up his hands in despair. "And that's the last straw."

"Actually, lad, it's only the first straw. There are many more to pass before you reach Crancularn. But reach it you must," he finished emphatically, "or I will surely perish from the pain, and any chance you have of returning home will perish with me."

"But I don't even know how big the Glittergeist is."

"Not all that big, as oceans go." Clothahump strove to sound reassuring. "It can be crossed in a few weeks. All you have to do is book passage on one of the many ships that trade between the mouth of the Glittergeist and distant Snarken."

"I've heard of Snarken. Big place?"

"A most magnificent city. So I have been told, never having visited there myself. Grander than Polastrindu. You'd find it fascinating."

"And dangerous."

"No journey is worthwhile unless it is dangerous, but we romanticize. I do not see any reason for anticipating trouble. You are a tourist, nothing more, embarked on a voyage of rest, relaxation, and discovery."

"Sure. From what I've seen of this world it doesn't treat tourists real well."

"That should not trouble an accomplished spellsinger like you."

The wizard was interrupted by the sound of another crash from the nearby storeroom, followed by a few snatches of drunken song.

"You also have your ramwood staff for protection, and you no longer are a stranger to our ways. Think of it as a holiday, a vacation."

"Why do I have this persistent feeling you're not telling me everything?"

"Because you are a pessimist, my boy. I do not criticize. That is a healthy attitude for one embarked on a career in magic. I am not sending you after trouble this time. We do not go to battle powerful invaders from the east. I am asking you only to go and fetch a handful of powder, a little medicine. That is all. No war awaits. True, it is a long journey, but there is no reason why it should be an arduous one.

"You leave from here, proceed south to the banks of the Tailaroam, book passage downstream. At its mouth where the merchant ships dock you, board a comfortable vessel heading for Snarken. Thence overland to Crancularn. A short jaunt, I should imagine."

"Imagine? You mean you don't know how far it is from Snarken to Crancularn?"

"Not very far."

"For someone who deals in exact formulas and spells,

you can be disconcertingly nonspecific at times, Clothahump.''

"And you can be unnecessarily verbose,'' the turtle shot
back.

"Sorry. My pre-law training. Never use one word where
five will fit. Maybe I would've ended up a lawyer instead
of a heavy-metal bass player.''

"You'll never know if you don't return to your own
world, which you cannot do unless . . .''

"I know, I know,'' Jon-Tom said tiredly. "Unless I
make the trip to this Crancularn and bring back the
medicine you need. Okay, so I'm stuck.''

"I would rather know that you had undertaken this
journey with enthusiasm, willingly, out of a desire to help
one who only wishes you well.''

"So would I, but you'll settle for my going because I
haven't got any choice, won't you?''

"Yes,'' said Clothahump thoughtfully, "I expect that I
will.''

II

He wasn't in the best frame of mind the morning he set off. Not that anything was keeping him occupied elsewhere, he told himself sourly. He had no place in this world and certainly no intention of setting himself up in practice as a professional spellsinger.

For one thing, that would put him in direct competition with Clothahump. Although the wizard thought well of him, Jon-Tom didn't think Clothahump would take kindly to the idea. For another, he hadn't mastered his odd abilities to the point where he could guarantee services for value received, and might never achieve that degree of expertise. He preferred to regard his spellsinging as a talent of last resort, choosing to rely instead on his staff and his wits to keep him out of trouble.

In fact, the duar provided him with far more pleasure when he simply played it for fun, just like his battered old Fender guitar back home. Now he played it to ease his mind as he walked into town, strumming a few snatches of very unmagical Neil Diamond while wishing he had Ted Nugent's way with strings. At the same time he had to be careful in his selections. Diamond was innocuous enough.

13

If he tried a little Nugent—say, "Cat Scratch Fever" or "Scream Dream"—there was no telling what he might accidentally conjure up.

At least the weather favored his journey. It was early spring. Deep within the Bellwoods, so named for the bell-shaped leaves which produced a tinkling sound when the wind blew through them, there was the smell of dew and new blossoms on the air. Glass butterflies flew everywhere, their stained-glass wings sending shafts of brilliant color twinkling over the ground. Peppermint bees striped in psychedelic hues darted among the flowers.

One hitched a ride on his indigo shirt. Perhaps it thought he was some kind of giant ambulatory flower. Jon-Tom examined it with interest. Instead of the yellow-and-black pattern he was accustomed to, his visitor's abdomen was striped pink, lemon yellow, orange, chocolate brown, and bright blue. Man and insect regarded one another thoughtfully for a long moment. Deciding he was neither a source of pollen or enlightenment, the bee droned off in search of sweeter forage.

Lynchbany Towne was unchanged from the first time Jon-Tom had seen it, on that rainy day when he, a stranger to this world, had entered it accompanied by Mudge the otter. It was Mudge he sought now. He had no intention of striking out across the Glittergeist alone, no matter how much confidence Clothahump vested in him. There was still far too much of the ways and customs of this place he was ignorant of.

Mudge's knowledge was of the practical and non-intellectual variety. Too, nothing was more precious to the otter than his own skin. He was sort of a furry walking alarm, ready to jump or take whatever evasive action the situation dictated at the barest suggestion of danger. Jon-Tom intended to use him the way the allies had used pigeons in World War I to detect the presence of poison gas.

Mudge would have considered the analogy unflattering,

but Jon-Tom didn't care what the otter thought. Despite his questionable morals and wavering sense of loyalty, the otter had been a great help in the past and could be so again.

Luck wasn't with Jon-Tom, however. There was no sign of Mudge in the taverns he normally frequented, nor word of him in the eating establishments or gambling dens. He hadn't been seen in some time in any of his usual haunts.

Jon-Tom finally found mention of him in one of the more reputable rooming houses on the far side of town, where the stink from the central open sewer was less.

The concierge was an overweight koala in a bad mood. A carved pipe dangled from her lips as she scrubbed the floor near the entrance.

"Hay, I've seen him," she told Jon-Tom. Part of her right ear was missing, probably bitten off during a dispute with an irate customer.

"I'd laik to know where he gone to much as you, man. He skip away owing me half a week's rent. That not bad as some have dun me, but I work hahd to run this place and every silver counts."

"Only a few days' rent, is it?" Jon-Tom squatted to be at eye level with the koala. "You know where he is, don't you? You're feeding me some story old Mudge paid you to tell anyone who came looking for him because he paid you to do so, because he probably owes everyone *but* you."

She wrinkled her black nose and wiped her paws on her apron. Then she broke out in a wide grin. "You a clever one, you are, man, though strange of manner and talk."

"I'm not really from around here," Jon-Tom confessed. "Actually my home lies quite a distance from Lynchbany. Nor am I a creditor or bill collector. Mudge is my friend."

"Is he now?" She dropped her scrub brush in the pail of wash water and rose. Jon-Tom did likewise. She reached barely to his stomach. That wasn't unusual. Jon-Tom was something of a giant in this world where humans barely topped five and a half feet and many others stood shorter.

"So you his friend, hay? That make you sort of unique. I wasn't aware the otter had any friends. Only acquaintances and enemies."

"No matter. I am his friend, and I need to get in touch with him."

"What for?"

"I am embarked on a journey in the service of the' great wizard Clothahump."

"Ah, that old fraud."

"He's not a fraud. Haven't you heard of the battle for the Jo-Troom Gate?"

"Yea, yea, I heard, I heard." She picked up the bucket of wash water, the scrub brush sloshing around inside. "I also know you never believe everything you read in the papers. This journey you going on for him. It going be a hard one, where someone might get deaded?"

"Possibly."

"Hay, then I tell you where the otter is and you make sure he go with you?"

"That's the idea."

"Good! Then I tell you where he is. Because I tell you true, man, he owe me half a week's rent. I just don't want to tell anyone else because maybe they get to him before me. But this is better, much better. Worth a few days' rent."

"About that rent," Jon-Tom said, jiggling the purse full of gold Clothahump had given him to pay for his passage across the Glittergeist.

The concierge waved him off. "Hay nay, man. Just make sure he go with you on this dangerous journey. More better I dream of him roasting over some cannibal's spit in some far-off land. That will give me more pleasure than a few coins."

"As you wish, madame." Jon-Tom put the purse aside.

"Only, you must be sure promise to come back here someday and regale me with the gory details. For that I pay you myself."

"I'll be sure to make it my business," Jon-Tom said dryly. "Now, where might I find my friend?"

"Not here. North."

"Oglagia Towne?"

"Hay nay, farther west. In Timswitty."

"Timswitty," Jon-Tom repeated. "Thanks. You know what business he has there?"

She let out a short, sharp bark, a koalaish laugh. "Same business that otter he have any place he go: thievery, deception, debauchery, and drunkenness. I wager you find him easy enough you keep that in mind."

"I will. Tell me. I've never been north of Lynchbany. What's Timswitty like?"

She shrugged. "Like heah. Like Oglagia. Like any of the Bellwoods towns. Backward, crowded, primitive, but not bad if you willing stand up for your rights and work hard."

"Thank you, madame. You're sure I can't pay you anything for the information you've given me?"

"Keep you money and make you journey," she told him. "I look forward to hearing about the otter's slow and painful death upon you return."

"Don't hold your breath in expectation of his demise," Jon-Tom warned her as he turned to leave. "Mudge has a way of surviving in the damndest places."

"I know he do. He slip out of heah without me smelling his going. I tell you what. If he don't get himself killed on this journey of yours, you can pay me his back rent when you return."

"I'll do better than that, madame. I'll make him pay it himself, in person."

"Fair enough. You have good traveling, man."

"Good day to you too, madame."

Jon-Tom had no intention of walking all the way to Timswitty. Not since Clothahump had provided him with funds for transport. The local equivalent of a stagecoach was passing through Lynchbany, and he bought himself a seat on the boxy contraption. It was pulled by four hand-some horses and presided over by a couple of three-foot-tall chimpmunks who cursed like longshoremen. They wore dirty uniforms and scurried about, wrestling baggage and cartons into the rear of the stage.

Jon-Tom had the wrong notion of who was in charge, however. As he strolled past the team of four, one of the horses cocked an eye in his direction.

"Come on, bud, hurry it up. We haven't got all day."

"Sorry. The ticket agent told me you weren't leaving for another fifteen minutes."

The mare snorted. "That senile bastard. I don't know what the world's coming to when you can't rely on your local service people anymore."

"Tell me about it," said the stallion yoked to her. "Unfortunately we were born with hooves instead of hands, so we still have to hire slow-moving fools with small brains to handle business details for us."

"Right on, Elvar," said the stallion behind him.

The discussion continued until the stage left the depot.

"All aboard?" asked the mare second in harness. "Hold on to your seats, then."

The two chipmunks squatted in the rear along with the luggage, preening themselves and trying to catch their breath. There was no need for drovers, since the horses knew the way themselves. The chipmunks were loaders and unloaders and went along to see to the needs of the team, who, after all, did the real work of pulling the stage.

This would have been fine as far as Jon-Tom and the other passengers were concerned except that the horses had an unfortunate tendency to break into song as they galloped, and while their voices were strong and clear, not a one of them could carry a tune in a bucket. So the passengers were compelled to suffer a series of endless, screeching songs all the way through to Timswitty.

When one passenger had the temerity to complain, he was invited to get out and walk. There were two other unscheduled stops along the way as well, once when the team got hungry and stopped to graze a lush meadow through which the road conveniently cut, and again when the two mares got into a heated argument about just who boasted the daintier fetlocks.

It was dark when they finally pulled into Timswitty.

"Come on," snapped the lead stallion, "let's get a move on back there. Our stable's waiting. I know you're all stuck with only two legs, but that's no reason for loafing."

"Really!" One of the outraged travelers was an elegantly attired vixen. Gold chains twined through her tail, and her elaborate hat was badly askew over her ears from the jouncing the stage had undergone. "I have never been treated so rudely in my life! I assure you I shall speak to your line manager at first opportunity."

"You're talking to him, sister," said the stallion. "You got a complaint, you might as well tell me to my face." He looked her up and down. "Me, I think you ought to thank us for not charging you for the extra poundage."

"Well!" Her tail swatted the stallion across the snout as she turned and flounced away to collect her luggage.

Only the fact that his mate restrained him kept him from taking a bite out of that fluffy appendage.

"Watch your temper, Dreal," she told him. "It doesn't do to bite the paying freight. Rotten public relations."

"Bet all her relations have been public," he snorted, pawing the ground impatiently. "What's slowing up those striped rats back there? I need a rubdown and some sweet alfalfa."

"I know you do, dear," she said as she nuzzled his neck, "but you have to try and maintain a professional attitude, if only for the sake of the business."

"Yeah, I know," Jon-Tom overheard as he made his way toward the depot. "It's only that there are times when I think maybe we'd have been better off if we'd bought ourselves a little farm somewhere out in the country and hired some housemice and maybe a human or two to do the dirty work.''

He was the only one in the office. The fox and the other passengers already had destinations in mind.

"Can I help you?" asked the elderly marten seated behind the low desk. With his long torso and short waist, the clerk reminded Jon-Tom of Mudge. The marten was slimmer still, and instead of Mudge's jaunty cap and bright vest and pantaloons he wore dark shorts and a sleeveless white shirt, a visor to shade his eyes, and bifocals.

"I'm a stranger in town."

"I suspect you're a stranger everywhere," said the marten presciently.

Jon-Tom ignored the comment. "Where would a visitor go for a little harmless fun and entertainment in Timswitty?"

"Well now," replied the marten primly, "I am a family man myself. You might try the Golden Seal. They offer folksinging by many species and occasionally a string trio from Kolansor."

"You don't understand." Jon-Tom grinned insinuatingly. "I'm looking for a good time, not culture."

"I see." The marten sighed. "Well, if you will go down the main street to Born Lily Lane and follow the lane to its end, you will come to two small side streets leading off into separate cul-de-sacs. Take the north close. If the smell and noise isn't enough to guide you further, look for the small sign just above an oil lamp, the one with the carving of an Afghan on it."

"As in canine or cloth?"

The marten wet his lips. "The place is called the Elegant Bitch. No doubt you will find its pleasures suitable. I wouldn't know, of course. I am a family man."

"Of course," said Jon-Tom gravely. "Thanks."

As he made his solitary way down the dimly lit main street, he found himself wishing Talea was at his side. Talea of the flame-red hair and infinite resourcefulness. Talea of the blind courage and quick temper. Did he love her? He wasn't sure anymore. He thought so, thought she loved him in return. But she was too full of life to settle down as the wife of an itinerant spellsinger who had not yet managed to master his craft.

Not long after the battle of the Jo-Troom Gate, she had regretfully proposed they go their separate ways, at least for a little while. She needed time to think on serious matters and suggested he do likewise. It was hard on him. He did miss her. But there was the possibility she was simply too independent for any one man.

He held to his hopes, however. Perhaps someday she would tire of her wanderings and come back to him. There wasn't a thing he could do but wait.

As for Flor Quintera, the cheerleader he'd inadvertently brought into this world, she had turned out to be a major disappointment. Instead of being properly fascinated by him, it developed that she lusted after a career as a sword-wielding soldier of fortune and had gone off with Caz, the tall, suave rabbit with the Ronald Colman voice and sophisticated manners. Jon-Tom hadn't heard of them in months. Flor was a dream that had brought him back to reality, and fast.

At least this was a fit world in which to pursue dreams. At the moment, though, he was supposed to be pursuing medicine. He clung to that thought as he turned down the tiny side street.

True to the marten's information he heard sounds of singing and raucous laughter. But instead of a single small oil lamp there were big impressive ones flanking the door, fashioned of clear beveled crystal.

Above the door was a swinging sign showing a finely coiffed hound clad in feathers and jewels. She was gazing back over her furry shoulder with a distinctly come-hither look, and her hips were cocked rakishly.

There was a small porch. Standing beneath the rain shield, Jon-Tom knocked twice on the heavily oiled door. It was opened by a three-foot-tall mouse in a starched suit.

Sound flooded over Jon-Tom as the doormouse looked him over.

"Step inside and enjoy, sir," he finally said, moving aside.

Jon-Tom nodded and entered. The doormouse closed the door behind him.

He found himself in a parlor full of fine furniture and a wild assortment of creatures representing several dozen species. All were cavorting without a care as to who they happened to be matching up with. There were several humans in the group, men and women. They moved freely among their intelligent furry counterparts.

Jon-Tom noted the activity, listened to the lascivious dialogue, saw the movement of hands and paws, and suspected he had not entered a bar. No question what kind of place this was. He was still surprised, though he shouldn't have been. It was a logical place to look for Mudge.

Still, he didn't want to take the chance of embarrassing himself. First impressions could be wrong. He spoke to the doormouse.

"I beg your pardon, but this is a whorehouse, isn't it?"

The mouse's voice was surprisingly deep, rumbling out of the tiny gray body. "All kinds we get in here," he muttered dolefully, "all kinds. What did you think it was, jack? A library?"

"Not really. There aren't any books."

The doormouse showed sharp teeth in a smile. "Oh, we have books, too. With pictures. Lots of pictures, if that's to your taste, sir."

"Not right now." He was curious, though. Maybe later, after he'd found Mudge.

"You look like you've been a-traveling, sir. Would you like something to eat and drink?"

"Thanks, I'm not hungry. Actually, I'm looking for a friend."

"Everyone comes to the Elegant Bitch in search of a friend."

"You misunderstand. That's not the way I mean."

"Just tell me your ways, sir. We cater to all ways here."

"I'm looking for a buddy, an acquaintance," Jon-Tom said in exasperation. The doormouse had a one-track mind.

"Ah, now I understand. No divertissements, then? This isn't a meeting house, you know."

"You're a good salesman." Jon-Tom tried to placate him. "Maybe later. I have to say that you're the smallest pimp I've ever seen."

"I am not small and I am not a pimp," replied the doormouse with some dignity. "If you wish to speak to the madam . . ."

"Not necessary," Jon-Tom told him, though he wondered not only what she'd look like but what she'd be. "The fellow I'm after wears a peaked cap with a feather in it, a leather vest, carries a longbow with him everywhere he goes, and is an otter. Name of Mudge."

The doormouse preened a whisker, scratched behind one ear. For the first time Jon-Tom noticed the small earplugs. Made sense. Given the mouse's sensitivity to sound, he'd need the plugs to keep from going deaf while working amid the nonstop celebration.

"I recognize neither name nor attire, sir, but there is one otter staying with us currently. He would be in room twenty-three on the second floor."

"Great. Thanks." Jon-Tom almost ran into the mouse's outstretched palm. He placed a small silver piece there and saw it vanish instantly.

"Thank you, sir. If there is anything I can do for you after you have met with this possible friend, please let me know. My name is Whort and I'm the majordomo here."

"Maybe later," Jon-Tom assured him as he started up the carved stairway.

He had no intention of taking the doormouse up on his

offer. Not that he had anything against the house brand of
entertainment. His long separation from Talea plagued him
physically as well as mentally, but this wasn't the place to
indulge in any lingering fancies of the flesh. It looked
fancy and clean, but you never could tell where you might
pick up an interesting strain of VD, and not only the
human varieties. In the absence of modern medicine he
didn't want to have to count on curing a good dose of the
clap with a song or two.

So he restrained his libido as he mounted the second-
floor landing and hunted for the right door. He was
interrupted in his search by a sight that reminded him this
was a real place and not a drug-induced excursion into a
dreamland zoo.

A couple of creatures had passed him, and he'd paid
them no mind. Coming down the hall toward him now was
an exceptionally proportioned young woman in her early
twenties. She was barely five feet tall and wore only a
filmy peach-colored peignoir. The small pipe she smoked
did little to blur the image of prancing, bouncing femininity.

"Well, what are you staring at, tall-skinny-and-hand-
some?"

It occurred to Jon-Tom this was not intended as a
rhetorical question, and he mumbled a reply that got all
caught up in his tongue and teeth. Somehow he managed
to shamble past her. Only the fact that Clothahump lay
dying in his tree along with any chance Jon-Tom had of
returning home kept him moving. His head rotated like a
searchlight, and he followed the perfect vision with his
eyes until she'd disappeared down the stairs.

As he forced himself down the hall, that image lingered
on his retinas like a bright light. Sadly, he found the right
door and knocked gently, sparing a last sorrowful glance
for the now empty landing.

"Mudge?" He repeated the knock, was about to repeat
the call, when the door suddenly flew open, causing him to
step back hastily. Standing in the opening was a female

otter holding a delicate lace nightgown around her. Her eyebrows had been curled and painted, and the tips of her whiskers dipped in gold. She was sniffling, an act to which Jon-Tom attached no particular significance. Otters sniffled a lot.

She took one look at him before dashing past his bulk down the hallway, short legs churning.

Jon-Tom stared after her, was about to go in when a second fur of the night came out, accompanied by an equally distraught third otter. They followed their sister toward the stairs. Shaking his head, he entered the dark room.

Faint light flickered from a single chandelier. Golden shadows danced on the flocked wallpaper. Nothing else moved. Two curved mirrors on opposing walls ran from floor to ceiling. An elegant china washbasin rested on a chellow-wood dresser. The door to the john stood half-agape.

A wrought-iron bed decorated with cast grapevines and leaves stood against the far wall. The headboard curved slightly forward. A pile of sheets and pillows filled the bed, an eruption of fine linen. Jon-Tom guessed this was not the cheapest room in the house.

From within the silks and satins came a muffled but still familiar voice. "Is that you, Lisette? Are you comin' back to forgive me, luv? Wot I said, that were only a joke. Meant nothin' by it, I did."

"That would be the first time," Jon-Tom said coolly.

There was silence, then the pile of sheets stirred and a head emerged, black eyes blinking in the darkness. "Cor, I'm 'aving a bloody nightmare, I am! Too much bubbly."

"I don't know what you've had," Jon-Tom said as he moved toward the bed, "but this is no nightmare."

Mudge wiped at his eyes with the backs of his paws. "Right then, mate, it is no nightmare. You're too damned big to be a nightmare. Wot the 'ell are you doin' 'ere, anyways?"

"Looking for you."

"You picked the time for it." He vanished beneath the linens. "Where's me clothes?"

Jon-Tom turned, searched the shadows until he'd located the vest, cap, pants and boots. The oversized bow and quiver of arrows lay beneath the bed. He tossed the whole business onto the mattress.

"Here."

"Thanks, mate." The otter began to flow into the clothes, his movements short and fast. " 'Tis a providence, it is, wot brings you to poor ol' Mudge now."

"I don't know about that. You actually seem glad to see me. It's not what I expected."

Mudge looked hurt. "Wot, not 'appy to see an old friend? You pierce me to the quick. Now why wouldn't I be glad to see an old friend?"

Something funny going on here, Jon-Tom mused warily. Where were the otter's usual suspicious questions, his casual abusiveness?

As if to answer his questions the door burst inward. Standing there backlit by the light from the hall was a sight to give an opium eater pause.

The immensely overweight lady badger wore a bright red dress fringed with organdy ruffles. Rings dripped from her manicured fingers, and it was hard to believe that the massive gems that encircled her neck were real. They threw the light back into the room.

A few curious customers crowded in behind her as she raised a paw and pointed imperiously at the bed.

"*There* he is!" she growled.

"Ah, Madam Lorsha," said Mudge as he finished his dressing in a hurry, "I 'ave to compliment you on the facilities of your establishment."

"That will be the last compliment you ever give anyone, you deadbeat. Your ass is a rug." She snapped her fingers as she stepped into the room. "Tork."

Bending to pass under the sill was the largest intelligent warmlander Jon-Tom had yet encountered. It was a shock to see someone taller than himself. The grizzly rose at least seven and a half feet, wore black-leather pants and shirt. He also wore what appeared in the bad light to be heavy leather gloves. Their true nature was revealed all too quickly.

Now, Jon-Tom did not know precisely what had transpired in the elegant room or beyond its walls or between his furry friend who was slipping on his boots in a veritable frenzy and the badger who was clearly the owner of the house of ill repute, but he suspected the sight of the full-grown grizzly adjusting the brass knuckles over his immense paws did not bode well for the future.

"I understand your concern, luv," said Mudge as he casually recovered his bow and quiver, "but now that me mate's 'ere everything will be squared away."

"Will it, now?" she said. The grizzly stood rubbing one palm with a massive fist and grinning. His teeth were very white. The badger eyed Jon-Tom. "Does he mean to say that you'll pay his bill?"

"Pay his bill? What do you mean, pay his bill?"

"He's been up here for three days without coming down, enjoying my best liquor and girls, and now he tells them he hasn't got a silver to his bastard name."

Jon-Tom glared back at Mudge. The otter shrugged, didn't appear in the least embarrassed. "Hey, at least I was honest about it, mate. I told 'em I was broke. But it's all right, ain't it? You'll pay for me, won't you?"

"You *are* his friend?" inquired the badger.

"Well, yeah." He brought out the purse Clothahump had given him and jiggled it. The gold inside jingled musically, and the badger and the bear relaxed.

She smiled at him. "Now that's more like it . . . sir. I can see that you are a gentleman, though I don't think much of your choice of friends." Mudge looked wronged.

"How much does he owe you?"

She didn't even have to think. "Two hundred and fifty, sir. Plus any damages to the linen. I'll have to check."

"I can cover it," Jon-Tom assured her. He turned to look darkly at Mudge, hefting his ramwood staff. "If you'd be kind enough to give me a moment alone with him, I intend to take at least some of it out of his hide."

The badger's smile widened. "Your pleasure is mine, sir." Again she snapped her fingers. The grizzly let out a disappointed grunt, turned, and ducked back through the doorway.

"Take your time, sir. If you need anything helpful— acid, some thin wooden slivers, anything at all—the house will be delighted to supply it."

The door closed behind her. As soon as they were alone, Jon-Tom began to search the room. There was only one window, off to the left. He tried to open it, found it wouldn't budge.

" 'Ere now, mate," said Mudge, ambling over, "wot's the trouble? Just pay the old whore and let's be gone from 'ere."

"It's not that simple, Mudge. That money is from Clothahump, to pay for our passage at least as far as Snarken. And I lied about the amount. No way is there two hundred and fifty there."

Mudge took a step backward as Jon-Tom strove to puzzle out the window. "Just a minute there, mate. Wot's that about payin' *our* way? Snarken, you said? That's all the way across the Glittergeist, ain't it?"

"That's right." Jon-Tom squinted at the jamb. "I think this locks from the outside. Clever. Must be a way to break through it."

Mudge continued backing toward the bed. "Nice of you to come lookin' for me, mate, but I'm afraid I can't go with you. And you say 'is wizardship is behind it?"

"That's right. He's sick and I have to go get him some medicine."

"Right. Give the old reptile me best wishes, and I 'ope he makes a speedy recovery. As for me, I've some travelin' to do for me 'ealth, and salt air doesn't agree with me lungs."

"You're not going anywhere unless it's with me,"
Jon-Tom snapped at him. "You take one step out that door
and I'll call the madam. I saw the look in her eyes. She'd
enjoy separating your head from the rest of you. So would
that side of beef that came in with her."

"I ain't afraid of no bag of suet wot communicates in
grunts," Mudge said.

Jon-Tom turned from the window. "Then maybe I ought
to call them. I can always find someone else to accompany
me."

Mudge rushed at him. "Take it easy, mate, 'old on. To
Snarken, you say?"

"Maybe beyond."

"Ain't no place beyond Snarken."

"Yes there is. Little town not too far inland from
there." He fumbled between the windowpanes, was rewarded
by a double clicking sound. "Ah."

He lifted the window slowly. Halfway up, something
loud and brassy began to clang inside the building.

"Shit! There's an alarm spell on this thing!" The
sounds of pounding feet came from the hall.

"No time for regrets, mate, and you'd best not stand
there gawkin'." Mudge was over the sill in a flash and
shinnying down the rainpipe outside. Jon-Tom followed
more slowly, envying the otter his agility.

By the time they reached the pavement, faces had
appeared at the open window.

"You won't get away from me, otter!" Madam Lorsha
yelled, shaking her fist at them as they ran up the side
street. At any moment Jon-Tom expected to hear the
grizzly's footsteps behind them, feel huge paws closing
around his throat. "I'll hunt you to the ends of the world!
No one runs out owing Madam Lorsha!"

"Funny what she said about the ends of the world,"
Jon-Tom murmured as he followed the otter down endless
alleyways and turns. He was sure Mudge had memorized

this escape route before stepping inside the brothel. "That's where we're going."

"There you go again, mate," said Mudge, "usin' them words like *we* and *us*."

"I need your help, Mudge."

They reached a main street and slowed to a walk as they joined the crowd of evening strollers. Timswitty was a good-sized town, much bigger than Lynchbany. It was unlikely Madam Lorsha's thugs would be able to find them. Jon-Tom tried to hunch over and mask his exceptional height.

"Clothahump is deathly ill, and we must have this medicine. I'm not any happier about making this trip than you are."

"You must be, mate, because I'm not goin' to make it. Don't get me wrongo. You just 'elped me clear out of a bad spot. I am grateful, I am, but she weren't worth enough to make me put me life on the line for you, much less for that old word-poisoner."

They edged around a strolling couple. "I need someone who knows the way, Mudge."

"Then you needs some other bloke, mate. I ain't never been to Snarken."

"I mean someone who knows the ways of the world, Mudge. I've learned a lot since I've been here, but that's nothing compared to what I don't know. I need your good advice as well as your unconventional knowledge."

"Sure you do." Mudge puffed up importantly in spite of knowing better. "You think you can flatter me into goin', is that it? Or did you think I'd forgotten your intentions to be a solicitor in your own world? Don't take me for a fool, mate."

"I have to have someone along I can trust," Jon-Tom went on. The otter's expression showed that was one ploy he wasn't expecting.

"Now that ain't fair, guv'nor, and you knows it."

"There will also," Jon-Tom added, saving the best for last, "be a good fee for helping me."

That piqued the otter's interest. " 'Ere now, why didn't you come out and say that t' begin with instead of goin' on with all this twaddle about 'ow 'is poor old 'ardheaded curmudgeonly 'oliness was 'aving an attack of the gout or whatever, or 'ow badly you need me unique talents." He moved nearer and put a comradely arm around Jon-Tom's waist, as high as he could comfortably reach.

"You 'ave a 'ell of a lot to learn about life, guv'nor." He rambled on as the evening fog closed in comfortingly around them, explaining that though he didn't know how it was in Jon-Tom's world, here it was gold that spoke clearest and bought one's trust. Not words.

Jon-Tom allowed as how things indeed were different, deferring to the otter's claims while privately disagreeing. It did not matter who was right, however. All that mattered was that Mudge had agreed to join him.

Mudge managed to steer them into a tavern in a high-class district. Having already flashed Clothahump's gold, Jon-Tom couldn't very well claim he didn't have the wherewithal to pay. So he went slowly through his own meal while the otter devoured a gigantic banquet more suitable to the appetite of Madam Lorsha's bouncer. As Mudge explained between mouthfuls, he'd burned up a lot of energy this past week and wanted to make certain he embarked on their long journey at full strength.

Only when the otter had finished the final morsel did he lean contentedly back in his chair.

"So you say we're goin' to distant Snarken, wot, and beyond, and I say there's nothin' beyond. Wot did 'is nibs say it would be like?"

"He didn't exactly say." Jon-Tom picked at a sweet dessert. "Just the town where the store with the medicine is kept."

"Yeah, I 'eard you say somethin' about a town. 'As it got a name?"

Jon-Tom decided the bittersweet berry dessert was to his taste, finished the last of it. "Crancularn."

"WOT?" Mudge suddenly was sitting bolt upright, dribbling the last traces of wrinklerry jelly from his lips as he gaped at the man sitting across the table from him. A few curious diners spared him a glance, returned to their business when they saw no fighting was involved.

Mudge wiped at his sticky whiskers and spoke more softly, eyeing Jon-Tom sideways. "Wot did you say the name o' this dump was, guv'nor?"

"Crancularn. I see you've heard of it."

" 'Eard of it, you're bloody well right I've 'eard of it. That's a place o' the dead, mate."

"I thought there wasn't anything beyond Snarken."

"Not supposed to be, mate, but then, nobody knows where this Crancularn is supposed to be either, except that it moves about from time to time, like lice, and that anyone who ever gets there never comes back. 'Tis the entrance to 'ell itself, mate. Surely you don't mean to go there."

"Not only do I mean to go there, I intend to make a small purchase and return safely with it. And you're coming with me. You promised."

" 'Ere now, mate, when I made this 'ere bargain, weren't nothin' said about Crancularn. I'm out." He stepped off the chair and discovered he was straddling the far end of Jon-Tom's ramwood staff, which had been slipped under the table earlier.

"Sit down," Jon-Tom ordered him. Gingerly, the otter resumed his seat. "You made a promise, Mudge. You agreed to accompany me. In a sense, you accepted the proffered fee. Where I come from an oral contract is enforceable when the details are known to both parties, and in this case the details are now known."

"But *Crancularn*, mate. Can't this medicine be got anywheres else?"

Jon-Tom shook his head. "I pressed Clothahump on that

point repeatedly, and he never wavered. The only place it can be bought is Crancularn.'' He leaned over the table, spoke almost angrily. "Look, do you think I want to go gallivanting halfway across a strange world in search of some old fart's pills? I like Clothahump, sure, but I have my own life to live. What's left of it. If he dies leaving me stuck here, I might as well be dead. It's interesting enough, your world, but I want to go *home,* damn it! I miss Westwood on the opening night of a Steven Spielberg movie, and I miss the bookstores on Hollywood Boulevard, and the beach, and bagels at the deli, and take-out Chinese food, and—''

"All right, mate, I believe you. Spare me your memories. So it's a contract, is it? At least you're learnin' 'ow to stick up for your rights.'' He smiled and tapped the staff.

Jon-Tom was taken aback. He'd acted almost exactly the way Mudge would have if their situations had been reversed. The thought was more than a little appalling.

"You'll keep your end of the bargain, then?''

"Aye.'' Mudge spoke with obvious reluctance. "I gave me word, so I'm stuck with it. Well, a short life but a happy one, they say. 'Tis better than dyin' in one's bed. Alone, anyway.''

"There's no need for all this talk of dying.'' Jon-Tom sipped at the mug of cold cider in front of him. "We are going to get to Crancularn, obtain the necessary medication, and return here. All we're doing is running an errand.''

"That's right, mate. Just an errand.'' He belched derisively, to the unconcealed disgust of the well-dressed diners nearby. "Wot a day it was for me when you tumbled into that glade where I was huntin' so peaceful. Why couldn't you 'ave settled on some other poor bloke besides old Mudge?''

"You were just lucky. As for your ill fortune, we don't know yet who's the fool in this play: you for agreeing to come with me or me for wanting you to.''

"You singe me privates, mate," said Mudge, looking wounded, an expression he had mastered.

"A wonder there's anything left to singe, after three days in that brothel. Finish up and let's find a place to sleep. I'm bushed."

III

It took six tries to finally wake Mudge. After three days of nonstop debauchery and the huge meal of the previous night, the otter had to be helped to the bathroom. He got his pants on backwards and his boots on opposite feet. Jon-Tom straightened him out and together they worked their way through Timswitty in search of transportation.

From a nervous dealer badly in need of business they rented a low wooden wagon pulled by a single aged dray lizard, promising to drop it off at the port of Yarrowl at the mouth of the Tailaroam. From Yarrowl it should be a simple matter to book passage on a merchantman making the run across the Glittergeist to Snarken.

They succeeded in slipping quietly out of town without catching the eye of Madam Lorsha or her hirelings and were soon heading south along the narrow trade road. Once within the forest Mudge relaxed visibly.

" 'Peers we gave the old harridan the slip, mate."

Jon-Tom's eyebrows lifted. "We?"

"Well now, guv'nor, since 'tis *we* who are goin' on this little jaunt and *we* who are goin' to risk our lives for the sake o' some half-dotty ol' wizard, I think 'tis fair enough

35

for me to say that 'tis *we* who escaped the clutches of her haunches.''

"Plural good and plural bad, is that it?" Jon-Tom chucked the reins, trying to spur the ancient lumbering reptile to greater speed. "I guess you're right."

"Nice of you to agree, mate," said Mudge slyly. "So 'ow's about lettin' me 'ave a looksee at *our* money?"

"I'll keep an eye on our travel expenses, thanks. I need your help with several matters, Mudge, but counting coin isn't one of them."

"Ah well, then." Mudge leaned back against the hard back of the bench, put his arms behind his head, and gazed through the tinkling branches at the morning sun. "If you don't trust me, then to 'ell with you, mate."

"At least if I end up there it'll be with *our* money intact."

They stopped for lunch beneath a tree with bell leaves the size of quart jars. Mudge unpacked snake jerky and fruit juice. The appearance of the fruit juice made the otter shudder, but he was intelligent enough to know that he'd overdone his alcoholic intake just a hair the past week and that the percentage in his blood could not be raised much higher without permanent damage resulting. He poured himself a glass, wincing as he did so.

Something glinted in the glass and he looked sharply to his right. Nothing amiss. Bell leaves making music with the morning breezes, flying lizards darting from branch to branch in pursuit of a psychedelic bee.

Still . . . Carefully he set down his glass next to the wagon wheel. The dray lizard snoozed gratefully in a patch of sunlight, resting its massive head on its forelegs. Jon-Tom lay in the shade of the tree. All seemed right with the world.

But it wasn't.

"Back in a sec, mate." Mudge reached into the back of the wagon. Instead of food and drink he grabbed for his bow and quiver. The crossbow bolt that rammed into the wood between his reaching hands gave him pause. He withdrew them slowly.

"A wise decision," said a voice from the trees.

Jon-Tom sat up fast. "Who said that?"

He found himself staring at the business ends of an assortment of pikes and spears, wielded by an unpleasant-looking assortment of furry assailants.

"Me fault," Mudge muttered, angry at himself. "I 'eard 'em comin', I did, but not quite soon enough."

"It wouldn't have mattered," said the voice which had spoken a moment before. "There are too many of us anyway, and though we are instructed to bring you in alive, it wasn't specified in what condition."

Stepping through the circle of armed warmlanders was a coatimundi nearly as tall as Mudge. His natural black striping had been enhanced with brown decorations painted on muzzle and tail. One front canine was missing, and the remainder of the long, sharp teeth were stained yellow. He rested one paw on the hilt of a thick, curved dagger belted at his waist. The dagger was also stained, but not yellow.

Jon-Tom thought rapidly. Like Mudge's bow, his own duar and ramwood staff lay in the bed of the wagon. If he could just get to them. . . . Well, what if he could? As this apparent leader of their captors had said, they were badly outnumbered.

"Right. Wot is it you want with us?" Mudge asked. "We're just a couple of innocent travelers, poor prospects for thieves."

The coati shook his head and glared at them over his long snout out of bright black eyes. "I'm not interested in your worldly possessions, whatever they might be. I've been ordered by my master to bring you in."

"So Lorsha found us out anyway," the otter muttered. He sounded wistful. "Well, them three days were almost worth dyin' for. You should've been with me, mate."

"Well, I wasn't, and they're not worth dying for from my viewpoint."

"Calm yourselves," said the coati. "No one's speaking of dying here. Cooperate and give me no trouble, and I'll give none back to you." He squinted at Mudge. "And what's all this chattering about someone named Lorsha?"

Mudge came back from his memories and made a face at the coati. "You ain't 'ere to take us back to Madam Lorsha of Timswitty?"

"No. I come from Malderpot."

"Malderpot?" Jon-Tom gaped at him.

"Big town," Mudge informed him, "full of dour folk and little pleasure."

"*We* like it," said a raccoon hefting a halberd.

"No offense," Mudge told him. "Who wants us in Malderpot?"

"Our master Zancresta," said the coati.

"Who's this Zancresta?" Jon-Tom asked him.

A few incredulous looks showed on the faces of their captors, including the coati.

"You mean you've never heard of the Master of Darkness and Manipulator of the Secret Arts?"

Jon-Tom shook his head. " 'Fraid not."

The coati was suddenly uncertain. "Perhaps we have made a mistake. Perhaps these are not the ones we were sent to fetch. Thile, you and Alo check their wagon."

Two of the band rushed to climb aboard, began going through the supplies with fine disregard for neatness. It took them only moments to find Jon-Tom's staff and duar, which Thile held up triumphantly.

"It's the spellsinger, all right," said the muskrat.

"Keep a close watch on his instrument and he'll do us no harm," the coati instructed his men.

"I mean you no harm in any case," said Jon-Tom. "What does your Zancresta want with us?"

"Nothin' good. You can be certain o' that, mate," said Mudge.

"So one of you, at least, has heard of our master."

"Aye, I've 'eard of 'im, though I don't mean to flatter

'is reputation by it.'' He turned to Jon-Tom. "This 'ere
Zancresta chap's the 'ead wizard not only for the town of
Malderpot but for much of the northern part o' the Bellwoods.
See, each town or village 'as its own wizard or sorcerer or
witch, and each o' them claims to be better than 'is
neighbor at the arts o' magickin'.''

"Zancresta *is* the best," said the coati. "He is the
master."

"I ain't goin' to argue the point with you," said Mudge.
"I 'ave no interest whatsoever in wizardly debates and
functions, for all that I seem to be gettin' repeatedly
screwed by 'em.

"Now, if it's the spellsinger 'ere you're come after, take
'im and let me go. I'm only a poor traveler tryin' 'is best
to make it down the windy road o' life, and I've 'ad a 'ard
enough time makin' ends meet as it is without gettin'
caught up again in the world's troubles."

"It may be true," said the coati, eyeing him unflatteringly.
"But I have my orders. They say I am to bring back the
spellsinger known as Jon-Tom and any who travel with
him. You will have the chance to plead your case before
the master. Perhaps he will let you go."

"And if 'e don't?"

The coati shrugged. "That's not my affair."

"Easy for you to say," Mudge grumbled.

Spears prodded Jon-Tom and Mudge into the back of the
wagon, where they sat with their hands tied behind their
backs. A couple of the coati's henchmen took over the
reins. The little procession swung back northward, slightly
west of Timswitty but also in the opposite direction from
Lynchbany and the River Tailaroam.

"This Zancresta 'as a bad reputation, mate," Mudge
whispered to his companion. "Mind now, I'm not denyin'
'is abilities. From wot I've 'eard 'e ain't bad at sorcerin',
but 'e's unscrupulous as 'ell. Cheats on 'is spells and
short-changes 'is incantations, but 'e's too powerful for
anyone to go up against. I've 'ad no dealin's with 'im

meself, and I stay clear o' folk from Malderpot. As I said, they ain't much for partyin'."

"From what you tell me about their chief wizard, I can see why they aren't."

"Right." Mudge nodded past the drivers. "Now, 'tis clear this 'ere ringtail knows nothin' o' wot 'is master wants with us. That may be somethin' we can turn to our advantage. So somehow we 'ave to get clear o' this charmin' bunch o' throat-slitters before we're brought up before Zancresta himself. If that 'appens, I 'ave this funny feelin' that we'll never see the shores o' the Glittergeist or any other calm water."

"Don't underestimate this one." Jon-Tom indicated the coati, who strolled along in the lead, talking with a couple of his band. "He seems more than the usual hired thug."

"Fancy clothes can't hide one's origin," said Mudge.

"No harm in trying." He raised his voice. "Hey, you, leader!"

"Shut up," snapped the muskrat from the driver's bench. He showed a short sword. "Or you will eat your own tongues for breakfast and can see how your words taste then."

"I just want a word with your chief. Surely one as illustrious as he can spare a prisoner a few minutes of his time."

Evidently the coati's ears were as sensitive as his nose, because he slowed his pace until he was walking alongside the wagon.

"I bear you no hatred, spellsinger. What do you wish to talk about? By the way, my name is Chenelska."

"Don't you have any idea what your master wants with us? What use has so great and powerful a wizard for a mere spellsinger like me?"

Chenelska considered a moment, then glanced past Jon-Tom to Mudge. "Tell me, water rat, is this tall human as ignorant as he appears or is he making fun of me?"

"No." Mudge spoke with sufficient conviction to persuade the coati that he was telling the truth. " 'E's as dumb as he looks.''

"Thanks, Mudge. Nice to know I can rely on your good opinion.''

"Don't mention it, mate.''

"Can it be,'' said the dumbfounded Chenelska, ''that you have never heard of the rivalry between our master and the one that you serve?''

"The one I serve? You mean Clothahump? I don't serve him. I'm not an apprentice or anything like that. He has another who serves him. We're just friends.''

"Indeed. Good enough friends that you undertake a long, dangerous mission on his behalf when he lies too ill to travel himself. A mission to cross the Glittergeist in search of a rare and precious medicine he requires to cure himself.''

"How the hell do you know that?'' Jon-Tom said angrily.

The coati grinned and laughed, a single sharp barking. "It seems that this Clothahump does have another who serves him. A true famulus. A fine, intelligent, hard-working apprentice who serves faithfully and well. Except when he's been treated to a few stiff sips of good belly-warmer.''

"Sorbl! That stupid big-eyed sot!''

The coati nodded, still grinning. "Not that we had to work hard at it, you understand. The poor little fellow merely wanted companionship, and other servants of my master provided it, whereupon the turtle's servant grew extremely talkative.''

"I'll bet he did,'' Jon-Tom mumbled disconsolately.

"It has always been a matter of great contention in this part of the world,'' the coati explained, ''as to who the greater wizard is. Clothahump of the tree or my master Zancresta. It didn't bother my master when opinion was divided and drifted back and forth. But it has lately become apparent that outside the immediate environs of

Malderpot, the consensus is that your Clothahump is the greater.'' He moved closer to the wagon and lowered his voice so that his band could not overhear.

"It's true that saving the whole world is a tough act to follow. When word came of the victory over the Plated Folk at the Jo-Troom Gate, and the part your master Clothahump played in it, there was very little my master could do to counteract the great shift in public opinion, and he has been in a murderous mood ever since.''

"As if Clothahump saved all the warmlands just to spite him," Jon-Tom said disgustedly.

"Be that as it may, wizards can be very touchy about such things. Zancresta dwells on evil spells and prepares toxic presents and calls down all who cross him. He has been dangerous to approach ever since this happened. The only way for him to regain his self-respect and cancel his shame is to do something to make himself again be considered the equal of the turtle of the tree. Yet he sees no way to do this. This Clothahump refuses all challenges and duels.''

"Clothahump," Jon-Tom explained politely, "doesn't think much of games.''

"Word travels that he does not because he is getting senile.''

Jon-Tom didn't reply. There was nothing to be gained by arguing with Chenelska and angering him.

"Therefore, my master is badly frustrated, since there is no way he can prove that he is truly the most skilled in the wizardly arts.

"Word arrived recently about this severe sickness Clothahump is suffering from and that he cannot cure with his own magic, that he needs medicine obtainable only from a land beyond Snarken. My master was delighted by it.''

"When we get out of this," Jon-Tom whispered to Mudge, "I'm going to string Sorbl up by his feet and hang him beak-first over an open bottle of brandy.''

"Mate, I truly 'ope you get that opportunity," said Mudge.

"Thanks to the information the wizard's famulus provided, we were able to locate and intercept you," said Chenelska.

"What does your master intend doing with us?"

"I do not know, man. For now, it would seem sufficient to prevent you from carrying out your mission and returning with the necessary medicine. Perhaps after he has weakened enough my master will take pity on him and travel south to allow him the privilege of begging for his help."

"Clothahump would never do that," Jon-Tom assured the coati. "He'll spit in Zancresta's face before he asks his help."

"Then I imagine he will die." The coati spoke without emotion. "It is of no import to me. I only serve my master."

"Yes, you're a good slave."

The coati moved closer to the wagon and slapped the sideboard angrily. "I am no slave!"

"A slave is one who unquestioningly carries out the orders of his master without considering the possible consequences."

"I know the consequences of what I do." Chenelska glowered at him, no longer friendly. "Of one consequence I am sure. I will emerge from this little journey far better off than you. You think you're smart, man? I was instructed in all the tricks a spellsinger can play. You can make only music with your voice and not magic without your instrument. If I choose to cut your throat, I will be safer still.

"As for the water rat that accompanies you, it may be that the master will free him. If he does so, I will be waiting for him myself, to greet him as is his due." With that, the coati left them, increasing his stride to again assume his place at the head of the little procession.

"I'm beginnin' to wish you'd left me at Madam Lorsha's," the otter said later that night.

"To Tork's tender mercies?" Jon-Tom snorted. "You'd be scattered all over Timswitty by now if I hadn't shown up to save you, and you know it."

"Better to die after three days o' bliss than to lie in some filthy cell in Malderpot contemplatin' a more mundane way o' passin'."

"We're not dead yet. That's something."

"Is it now? You're a fine one for graspin' at straws."

"I once saw a man start a fire with nothing more than a blade of dry grass. It kept both of us warm through a night in high mountains."

"Well 'e ain't 'ere and neither is 'is fire."

"You give up too quickly." Jon-Tom looked ahead, to where Chenelska strode proudly at the head of his band. "I could put in for a writ of habeas corpus after we arrive, but somehow I don't think it would have much sway with this Zancresta."

"Wot's that, mate? Some kind of otherworldly magic?"

"Yes. We're going to need something like it to get out of this with our heads in place. And let's not forget poor Clothahump for worrying about our own skins. He's depending on us."

"Aye, and see 'ow well 'is trust is placed."

They kept to back roads and trails, staying under cover of the forest, avoiding intervening communities. Chenelska intended to avoid unnecessary confrontations as well as keep his not always reliable troops clear of civilization's temptations. So they made good time and after a number of days arrived on the outskirts of a town too small to be a city but too large to be called a village.

A crudely fashioned but solid stone wall encircled it, in contrast to the open city boundaries of Lynchbany and Timswitty. It wasn't a very high wall, a fact Jon-Tom commented on as they headed west.

A small door provided an entrance. The prisoners were

hustled quickly down several flights of stone stairs, past crackling torches smelling of creosote, and thrust into a dark, odiferous cell. An obese porcupine turned the large key in the iron lock and departed, leaving them alone in the near blackness.

"Still optimistic, mate?" Mudge leaned against a dank wall and sniffed. "Cast into a dungeon without hope of rescue to spend our last hours talkin' philosophy."

Jon-Tom was running his fingers speculatively over the mossy walls. "Not very well masoned or mortared."

"I stand corrected," said Mudge sardonically. "Talkin' about architecture."

"Architecture's an interesting subject, Mudge. Don't be so quick to dismiss it. If you know how something is put together, you might learn how to take it apart."

"That's right, guv'nor. You find us a loose stone in the wall, take it out, and bring the whole stinkin' city down on top o' us. Then we'll be well and truly free." He slunk off toward a corner.

"Not even a chamber pot in this cesspool. I 'ope they kill us fast instead o' leavin' us to die with this smell." He moved back to grab the bars of the cell, shouted toward the jailer.

"Hey mate, get your fat ass over 'ere!"

In no hurry, the porcupine ambled across the floor from his chair. When he reached the bars he turned his back, and Mudge backed hastily away from the two-foot-long barbed quills.

"I will thank you to be a little more polite."

"Right, sure, guv. Take 'er easy. No offense. You can imagine me state o' mind, chucked in 'ere like an old coat."

"No, I cannot," said the jailer. "I do my job and go home to my family. I do not imagine your state of mind."

"Excuse me," said Jon-Tom, "but have you any idea how long we are to be held in here?"

"Ah, no."

Slow. Their jailer was a little slow in all areas. It was a
characteristic of all porcupines, and this one was no
exception. That didn't mean he was a moron. Tread
slowly, Jon-Tom warned himself.

"Our possessions have become separated from us," he
went on. "Do you know what was done with them?"

Lazily, the porcupine pointed upward. "They are in the
main guard chamber, to be taken out and sent along with
you when word comes for you to be moved."

"Do you know what's going to happen to us?"

The porcupine shook his head. "No idea. None of my
business. I do my job and stay out of other people's
business, I do."

Mudge instantly divined his companion's intentions,
said sadly, "We were searched before we were sent down
here. I wonder if they found your sack o' gold, mate?"

"Sack of gold?" Evidently the porcupine wasn't all that
slow. For the first time the half-lidded eyes opened fully,
then narrowed again. "You are trying to fool me. Chenelska
would never leave a sack of gold in a place where others
could find it and steal it."

"Yeah, but wot if 'e didn't think to look for somethin'
like that?" Mudge said insinuatingly. "We just don't want
'im to get 'is 'ands on it, after 'im throwin' us down 'ere
and all. If you wanted to find out if we were lyin' or not,
all you'd 'ave to do is go look for yourself, mate. You 'ave
the keys, and we ain't 'ardly goin' to dig our way out o'
this cell while you're gone."

"That is true." The jailer started for the stairs. "Do not
get any funny ideas. You cannot cut through the bars, and
there is no one else here but me."

"Oh, we ain't goin' anywhere, we ain't," Mudge insisted.

"By the way," Jon-Tom added offhandedly, "as long as
you're going upstairs, maybe you could do something for
us? This is an awfully dank and somber place. A little
music would do a lot to lighten it up. Surely working

down here day after day, the atmosphere must get pretty depressing after a while.''

"No, it does not," said the porcupine as he ascended the stairs. "I like it dank and somber and quiet, though I would be interested in hearing the kind of music you could play. You see, Chenelska told me you were a spellsinger.''

Jon-Tom's heart sank. "Not really. I'm more of an apprentice. I don't know enough yet to really spellsing. I just like to make music.''

"Nonetheless, I cannot take the chance.''

"Wait!" Jon-Tom called desperately. "If you know what spellsinging's all about, then surely you know that a spellsinger can't make magic without his instrument.''

"That is so.'' The porcupine eyed him warily.

"Well then, how about this? You bring down my duar, my instrument, but after you give it to me you chain my hands so I can't pull them back through these bars. That way if I tried to sing anything that sounded dangerous to you, you could yank the duar away from me before I could finish and I couldn't do a thing to stop you from doing so.''

The jailer considered, wrestling with unfamiliar concepts. Jon-Tom and Mudge waited breathlessly, glad of the darkness. It helped to conceal their anxiety.

"Yes, I think that would be safe enough,'' the jailer said finally. "And I *am* curious to hear you sing. I will see if your instrument is with your other possessions. While I look for the sack of gold.''

"You won't regret it!" Jon-Tom called after him as he disappeared up the stairway. As soon as he'd left, Mudge looked excitedly at his friend.

"Cor, mate, can you really do anythin' tied like that?''

"I don't know. I have to try. It's clear he wasn't just going to hand me the duar without some kind of safeguard. I just don't know what I could sing that could help us out of here before he decided it sounded threatening and took the duar away from me. Not that I ever know what to sing.

I had the same problem in my own world. But it was all I could think of.''

"You better think o' somethin', mate, or it'll be two worlds that'll be missin' you permanent. I don't know what this Zancresta has planned for us, but as much as 'e hates Clothahump, I don't figure on 'im bein' overly polite to a couple o' the turtle's servants.''

"We're not his servants. At least, you're not.''

"Aye, an' you saw 'ow far that got me with Chenelska. I'm stuck with the bedamned label just like you are, like it or not. So *think* of somethin'. Somethin' effective, and fast.''

"I don't *know*." Jon-Tom fought with his memory. "Practically everything I know is hard rock."

Mudge gestured at the walls. "Strikes me as damned appropriate.''

"Not like that,'' Jon-Tom explained impatiently. "It's a name for a kind of popular music. You've heard me sing it.''

"Aye, an' I don't pretend to understand a word o' it.''

"Then you have something in common with my parents.''

Footsteps coming down the stairs interrupted them momentarily.

"You'd better think up somethin' quick, mate.''

"I'll try.'' He stuck his arms out between the bars, waiting expectantly. His spirits were boosted by the sight of the undamaged duar dangling from one of the jailer's paws.

"There was no gold,'' the porcupine declared sourly.

"Sorry.'' Mudge sighed fitfully. "About wot one would expect from a snurge like Zancresta. Still, 'tweren't no 'arm in lookin', were there?''

"What were you two talking about while I was gone? I heard you talking.'' The porcupine looked suspicious.

"Nothin' much, mate. Just makin' conversation. We talk while you're right 'ere, too, don't we?''

"Yes, that is so. Very well.'' He stepped forward and

made as if to hand the duar to Jon-Tom, then hesitated. "I do not know."

"Oh, come on," Jon-Tom urged him, a big smile frozen on his face. "A little music would be nice. Not everyone has the chance to hear an apprentice spellsinger make music just for pleasure."

"That is what concerns me." The jailer stepped back and rummaged through a wooden chest. When he returned it was to clap a pair of thick leather cuffs on Jon-Tom's wrists. They were connected to one another by a chain. He also, to Jon-Tom's dismay, tied a thick cord around the neck of the duar.

"There," he said, apparently satisfied, and handed over the instrument. Jon-Tom's fingers closed gratefully over the familiar wooden surface, lightly stroked the double set of strings.

The porcupine returned to his chair, keeping a firm grip on his end of the cord. "Now if you try anything funny I don't even have to run over to you. All I have to do is pull this rope." He gave the cord an experimental yank, and Jon-Tom had to fight to hold onto the duar.

"I need a little slack," he pleaded, "or I won't be able to play at all."

"All right." The jailer relaxed his grip slightly. "But if I think you are trying to trick me I will pull it right out of your hands and smash it against the floor."

"Don't worry. I wouldn't try anything like that. Would I, Mudge?"

"Oh, no, sor. Not after you've all but given this gentlebeing your word." The otter assumed an air of mock unconcern as he settled down on the floor to listen. "Play us a lullaby, Jon-Tom. Somethin' soothin' and relaxin' to 'elp us poor ones forget the troubles we face and the problems o' the world."

"Yes, play something like that," asked the porcupine.

Jon-Tom struggled with himself. Best to first play a couple of innocuous ditties to lull this sod into a false

sense of security. The trouble was, being mostly into
heavy metal, he knew about as many gentle tunes as he did
operatic arias. Somehow something by Ozzy Osbourne or
Ted Nugent didn't seem right, nor did anything by KISS.
He considered "Dirty Deeds Done Dirt Cheap" by AC/DC,
decided quickly that one stanza would cost him control of
the duar permanently.

He decided to take a chance with some golden oldies.
Maybe a few of Roy Orbison's songs, even if his voice
wasn't up to it. It seemed to work. The porcupine lazed
back in his chair, obviously content, but still holding tight
to the cord.

Jon-Tom segued into the part of one song where the
lyrics went "the day you walked out on me" and the jailer
didn't stir, but neither did the walls part to let them
through. Discouraged, he moved on to "America" by Neil
Diamond. A few faint images of the Statue of Liberty and
Ellis Island flickered fitfully in the cell, but Jon-Tom did
not find himself standing safe at either location.

Then he noticed Mudge. The otter sat back in the shadows making long pulling and throwing motions. It took
Jon-Tom a moment to understand what his companion was
driving at. In the middle of humming "Won't Get Fooled
Again," he figured the otter's movements out.

The porcupine had tied the cord to the duar in order to
be able to jerk it quickly out of Jon-Tom's hands. If they
could somehow gain control of the rope, they might be
able to make a small lasso and cast it toward a weapon or
even the big keyring lying on the table.

In order to try that, of course, they had to somehow
incapacitate their jailer. Since he seemed half-asleep already, Jon-Tom softened his voice as much as possible and
sang the sweetest ballads he could think of, finishing with
"Sounds of Silence" by Simon and Garfunkel. That particularly apt selection set the porcupine to snoozing. To
make sure, he added a relaxing rendition of "Scarborough
Fair."

Carefully, he tugged gently on the cord. Two half-witted eyes popped wide open and the line went taut.

"I told you not to try anything," the porcupine growled.

For an instant Jon-Tom was sure they'd lose the duar along with their last hope. "I didn't mean anything!" he said desperately. "It's only that playing in the same position all the time hurts my arms. I wasn't doing anything else."

"Well . . ." The jailer slumped back in his chair. "See that you don't do it no more. Please play another song. I never heard anything like them. Pretty."

Despairingly, Jon-Tom simply sang the first thing that came to mind, the theme song from one of the *Rocky* films. Maybe it was his frustration, perhaps his sudden indifference. Whatever the reason, he almost thought he could feel the power running through him. He tried to focus on it, really working himself into the useless song in the hope it might lead to something better.

A faint smell of ozone began to filter into the air of the dungeon. Something crackled near the ceiling. Mudge scrambled warily back into the farthest corner of the cell. Jon-Tom jumped as an electric shock ran up his wrists. He tried to pull back into the cell, found he was trapped against the bars by the leather wristcuffs and linking chain.

Oh, shit, he mumbled silently. I've gone and done something weird again.

Only this time he was trapped up against whatever it was. Something was materializing in the air next to him. He tugged futilely at the leather cuffs, dropping the duar in the process. The instrument was glowing brightly as it bounced around on the floor like a toad at a disco.

The slow-moving porcupine was on his feet and staring. He'd abandoned the cord in favor of edging 'round toward the rack of weapons. Selecting a long spear, he aimed it at the cell. Jon-Tom was uncomfortably aware of the fact that if the jailer so chose, he could run him through where he stood.

"What are you doing, spellsinger? Stop it!"

"I'm not doing anything!" Jon-Tom prayed his hysteria was as convincing as it was heartfelt. "Untie my hands!"

The jailer ignored him, gazing in stupefied fascination at the slowly rotating cylinder of fluorescent gas that had gathered inside the cell. "Don't lie to me. Something is happening. Something is happening!"

"I know something's happening, you moron! Let me loose!" He wrenched uselessly at his bonds.

The jailer continued to keep his distance. "I am warning you, spellsinger. Put an end to this magic right now!" Keeping his thorny back against the walls, he edged around until he was standing close to the bars. From there he was able to prod the prisoner with the tip of his spear. It was extremely sharp.

"I can't stop it! I don't know what I did and I don't know what's happening."

"I do not believe you." The jailer's voice had turned shrill and he was jabbing seriously with the spear.

Suddenly a loud *bang* came from the cloud of gas. The glowing cylinder dissipated to reveal a massive, powerful form at least seven feet tall standing in the center of the jail cell. It had to crouch to keep from bumping its head against the ceiling.

Mudge quailed back against the wall while Jon-Tom thought wildly about his last song. The indifferently sung song which apparently had been far more effective than all its anxiety-laden predecessors. The theme song from that *Rocky* film . . . what was it?

Oh, yeah. The "Eye of the Tiger."

IV

Actually there were two of them, and they glared around in bewilderment. Jon-Tom had never seen a white tiger before, much less one that wore armor and stood on two legs. Leather and brass strips made a skirt which covered the body from waist to the knees. Additional armor protected the back of arms and legs, was secured over the legs with crisscrossing leather straps. A finely worked brass helmet shielded the head, and an intricate inscription covered the thin nose guard. Holes cut in the top of the helmet allowed the ears to protrude.

The huge furry skull glanced in all directions, taking in unanticipated surroundings. White and black ears flicked nervously as a quarter ton of tiger tried to orient itself. Paws dropped to sheaths, and in an instant each one held a five-foot-long sword with razor-sharp serrated edges.

"By all the nine feline demons, what's going on heah? I declare I'll have some answers right quick or there'll be hell to pay." Slitted eyes fixed on the bars. She took a step forward and glared down at the quivering porcupine. "You! What is this place? Why am ah locked up? Y'all

53

answer me fast or ah'll make a necklace out of yo backbone!''

"G-g-g-guards," the porcupine stammered. It came out as a whisper. Aware his cry wasn't reaching very far, he raised his voice. "Guards!"

"Quit stahling and talk to me." Feminine, Jon-Tom decided. Thunderous, but undeniably feminine. The conjuration was a she. She turned to eye Mudge. "Yo theah. Why won't he talk to me?"

"You talkin' to me, m'dear?" Mudge inquired reluctantly.

She reached down and lifted him easily off the floor with one paw, setting her second sword aside but within easy reach. Fully extended, her claws were nearly as long as Mudge's fingers.

"Now, who else would ah be talking to, you little sponge?"

"Blimey, m'dear, I ain't considered the possibility."

"Guards!" Suddenly it occurred to the porcupine that since he wasn't having much luck obtaining help with his voice, it might be efficacious to employ his feet. He raced up the stairs with unexpected speed. "Guards, help me!"

"Hey, yo!" The tigress dropped Mudge, who promptly retreated to the back of the cell. "Come back heah! Yo heah me?"

"He thinks you're a threat to him."

"What's that?" For the first time she focused her attention on Jon-Tom.

"I said, he thinks you're a threat to him. Because you're in here with us."

"Y'all are awfully big fo a human."

"And you're awfully big period." He continued struggling with the cuffs that bound him to the bars of the cell.

"What is this place?" She turned slowly to make a more careful inspection of the prison. She did not appear frightened. Only irritated.

"We're in a dungeon in a town called Malderpot."

"Nevah heard of it," said the feline amazon. "A dungeon, you say. I can see that fo mahself, honey.'' She eyed his restraints. ''Why ah yo tied up like that?''

''I'm a spellsinger,'' he explained. ''I've been doing a little singing and I think I accidently brought you here.''

''So that's it!'' Jon-Tom did his best not to cower away from those burning yellow eyes. She stepped back and hefted both her swords. ''Well then, y'all can just send me back.''

He squirmed against the bars. ''I, uh, I'm afraid I can't do that. I don't know how I brought you here. I can try later, maybe. But not without my duar.'' He pointed into the room. ''And I can't play it with my hands tied like this.''

''Well, that much is obvious. Ah've got eyes, yo know.''

''Very pretty eyes, too.''

''Huh,'' she said, a little more softly. ''Spellsingah, yo say? Yo sound moah like a solicitah to me.'' Jon-Tom didn't inform her about his legal training, not being sure of her opinion of solicitors.

One sword suddenly cut forward and down. Mudge let out a half moan, half squeak, and Jon-Tom closed his eyes. But the sword passed between the bars to delicately cut the chain linking his wrist cuffs. A couple of quick twists of a clawed paw and his hands were free. He spoke as he rubbed the circulation back into his wrists.

''I still need the duar.'' Loud noises reached them from somewhere on the level above, and he hurried his introductions. ''That's Mudge, I'm Jon-Tom Meriweather.'' He recalled the song he'd sung prior to ''Eye of the Tiger.'' ''By any chance would your name be Sage, Rosemary, or Thyme?'' Somehow Scarborough didn't seem a possibility.

''Close enuf. Ah am called Roseroar.''

Jon-Tom nodded to himself. Once again his songs and his desires had gotten themselves thoroughly mixed. He took a deep breath, repeated the gist of a by now familiar story.

"We're trying to help a wizard who is dying. Because of that a jealous wizard is trying to prevent us from doing so. He had us captured, brought here, and locked up."

"That's no business of mine," said the tigress. "Yo really think mah eyes are pretty?"

"Extremely so." Why didn't Mudge chip in with a word or two? he wondered. He was better at this sort of thing. But the otter hugged his corner of the cell and kept his mouth shut. Jon-Tom plunged on. "Like topaz."

"Yo have a gift of words as well as music, don't yo? Well, let me tell yo, ah am not subject to the simple flattery of the male of any species!"

"Of course you're not. I didn't mean for you to think I was intentionally flattering you, or anything like that. I just made a simple statement of fact."

"Did y'all, now? Where do yo have to go to help this dying friend of yours?"

"Across the Glittergeist Sea."

"So ah'm that fah west, am ah?" She shook her head in wonder. "It's a peculiah world we live in."

"You don't know the half of it," Jon-Tom muttered.

"Ah've nevah been to an ocean, much less the Glittergeist." She looked out through the bars. "So that's yo instrument fo making magic?"

"It is. Also, the keys are on the table nearby. If we could get ahold of the rope attached to the duar, we could maybe drag the keys over here." He eyed the stairwell. "But I don't think we've got much time."

"Well, sugah, if it's the keys you want . . ." Roseroar put one paw on a bar to the left, the other on the bar immediately opposite, inhaled mightily, and pushed. Muscles rippled beneath the armor.

There was a groan and the metal bent like spaghetti. The tigress stepped through the resultant gap, walked over to the table, and picked up the keyring.

"Yo still want these?"

Mudge was already out in the corridor. Jon-Tom was

right on his heels. He snatched the duar and slung it over his shoulder.

"I think we'll be able to manage without them. Roseroar, you're quite a lady."

"Aye, with a delicate and ladylike touch," Mudge added.

"Ah think ah like you two," she said thoughtfully, staring at Mudge, "though ah can't decide if y'all are trying to be funny or flattering." She gestured with the two heavy swords. "Ah hope fo yo sake y'all are trying to be funny."

Jon-Tom hastened to reassure her. "You've got to take whatever Mudge says with a grain of salt. Comments like that are part of his nature. Sort of like a disease." He turned to bestow a warning look on the otter.

"Ah can see that," said the tigress. "Well, ah don't know how ah'm going to get home, but ah sure don't fancy this hole. Let's go somewhere quiet and talk."

"Suits me," said Jon-Tom agreeably.

At that moment the porcupine appeared at the top of the stairs, preceded by a pair of big, heavily armed wolves. They saw Roseroar about the time she saw them. She emitted a battle cry, a mixture of roar and curse, that shook moss from the ceiling. Waving both swords like propellers, she charged the stairway, which cleared with astonishing speed.

Mudge executed a little bow and gestured with his right hand. "After you, master o' magic and spellsinger extraordinaire."

Jon-Tom made a face at him, hurried to follow Roseroar upward. From ahead sounded shouts, screams, frantic cries, and yelps. Above all rose the tigress's earthshaking growls.

"Don't be so quick to compliment me," Jon-Tom told the otter. "She's not what I was trying to conjure up."

"I know that, guv'nor," said Mudge, striding along happily in his companion's wake. "It never is, wot? But even though you never get wot you're after with your spellsingin', wotever you gets always seems to work out.''

"Tell me that again when she finds out there's no way I can send her home.''

"Now, mate,'' Mudge told him as they started up to the next level, "wot's the use o' creatin' worry where there ain't none? Besides,'' he went on, his grin widening, "if she turns quarrelsome, you can tell 'er 'ow beautiful 'er eyes are.''

"Oh, shut up.''

They emerged into the main guardroom, which looked as if a modest typhoon had thundered through it. Every table was overturned and broken furniture littered the floor. Broken spears and pikes sopped up spilled liquid from shattered jugs. A couple of the guards remained, decoratively draped over the broken furniture. None offered a protest as Jon-Tom and Mudge began to search the still intact chests and drawers.

One yielded Mudge's longbow and arrows, another Jon-Tom's ramwood fighting staff. There was no sign of the full purse Clothahump had given him, nor did he expect to find it. Mudge was more disappointed than his companion at the absence of the gold.

"Bloody bedamned stinkin' thieves,'' he mumbled, ignoring the fact that he'd lifted a purse or two in his own time.

"Be quiet.'' Jon-Tom led him up the next flight of stairs. "From the way you're carrying on, you'd think this was the first time you'd ever been penniless.''

"I'm not sayin' that, mate,'' replied Mudge, putting a leash on his lamentations, "but when I gets friendly with a bit o' gold or silver and it ups and disappears on me, I feel as if I've lost a good friend. The loss strikes me to the quick.''

"One of these days it'd be nice to see you get so emotional over something besides money.''

"You do me an injustice, mate.'' Mudge carried his bow

in front of him, a hunting arrow notched and ready to fire. If the fates were kind they'd give him one clear shot at Chenelska or his bullyboys. Nothing would please him more than to be able to give the coati the shaft.

"You want emotional?" he continued as they climbed. "You should've seen me at Madam Lorsha's."

"I'm talking about honest emotion, about caring. Not lust."

"Cor, you mean there's a difference?"

The third landing was the last. They emerged into a small open square lit by torches and oil lamps. To their left was the city wall, to the right the outermost buildings of the town. The light danced wildly as sources of illumination were hastily moved to different positions. Shouts and yells filled the air.

Jon-Tom ducked as a wolf whizzed over his head. It pinwheeled once before striking the wall with a sickening thud.

Roseroar's efforts threw everything into confusion. Horns and shouts were beginning to rouse a whole section of the community. Lights were starting to appear in nearby windows as residents were awakened by the commotion.

Mudge bounced gleefully up and down, pointing at the evidence of the chaos the tigress was causing. "Wot a show! The poor buggers must think the 'ole bloomin' city is under attack."

"Maybe they're right." Jon-Tom started forward.

"Hey, you two!" Roseroar called to them as she idly batted aside a large rat armed with a short sword who had tried to sneak under her guard. The rodent went skidding across the paving stones, shedding bits and pieces of armor and flesh as he went. "Ovah heah! This way!"

They ran toward her. Jon-Tom placed his staff in front of him while Mudge ran backward to guard their rear, his short legs a blur. As they ran they dodged spears and arrows. Mudge responded to each attack individually, and they were rewarded as one figure after another fell from the wall above.

Snarling, a hyena draped in heavy chain mail headed right for Jon-Tom, swinging a viciously studded mace over his head. Jon-Tom blocked it with his staff, and the ramwood held as the mace's chain wrapped around it. He pulled and twisted in one motion, bringing the knobbed end of the staff down on his assailant's helmet. The hyena dropped like a stone. They ran on, Jon-Tom unwrapping the chain from his staff.

Then they were up against the thick wooden door in the city wall. Crossbow bolts thudded into the wood or splintered against the rock as the wall's garrison struggled to regroup.

Mudge inspected it rapidly. "Locked, damn it, from the other side!"

"Pahdon me," said Roseroar. While they covered her she put her back against the door, dug her feet into the pavement, and shoved. The door broke with a snap, the wood holding but not the iron hinges. It fell with a crash. The trio ran out, pursued by yells and weapons. No one chose to pursue beyond the city wall in person. The tigress had demonstrated what she could do at close range, and Malderpot's soldiery had taken the lesson to heart. They held back, waiting for someone higher up to give the necessary orders, and praying those directions would take their time arriving.

Before they did, the fugitives were deep within the concealment offered by the Bellwoods and the night. Eventually they located a place where several giant trees had fallen, forming a natural palisade, and settled in behind the wooden barricade nature had so thoughtfully provided.

The long run hadn't troubled Jon-Tom, who was a good distance runner, nor Mudge, who was blessed with inexhaustible energy, but Roseroar was tired. They waited while she caught her breath.

There in the moonlight she pulled off her helmet, undid

the thick belt that held both swords, and put it aside. Then she leaned back against one fallen trunk. Her bright yellow eyes seemed to glow in the darkness. Physically she was unharmed by the fighting, though her armor showed plenty of cuts and dents.

"We owe you our lives," he finally told her.

"Yes, ah expect that's so. Damned if ah know how ah'm going to collect on that debt. Yo told me yo didn't mean to conjuh me up in the first place?"

"That's right," he confessed. "It was an accident. I was trying to put our jailer to sleep. When it didn't work I got upset and spellsang the first thing that came to mind and—poof—there you were."

"Ah was the first thing that came to yo mind?"

"Well, not exactly. Matter of fact, I've never seen anybody like you. This kind of thing happens to me a lot when I try to spellsing."

She nodded, turned to look to where Mudge was already searching the bushes for something edible. "Is he telling the truth, squirt?"

"Me name is Mudge, lady o' the long tooth," said the voice in the bushes, "and I'll make you a deal right now. You can like me o' not, but you don't call me names and I'll respond likewise."

"Ah favor politeness in all things, being a lady of refined tastes," she replied evenly.

Mudge restrained the first reply that came to mind, said instead, "Aye, 'e's tellin' you the truth. A powerful spellsinger 'e is. Maybe the most powerful ever, though we ain't yet sure o' that. 'E certainly ain't. See, 'e 'as this bad 'abit o' tryin' to do one thing and 'e ends up doin' something total unexpected."

Jon-Tom spread his hands in a gesture of helplessness. "It's true. I have this ability but I don't seem able to control it. And now it's caused me to go and inconvenience you."

"That's a fine, politic way of putting it, suh. Going to the Glittergeist, yo said?"

"And across it. We have to get to Snarken."

"Ah've heard of Snahken. It's supposed to be an interesting place, rich in culture." She thought a long moment, then sighed. "Since yo say y'all can't send me home, ah guess ah maht as well tag along with y'all. Besides, ah kind of like the way you have with words, man." Her eyes glittered and Jon-Tom felt suddenly uncomfortable, though he wasn't sure why.

"Oh, 'e's a fine one with words 'e is, luv," Mudge said as he reappeared. He was carrying an armful of some lime-green berries. Jon-Tom took a few, bit into one, and found the taste sweet. More out of politeness than any expectation of acceptance, the otter offered some to the tigress.

"Bleh!" she said as she pulled back. She smiled widely, displaying an impressive array of cutlery. "Suh, do ah look like the kind to enjoy weeds?"

"No you don't, luv, but I thought I'd be polite, since you place such store by it."

She nodded thankfully as she scanned the surrounding woods. "Come the morning ah'll find mahself something to eat. This appeahs to be good game country. Theah should be ample meat about."

Jon-Tom was glad she wasn't looking at him when she said that. "I'm sure we'll run across something edible." He turned to the otter. "What about our pursuit, Mudge?"

The otter responded with his ingratiating, amused bark. "Why, them sorry twits will be all night just tryin' t' get their stories straight. From wot I saw on our way out, most of 'em were your typical city guard and likely ain't in Zancresta's personal service. It'd be that arse'ole Chenelska who'd be put in charge o' organizin' any kind o' formal chase. By the time 'e gets the word, gets 'is conflictin' reports sorted out, and puts together anythin' like a formal pursuit, we'll be well out o' it."

"Then you don't think they'll be able to track us down?"

"I've been seein' to the coverin' o' our tracks ever since we left that cesspool o' a town, mate. They won't find a sign o' us."

"What if they do come after us, though? We can't conceal all of Roseroar's petite footprints."

Mudge assumed a crafty mien. "Aye, that they might, guv. They'll likely comb a wide front to the south, knowin' that we're to be headin' for the ol' Tailaroam. They can run up every tree in the Bellwoods without findin' sign o' us, because we ain't goin' t' go south. We'll fool 'em inside out by goin' west from 'ere. We're so far north o' the river we might as well do it anyhows."

Jon-Tom struggled to recall what he'd been taught of the local geography. "If you go far enough west of here, the forest disappears and you're into the Muddletup Moors."

"You got it, mate. No one would think t'ave a looksee for us there."

"Isn't that because no one ever does go in there?"

"That's right. Wot better place o' safety t' flee to?"

Jon-Tom looked doubtful as he sat back against a fallen trunk. "Mudge, I don't know about your thinking."

"I'm willin' enough to entertain alternative suggestions, m'lord warbler, but you're 'ardly in shape for some straight arguin'."

"Now, that I won't argue. We'll discuss it in the morning."

"In the mornin', then. Night to you, mate."

The thunder woke Jon-Tom. He blinked sleepily and looked up into a gray sky full of massive clouds. He blinked a second time. White clouds were common enough in this world, just as they were in his own. But not with black stripes.

He tried to move, discovered he could not. A huge furry arm lay half on and half off his chest while another curved behind his head to form a warm pillow. Unfortunately, it was also cutting off the circulation to his throbbing left arm.

He tried to disengage himself. As he did so the thunder of Roseroar's purring was broken by a coughing snarl. She stirred, but her arms did not budge.

Another shape moved nearby. Mudge was sitting up on the bed of leaves he'd fashioned for himself. He looked over toward Jon-Tom as he stretched.

"Well, don't just sit there, damn it. Give me a hand here!"

"Wot, and interrupt a charmin' domestic tableau like that?"

"Don't try to be funny."

"Funnier than that?" He pointed at the helpless spell-singer. "Couldn't be if I tried, mate."

Glaring at him, Jon-Tom tried again to disengage himself, but the weight was too much for him. It was like trying to move a soft mountain.

"Come on, Mudge. Have a heart."

"Who, me? You know me better than that, mate." As he spoke Roseroar moved in her sleep, rolling partly across Jon-Tom's midsection and chest. He gasped and kicked his legs in a frantic attempt to extricate himself. The tigress purred thunderously atop him.

Mudge took his time getting to his feet, ambled lazily over to eye the arrangement thoughtfully. "Our dainty lady friend sounds 'appy enough. Best not to disturb 'er. I don't see wot you're fussin' about. It's not like she's got a 'and over your mouth. From where I stands it looks almost invitin', though I can't say as 'ow I'd trade places with you. I'd be lost under 'er."

Jon-Tom put a hand on the tigress's face and pushed. She stirred, moved slightly, and nearly bit his fingers off. He withdrew his hand quickly. She'd moved enough for him to breathe again, anyway.

"Any signs of pursuit?"

" 'Aven't smelled or 'eard a thing, mate. I think they're

still too disorganized. If they are lookin' for us, you can be sure 'tis to the south o' Malderpot and not 'ere. Still, the sooner we're on our way, the better." He turned, began gathering up his effects.

"Come on now, lad. No time to waste."

"That's real funny, Mudge. How am I supposed to get her off me?"

"Wake 'er up. Belt 'er one, mate."

"No thanks. I like my head where it is. On my shoulders. I don't know how'd she react to something like that in her sleep."

Mudge's eyes twinkled. "Be more interestin' to see wot she might do while she's awake."

There was no need to consider extreme action, however. All the talking had done its job. Roseroar snorted once and opened those bottomless yellow eyes.

"Well, good morning, man."

"Good morning yourself. Roseroar, I value your friendship, but you're breaking my arm."

Her expression narrowed. "Suh, are you insinuatin' that ah am too heavy?"

"No, no, nothing like that." Somewhere off in the bushes Mudge was attending to necessary bodily functions while trying to stifle his laughter. "Actually, I think you're rather svelte."

"Svelte." Roseroar considered the word. "That's nice. Ah like that. Are you saying I have a nice figure?"

"I never saw a tiger I didn't think was attractive," he confessed, honestly enough.

She looked mildly disappointed as she rolled off him. "What the fuzz-ball said is true. Yo ah at least half solicitah."

Jon-Tom rolled over and tried shaking his left arm, trying to restore the circulation at the same time as he was dreading its return. Pins and needles flooded his nerves and he gritted his teeth at the sensation.

"I did study some law in my own world. It might be my profession someday."

"Spellsinging's better," she rumbled. "Svelte?"

"Yeah." He sat up and began pulling on his boots.

"Nice. Ah think ah like yo, man."

"I like you, too, Roseroar."

"Svelte." She considered the new word thoughtfully. "Want to know mah word fo yo?" She was putting on her armor, checking to make sure each catch and strap was fastened securely. She grinned at him, showing six-inch fangs. "Cute. Yo ah kind o' cute."

"Gee." Jon-Tom kept his voice carefully neutral as he replied. "That's nice."

Mudge emerged from the woods, buttoning his shorts. "Gee, I always thought you were cute, too, mate."

"How'd you like your whiskers shoved up your ass?" Jon-Tom asked him softly.

"Calm down, mate." Somehow Mudge stifled his laughter. "Best we get goin' westward. We've given 'em the slip for the nonce, but sooner o' later the absence o' tracks o' mention of us south o' 'ere will hit 'im as distinctly peculiar and they'll start 'untin' for us elsewhere."

Jon-Tom slung the duar over his shoulder and hefted his staff. "Lead on."

Mudge bowed, his voice rich with mock servility. "As thy exalted cuteness decrees."

Jon-Tom tried to bash him with the staff, but the otter was much too fast for him.

V

It took several days for them to reach the outskirts of the Moors, a vast and, as far as anyone knew, uninhabited land which formed the western border of the Bellwoods and reached south all the way to the northern coast of the Glittergeist Sea. After a day's march into the Moors' depths, Mudge felt safe enough to angle southward for the first time since fleeing the city.

Transportation across the ocean was going to present a problem. No ports existed where the ocean met the southern edge of the Moors, and Jon-Tom agreed with the otter that it would be a bad idea to follow the shoreline back eastward toward the mouth of the Tailaroam. Chenelska would be sure to be looking for them in ports like Yarrowl.

As for the Moors themselves, they looked bleak but hardly threatening. Jon-Tom wondered how the place had acquired its widespread onerous reputation. Mudge could shed little light on the mystery, explaining only that rumor insisted anyone who went into the place never came out again, a pleasant thought to mull over as they hiked ever deeper into the foggy terrain.

It was a sorry land, mostly gray stone occasionally

stained red by iron. There were no trees, few bushes, a little grass. The sky was a perpetual puffy, moist gray.

Fog and mist made them miserable, except for Mudge. Nothing appeared to challenge their progress. A few mindless hoots and mournful howls were the only indications of mobile inhabitants, and nothing ever came close to their camps.

They marched onward into the heart of the Muddletup, where none penetrated. As they moved ever deeper into the Moors the landscape began to change, and not for the better. The last stunted trees disappeared. Here, in a place of eternal dampness and cloud cover, the fungi had taken over.

Enormous mushrooms and toadstools dripped with moisture as Jon-Tom and his companions walked beneath spore-filled canopies. Some of the gnarled, ugly growths had trunks as thick as junipers, while others thrust delicate, semi-transparent stems toward the sodden sky. There were no bright, cheerful colors to mitigate the depressing scene, which was mostly brown and gray. Even the occasional maroon or unwholesomely yellow specimen was a relief from the monotonous parade of dullness.

Some of the flora was spotted, some striped. One displayed a checkerboard pattern that reminded Jon-Tom of a non-Euclidian chessboard. Liverworts grew waist-high, while lichens and mosses formed a thick, cushiony carpet into which their boots sank up to the ankles. Clean granite was disfigured by crawling fungoid corruption growing on its surface. And over this vast, wild eruption of thallophytic life there hung a pervasive sense of desolation, of waste and fossilized hope.

The first couple of days had seen no slowing of their progress. Now their pace began to degenerate. They slept longer and spent less time over meals. It didn't matter what food they took from their packs or scavenged from the land: everything seemed to have lost its flavor. Whatever they consumed turned flat and tasteless in their mouths and sat heavy in their bellies. Even the water which fell fresh from the clouds had acquired a metallic, unsatisfying aftertaste.

They'd been in the Moors for almost a week when Jon-Tom tripped over the skeleton. Like everything else lately its discovery provoked little more than a tired murmur of indifference from his companions.

"So wot?" muttered Mudge. "Don't mean a damn thing."

"Ah'm sitting down," said Roseroar. "Ah'm tired."

So was Jon-Tom, but the sight of the stark white bone peeping out from beneath the encrusting rusts and mildews roused a dormant concern in his mind.

"This is all wrong," he told them. "There's something very wrong going on here."

"No poison, if that's wot you're thinkin', mate." Mudge indicated the growths surrounding them. "I've been careful. Everythin' local we've swallowed 'as been edible, even if it's tasted lousy."

"Lucky yo'," said Roseroar. "No game at all fo me. Ah find mahself reduced to eating not just weeds, but this crap. Ah declah ah've nevah been so bored with eating in all mah life."

"Boring, tired, tasteless . . . don't you see what's happening?" Jon-Tom told them.

"You're gettin' worked up over nothin', mate." The otter was lying on a mound of soft moss. "Settle yourself down. 'Ave a sip o' somethin'."

"Yes." Roseroar slipped off her swordbelt. "Let's just sit heah and rest awhile. There's no need to rush. We haven't seen a sign of pursuit since we left that town, and ah don't think we're likely to encounter any now."

"She's right, mate. Pull up a soft spot and 'ave a sit."

"Both of you *listen* to me." Jon-Tom tried to put some force into his voice, was frightened to hear it emerge from his lips flat and curiously empty of emotion. He felt sad and utterly useless. Something had begun to afflict him from the day they'd first set foot in the Moors. It was something more than just boredom with their surroundings, something far more penetrating and dangerous. It was a grayness of the heart, and it was digging its insidious way deeper and deeper into their thoughts, killing off determination and assurance as it went. Eventually, it would ruin their bodies as well. The skeleton was proof enough of that. Whatever was into them was patient and clever, much too calculating, it occurred to Jon-Tom, to be an accident of the environment.

He tried to find the enthusiasm to fight back as he turned to scream at the landscape. "Who are you? Why are you doing this to us? What is it you *want*?"

He felt like a fool. Worse, he knew his companions might think he was becoming unhinged. But they said nothing. He would've welcomed some outcry of skepticism. Instead, the sense of hopelessness settled ever deeper around them.

Nothing moved within the Moors. Of one thing he was fairly confident: this wasn't wizardry at work. It was too slow. He had to do something, but he didn't know what. All he could think of was how ironic it would be if, after surviving Malderpot, they were to perish here from a terminal case of the blahs.

So he was startled when a dull voice asked, "Don't you understand it all by now?"

"Who said that?" He whirled, trying to spot the speaker. Nothing moved.

"I did."

The voice came from an eight-foot-tall mushroom off to his left. The cap of this blotchy ochre growth dipped slightly toward him.

"Not that I couldn't have," said another growth.

"Nor I," agreed a third.

"Mushrooms," Jon-Tom said unsteadily, "don't talk."

"What?" said the first growth. "Sure, we're not loquacious, but that's a natural function of our existence. There isn't much to talk about, is there? I mean, it's not just a dull life, man, it's boring. B-o-r-i-n-g.''

"That's about the extent of it," agreed the giant toadstool against which Roseroar rested. She moved away from it hastily, showing more energy than she had in the previous several days, and put a hand to the haft of each sword.

"I mean, give it some thought." The first mushroom again, which was taking on something of the air of a fungoid spokesman. Jon-Tom saw no lips or mouth. The words, the thoughts, came fully formed into his mind through a kind of clammy telepathy. "What would we talk about?"

"Nothing worth wasting the time discussing," agreed another mushroom with a long, narrow cap in the manner of a morrel. "I mean, you spend your whole existence sitting in the same spot, never seeing anything new, never moving around. So what's your biggest thrill? Getting to make spores?"

"Yeah, big deal," commented the toadstool. "So we don't talk. You never hear us talk, you think fungoids don't talk. Ambulatories are such know-it-alls."

"It doesn't matter," said the second mushroom. "Nothing matters. We're wasting our efforts."

"Wait." Jon-Tom approached the major mushroom, feeling a little silly as he did so. "You're doing something to us. You have been ever since we entered the deep moors."

"What makes you think we're doing anything to you?" said the spokesthing. "Why should we make the effort to do anything to anyone?"

"We've changed since we entered this land. We feel different."

"Different how, man?" asked the toadstool.

"Depressed. Tired, worn-out, useless, hopeless. Our outlook on life has been altered."

"What makes you think we're responsible?" said the

second mushroom. "That's just how life is. It's the normal state of existence. You can't blame us for that."

"It's *not* the normal state of existence."

"It is in the Moors," argued the first mushroom.

Jon-Tom held his ground. "There's some kind of telepathy at work here. We've been absorbing your feelings of hopelessness, your idea that nothing's worth much of anything. It's been eating at us."

"Look around you, man. What do you see?"

Jon-Tom turned a slow circle. Instead of the half-hoped-for revelation, his gaze swept over more of what they'd seen the past dreary days—rocks, mushrooms, lichens and mosses, mist and cloud cover.

"Now, I ask you," sighed the first mushroom, "is that depressing or what? I mean, it is de-press-ing."

Jon-Tom could feel his resolve slipping dangerously. Mudge and Roseroar were half-asleep already. He had the distinct feeling that if he joined them, none of them would ever wake up again. The sight of white bone nearby revitalized him. How long had it taken the owner of that skeleton to become permanently depressed?

"I guess you *might* consider your existence here depressing."

"Might consider?" moaned the toadstool. "It *is* depressing. No maybes about it. Like, I'm a *fungus*, man. That's depressing all by itself."

"I've eaten some mushrooms that were downright exciting," Jon-Tom countered.

"A cannibal, too," said the tall toadstool tiredly. "How depressing." It let out a vast telepathic sigh, a wave of anxiety and sadness that rolled over Jon-Tom like a wave.

He staggered, shook off the cobwebs that threatened to bind his mind. "Stop that."

"Stop what? Why sweat it? Just relax, man. You're full of hurry, and desire, and all kinds of useless mental baggage. Why knock yourself out worrying about things that don't matter? Nothing matters. Lie down here, relax, take it easy. Let your foolish concerns fly bye-bye. Open yourself to the true blandness of reality and see how much better you'll feel for it.''

Jon-Tom started to sit down, wrestled himself back to an upright stance. He pointed toward the skeleton.

"Like that one?"

"He was only reacting sensibly," said the toadstool.

"He's dead." Jon-Tom's voice turned accusing. "You killed him. At least, this place killed him."

"Life killed him. Slain by dullness. Murdered by monotony. He did what comes naturally to all life. He decayed."

"Decayed? You flourish amidst decay, don't you? You thrive on it."

"He calls this thriving," mumbled another toadstool. "He went the way of all flesh, that's all. Sure, we broke down his organic components. Sometimes I wonder why we bother. It's all such a waste. We live for death. Talk about dull, man. It's, like, numbsville."

Jon-Tom turned and walked over to shake Roseroar, shoving hard against the enormous shoulder. "Wake up, Roseroar. Come on, wake up, damn it!"

"Why bother?" she murmured sleepily, eyeing him through half-closed eyes. "Let me sleep. No, don't let me sleep." The feeble plea hit him like a cry for help.

"Don't worry, I won't. Wake up!" He continued to shake her until she sat up and rubbed at her eyes.

He moved over to where Mudge lay sprawled on his side, kicked the otter ungently. "Move it, water rat! This isn't like you. Think about where we're going. Think of the ocean, of clear salt air."

"I'd rather not, mate," said the otter tiredly. "No point to it, really."

"True true, true," intoned the fungoid chorus of doom.

"I'll get up in a minute, guv'nor. There's no rush, and we're in no 'urry. Let me be."

"Like hell, I will. Think of the food we've enjoyed.

Think of the good times ahead, of the money to be made. Think,'' he said with sudden alacrity, ''of the three days you spent at the Elegant Bitch.''

The otter opened his eyes wide, smiling weakly. ''Aye, now that's a memory t' 'old tight to.''

''Useless, useless, useless,'' boomed the a cappella ascomycetes.

'' 'Tis kind o' pointless, mate,'' said the otter. For an instant Jon-Tom despaired, fearing he'd lost his friend for good. Then Mudge sprang to his feet and glared at the surrounding growth. ''But 'tis also one 'ell of a lot o' fun!''

''Help Roseroar,'' Jon-Tom ordered him, a great relief surging through him. He turned his attention back to their subtle, even indifferent, assailants.

''Look, I can't help what you are and I can't help it if you find your existences so depressing.''

''It's not how we find them,'' said the first mushroom. ''It's how they are. Don't you think we'd change it if we could? But we can't. This is life: boring, dull, unchanging, gray, depressing, decay . . .''

''But it doesn't have to be that way. It's you who let it remain so.'' Unslinging the duar, he launched into the brightest, cheeriest song he could think of: John Denver's ''Rocky Mountain High.'' He finished with Rick Springfield's ''We All Need the Human Touch.'' The gray sky didn't clear, the mist didn't lift, but he felt a lot better.

''There! What did you think of that?''

''Truly depressing,'' said the toadstool. ''Not the songs. Your voice.''

Eighty million mushrooms in the Muddletup Moors, Jon-Tom mused, and I have to get a music critic. He laughed at the absurdity of it, and the laughter made him feel better still.

''Isn't there anything that can lighten your existence, make your lives more bearable so you'll leave us alone?''

''We can't help sharing our feelings,'' said the second

mushroom. "We're not laying all this heavy stuff on you to be mean, man. We ain't mean. We're indifferent. What's bringing you down is your own knowledge of life's futility and your own inability to do anything about it. Face it, man: the cosmos is a downer."

Hopeless. These beings were hopeless, Jon-Tom told himself angrily. How could you fight something that didn't come at you with shields and swords and spears? What could he employ against a broadside of moroseness, a barrage of doubt?

They sounded so sure of themselves, so confident of the truth. All right then, he'd show them the truth! If he couldn't fight them by differing with them, maybe he could win by agreeing with them.

He took a deep breath. "The trouble with you is that you're all manic-depressives."

A long silence, an atmosphere of consideration, before the toadstool inquired, "What are you talking about, man?" In the background a couple of rusts whispered to one another, "Talk about a *weird* dude."

"I haven't had that much psychology, but pre-law requires some," Jon-Tom explained. "You know, I'll bet not one of you has ever considered psychoanalysis for your problems."

"Considered what?" asked the first mushroom.

Jon-Tom found a suitable rock—a hard, uncomfortable one sure to keep him awake. "Pay attention now. Anybody here ever heard of Franz Kafka?"

Several hours passed. Mudge and Roseroar had time to reawaken completely, and the mental voices surrounding them had become almost alive, though all were still flat and tinged with melancholy.

". . . And another thing," Jon-Tom was saying as he pointed upward, "that sky you're all always referring to. Nothing but infantile anal-retentive reinforcement. Well, maybe not exactly that," he corrected himself as he reminded himself of the rather drastic anatomical differences between himself and his audience, "but it's the same idea."

"We can't do anything about it," said the giant toadstool. "The mist and clouds and coolness are always with us. If they weren't, we'd all die. That's depressing. And what's even more depressing is that we don't particularly *like* perpetual mist and clouds and fog."

Jon-Tom struggled desperately for a reply, feeling victory slipping from his grasp. "It's not the fact that it's cloudy and damp all the time that matters. What matters is your outlook on the fact."

"What do you mean, our outlook?" asked a newcomer, an interested slime mold. "Our outlook is glum and miserable and pointless."

"Only if you think of it that way," Jon-Tom informed it. "Sure, you can think of yourselves as hopeless. But why not view your situation in a positive light? It's just a matter of redirecting your outlook on life. Instead of regarding your natural state as depressing, think of the constancy of climate and terrain as stabilizing, reassuring. In mental health, attitude is everything."

"I'm not sure I follow you, man," said another mushroom.

"Me neither, mate."

"Be quiet, Mudge. Listen, existence is what you make of it. How you view your surroundings will affect how you feel about them."

"How can we feel anything other than depressed in surroundings like these?" wondered the liverworts.

"Right, then. If you feel more comfortable, go with those thoughts. There's nothing wrong with being depressed and miserable all the time, so long as you feel *good* about it. Have you ever felt bright and cheery?"

"No, no, no," was the immediate and general consensus.

"Then how do you know that it's any better than feeling depressed and miserable? Maybe one's no better than the other."

"That's not what the other travelers who come our way

say," murmured the toadstool, "before they relax, see it our way, and settle down for a couple of months of steady decomposition."

Jon-Tom shivered slightly. "Sure, that's what they say, but do they look any better off, act any more contented, any more in tune with their surroundings than you do?"

"Naturally they're not as in tune with their surroundings," said the first mushroom, "but these surroundings are . . ."

". . . Damp and depressing," Jon-Tom finished for it. "That's okay if you accept it. It's all right to feel depressed all the time if you feel good about it. Why can't it be fun to feel depressed? If that's how your environment makes you feel, then if you feel that why it means you're in tune with your environment, and that should make you feel good, and secure, and confident."

Roseroar's expression reflected her confusion, but she said nothing. Mudge just sat quietly, shaking his head. But they were thinking, and it kept them from growing dangerously listless again.

"Hey," murmured a purple toadstool, "maybe it is okay to feel down and dumpy all the time, if that's what works for you."

"That's it," said Jon-Tom excitedly. "That's the point I'm trying to make. Everything, every entity, is different. Just because one state of mind works for us ambulatories doesn't mean it ought to work the same way for you. At least you aren't confused all the time, the way most of my kind are."

"Far fucking out," announced one enlightened truffle from beneath a clump of shelf fungi. "Existence is pointless. Life is decrepit. Consciousness sucks. And you know what? I feel *good* about it! It all fits."

"Beautiful," said Jon-Tom. "Go with that." He put his hands on his hips and turned a circle. "Anybody else here have any trouble dealing with that?"

"Well, we do," said a flotilla of mushrooms clinging to a scummy pile of dead weeds near a small pool.

"Tell me about it," said Jon-Tom coaxingly.

"It started when we were just spores. . . ."

It went on like that all through the night. By morning, Jon-Tom was exhausted, but the fungoid forest surrounding him was suffused with the first stages of exhilaration . . . in a maudlin manner, of course. But by and large, the group-therapy session had been wildly successful.

Mudge and Roseroar had recovered completely from their insidiously induced lethargies and were eager to set out again. Jon-Tom held back. He wanted to make certain the session would have at least a semipermanent effect, or it wouldn't last them through the Moors to the Glittergeist.

"You've certainly laid a heavy trip on us, man," said the large mushroom that served as speaker for the rest of the forest.

"I'm sure that if you hold to those thoughts, go with the flow, make sure you leave yourselves enough mental space, you'll find that you'll always feel better about your places in existence," Jon-Tom assured it.

"I don't know," said the big toadstool, and for an instant the veil of gloom which had nearly proved lethal descended about Jon-Tom all over again. "But just considering it makes me more inclined to accept it."

The cloud of despair dissipated. "That's it." Jon-Tom grew aware of just how tired he was. "I'd like to stay and chat some more, but we need to be on our way to the Glittergeist again. You wouldn't happen to know in which direction it lies?"

Behind him, the shapes of three giant amanitas crooked their crowns into the mist. "This way, friend. Pass freely from this place . . . though if you'd like to join us in our contented dissolution, you're more than welcome to remain and decompose among us."

"Couldn't think of it," Jon-Tom replied politely, falling

in behind Mudge and Roseroar as they started southward.
"See, I'm not into decomposition."

"Tell us about it," several rusts urged him.

Worrying that he might be leaving behind a forest full of
fungoid Frankensteins, Jon-Tom waved it off by saying,
"Some other time."

"Sure, that's it, go on and leave," snapped the toadstool. "We're not worth talking to."

"I've just spent a whole night talking to you. Now
you're bringing out new feelings of insecurity."

"No I'm not," said the toadstool, defensive. "It's the
same thing as depression."

"Isn't. Why don't you discuss it for a while?" A rising
mental susurration trailed in his wake as he hastened after
his companions.

Word of the therapy session preceded them through the
Muddletup. The intensity of the depression around them
varied considerably in strength according to the success of
Jon-Tom's therapy. They detoured around the worst areas
of despair, where the mental aura bordered on the comatose, and as a result they were never again afflicted with
the urge to lie down and chuck it all.

Eventually the fungi gave way to blossoming bushes and
evergreens. The morning they emerged from the woods
onto a wide, gravelly beach formed of wave-polished
agates and jade was one of the happiest of Jon-Tom's life.

Pushing his ramwood staff into the gravel, he hung his
backpack from the knobbed end, sat down, and inhaled
deeply of the sea air. The sharp salty smell was heartbreak-
ingly familiar.

Mudge let out a whoop; threw off his bow, quiver, pack,
and clothes; and plunged recklessly into the warm surf.
Jon-Tom felt the urge to join him, but he was just too
damn tired. Roseroar sat down next to him. Together they
watched the gleeful otter porpoise gracefully through the
waves.

"I wish I had my board," Jon-Tom murmured.

"Yo what?" Roseroar looked down at him.

"It's a flat piece of fiberglass and epoxy resin. It floats. You stand on it and let the waves carry you toward shore."

Roseroar considered, decided. "That sounds like fun. Do y'all think yo could teach me?"

He smiled apologetically. "Like I said, I don't have my board with me."

"How big a board do yo need?" Rising, she started stripping off her armor. "Surely not biggah than this?"

"Now, wait a minute, Roseroar. I thought cats hated the water."

"Not tigahs, sugah. Come on. Ah'll race yo to the beach."

He hesitated, glanced up and down the gravel as though somone might appear on this deserted section of shore.

What the hell, he told himself.

The clean tropical salt water washed away the last lingering feelings of depression. Though Roseroar's back wasn't as even as waxed fiberglass, his toes found plenty of purchase in the thick white fur. The tigress's muscles shifted according to his instructions as she steered easily through the waves with powerful arms and legs. It took no time at all to discover that surfing on the back of a tiger was far more exhilarating than plying the waves on a hunk of inanimate resin.

As the afternoon drew to a close, they lay on the warm beach and let the sun dry them. Clean and refreshed, Jon-Tom made a fire and temporary shelter of driftwood while Mudge and Roseroar went scavenging. Life in abundance clung to the shore.

The two unlikely hunters returned with a load of crustaceans the size of king crabs. Three of these—killed, cracked, and cooked over an open fire—were sufficient to fill even the tigress's belly. This time Jon-Tom didn't even twitch as he snuggled up against the amazon's flank. Mudge curled up on the far side of the fire. For the first time since they'd fled Malderpot, they all slept peacefully.

VI

As usual, Mudge woke first. He sat up, stretched, and yawned, his whiskers quivering with the effort. The sun was just up and the last smoke fleeing the firepit. Something, some slight noise, had disturbed the best night's rest he'd had in weeks.

He heard it again, no mistake. Curious, he dressed quickly and tiptoed past his still somnolent companions. As he made his way over a sandy hillock flecked with beach grass, he slowed. A cautious glance over the crest revealed the source of the disturbance.

They were not alone on the beach. A small single-masted sailing craft was grounded on the gravel. Four large, ugly-looking specimens of varying species clustered around a single, much smaller individual. Two of them were arguing over a piece of clothing. Mudge shrugged mentally and prepared to retreat. None of his business. What had awakened him was the piteous cry for help of the person trapped among the ruffians. It was an elderly voice but a strong one.

There was a touch on his shoulder. Inhaling sharply, he

rolled and reached for his short sword, then relaxed. It was Jon-Tom, with Roseroar close behind.

"What's happening?"

"Nothin', mate. None o' our business, wot? Let's leave it be. I'm ready for breakfast."

"Is that all you ever think of? Food, money, and sex?"

"You do me a wrong, guv'nor. Sometimes 'tis sex, food, and money. Then again at times 'tis—"

"Never mind," said the exasperated Jon-Tom.

"Foah against one," muttered Roseroar angrily, "and the one looks none too strong. Not very gallant."

"We've got to do something," Jon-Tom murmured. "Mudge, you sneak around behind the trees off to the left and cover them from there. I'll make a frontal assault from here. Roseroar, you . . ." But the tigress was already over the hill and charging down the slope on the other side.

So much for careful tactics and strategy, Jon-Tom thought.

"Come on, Mudge!"

"Now wait a minim, mate." The otter watched Jon-Tom follow in Roseroar's wake, waving his staff and yelling at the top of his lungs. "Bloody fools!" He notched an arrow into his bow and followed.

But there was to be no fight. The assailants turned to see all seven feet and five hundred pounds of white tigress bearing down on them, waving twin swords and bellowing fit to shake the leaves off the nearby trees. There was a concerted rush for the boat.

The four paddled like fiends and were out of sword range before she entered the water in angry pursuit, throwing insults and challenges after them. Mudge might have reached the boat with an arrow or two, but saw no point in meaningless killing or antagonizing strangers. As far as he was concerned, the best battle was the one that never took place.

Meantime Jon-Tom was bending solicitously over the exhausted subject of their rescue. He put an arm beneath the slim furry neck and helped it sit up. It was a ferret, and an old one, distant kin to Mudge's line but thinner still. Much of the normally brown fur was tipped with silver. So was the black mask that ran across the face.

The stranger was clad in beige shorts and vest and wore sandals instead of boots. A plain, floppy hat lay trampled in the sand nearby, next to a small leather sack. Several other similar sacks lay scattered along the beach. All looked empty.

Gradually the elderly ferret's breathing slowed. He opened his eyes, saw Jon-Tom, then looked around wildly.

"Easy, easy, friend. They re gone. We saw to that."

The ferret gave him a disbelieving look, then turned his gaze toward the beach. His eyes settled on the scattered leather sacks.

"My stock, my goods!" He broke away from Jon-Tom, who watched while the oldster went through each sack, one at a time. Finally he sat down on the sand, one sack draped across his lap. He sighed listlessly, threw it aside.

"Gone." He shook his head sadly. "All gone."

"Wot's all gone, senior?" Mudge prodded one of the sacks with a boot.

The ferret didn't look up at him. "My stock, my poor stock. I am . . . I was, a humble trader of trinkets, plying my trade along the shores east of here. I was set upon by those worthless brigands"—he nodded seaward, to where the retreating boat had raised sail and was disappearing toward the horizon—"who stole everything I have managed to accumulate in a short, unworthy life. They kept me and forced me to do their menial work, to cook and clean and wash for them while they preyed upon other unsuspecting travelers.

"They said they would let me go unharmed. Finally they tired of me, but instead of returning me to a place of civilization they brought me here to this empty, uninhabited shore, intending to maroon me in an unknown land where I might starve. They stole what little I had in this world, taunted me by leaving my stock bags, and would have stolen my life as well at the last moment had you not come along, for I was refusing to be abandoned.''

"Don't give us too much credit,'' Jon-Tom advised him. "Our being in a position to rescue you was an accident.''

"You can say that again, mate,'' growled the disgusted Mudge as he slung his bow back over his shoulder.

Jon-Tom ignored the otter. "We're glad we could help. I don't like seeing anyone taken advantage of, especially senior citizens.''

"What?''

"Older people.''

"Ah. But how can I thank you, sir? How can I show my gratitude? I am destitute.''

"Forget it.'' The ferret's effusiveness was making Jon-Tom uncomfortable. "We're glad we could help.''

The ferret rose, wincing and putting one hand against his back. "I am called Jalwar. To whom do I owe my salvation?''

"I'm Jon-Tom. I'm a spellsinger. Of sorts.''

The ferret nodded gravely. "I knew at once you were mighty ones.''

Jon-Tom indicated the disgruntled Mudge. "That ball of fuzzy discontent is my friend Mudge.'' The otter grunted once. "And this tower of cautionless strength is Roseroar.''

"I am honored to be in your presence,'' said the ferret humbly, proceeding to prostrate himself on the beach and grasping Jon-Tom's boots. "I have nothing left. My stock is gone, my money, everything save the clothes I wear. I owe you my life. Take me into your service and let me serve you.''

"Now, wait a minute.'' Jon-Tom moved his boots out of the ferret's paws. "I don't believe in slavery.''

" 'Ere now, mate, let's not be 'asty.'' Mudge was quick to intervene. "Consider the poor suck—uh, this poor unfortunate chap. 'E's got nothin', 'e 'asn't. 'E'll need protection, or the next bunch 'e runs into will kill 'im for sure, just for 'is clothes.'' He eyed the ferret hopefully. "Wot about it, guv? Can you cook?''

"I have some small talent in the kitchen, good sir.''

"Mudge . . .'' Jon-Tom said warningly. The otter ignored him.

"You said you washed clothes.''

"That I did, good sir. I have the ability to make even ancient attire smell sweet as clover again, with the slightest of cleansing materials. I am also handy at repairing garments. Despite my age, I am not a weakling. I can more than carry my weight.''

Mudge strutted about importantly. " 'Ere then, friend, I think we should take pity on you and admit you to our company, wot?''

"Mudge, you know how I feel about servants.''

"It wouldn't be like that at all, Jon-Tom. 'E *does* need our protection, and 'e'll never get out o' this place without our 'elp, and 'e's more than willin' to contribute 'is share.''

The ferret nodded enthusiastically. "Please accept my service, good sir . . . and madame. Allow me to accompany you. Perhaps being proximate to such mighty ones as yourselves will improve my own ill fortune.''

"I'll bet you were a good trader,'' Jon-Tom commented. "Okay, you can come with us, but as an equal. Not as a servant or slave. We'll pay you a decent wage.'' He remembered the purse filled with gold, stolen by Zancresta's thugs. "As soon as we can afford it, that is.''

"Food and shelter and protection is all I ask, great sir.''

"And stop calling me sir,'' said Jon-Tom. "I've introduced you to everyone by name.''

"As you wish, Jon-Tom.'' The ferret turned to look down the beach. "What do we now? I presume you are bound to the east, for if one walks long enough one will come 'round again to the lands bordering the Bellwoods and the River Tailaroam, where civilization is to be encountered.''

"Don't I wish,'' Mudge grumbled.

Jon-Tom shook his head. "We don't go to the east,
Jalwar. We go southwest, to Snarken."

"Across the Glittergeist? Sir . . . Jon-Tom . . . I have lived
long and seen much. The voyage to Snarken is long and
fraught with danger and difficulty. Better to begin the long
trek to the mouth of the Tailaroam. Besides, how could
one take ship from this deserted land? And north of here
lie the Muddletup Moors, where none may penetrate."

"*We* penetrated," said Mudge importantly.

"Did you? If you say it so, I doubt it not. Still, this far
north places us well away from the east–west trade routes.
We will encounter no vessels here."

"You won't get any arguments from me on that score,
mate," said Mudge. "Best to do as you say, go back to the
Bellwoods and the Tailaroam and start over. Likely
Chenelska's give up on us by now."

"No," said Jon-Tom firmly. "I am not going back and I
am not starting over. We've come too far."

Mudge squinted up at him. "Well now, you've just
'eard this wise old chap. 'Ow do you propose to get us
across that?" He pointed to the broad, sailless expanse of
the Glittergeist. "I like to swim, lad, but I prefer swimmin'
across water I can cross."

"What can yo do, Jon-Tom?" Roseroar asked him.

He stood fuming silently for a moment before blurting
out, "I can damn well conjure us up a boat, that's what!"

"Uh-oh." Mudge retreated toward the trees, searching
for a boulder of appropriate size to conceal himself behind.
" 'Is nibs is pissed off and 'e's goin' to try spellsingin'
again."

Roseroar eyed the otter curiously. "Isn't that his business, fuzzball?"

"That may be wot some calls it. Me, I'd as soon brush
a crocodile's teeth than 'elp 'im with 'is work."

"Ah don't understand. Is he a spellsinger or not?"

" 'E is," Mudge admitted. "Of that there's no longer
any doubt. 'Tis just that 'e 'as this disconcertin' tendency

to misfire from time to time, and when it 'appens, I don't want to be in the line o' fire."

"Go on, Roseroar," Jon-Tom told her. "Get back there and hide behind a rock with him." He was mad at the otter. Hadn't he, Jon-Tom, helped to bring about the great victory at the Jo-Troom Gate? Purely by accident of course, but still . . .

"No suh," said the tigress, offended. "If'n y'all don't mind, I'll stand right heah."

"Good for you." Jon-Tom unlimbered his duar, turned away to confront the open sea, where soon he hoped to see a proper ship riding empty at anchor. Turning also kept Roseroar from seeing how nervous he was.

Once before on a far-distant river he'd tried to bring forth a boat to carry himself and his companions. Instead, he'd ended up with Falameezar, the Marxist dragon. That misplaced conjuration had produced unexpectedly benign results, but there was no guarantee he'd be as fortunate if he fouled up a second time.

It was too late to back down now. He'd already made his boast. He felt Roseroar's gaze on the back of his neck. If he backed down now he'd prove himself an incompetent to Mudge and a coward to the tigress. He had to try.

He considered several songs and discarded them all as unsuitable. He was beginning to grow frantic when a song so obvious, so simple, offered what seemed like an obvious way out.

His fingers tested the duar's strings and he began to sing.

Flecks of light sprang to instant life around him. It was as though the sand underfoot had come to glowing life. The lights were Gneechees, those minute ultrafast specks of existence that were drawn irresistibly to magic in motion. They coalesced into a bright, dancing cloud around him, and as usual, when he tried to look straight at any of them, they vanished. Gneechees were those suggestions of something everyone sees out of the corner of an eye but aren't there when you turn to look at them.

But he sensed their presence. So did Roseroar and the others. It was a good sign, an indication that the spellsinging was working. Certainly the tune he played seemed harmless enough, even to the wary Mudge, whose opinion of Jon-Tom's musical tastes differed little from that of the average PTA president.

The otter had to admit that for a change the otherworldly ditty Jon-Tom was reciting was easy on the ears, even if the majority of the words, as was true of all of Jon-Tom's songs, were quite incomprehensible.

Jon-Tom had chosen the song as much out of desperation as need. The song was "Sloop *John B.*," by the Beach Boys. Given their present needs, it was a logical enough choice.

Nothing happened right away. But before long, Jalwar was making protective signs over his face and chest while cowering close to Mudge for protection, while the otter waited nervously for the unexpected to manifest itself. Despite her own awe at what was taking place on the beach, Roseroar stood her ground.

Mudge was worrying needlessly. For once, for the very first time, it looked like Jon-Tom's efforts were to be rewarded with success. For once it appeared that his spellsong was going to produce only what he wanted. The otter moved hesitantly out from behind the shelter of the boulder, while simultaneously holding himself ready to rush for the trees at the first hint of trouble.

"Bugger me for a blue-eyed bandicoot," he muttered excitedly. "The lad's gone an' done it!"

Rocking gently in the waves just beyond the breaking surf was a single-masted sloop. The stern faced shoreward and on the name-plate everyone could clearly make out the words JOHN B.

Jon-Tom let the last words of the song trail away. With it went the Gneechees and the cloud of blue fog from which the boat had emerged. It bobbed gently at anchor, awaiting them.

Roseroar put a proud paw on Jon-Tom's shoulder. "Sugah, bless mah soul if it isn't a spellsingah yo are. That's a fine-looking ship, for all that her lines are strange to me, and ah've sailed many a craft."

Jon-Tom continued to pluck fitfully at the duar as if fearful that the sloop, solid as she looked, might disappear at any moment in a rush of fog.

"Glad you think so. Me, I've never been on anything bigger than a surfboard in my life."

"Not to worry. Ah don't recognize the mannah of ship, but if she sails, ah can handle her."

"So can I." Jalwar appeared behind them. "In my youth I spent much time sailing many kinds of ships."

"See?" said Mudge, joining them on the beach. "The old fur's provin' 'imself valuable already."

"Okay." Jon-Tom nodded reluctantly. "Let's see what she's like on board."

Mudge led them out to the boat, as at home in the water as he was on land. The others followed. By the time Jon-Tom reached the bottom of the boarding ladder, the otter had completed a preliminary inspection.

"She's fully stocked, she is, though the packin's bloody strange."

"Let me have a look." Jon-Tom went first to the galley.

Cans and packages bore familiar labels like Hormel, Armor, Oscar Mayer, and Hebrew National. There was more than enough food for an extensive journey, and they could fish on the way. The tank for the propane stove read full. Jon-Tom tried a burner, was rewarded with a blast of blue flame that caused Roseroar to pull back.

"Ah don't see no source of fire."

"The ship arrives already fully spelled for traveling," Jalwar murmured appreciatively. "Impressive."

"In the song she's supposed to be on a long voyage," Jon-Tom explained.

There was a diesel engine meant to supplement the sails.
Jon-Tom didn't try it. Let it wait until they were becalmed.
Then he could dazzle them with new magic.

"Roseroar, since you're the most experienced sailor
among us, why don't you be captain?"

"As you wish, Jon-Tom." She squeezed through the
hatchway back onto the deck and began familiarizing
herself with the unusual but not unfathomable rigging. As
with any modern sailing ship, the sloop would almost run
the sails up and down the masts all by itself. It didn't take
the tigress long to figure it out.

An electric winch made short work of the anchor.
Roseroar spun the wheel, the sloop hove around with a
warm breeze filling its sails, and they headed out to sea.
Within an hour they had left the gravel beach and the
Muddletup Moors with its confused fungoid inhabitants far
behind.

"Which way to Snarken?" she asked as she worked the
wheel and a hand winch simultaneously. The mainsail
billowed in the freshening wind.

"I don't know. You're the sailor."

"Sailor ah confess to, but ah'm no navigator, man."

"Southwest," Mudge told her. "For now that's good
enough."

Roseroar adjusted their heading, brought it in line with
the directions supplied by the compass. "Southwest it is."
The sloop changed directions smoothly, responding instantly
to the tigress's light touch on the wheel.

Feeling reasonably confident that at last all was right
with the world, Jon-Tom reprised the song and for good
measure added a chorus of the Beach Boys' "Sail On, Sail
On, Sailor." The sun was warm, the wind steady, and
Snarken seemed just over the near horizon.

Putting up the duar, he escorted Jalwar down to the
galley, there to explain the intricacies of the propane stove
and such otherworldly esoterica as Saran Wrap and can

openers to their designated chef. That and the rest of a fine day well done, he allowed himself to be first to bed.

To be awakened by rough hands shaking him violently.

"Get up, get up, spellsinger!"

Feeling very strange, Jon-Tom rolled over, to find himself staring into the worried face of the ferret.

"What . . . whash wrong?" He was startled by the sound of his own voice, unnaturally thick and slurred. And the boat seemed to be rolling in circles.

"We are in bad trouble, spellsinger. Bad trouble." Jalwar disappeared.

Jon-Tom sat up. It took three tries. Then he tried to get out of the bunk and discovered he couldn't tell the floor from the ceiling. The floor found him.

"Wot was that?" said a distant voice.

He struggled to get up. "I don't . . ." He reached for the railing of the lower bunk and tried to pull himself upright. "Wheresh the . . . ?" Somehow he managed to drag himself to a standing position. He stood there on shaky knees that felt determined to go their own way, exclusive of any contrariwise instructions from his brain.

"Whash wrong with me?" he moaned.

Two faces appeared in the doorway, one above the other. Both were blurred.

"Shee-it," said Roseroar. "He's drunk! Ah didn't see him get into any liquor."

"Nor did I," said Mudge, trying to push past her. "Give me room, you bloody great amazon!" He put his hands on Jon-Tom's shoulders and gripped hard. Jon-Tom staggered backward.

"Blister me for a brown vole if you're not. Where'd you find the hootch, guv'nor?"

"What hoosh?" Jon-Tom replied thickly. "I didn't . . ." The floor almost went out from under him. "Say, whoosh driving thish bush?"

A disgusted Mudge stepped back. "Can't abide anyone who can't 'old 'is booze."

"Leave him fo now," said Roseroar. "We'll have to handle this ourselves." They turned to leave.

"Hey, wait!" Jon-Tom yelled. He took a step forward, and the boat, sly and tricky craft that it was, deliberately yanked the floor out from under him. He slammed into the door, hung on for dear life.

Mudge was right, he realized through the glassy haze that had formed over his eyeballs. I *am* drunk. Try as he might, he couldn't remember imbibing anything stronger than orange juice at supper. After reprising a couple of choruses of "Sloop *John B*." to make sure the boat didn't dematerialize out from beneath them in the middle of the night, he'd gone to bed. Jalwar was awake and alert. Everyone was except him.

Suddenly he found himself in desperate need of a porthole, barely located one in time to stick his face out and throw his guts all over the equally upset ocean. When he finally finished puking he was soaking wet from the spray. He felt a little less queasy but not any soberer.

Somehow he managed to slam the porthole shut and refasten it. He staggered toward the gangway, pulled himself toward the deck.

Wind hit him hard the instant he stepped out on the teak planking, and rain filled his vision. Roseroar was holding the wheel steady with grim determination, but Mudge and Jalwar were having a terrible time trying to wrestle the mainsail down.

"Hurry it up!" the tigress roared, her voice barely audible above the storm, "or we'll lose it fo sure!"

"I don't care if we do," Jon-Tom moaned, putting both hands to the sides of his head, "just let's not shout about it, shall we?"

"Tell it to the sky, spellsinger," pleaded Jalwar.

"Yeah, use your magic, mate," added Mudge. "Turn this bloomin' weather back to normal!" Jon-Tom noticed that both of them were soaked. "Get rid of this bloody bedamned storm!"

"Anything, anything," he told them, "if you'll just stop shouting." He staggered and nearly went careening overboard, just managed to save himself by grabbing on to a stay. "I don't unnershtand. It wash so calm when I went to bed."

"Well 'tis not calm now, mate," snapped Mudge, wrestling with the heavy, wet sail.

"Ah've nevah seen a storm like this come up so quickly." Roseroar continued fighting with the wheel.

"The words," Jalwar muttered. "The words of the spellsinging! Don't you remember?" He looked straight at Jon-Tom. "Don't you remember the words?"

"But ish just the chorush," Jon-Tom groaned. "Jusht the chorush." He mumbled them again. " 'Thish ish the worsht trip, I've ever been on.' I didn't mean that part of the shong."

The ferret was nodding. "So you sang. The spirits cannot distinguish between what you sing and mean and what you sing and do not mean. They have a way of taking everything literally."

"But ish *not* the worsht trip I've ever been on!" Jon-Tom stood away from the rail on rubbery legs and screamed his protest at the skies that threatened to swamp them. "Ish *not!*"

The skies paid him no heed.

For hours they battled the winds. Twice they were in danger of being swamped. They were saved only by the unmagical efforts of the sloop's pump. Somehow Jon-Tom got it started, though the effort made him upchuck all over the engine room. That wouldn't happen again, though. His stomach was empty.

If only it would *feel* empty.

Soon after they pumped out the second holdful of water, the storm began to abate. An hour later the mountainous seas started to subside. And still there was no real relief, because thunder and lightning gave way to a thick, impenetrable fog.

Mudge was leaning on the rail, grumbling. "We'd better not be near any land, mates." He glanced upward. A faint glow suffused the upper reaches of the fog bank, which had not thinned in the slightest. "I know you're up there, you great big ugly yellow bastard! Why don't you burn this driftin' piss off so we can see to be on our way!"

"The words of the song," Jalwar murmured. Mudge snarled at him.

"And you pack in it, guv'nor, or I'll do it for you."

It was morning. Somewhere the sun was up there, probably laughing at them. The compass still showed the way, but the wind had vanished with the storm, and none of Jon-Tom's feeble coaxing could induce the shiny new diesel engine to perform.

The restored sail hung limp against the mast. The sloop was floating through glassy, smooth, shallow water. A sandy bottom occasionally rose dangerously close to the keel, only to fall away again into pale blue depths each time it looked like they were about to ground. Roseroar steered as best she could, and with an otter and a ferret aboard there was at least no shortage of sharp eyesight.

But as the day wore on and the fog clung tenaciously to them, it began to look as if Jon-Tom's song was to prove their simultaneous salvation and doom. The wind remained conspicuous by its absence. Sooner or later the shallows would close in around them and they would find themselves marooned forever in the midst of a strange sea.

The tension was taking its toll on everyone, even Roseroar. Their spellsinger, who had conjured up this wonderful craft, was of no use to anyone, least of all himself. Thankfully he no longer threw up. Yet despite his unarguable abstinence from any kind of drink, he remained falling-down drunk. Smashed. Potted.

If anything, his condition had worsened. He strolled about the deck muttering songs so incomprehensible and slurred none of his companions could decipher them.

Just as a precaution, Mudge had sequestered Jon-Tom's

duar in a safe place. He'd gotten them into this situation while sober. It was terrifying to contemplate what might happen if he started spellsinging while drunk.

"We have one chance," Jalwar finally declared.

"Wot's that, guv'nor?" Mudge sat on the port side of the bow, keeping his eyes on the threatening shallows.

"To turn around. We aren't that far yet from the beach where this unfortunate turn of events began. We can return there, land, or use this craft, provided the wind will return, to take us back to the mouth of the Tailaroam and civilization."

"I'm tempted, guv, but 'e'll never stand for it." He nodded back to where Jon-Tom lay sprawled on his back on the deck, alternately laughing and hiccuping at the fog.

"How can he object to stop us?" wondered Jalwar. "He has the gift, but no control over it."

"That may be, guv. I'm sure as 'ell no expert on spellsingin', but this I do know. 'E's me friend, and I promised 'im that I'd see 'im through this journey to its end, no matter wot 'appens."

Besides which, the otter reminded himself, if they returned without the medicine, there would be no rich reward from a grateful Clothahump. Mudge had endured too much already to throw that promise away now.

"But what else can we do?" Jalwar moaned. "None of us is a wizard or sorcerer. We cannot cure his odd condition, because it is the result of his own spellsinging."

"Maybe it'll cure itself." Mudge tried to sound optimistic. He watched sadly as Jon-Tom rolled over on the center cabin and tried to puke again. "I feel sorry for 'im. 'Tis clear 'e ain't used to liquorish effects." As if to reinforce the otter's observation, Jon-Tom rolled over again and fell off the cabin, nearly knocking himself out on the deck. Lifting himself to a sitting position, he burst out laughing. He was the only one on the boat who found the situation amusing.

Mudge shook his head. "Bleedin' pitiful."

"Yes, it is sad," Jalwar agreed.

"Cor, but not the way you think it is, mate. 'Ere 'e is, sufferin' from one o' the finest binges I've ever seen anybody on, and 'e ain't even had the pleasure o' drinkin' the booze. Truly pitiful." A glance downward showed sand looming near.

"Couple o' degrees to starboard, luv!" he called sternward.

"Ah heah y'all." Roseroar adjusted the boat's heading. The sandy bottom fell away once again.

"It'll wear off," the otter mumbled. "It *'as* to. Ain't nobody can stay drunk this long no matter 'ow strong a spell's been laid on 'is belly. I wonder when 'e did it?"

"The same time he did everything else," Jalwar explained. "Don't you remember the song?"

"You mean that part about it bein' 'the worst trip I've ever been on'?"

"Not just that. Remember that he made the tigress captain because she was the best sailor among us? That would leave him as next in command, would it not?"

"Beats me, mate. I'm not much on ships and their lore."

"He reduced himself to first mate," Jalwar said positively. "That was in the song, too. A line that went something like 'The first mate, he got drunk.' "

"Aye, now I recall." The otter nodded toward the helpless spellsinger, who remained enraptured by a hysteria perceptible only to himself. "So 'e spellsung 'imself into this condition without even bein' aware o' doin' it."

"I fear that is the case."

"Downright pitiful. Why couldn't 'e 'ave made me first mate? I'd 'andle a long drunk like this ten times better than 'e would. 'E's got to come out of it sometime."

"I hope so," said Jalwar. He glanced at the sky. "Perhaps we will lose this infernal fog, anyway. Then we might pick up a wind enabling us to turn back."

"Now, I told you, guv," Mudge began, only to be interrupted by a shout.

What stunned him to silence, however, was not the fact

of the shout but its origin. It came from the water off to starboard.

It was repeated. "Ahoy, there! You on the sloop! What's happenin'!"

"What's happenin'?" Roseroar frowned, tried to see into the fog. "Jon-Tom, wake up!" The sails continued to luff against the mainmast.

"Huh? Wash?" Jon-Tom laughed one more time, then struggled to stand up.

"Ahoy, aboard the sloop!" A new voice this time, female.

"Wash . . . whosh that?" He stumbled around the center cabin and tried to squint into the fog. Neither his eyesight nor his brain was functioning at optimum efficiency at the moment.

A second boat materialized out of the mist. It was a low-slung outboard with a pearlescent fiberglass body. Three . . . no, four people lounged in the vinyl seats. Two couples in their twenties, all human, all normal size.

"What's happenin', *John B.*?" asked the young man standing behind the wheel. He didn't look too steady on his feet himself. A cooler sat between the front seats, full of ice and aluminum cans. The cans had names like Coors and Lone Star on them.

Jon-Tom swayed. He was hallucinating, the next logical step in his mental disintegration. He leaned over the rail and tried to focus his remaining consciousness on the funny cigarette the couple in the front of the boat were passing back and forth.The other pair were exchanging hits on a glass pipe.

The big outboard was idling noisily. One girl leaned over the side to clean her Foster Grants in the ocean. Next to the beer cooler was a picnic basket. A big open bag of pretzels sat on top. The twisted, skinny kind that tasted like pure fried salt. Next to the bag was a two-pound tin of Planter's Redskin Peanuts, and several brightly colored tropical fruits.

He tried to will himself sober. If anything could have cleared his mind, it should have been the sight of the boat and its occupants. But the uncontrollable power of his own spellsinging held true. Despite everything he tried, the self-declared first mate still stayed drunk. He swallowed the words on his tongue and tried a second time.

"Who . . . who are you?"

"I'm Charlie MacReady," said the boat's driver cheerily, through a cannabis-induced fog of his own. He smiled broadly, leaned down to speak to his girlfriend. "Dig that getup that guy's got on. Must've been a helluva party!"

Jon-Tom briefly considered his iridescent lizard-skin cape, his indigo shirt, and the rest of his attire. Subdued clothing . . . for Clothahump's world.

The girl in the front was having a tough time with her sunshades. Maybe she didn't realize that the glasses were clean and that it was her eyes that needed washing out. She leaned over again and nearly tumbled into the water.

Her boyfriend grabbed the strap of her bikini top and pulled hard enough to hold her in the boat. Unfortunately, it was also hard enough to compress certain sensitive parts of her anatomy. She whirled to swing at him, missed badly thanks to the effects of what the foursome had been smoking all morning. For some unknown reason this started her giggling uncontrollably.

Jon-Tom wasn't laughing anymore. He was battling his own sozzled thoughts and magically contaminated bloodstream.

"Who *are* you people?"

"I told you." The boat's driver spoke with pot-induced ponderousness. "MacReady's the name. Charles MacReady. I am a stockbroker from Manhattan. Merrill Lynching. You know, the bull?" He rested one hand on the shoulder of the suddenly contemplative woman seated next to him. She appeared fascinated by the sheen of her nail polish.

"This is Buffy." He nodded toward the front of the boat. "The two kids up front are Steve and Mary-Ann.

Steve works in my office. Don't you, Steve?'' Steve didn't reply. He and Mary-Ann were giggling in tandem now.

The driver turned back to Jon-Tom. "Who are you?"

"One hell of a good question," Jon-Tom replied thickly. He glanced down at his outrageous costume. Is this what happens when you get the DTs? he wondered. Somehow he'd always imagined having the DTs would involve stronger hallucinations than a quartet of happily stoned vacationers loaded down with pot and pretzels.

"My name . . . my name . . ." For one terrible instant there was a soft, puffy blank in his mind where his name belonged. The kind of disorientation one encounters in a cheap house of mirrors at the state fair, where you have to feel your way through to the exit by putting your hands out in front of you and pushing through the nothingness of your own reflections.

Meriweather, he told himself. Jonathan Thomas Meriweather. I am a graduate law student from UCLA. The University of California at Los Angeles. He repeated this information slowly to the driver of the boat.

"Nice to meet you," said MacReady.

"But you, you, you, where are you? Where are you from?" Jon-Tom was aware he was half crying, but he couldn't stop himself. His desperation overwhelmed any suggestion of self-control.

The song, the song, that seemingly innocuous song so full of unforeseen consequences. First the boat, then the storm and his drunkenness, and now . . . where in the song had the sloop *John B.* been going?

The stockbroker from Manhattan pointed to his right. "Just out for the afternoon from the Nassau Club Med. You know, man. The Bahamas? You lost out of Miami or what?" He jiggled the chain of polyethelene beads that hung from his neck.

"Wanna come back in with us?"

"It can't be," Jon-Tom whispered dazedly. "It can't be this easy." The song he'd repeated over and over, what was the phrasing? "Around Nassau Town we did roam ... I wanna go home, I wanna go home ... this is the worst trip, I've ever been on."

"*I wanna go home,*" Jon-Tom sang in his mind. "*Around Nassau Town.* Yes ... yes, we'll follow you back! We'll follow you back." He clung to the rail for dear life, his eyes locked on the big Evenrude rumbling at the stern of the ski boat.

"You coming over here or you just going to follow us in?"

"We'll follow you," Jon-Tom mumbled. "We'll follow." He turned to the helm. "Roseroar, put on all sail ... no, wait." It was still windless. "The engine. I'll get that engine started and we'll follow them in!" He took a wild step toward the hatchway, felt himself going backward over the rail, tumbling toward a waiting pane of glass that wasn't there.

An immense paw had hold of him, was pulling him back on deck. "Watch yourself, sugah," Roseroar told him quietly. She'd cleared the distance to him from her position at the wheel in one leap.

Now she stared across the water. "Who are these strange folk? Ah declare, ah can't make top no bottom of their words."

"Tell them," Jon-Tom moaned weakly toward the ski boat, "tell them who you are, tell them where we are!"

But Charles MacReady, stockbroker on vacation, seven days, six nights, $950 all-inclusive from LaGuardia, not counting the fact that he expected to get laid tonight, did not reply. He was staring at the boat where seven feet of white tigress dressed in leather and brass armor stood on hind legs staring back at him.

Giggling rose from the floorboards in the front of the boat. MacReady's girlfriend had progressed from an intimate examination of her nails to her toes, which she was regarding now with a Buddha-like glassy stare.

MacReady dazedly flipped the butt of the sansemilla

stick over the side as though it had been laced with cyanide and said clearly, "Holy shit." Then he sat down hard in the driver's seat and fired up the big outboard.

"No wait," Jon-Tom screamed, "wait!" He tried to dive over the side, and it took all of Roseroar's considerable strength to prevent him from drowning himself. In his current state he couldn't float, much less swim.

"Easy there, Jon-Tom. What's gotten into y'all?"

He wrenched away from her, tore down the hatchway into the hold, and fumbled with the diesel. It took three tries but this time it started up. Then he was running, crawling back up the stairs and flying for the steering wheel console. The compass rocked. He stabbed a button. A gargling came from underneath the ship, hesitated, died. He jabbed the button again. This time the sound was a *whir, whir*.

Mudge raced back from the bow. "Wot the bloody 'ell is goin' on back 'ere?"

Roseroar stood aside, guarding the railing, and eyed the otter uncertainly. "There ah people in a boat. We must be neah some land."

"I 'eard. That's bloody marvelous. They goin' to lead us in?"

"I think they're frightened of something," Roseroar told him.

Jon-Tom was crying, crying and jabbing away at the starter. "You don't understand, you don't understand!" The sound of the ski boat's outboard was fading with distance. Still the engine refused to turn over.

Then there was a deep growl. Roseroar jumped and grabbed the rail as the boat began to move.

"Where are they?" Jon-Tom cried, trying to steer and search the fog at the same time. "Which way did they go?"

"I do not know, Jon-Tom," said Jalwar helplessly. "I did not see." He pointed uncertainly into the fog off the bow. "That way, I think."

Jon-Tom increased their speed and the diesel responded efficiently. They couldn't be far from the town of Nassau. The foursome from New York had been out for the afternoon only. Hadn't the stockbroker said so? Besides, they wore only swim suits and carried little in the way of supplies. Surely he was near enough to hit the island! And from Nassau it would be a short flight to the Florida coast. To home, to Miami, Disneyworld, hotels, and soap operas on TV in the afternoon. Images shoved purposefully into the back of his mind sprang back to the fore: home.

He was home.

So crazed was he with hope and joy that he didn't think what the reaction would be to his arriving in Nassau with the likes of Mudge and Jalwar and Roseroar in tow. But none of that mattered. None.

Unintentionally and quite without intending to do so, he'd spellsung himself home.

VII

He clung desperately to that thought as day gave way to night. Still no sign of Nassau or any of the Bahamas. No hint of pleasure boats plying the placid Caribbean. No lights on shore to guide them in. Only the ever-present fog and an occasional glimpse of a half-moon glittering on high, keeping a watchful silver eye on his waning hopes.

He was still at the wheel the next morning. The fog had fled from the sky only to settle heavily inside his heart. You could see for miles in every direction. None yielded a glimpse of a coconut palm, a low-lying islet, or the warm glass-and-steel face of a Hilton Hotel. Only when the diesel finally sputtered to a halt, out of fuel, did he sit away from the helm, exhausted.

Worst of all, he was sober. Desperation and despair had driven the spellsong-induced drunkenness from his body. It was sour irony: he had regained the use of his senses when he no longer had need of them.

Roseroar assumed the wheel again, said nothing. With the disappearance of the fog had come the return of the wind. The sails filled.

"Wheah shall I set course for, Jon-Tom?" she asked gently. He didn't reply, stared blankly over the side.

Mudge watched him closely. "Snarken, luv. You know the way." Roseroar nodded, swung the wheel over.

"What's wrong with him?"

Mudge replied thoughtfully. " 'E believed for a few minutes last night 'e might 'ave been 'ome, back in 'is own world. Now, me, I don't believe we went from one world to another that simple, even if that was a peculiar boat full of mighty odd-lookin' 'umans. The birds were sharp enough lookin', though. I'll give 'em that."

Roseroar gave him a look of distaste. "Y'all are disgustin'. Yo friend is heartsick and all yo can thank of, yo scummy little degenerate pervert, is intercourse."

"Blow it out your striped arse, you self-righteous bitch! I'd swear on me mother's 'ead that 'alf an army's done proper work under that tail."

Roseroar lunged for the otter. A ghost of a voice made her pause.

"Don't. Please." For the first time in days a familiar face swung around to face both of them. "It's not worth it. Not on my behalf."

Roseroar reluctantly returned to her station behind the wheel. "Blimey, mate," said Mudge softly, "you really do think we went over into your world, don't you?"

He nodded. "It was in the song. I didn't mean it to happen that way, but yes, I think we crossed over. And I was too drunk to do anything about it."

"Maybe we're still in yo world," said Roseroar.

Mudge noticed movement in the water. " 'Ang on. I think I know 'ow to find out." He headed toward the bow.

Jon-Tom rose, swayed slightly. Roseroar put out a hand to steady him but he waved her off with a smile. "Thanks. I'm okay now. Stone-cold sober."

"Yo drunkenness did come from yo song, then?"

"Something else I didn't plan on. It's worn off. That's why I don't think we're still in my world. The good wears off along with the bad." His voice fell to a whisper. "I was *home,* Roseroar! Home."

"Ah am sorry fo yo, Jon-Tom. Ah really and truly am."

"You've got a big heart, Roseroar. Along with every-thing else." He smiled at her, then walked toward the front of the boat. Maybe he was wrong. Maybe there was still a chance, however faint that seemed now.

The otter was leaning over the side. "How are you going to find out where we are?" Jon-Tom asked.

Mudge glanced up at him. "That's easy enough, guv'nor. All you 'ave to do is ask." He turned his face to the water racing past the prow and shouted, "Hey, you, where are we?"

Jon-Tom peered over the railing to see the playful, smooth, gray-backed shapes sliding easily through the water, hitching a free ride on the boat's bow-wave. One of them lifted its bottle-nose clear of the surface and squeaked a reply.

"You're at half past a quarter after." Giggles rose from around the speaker as the rest of the dolphins vented their appreciation of the little joke.

Mudge gave Jon-Tom an apologetic look. "Sorry, mate, but tain't easy gettin' a straight answer out o' this bunch o' sea-goin' comedians."

"Never mind," Jon-Tom sighed. "The fact that it answered at all is proof enough of which world we're in."

"Hey-ya," said another of the slim swimmers, "have you guys heard the one about the squid and the Third Mistress of Pack Thirty?"

"No." Mudge leaned forward, interested.

The dolphin now speaking sidled effortlessly up to the side of the speeding sloop. "It seems she . . ." Jon-Tom abandoned the ongoing display of oceanic vulgarity and climbed the central cabin to contemplate the horizon.

No, he wasn't home anymore. Maybe he'd hallucinated the whole incident. Maybe there'd been no ski boat full of

stoned stockbrokers from New York. Maybe the entire
episode was nothing more than the result of his drunkenness.

Except that Mudge and Roseroar and Jalwar had seen
them also.

The last vestiges of inebriation left him frighteningly
cold inside. It was bad enough that fate had dumped him
in this alien otherworld. Now it had chosen to tease him
with a glimpse of reality, of home. He felt like a poor kid
forced to stand in front of the main display window at
F.A.O. Schwarz the night before Christmas.

Slipping the duar around in front of him, he tried the
song again, tried altering the inflection in his voice, the
volume of each stanza. Tried until his throat was dry and
he could hardly speak. Nothing worked. The song remained
a song and nothing more.

He tried other songs, with the same result. He sang
everything he could remember that alluded however vaguely
to going home, to returning home, to longing for home.
The sloop *John B.* cut cleanly through the waves, running
southwestward under Roseroar's expert guidance. There
was no sign of land to cheer him. Only the dolphins with
their endless corny jokes.

"Sail ahead!" Jalwar yelled from the top of the mainmast. Jon-Tom shoved his own concerns aside as he joined
Mudge near the bowsprit. Stare as he might, he saw only
empty horizon. Mudge had no difficulty in matching the
ferret's vision.

"I see 'er, mate."

"What does she look like?"

"Rigged normal, not like this thing." The last of
Jon-Tom's hopes vanished. Not a speedboat, then. "Big,
two rows of oars. That I don't like."

"Why not?"

"Think about it, mate. Only a fool would try rowin'
across an ocean. Only a fool . . . and them that's given no
choice in the business."

The visitor was bearing down on them fast. Soon

Jon-Tom could make out the silhouette. "Can you see a flag?"

Mudge stared hard. Then he began to shake. "That's all she wrote, mate. There's a 'eart with a knife through it flyin' from the yardarm. Pirates." He raced sternward, Jon-Tom hurrying after him.

"I thought only traders traveled the Glittergeist."

"Aye, traders and them that preys on 'em." The otter was dancing frantically around Roseroar. "Do somethin', you bloody great caricature of a courtesan!"

Roseroar put the wheel hard over, said evenly, "They've probably seen us already."

"Jon-Tom, spellsing us out o' 'ere!" By now the huge, swift shape of the pirate ship was bearing down on their stern. Strange figures lined the rails and the double rows of oars dipped in unison.

"There's not enough wind," Roseroar observed. "What there is, is at our back, but they're supplementin' their own sails with those oahs."

Jon-Tom was trying to untangle his duar from around his neck. "Our engine's out of diesel." He found himself eyeing the approaching behemoth in fascination. "Interesting lines."

"Interestin' my arse!" Mudge was saying frantically. "You'll see 'ow interestin' it can be if they take us!"

"I'm afraid I don't know many songs about boats," Jon-Tom muttered worriedly, trying to concentrate, "and none at all about pirates. See, where I come from they're a historical oddity. Not really a valid subject for contemporary songwriters."

"Screw wot's contemporary!" the otter pleaded with him. "Sing something!"

Jon-Tom tried a couple of hasty, half-remembered tunes, none of which had the slightest effect on the *John B.* or the approaching vessel. It was hard to remember anything, what with Jalwar moaning and genuflecting to the north

and Mudge hopping hysterically all over the boat when he
wasn't screaming in Jon-Tom's face.

Then there was no time left to think as Roseroar rumbled, "Stand by to repel boarders, y'all!"

Jon-Tom put the duar aside. No time for playing. The
upper deck of the pirate ship loomed over them. Arrayed
along the rail was the oddest assortment of creatures he'd
encountered since finding himself in this world.

One massive dirty-furred polar bear missing an ear stood
alongside three vicious-looking pikas armed with four-
foot-long lances. A pair of lynxes caressed chipped battle-
axes and prepared to swing down on ropes dangling from a
boom. Next to them a tarsier equipped with oversized
sunglasses aimed a bow at the sloop.

"Take 'em!" snarled a snaggle-toothed old bobcat. He
leaped boldly over the side, swinging a short scimitar over
his ears, and landed on the club end of Jon-Tom's ramwood
staff. He made a strangled sound as the breath went out of
him and there was a cracking sound as a rib went.

As the bobcat slid over the side a coyote came down
a rope dangling above Roseroar, intent on splitting her
skull with a mace. The tigress's swords flashed in unison.
Four limbs went their separate ways as the coyote's limb-
less torso landed soundlessly on the deck, spraying blood
in all directions. It twitched horribly.

Jon-Tom fought for control of his stomach as the attackers
began swarming over the side in earnest. He found himself
backing away from a couple of armored sloths whose
attitudes were anything but slothful and, rather shockingly,
a middle-aged man. The sloths carried no weapons, relying
instead on their six-inch-long foreclaws to do damage.
They didn't move as fast as the others, but Jon-Tom's
blows glanced harmlessly off their thick leather armor.

They forced him back toward the railing. The man
jumped between the two sloths and tried to decapitate
Jon-Tom with his axe. Jon-Tom ducked the blow and
lunged, catching one of the sloths square on the nose with

the end of his staff. He heard the bone snap, felt the carti-
lage give under his weight. As the sloth went down, its face
covered with blood, its companion moved in with both paws.

Jon-Tom spun the staff, touched the hidden switch set in
the wood, and six inches of steel emerged from the back
end of the shaft to slide into the sloth's throat. It looked at
him in surprise before crumpling. The man with the axe
backed off.

Jalwar and Mudge were trying to hack loose the grap-
pling hooks that now bound the sloop to the larger vessel,
but they couldn't do that and defend themselves as well.
Both went down under a wave of attackers. Roseroar had
been backed up to the stern. She stood there, enclosed by a
picket line of spears and lances. Every time someone made
a move to get under her guard, they ended up with their
insides spilling all over the deck.

Finally one of the mates barked an order. The spearmen
backed off, yielding their places to archers. Arrows were
aimed at the tigress. Being a brave warrior but not a
suicidal one, she nodded and handed over her weapons.
The pirates swarmed over her with chains and steel bands,
binding her in such a way that if she tried to exert pressure
on her bonds she would only end up choking herself. They
were much more casual in tying up Jon-Tom.

A towline was attached to the sloop as the prisoners
were marched up a gangplank onto the capturing craft.
They formed a sullen quartet as they were lined up for
review. The rest of the crew stood aside respectfully as an
unbloodied figure stepped forward and regarded the captives.

The leopard was as tall as Jon-Tom. His armor was
beautiful as well as functional, consisting of intricately
worked leather crisscrossed with silver metal bands. His
tail emerged from a hole in the back of the armor. The last
half of the tail looked like a prosthesis, but Jon-Tom
decided it would be impolitic to inquire about it just now.
Four long knives were attached to the belt that ran around

the upper part of the big cat's waist. No armor covered the muscular arms.

Leather gloves with the tips cut out to permit the use in battle of sharp claws showed many patches and deep cuts from previous fights. A deep gash across the black nose had healed imperfectly. Jon-Tom took all this in as the leopard strutted silently past them. The rest of the crew murmured restlessly.

"You fought well," their inspector finally growled. "Very well. Too well, thinks I." He glanced significantly toward the sloop which bobbed astern of the bigger ship.

"Too many shipmates lost in taking such a small prize." Green eyes flashed. "I don't believe in trading good mates for scum, but we were curious about your strange craft. Where do you come from and how come you by such a peculiar vessel? 'Tis not fashioned of wood. I'm sure of that."

"It's fiberglass."

The leopard's eyes snapped toward Jon-Tom. "Are you the owner of the craft?"

Jon-Tom nodded affirmatively. "I am."

Something stung his face and he staggered, temporarily blinded. His hand went instinctively to his face and came away with blood. He could feel the four parallel cuts the leopard's claws had made. They were shallow, if messy. A little lower and he would have lost both eyes.

Roseroar made a dangerous noise deep in her throat while Mudge muttered a particularly elegant curse. The leopard ignored them both as it stepped forward. It's nose was almost touching Jon-Tom's.

"I am . . . *sir*," it said dangerously. Mudge mumbled something else, and immediately the leopard's gaze flashed toward the otter. "Did you say something, dung-eater?"

"Wot, me? Just clearin' me throat . . . sir. Dried out it were by a hot fight."

" 'Tis going to get hotter for you, thinks I." The big cat

returned his attention to Jon-Tom, who stood bleeding silently. "Any complaints?"

Jon-Tom lowered his gaze from the leopard's face, feeling the blood trickling down his face and wondering if the scarring would be permanent.

"No, sir. No complaints, sir."

The leopard favored him with a thin smile. "That's better."

"Are you the captain of this ship . . . sir?"

The leopard threw back his head and roared. "I am Sasheem, first mate." He looked to his right, stepped aside. "Here comes the captain now."

Jon-Tom didn't know what to expect. Another bear, perhaps, or some other impressive figure. He forgot that captains are fashioned of brain as well as brawn, mind as much as muscle. The sight of the captain surprised but did not shock him. It seemed somehow perversely traditional.

Captain Corroboc was a parrot. Bright green, with patches of blue and red. He stood about four feet tall. The missing right leg had been replaced with one of wood. Metal springs enabled it to bend at the knee. A leather patch covered the one empty eye socket.

As was the fashion among the feathered citizens of this world, Corroboc wore a kilt. It was unpatterned and blood red, a perfect match to his crimson vest. The absence of a design showed that he had abandoned his clanship. Unlike many of the other fliers Jon-Tom had encountered, he wore no hat or cap. A narrow bandolier crossed the feathered breast. Sun glinted off the dozen tiny stilettos it held.

A member of the crew later informed them that the captain could throw four of the deadly little blades at a time: one with each flexible wingtip, one with his beak, and the last with his remaining foot. All this with lethal accuracy while balancing on the artificial leg.

The remaining bright blue eye flicked back and forth between the prisoners. Above and below the eye patch the skin showed an unwholesome yellow where feathers were missing.

"These be all the crew of our prize?" He looked up at the first mate, and Jon-Tom was surprised to see the powerful leopard flinch back. Corroboc made eye contact with each of his own crew in turn.

"A brave bunch you are. A bloodthirsty death-dealing collection . . . of infants!" His tail quivered with his anger. "Infants, the lot of you!" Not only Sasheem, but the rest of the cutthroats were completely cowed by this battered green bird. Jon-Tom determined not to cross him.

"Four against nearly a hundred, was it? A fine lot you are!" He cocked his head sideways to gaze at the prisoners. "Now then. Where be you four bound?"

"Just a few days out from the Tailaroam," Mudge volunteered ingratiatingly. "We were just on a little fishin' trip, we were, and—"

The wooden leg was a blur. It caught the otter between his short legs. Mudge turned slightly the color of the captain as he grabbed himself and collapsed on the deck. Corroboc eyed him indifferently.

"The Emir of Ezon has a tradition of employing eunuchs to guard his palace. I haven't decided what to do with any of you yet, but one more lie like that and you'll find yourself a candidate for the knife o' the ship's doctor."

Jon-Tom tried to pick a likely candidate for ship's physician out of the surrounding collection of cutthroats and failed, though he imagined that whoever that worthy might be, he hadn't taken his internship at the Mayo Clinic.

Mudge held his peace, along with everything else. The blue eye fastened on Jon-Tom. "Perhaps you be smarter than your sour-whiskered companion. Where be you bound, man?"

"Snarken," Jon-Tom replied without hesitation.

Corroboc nodded. "Now, that makes sense. A sensible

one. You be a strange specimen, tall man. Be you from the region o' the Bellwoods?''

"I am." He had to risk the falsehood. It was true enough now, anyway.

The parrot blew his nose on the deck, sniffed. "Fortunately for you I am in a good humor this morning." Jon-Tom decided he did not want to encounter him when he was in a bad mood. "You two"—he indicated Mudge and Jalwar—"can start cleaning out the bilges. That's a job long overdue and one I am certain you'll find to your liking. Won't you?"

Uncertain whether to say yes sir, no sir, or nothing at all, Jalwar stood and shook in terror. Mudge wasn't up to commenting. Corroboc was apparently satisfied, because he nodded absently before moving down to stare fearlessly up at the towering Roseroar.

"As for you, I'd be pleased to make you one of my crew. 'Tis plain enough to see you're no stranger to a life of fighting. You'd make a valuable addition."

"Ah'll think it ovah, suh."

Good girl, Jon-Tom thought. There was no point in making the pirate parrot mad with an outright refusal, though he found himself wishing her reply hadn't been quite so convincing. Surely she wasn't seriously considering the offer? But why not? Nothing bound her to Jon-Tom. In fact, she had reason enough to abandon him. Hadn't he yanked her unwillingly from her homeland and involved her in dangers in which she had no interest? If she were forced to throw in with some stranger, why not this captain as easily as some unsteady, homesick spellsinger?

Spellsinger! He'd almost forgotten his own abilities. Not a one of this band of murderers knew of his avocation. He prayed his companions would keep the secret and not blurt it out in a thoughtless moment. He was particularly worried about the elderly Jalwar, but the trader stood petrified and volunteered nothing.

As if reading his thoughts, the pirate captain turned his

attention back to him. "And you, tall man. What be you good for?"

"Well, I can fight, too." Corroboc glanced toward his first mate.

Sasheem muttered an opinion, reluctantly. "Passing well."

Corroboc grunted and Jon-Tom added, "I am also an entertainer, a troubadour by trade."

"Huh! Well, 'tis true we could do with a bit o' song on this scow from time to time." He gave his crew a look of disgust. "I gets tired o' listening to the drunken prattling o' this uncultured bunch."

Fighting to conceal his anxiety, Jon-Tom went on. "My instrument's on board our ship, along with the rest of our personal effects."

"Is it, now?" Corroboc was sweating him with that one piercing eye. "I expect we'll find it in due course. You in a rush to demonstrate your talents?"

"At your leisure, sir." Jon-Tom felt the back of his indigo shirt beginning to cling damply to his skin. "It's only that it's a fine instrument. I'd hate to see one of your refined crew reduce it to kindling in hopes of finding gold or jewels inside. They wouldn't."

Corroboc snorted. "Rest assured they'll mind their stinking manners." He addressed the leopard. "Take 'em below and lock 'em in the brig. Let them stew there for a bit."

"These two also?" Sasheem pointed to Jalwar and Mudge.

"Aye, the bilges will wait. Let them share each other's filth for a while. By the time I decide to let them out they'll be clamorin' to get to work."

This sophisticated sally brought appreciative laughter from the crew as they sloughed away to their posts. The pirate ship turned westward with the sloop trailing obediently behind it.

As they were herded below, Jon-Tom had his first glimpse of the rowers. Most were naked save for their own fur. They were a cross section of species, from humans to rodents. All exhibited the last stages of physical and mental degeneration.

That's where we'll all end up, on the rowing benches, he thought tiredly. Unless we can figure out some way out of this.

At the moment, entry into paradise seemed the more likely route. If he could only get his hands on his duar, there might be a chance. However fickle his spellsinging, however uncertain he was of what he might sing, he was sure of one thing: he'd fashion *some* kind of magic. And the first try would be his last. He was sure of that much. Corroboc wasn't stupid, and the captain would give him no second chance to try his hand at wizardry.

Roseroar suddenly twisted to look back over her shoulder, one paw going to her rump. The first mate was grinning back at her.

"Put yo hands on me like that again, cub, and ah'll make music with yo bones."

"Gentle now, big one," said the amused leopard. "I have no doubt you'd do just that if given the chance. But you won't be given the chance. It'll go easier on you in the long run if you mind your manners and be nice to Sasheem. If not, well, we have an ample supply of chain on this boat, we do. Your heart may be made of iron, but the rest of you is only flesh and bone. Nice flesh it is, too. Think over your options.

"If I ask him nicely, Corroboc will give you to me."

She glared back at him. "Ah won't be a comforting gift."

Sasheem shrugged. "Comforting or unforgiving, it won't matter. I aim to have you. Willingly if possible, otherwise if not. You may as well settle your mind to that." They were herded into a barred cell. Sasheem favored Roseroar with a departing smirk as he joined the rest of his companions in mounting the gangway.

Roseroar sat down heavily, her huge paws clenching and

unclenching. "That furred snake. Ah'd like to get my claws into his—"

"Not yet, Roseroar," Jon-Tom cautioned her. "We've got to be patient. They don't know that I'm a spellsinger. If I can just get my hands on my duar, get one chance to play and sing, we'll have a chance."

"A chance at wot, mate?" Mudge slumped dispiritedly in a corner. "For you to conjure up some poor dancin' girl to take Roseroar's place? To bury this slimy tub in flowers?"

"I'll do *something*," Jon-Tom told him angrily. "You see if I don't."

"I will that, guv." The otter rolled over, ignoring the fact that the floor of their cage was composed of rank straw stained dark by the urine of previous captives.

"What are you doing?"

"I'm goin' to 'ave a sleep, mate."

"How can you sleep now?"

"Because I'm tired, mate." The otter glanced up at him. "I am tired of fightin', tired with fear, and most of all I'm tired o' listenin' to wot a wonderful spellsinger you are. When you're ready to magic us out o' this 'ole and back to someplace civilized, wake me. If not, maybe I'll be lucky and not wake up meself."

"One should never ride the wave of pessimism," Jalwar chided him.

"Close your cake 'ole, you useless old fart. You don't know wot the 'ell you're talkin' about." Hurt, the old ferret lapsed into silence.

Jon-Tom had moved to the barrier and held a cell bar in each hand. They were fixed deep into the wood of the ship. Small scavenger lizards and dauntingly big bugs skittered about in the dark sections of the hold while others could be heard using the rafters for pathways.

Then he turned to walk over to Roseroar and put a comforting hand on her head, stroking her between the ears. She responded with a tired, halfhearted purr.

"Don't worry, Roseroar. I got you into this. Maybe I can't get myself home, but I can damn well get you out of it. I owe you that much. I owe all of you that much."

Mudge was already asleep and didn't hear the promise. Jalwar squatted in another corner picking resignedly at strands of hay.

I just don't know *how* I'm going to get you all out of this, Jon-Tom mused silently.

VIII

Somehow the concept of "swabbing the deck" was tinged with innocence; a reflection of childhood memories of stories about wooden ships and iron men.

The reality of it was something else.

You rested on your hands and knees on a rough planked deck, stripped to the waist beneath a hot sun that blistered your neck and set the skin to peeling off your back. Sweat flowed in streams from under your arms, from your fore-head and your belly. Anything small and solid, be it a speck of dust or one of your own hairs, that slipped into your eye made you want to run screaming for the railing to throw yourself over the side.

Salt air worsened your situation, exacerbating the sore spots, making them fester and redden faster. Splinters stung the exposed skin of hands and ankles while your palms were raw from pushing the wide brushes soaked with lye-based cleaning solution.

Meanwhile you advanced slowly the length of the deck, making sure to remove each bloodstain lest some laughing member of the crew remind you of its presence by pressing a heavy foot on your raw fingers.

By midday Jon-Tom no longer cared much if they were rescued or if he were thrown over the rail to be consumed by whatever carnivorous fish inhabited this part of the Glittergeist. He didn't have much hope left. Already he'd forgotten about Clothahump's illness, about returning home, forgotten about everything except surviving the day.

By late afternoon they'd finished scrubbing every square foot of the main deck and had moved up to the poop deck. The helmsman, a grizzled old warhog, ignored them. There was no sign of the captain, for which Jon-Tom was unremittingly grateful.

A crude, temporary shelter had been erected off to the left, close by the captain's perch. Huddled beneath the feeble shade this provided was a girl of sixteen, maybe a little older. Once she might have been pretty. Now her long blonde hair was so much pale seaweed clinging to her face. She was barely five feet tall. Her eyes were a washed-out blue. Excepting the heavy steel manacle that encircled her neck and was attached to a chain bolted to the deck, she was stark naked.

It provided her with a radius of movement of about ten feet. No more. Just enough to get from the shelter to the rail, where she would have to perform any personal bodily functions in full view of the crew. Jon-Tom had no trouble following the whip welts, casual burns, and bruises that covered most of her body.

She sat silently within the shelter, her legs extended to one side, and said nothing as they approached. She just stared.

Jon-Tom used a forearm to wipe the sweat from around his lips. They were alone on the deck except for the old helmsman. He risked whispering.

"Who are you, girl?" No reply. Only those empty blue eyes, staring. "What's your name?"

"Leave 'er be, mate," said Mudge softly. "Can't you see there's not much left o' 'er? She's mad or near enough, or maybe they cut out 'er tongue to keep 'er from screamin'."

"None of those," said the helmsman. He spoke without taking his eyes from the ship's course. "That's Folly, the captain's toy. He took her off a ship that sank several months ago. She's been nuthin' but trouble since. Uncooperative, unappreciative when the captain tried bein' nice to her. I don't know why he doesn't throw her overboard and be done with it. It was folly to bring her aboard, and folly to keep her, so Folly's been her name."

"But what's her real name?"

A thin, barely audible reply came from within the shelter. "I have no name. Folly's as good as any."

"You can talk. They haven't broken you yet."

She glared bitterly at Jon-Tom. "What do you know about anything? I've been watching you." Her mouth twisted. "You're hurting now. I watched when they took your boat and brought you aboard. The tigress will be around awhile. The old one won't last two weeks. The otter a little longer, if he keeps his mouth shut.

"As for you," she eyed Jon-Tom contemptuously, "you'll say the wrong thing and lose your tongue. Or worse."

"What happened to you?" Jon-Tom was careful to keep his voice down and his arms moving lest Sasheem or one of the other mates take note of the conversation.

"What does it matter?"

"It matters to me. It should matter to you, because we're going to get off this ship." If the helmsman overheard he gave no sign.

The girl laughed sharply. "And you thought I'd gone mad." She glanced at Roseroar. "The man is crazy, isn't he?" Roseroar made no reply, bending to her work.

"And you'll come with us," he went on. "I wouldn't leave you here."

"Why not? You've got your own business to attend to. Why not leave me here? You don't know me, you don't owe me." She spat at the deck. "This is a stupid conversation. You're not going anywhere."

"What happened?" he prodded gently.

A tiny bit of the hardness seemed to go out of her, and she looked away from him. "My family and I were on a trading packet bound from Jorsta to the Isles of Durl when we ran afoul of these bastards. They killed my father along with the rest of the males and later, my mother. Since my little sister was too young to be of any use to them, they threw her overboard. They killed everyone, except for me. For some reason that unmentionable thing they call their captain took a fancy to me. I imagine he saw future profit in me." She shrugged. "I've taken care to give them nothing but trouble since. Hence my name, a gift of the crew."

"Been less troublesome lately," grunted the helmsman significantly.

"Have you tried to escape?"

"Escape to where? Yes, I tried anyway. Better drowning or sharks than this. At least, I tried before they put this chain on me. I only tried once. There are worse things than being beaten. As you may find out."

He lowered his voice to make certain the helmsman couldn't overhear. "I don't intend to. We're getting off this ship. Will you come with us when we do?"

"No." She stared straight back at him. "No. I won't. I don't want to be hurt anymore."

"That's why I'm taking you with us." She turned away from him. "What's wrong?"

Mudge gave him a gentle nudge. "Watch your mouth, lad. 'Tis the captain, may 'e rot in 'is own excrement."

"How goes she, Pulewine?" Corroboc inquired of his helmsman.

"Steady on course, Captain."

Jon-Tom kept his attention on his scrub brush, heard the *thunk* of the captain's wooden leg move nearer.

"And how be our fine cleaning crew this bright morning? Are they working like the elegant fighters we brought aboard?"

"No, Captain." The helmsman allowed himself a grunting

laugh. "As anyone can see, they're working like the scum that they are."

"That's good." Corroboc walked around Jon-Tom until the parrot was standing between him and Folly's shelter. He turned his good eye on the man. "Now then, mayhap we each understand our place in the order o' things, har?"

"Yes, Captain," murmured Jon-Tom readily enough.

"Aye, that be the way to answer. Keep that tone about you and you'll live to do more service." He cast a glance into the shelter and Jon-Tom went cold as he saw the look that came over Folly's face as she drew back into the shadows.

"Chatting with the young she, have you?"

Since the helmsman had been privy to much of their conversation, Jon-Tom could hardly deny it had taken place.

"A word or two, sir. Harmless enough."

"Har, I be sure o' that! A cute little specimen of her species, though not marketable in her present condition, fears I. A consequence of noncooperation." Jon-Tom said nothing, scrubbed harder, trying to push the brush through the wood.

"That's it, boy. Scrub well and we'll see to giving you a chance to entertain us when you've finished." He shared a laugh with the helmsman. "Though not the kind you think, no. The two of you can entertain us together."

"I wouldn't get under that whey-faced stringbean if you shot me with pins," Folly snapped.

Corroboc turned that merciless eye on his prisoner. "Now, what make you think you'd be having any choice in the matter, Folly? It'll be a pleasant thing to work out the geometry of it." He lashed out suddenly with his one good foot. The sharp claws cut twin bloody gouges up her thigh and she let out a soft cry.

Jon-Tom dug his fingernails into the wood of the brush.

"That be better now, and we'll be having no more arguments, will we?" Folly clung to the shadows and whimpered, holding her injured leg. "You've been disappointment enough to me. As soon as we make land I'll rid myself of you, and I'll make certain your buyer is of a similar mind when it comes to staging entertainments. Then perhaps you'll yearn for the good old days back aboard Corroboc's ship, har?" He turned back to the deck cleaners.

"Keep at it, slime." He addressed his helmsman. "When they've finished the deck, run them forward and set them to scrubbing the sides. Sling them over in nets. If one of them falls through, it will serve as a fine lesson to the others."

"Aye, Captain," said the helmsman.

Corroboc rose on bright green wings to glide down to the main deck. The warthog cast a wizened eye at Jon-Tom.

"Watch thy tongue and mind thy manners and thee might live as much as a year." This admonition was finished off with a thick, grunting laugh. "Still going to escape?"

You bet your porcine ass we are, Jon-Tom thought angrily as he attacked the decking. The wood was the only thing he could safely take out his fury on. We'll get out of this somehow and take that poor battered girl with us.

Without his realizing it, the sight of Folly had done something their own desperate situation had not: it forced him to realize how selfish he'd been these past hours, moping around bemoaning his fate. He wasn't the only one who had problems. Everyone else was depending on him—Mudge and Jalwar and Roseroar, and Clothahump sick and hurt back in his tree, and now Folly.

So he hadn't made it back to his own world. Tough. Self-pity wouldn't get him any closer to L.A. He had friends who needed him.

Mudge noticed the change in his friend's attitude immediately. He scrubbed the deck with renewed enthusiasm.

"Work 'ard and 'ave confidence, mates," he whispered

to Jalwar and Roseroar. "See that look on me pal's face? I've seen it afore. 'E may be 'alf bonkers, but sometimes 'tis the 'alf bonkers, part crazy part that sees a way out where none's to be seen."

"I pray it is so," whispered Jalwar, "or we are well and truly doomed."

"'Alf a chance," Mudge muttered. "That's all 'e needs is 'alf a chance."

"They may not give it to him," commented Roseroar.

While his companions slept the sleep of the exhausted that night, Jon-Tom planned and schemed. Corroboc was going to let him sing, out of curiosity if naught else. Songs would have to be chosen carefully, with an eye toward suppressing any suspicions the captain might have. Jon-Tom had no doubt that the homicidal parrot would watch him carefully.

His recital should be as bland and homogenous as possible. Somehow he would have to find an effective tune that would have the hoped-for results while sounding perfectly innocent. The lyrics would have to be powerful but nonthreatening.

Only when he'd arranged a program in his mind did he allow himself to fall into a troubled, uneasy sleep.

The first mate had them scrubbing the base of the mainmast the next morning. Corroboc strolled past without looking at the work, and Jon-Tom turned slowly toward him, keeping his tone deferential.

"Your pardon, Captain."

The parrot turned, wingtips resting on slim bird hips. "Don't waste my time, boy. You've plenty to do."

"I know that, Captain sir, but it's very much the wrong kind of work. I miss my chosen avocation, which is that of minstrel. My knowledge of songs of far lands is unsurpassed."

"Be that so, boy?"

Jon-Tom nodded vigorously. "I know wondrous chords and verse of great beauty, can bring forth the most mellifluous

sounds from my instrument. You would find that they fall
lightly on the ears and sometimes, I am embarrassed to say
it, risquely.'' He risked a knowing wink.

"I see," was all Corroboc said at first. Then, "Can it
be that after only a day you know where your true interests
lie? Har, truth and a little sun can do that to one. You'd
rather sing for your supper now than scrub for it, har?''

"If you would allow me, Captain." Jon-Tom tried to
look hopeful and compliant at the same time.

"Far lands, you say? 'Tis been a longish time since
there's been any music aboard this tub other than the
screaming of good citizens as they made their way over the
side." He glanced to his left. Mudge, Jalwar, and Roseroar
had been set to varnishing the railings.

"And what of your mates? How do you think they'll
react if they have to do your labor as well as their own?''

Licking his lips, Jon-Tom stepped forward and smiled
weakly, concealing his face from sight of his companions.
"Look, sir, I can't help what they think, but my back's
coming apart. I don't have any fur to protect me from the
sun the way they do, and they don't seem to care. So why
should I care what they think?''

"That be truth, as 'tis a poor naked-fleshed human you
be. Not that it matters to me. However—" he paused,
considering, while Jon-Tom held his breath, "we'll give
you a chance, minstrel. Har. But," he added dangerously,
"if you be lying to me to get out of a day's work, I'll put
you to polishing the ship's heads from the inside out.''

"No, Captain, I wouldn't lie to you, no sir!'' He added
disingenuously, "If I weren't a minstrel, what would I be
doing carrying a musical instrument about?''

"As a master practitioner of diverse perversions I might
suggest any number of things, har, but I can see you
haven't the necessary imagination." He turned and shouted.
"Kaskrel!" A squirrel with a ragged tail hurried to obey.
"Get belowdecks and fetch the instrument from my cabin.
The one we took from this man's prize.''

"Aye sir!" the squirrel squeaked, disappearing down a hatch.

"Come with me, tall man." Jon-Tom followed Corroboc up onto the poop deck. There the captain settled himself into a wicker chair that hung from a crossbeam. The top of the basket chair doubled as a perch, offering the captain a choice of resting positions. This time he chose to sit inside the basket.

The squirrel appeared momentarily, carrying Jon-Tom's duar. He tried not to look at the instrument with the longing he felt, particularly since a curious Sasheem had followed the sailor up the ladder. The squirrel handed it over and Jon-Tom caressed it lovingly. It was undamaged.

He was about to begin playing when a new voice interrupted him.

At first he thought both of the dog's ears had been cropped. Then he saw that they were torn and uneven, evidence of less refined surgery. The dog limped and leaned on a crutch. Unlike Corroboc he still had the use of both legs. It was just that one was a good foot shorter than the other. Jowls hung loosely from the canine face.

"Don't do it, Cap'n."

Corroboc eyed the arrival quizzically. "Now what be your objection, Macreeg?"

The old dog looked over at Jon-Tom. "I don't like it, sir. Better to keep this one swabbing the decks."

Corroboc kicked out with his wooden leg. It caught the sailor's crutch and sent him stumbling in pursuit of new support, only to land sprawling on his rump, accompanied by the derisive laughter of his fellow sailors.

"Har, where be your sense of refinement, Macreeg? Where be your feeling for culture?"

Neither perturbed nor intimidated, the old sailor slowly climbed back to his feet, stretching to his full four and a half feet of height.

"I just don't trust him, Cap'n. I don't like the look of him and I don't like his manner."

"Well, I be not in love with his naked features either, Mister Macreeg, but they don't upset me liver. As for his manner"—he threw Jon-Tom one of his disconcertingly penetrating glances—"what of your manner, man?"

"Anything you say, Captain sir," replied Jon-Tom as he dropped his eyes toward the deck.

The parrot held the stare a moment longer. "Har, that be adequate. Not quite servile enough yet, but that will come with time. You see?" He looked toward the old sailor. "There be nothing wrong in this. Music cannot harm us. Can it, tall man? Because if I were to think for one instant that you were trying to pull something peculiar on me . . ."

"I'm just a wandering minstrel, sir," Jon-Tom explained quickly. "All I want is a chance to practice the profession for which I was trained."

"Har, and to save your fragile skin." Corroboc grunted. "So be it." He leaned back in the gently swaying basket chair. Sasheem stood nearby, cleaning his teeth with what looked like a foot-long icepick. Jon-Tom knew if he sang anything even slightly suggestive of rebellion or defiance, that sharp point would go through his offending throat.

He plucked nervously at the duar, and his first words emerged as a croak. Fresh laughter came from the crew. Corroboc obviously enjoyed his discomfiture.

"Sorry, sir." He cleared his throat, wishing for a glass of water but not daring to chance the request. "This . . . this particular song is by a group of minstrels who called themselves the Eagles."

Corroboc appeared pleased. "My cousins in flight, though I chose to fly clanless. Strong, but weak of mind. I never cared much for their songmaking, as their voices be high and shrill."

"No, no," Jon-Tom explained. "The song is not by eagles, but by men like myself who chose to call themselves that."

"Strange choice of names. Why not call themselves the

Men? Well, it be of no matter. Sing, minstrel. Sing, and lighten the hearts of my sailors and myself.''

"As you command, Captain sir," said Jon-Tom. And he began to sing.

The duar was no Fender guitar, but the words came easily to him. He began with "Take It Easy." The long high notes rolled smoothly from his throat. He finished, swung instantly into the next song he'd carefully chosen. Corroboc's eye closed and the rest of the crew started to relax. They were enjoying the music. Jon-Tom moved on to "Best of My Love," then a medley of hits by the Bee Gees.

Nearby, Mudge blinked as he slapped varnish on wind-scoured wood. "Wot's 'e tryin' to do?"

"Ah don't know," said Roseroar. "Ah heah no mention of powerful demons oah spirits."

Only Jalwar was smiling as he worked. "You aren't supposed to, and neither are the ruffians around us. Listen! Don't you see what he's up to? Were he to sing of flight or battle that leopard would lay open his throat in an instant. He knows what he's doing. Don't listen to the words. They're doing as he intends. Look around you. Look at the crew."

Mudge peered over his shoulder. His eyes widened.

"Blimey, they're fallin' asleep!"

"Yes," said Jalwar. "They wait ready for the slightest hint of danger, and instead he lulls them with lullabies. Truly he is a master spellsinger."

"Don't say that, mate," muttered Mudge uneasily. "I've seen 'is nibs go wrong just when 'e thought 'e 'ad it right." But though he hardly dared believe, it was looking more and more as if Jon-Tom was going to bring it off.

The spellsinger was now wending his lilting way through "Peaceful Easy Feeling." "See," whispered Jalwar excitedly through clenched, sharp teeth, "even the armpit of a captain begins to go!"

No question but that Corroboc was slumped in the chair.

Sasheem yawned and sat down beside him. They made an unlovely couple.

All around the deck the crewmembers were blinking and yawning and falling asleep where they stood. Only the three prisoners remained awake.

"We are aware of what he is doing," Jalwar explained, "and in any case the magic is not directed at us."

"That's good, guv'nor." Mudge had to work to stifle a yawn, blinked in surprise. "Strong stuff 'e's workin'."

By the time Jon-Tom sang the final strains of "Peaceful Easy Feeling," the pirate ship was sailing aimlessly. Its bloodthirsty crew lay snoring soundly on the deck, in the hold below, and even up in the rigging. He took a step toward Corroboc and ran his eyes over the captain's attire without finding what he was hunting for. Then he joined his friends.

"Did any of you see where he put his keyring?"

"No, mate," Mudge whispered, "but we'd best find 'em fast."

Jon-Tom started for the door leading to the captain's cabin, then hesitated uncertainly. Once inside, where would he look? There might be a sealed chest, many drawers, a hidden place beneath a nest or mattress, and the keyring might not even be kept in the cabin. Maybe Sasheem had charge of the keys, or maybe one of the other ship's officers.

He couldn't go looking for them and still sing the sleep spell. Already some of the somnolent crew were beginning to stir impatiently. And he didn't have the slightest idea how long the spellsong would remain in effect.

"Do somethin', mate!" Mudge was tugging uselessly on his own ankle chains.

"Where should I look for the keys? They're not on the captain." Suddenly words in his mind, suggestive of something once remembered. Not suggestions of a place to hunt for keys, but snatches of a song.

A song about steel cat eyes and felines triumphant. About "The Mouse Patrol That Never Sleeps," a lethal little bloodthirsty ditty about an ever-watchful carnivorous kitty. Or so he'd once described it to a friend.

He sang it now, wishing Ian Anderson were about to accompany him on the flute, the words pouring rapidly from his lips as he tried to concentrate on the tune while keeping a worried eye on the comatose crew.

The section of anchor chain that had been used to bind Roseroar suddenly cracked and fell away. She looked in amazement at the broken links, then up at Jon-Tom. Wordlessly, she went to work on the much thinner chains restraining her companions. Mudge and Jalwar were freed quickly as immense biceps strained. They vanished below-decks as she worked on Jon-Tom's bindings. By the time she'd finished freeing him, the otter and ferret had reappeared. Mudge's longbow was slung over his shoulder and his face was almost hidden by the burden of the tigress's armor. Jalwar dragged her heavy swords behind him, panting hard.

They turned and raced for the tow rope attached to the *John B*. Only Jon-Tom lingered.

"Come on," Roseroar called to him. "What ah yo waitin' fo?"

He whispered urgently back to her. "The girl! I promised."

"She don't care what yo do. She'll only be trouble."

"Sorry, Roseroar." He turned and rushed for the nearest open hatch.

"Damn," the tigress growled. She pushed past him, vanished below. While he waited he sang, but the spellsong was beginning to surrender its potency. Several sailors rolled over in their sleep, snuffling uneasily.

Then a vast white-and-black shape was pushing past him, the limp naked form of Folly bouncing lightly on one shoulder like a hunting trophy. Jon-Tom's heart stopped for a second, until he saw that her condition was no different from that of the rest of the ship's complement. His spell-singing had put Folly to sleep also.

"Satisfied?" Roseroar snarled.

"Quite." He muffled a grin as he raced her to the stern.

Mudge and Jalwar were just boarding the sloop, Mudge having negotiated the short swim with ease, while Jalwar displayed typical ferret agility by walking the swaying tow rope all the way down to the boat. Roseroar was about to step over the side when she saw Jon-Tom hesitate for the second time.

"*Now* what's the mattah?"

"I've done a lot of running, Roseroar, and I'm a pretty good swimmer, but the sea's rough and my shoulders are so sore from pushing that damn scrub brush that I'm not sure if I can make it. You go on. I'll try and catch up. When you cast off the line you can swing her 'round and pick me out of the water."

She shook her head. "Ah declah, ah nevah heard anyone, not even a human, talk so damn much. Grab hold." She turned her back to him.

Deciding this wasn't the time to salvage whatever remained of his already bruised male ego, he put both arms around her neck, using one to help balance Folly. Roseroar ignored her double burden as she went hand over hand down the towrope until all of them were standing safe on the deck of the *John B*.

"Cast off!" Jon-Tom shouted at Mudge as he ran for the stern. "I'll take the wheel. Roseroar, you run the sails up."

"With pleasure." She dumped Folly's unconscious form onto the deck. Jon-Tom winced as it hit, decided that one more black and blue mark wouldn't show up against the background of bruises that covered the girl's entire body.

Roseroar worked two winches at once while Mudge hacked away with his short sword at the thick hauser linking them to the pirate ship. In seconds the sloop swung clear. Her sails climbed the mast, caught the wind. Jon-

Tom turned her as confused shouts and cries of outrage began to sound from the deck of the larger vessel.

"Not a moment too soon." Jalwar spoke admiringly from his position atop the center cabin. "You have the gift, it is certain."

Jon-Tom shrugged off the compliment and concentrated on catching as much wind as possible. "I didn't study for it and I didn't plan on it. It's just a lucky combination of my musical training and something I've picked up in this world."

"Nonetheless, it cannot be denied. You have the gift."

For an instant it was as if the years had left the ferret and a different being entirely was standing next to the mainmast looking down at Jon-Tom. He blinked once, but when he looked again it was just the same Jalwar, aged and stooped and tired. The ferret turned away and stumbled toward the bow to see if he could help Mudge or Roseroar.

The tigress had the rigging well in hand, and at Jon-Tom's direction, Mudge was breaking out the sloop's spinnaker. Behind them, furious faces lined the port side of the pirate ship. Rude gestures and bloodthirsty curses filled the air. Above all sounded a thunderous cackling from Corroboc. The faces fled the railing, to reappear elsewhere on the ship as the crew swarmed up the masts. Oars began to dip as dull-eyed galley slaves took up the cue provided by whip and drum. The big ship began to come about.

But this time the sloop was sailing with the wind to port. The square-rigged pirate craft could not tack as well as the modern, fore-rigged sloop, nor could it overtake them on oar power. Still, with the galley slaves driven to collapse, it looked for a moment as if Corroboc might still close the distance between vessels. Then Mudge finally puzzled out the rigging that lifted the spinnaker. The racing sail ballooned to its full extent filled with wind, and the sloop fairly leaped away from its pursuers.

"We made it, we're away!" Jon-Tom shouted gleefully. Mudge joined him in the stern. The otter balanced precariously on the bobbing aft end railing, turned his back to the pirate ship, and pulled down his pants. Bending over, he made wonderfully insulting faces between his legs. The pirates responded with blood-chilling promises of what they'd do if they caught the sloop, but their words, like their ship, were rapidly falling astern.

"Yes, we made it." Jalwar glanced speculatively up at the billowing sails. "If the wind holds."

As soon as his audience had dropped out of sight, Mudge ceased his contortions and jumped to the deck, buttoning his shorts.

"We'll make it all right, guv'nor." He was smiling broadly as he gave Jon-Tom a friendly whack on the back. "Bake me for a brick, mate, but you sure 'ad me fooled! 'Ere I was expectin' you to conjure up somethin' like a ten-foot-tall demon to demolish them bastards, and instead you slickered me as well as them."

"I knew that if I tried anything overt, Corroboc would have me riding a pike before the day was out." Jon-Tom adjusted their heading.

"Aye, that 'e would. Crikey but that were a neat slip o' thought, puttin' 'em all gentle to beddy-bye like you did, and then freein' up the monster missus there." He nodded in Roseroar's direction.

"Actually I'd intended to go looking for the key," Jon-Tom told him, trying to hide his embarrassment. "When I realized I didn't have the slightest idea where Corroboc's keyring was hidden I knew the only chance we had left was to free Roseroar."

The tigress stepped down from the mast to join them, staring back over the stern. "Ah only wish ah'd had a few minutes to mahself on that boat." Her eyes narrowed and she growled low enough to chill the blood of her companions. "That fust mate, fo example. Wouldn't he have been surprised when he'd woke up without his—"

"Roseroar," Jon-Tom chided her, "that's no way for a lady to talk."

She showed sharp teeth, huge fangs. "That depends on the lady, don't it, Jon-Tom?" Suddenly she pushed past him, frowning as she squinted into the distance.

"What's wrong?" he asked, turned to look aft.

She spoke evenly, unafraid, and ready.

"Looks like we ain't finished with ol' Corroboc yet."

IX

"Get below, Jalwar," Jon-Tom told the ferret. "You'll be of no use to us on deck."

"I must disobey, sir." The oldster had picked up a long fishing gaff and was hefting it firmly. "I am not going back onto that floating purgatory. I'd rather die here."

Jon-Tom nodded, held his staff ready in front of him. In planning and executing their subtle flight from the pirate ship he'd forgotten one thing. Forgotten it because he'd been in this strange world so long he'd come to think of it as normal. So when he'd planned their escape he hadn't considered that they might have to deal with the fact that Corroboc and several of his crew could fly.

There were only six of them. The captain must have threatened all of them with dismemberment to force so small a group to make the attack. Behind the parrot flew a couple of big ravens, a hawk, and a small falcon. They were armed with thin spears and light swords.

Jon-Tom set the sloop on automatic pilot, which left him free to join the fight. Jalwar thought the flashing red light of this new magic fascinating.

The fliers were fast and agile. Corroboc in particular

might be short an eye and a leg, but there was nothing wrong with his wings. He dove and twisted as he thrust, keeping just out of range of his former prisoner's weapons. Nevertheless, it soon became clear that the pirates were overmatched.

Corroboc's strategy was good. It called for his crew to stay just beyond sword range while striking with their needlelike spears. It might even have worked except for the one joker in the sloop's deck. With his longbow, Mudge gleefully picked off first the falcon and then wounded one of the ravens.

This forced the attackers to close with their quarry, and their agility couldn't compensate for their relatively small size. One of Roseroar's spinning swords sliced the wounded raven in half. Then another of Mudge's arrows pierced the hawk's thin armor. When he saw that he couldn't hope to win either at long range or in close, Corroboc ordered a retreat.

"Have a care for your gullets, scum!" the parrot shouted at them as he danced angrily in the air just out of arrow range. "I swear your fate be sealed! The oceans, nay, the whole world be not big enough to hide you from me. Wherever you run to old Corroboc will find you, and when he do, you'll wish you'd never been borned!"

"Blow it out your arse, mate!" Mudge followed this with a long string of insulting comments on the captain's dubious ancestry. Roseroar listened with distaste.

"Such uncouthness! Ah do declah, it makes me queasy all ovah. Ah do so long fo the refined conversation of civilized company."

The otter overheard and cast a dignified eye back at her. "Cor! I'll 'ave you know, me elephantine kitten, that me language is as fucking refined as anyone's!"

"Yes," she agreed sweetly. "Ah surely don't know how ah could have thought otherwise."

Jon-Tom stepped between them. "What are you two

arguing about this time? We won, and we're safely on course again."

A shaky, no longer cocky voice came from the gangway. "What . . . what did we win? Who won?"

Jon-Tom remembered Folly. "Take the wheel, Roseroar."

"Jon-Tom, if'n yo want mah opinion, ah think—!"

He disengaged the autopilot. The boat heeled sharply to port, and Roseroar was forced to grab the wheel to keep it from spinning wildly.

Jon-Tom searched the gangway, finally discovered Folly huddled far back in a lower bunk. Within the sloop's clean, quiet confines she looked suddenly fragile. The iron collar was an ugly dark stain around her pale neck.

He studied it thoughtfully. The sloop was well stocked. If he searched, he was certain he could find a hacksaw or something with which to cut the metal.

"Relax, calm yourself." He spoke gently, soothingly. "You're free. Just as I promised. Well, not completely free," he corrected himself, smiling encouragingly. "You're still stuck with us. But you can forget about Corroboc. You'll never have to worry about him again. I spellsang them to sleep. You too. While they all slept, we escaped."

Her reply was halting. "Then . . . you are a wizard. And I doubted you."

"Forget it. Sometimes I doubt it myself." She was swaying on the bunk and he was suddenly concerned. "Hey, you don't look so good."

"I'm so tired. . . ." She put her hand to her forehead and fell over into his arms. He was acutely aware of her nakedness. Not to mention her smell. Corroboc's ship was no paragon of good hygiene. Folly likely hadn't bathed since she'd been taken captive.

He slipped a supportive arm around her back. "Come with me." He helped her stumble toward the ship's head. "We'll let you get cleaned up. Then we'll find some way to get that chunk of iron off you. While you're showering

I'll see if I can find something for you to wear. There must be clothes in one of the ship's storage lockers.''

"I thank you for your kindness, sir."

He smiled again. "That's better. Just call me Jon-Tom." She nodded, leaning against him. For a minute he thought she was going to break down in his arms. She didn't. Not then, and not later. The first thing she'd lost on Corroboc's ship was the ability to cry.

While she washed, he searched the ship's cabinets. One contained familiar clothing. Familiar to him, but not to any of his companions. He made a few selections and left them outside the shower, along with a hacksaw and a file.

He'd expected to see an improvement, but he was still shocked when she reappeared on deck later that afternoon.

She'd removed the iron collar. Her hair was combed out and pulled back behind her. She stood there and looked down at herself uneasily.

"I must look passing strange in these peculiar garments."

"You'll get no argument on that from me, luv." The flabbergasted Mudge moved closer to inspect the odd attire. "Strange sort o' material." He ran a paw over one leg, reached higher. " 'Ere too."

"That's not material," she said angrily, knocking his questing fingers away.

Mudge grinned as he dodged. "Fine-feelin' material to me, luv."

"You try that again, water rat, and I'll . . ."

Jon-Tom ignored them. The argument wasn't serious. Mudge was being his usual obnoxious self, and he thought Folly realized it. Besides which he was busy enough trying to sort out his own jumbled feelings.

Folly was gorgeous. There was no other word for it. Young, but beautiful, standing there on the deck in old Levi's and a worn sweatshirt that had SLOOP JOHN B. printed across the back. She looked so achingly normal, so much like any girl he might encounter on the beach back home, that for a moment he was afraid he would be the one to cry.

Only the fading but still visible bruises on her face and the ring the collar had left around her neck reminded him of where he'd found her. He would have to hunt for the sloop's first-aid kit. Or maybe he could think of a good healing song, something more effective here than bandages and ointments.

Roseroar gave the new arrival a cursory once-over and snorted. "Skinny little thing. Yo humans . . ." She turned her gaze to the stars that were coming out. Jalwar was already asleep somewhere below, the poor old ferret exhausted by the strenuous events of the past few days. The horizon astern was clear, the pirate ship having dropped out of sight long ago. The wind off the waves still blew them steadily toward Snarken, a goal temporarily lost and now within reach again.

Snarken itself proved easy to locate. As soon as they sailed within fifty miles of the city there was a perceptible increase in the volume of surface traffic around the sloop. All they had to do was hail a couple of merchant ships bound for the same destination and follow them in.

A long range of hills that rolled down to the sea was split by a wide but crowded inlet. Once through they found themselves in a spacious bay ringed by lush green slopes that climbed several hundred feet above the harbor. Still higher land was visible off in the distance.

Wharves and docks crowded together on the far side of the bay. These were home to dozens of vessels that docked here from lands known and alien. Snarken was the principal port on the Glittergeist's southwestern shore.

Jon-Tom steered them through the merchantmen, in search of an empty dock. Many of the wharves were constructed of stone. The rocks were smooth and rounded, evidence that they had been carried down to the beach by glaciers some time far in the past. The stones were cemented tightly together and topped with planks.

They finally located an open slip. Mudge dickered with the dockmaster until a fee was settled on. This brought up the matter of their Malderpot-induced impecuniousness. A solution was found in the form of several stainless steel hammers taken from the sloop's toolbox. These the avaricious dockmaster eagerly accepted in payment.

"What do you think, Mudge?" Jon-Tom asked the otter as they walked up the pier. "Will he leave the ship alone?"

"An 'onest bloke's easy enough to spot, bein' a rare sort o' bird. She'll be safe in our absence. For one thing, the greedy bugger's terrified of 'er."

Jon-Tom nodded, paused as they stepped off the pier onto the cobblestone avenue that fronted the harbor. Lizard-drawn wagons piled high with goods clanked and rumbled all around them. Strange accents and aromas filled the air.

"That bit o' business do bring one problem to mind, mate."

"What's that, Mudge?"

"Wot are we goin' to do for money? We can't keep tradin' away ship's tools."

Jon-Tom rubbed his chin thoughtfully. "Right you are. We're going to have to buy supplies for the trek to Crancularn, too. We're going to need a lot."

"I'll say!" said Folly impatiently. "I need some real clothes. I can't walk around in this silly otherworldly stuff. People will laugh at me. Besides"—she ran her hands over the too-tight seat of her jeans—"it binds me most strangely."

Mudge stepped toward her. " 'Ere now, luv, let me 'ave a looksee. Might be we could loosen this 'ere. . . ."

She jumped away from his outstretched fingers. "Keep your hands to yourself, water rat, or you're liable to lose them."

Mudge pursed his lips hurtfully, turned to Jon-Tom. "Now, 'ere's an idea, mate. Why don't we sell 'er? That were probably the best idea that ever occurred to that rancid bag o' feathers Corroboc. Now that she's cleaned up 'alfway decent, she'd likely bring a nice bit o' change. It would solve two of our problems at once, wot?''

Despite his speed, the otter barely succeeded in ducking under Jon-Tom's swing. The chase shifted to a cluster of big wooden barrels, but Jon-Tom was unable to run the tireless otter down. He wore him out pretty good, though.

"Take it easy, mate." Both man and otter fought to catch their breath. Mudge looked out from behind a barrel. "Let's not kill each other over it. It were just a thought."

"Okay. But let's not have any more idiotic talk about selling Folly or anyone else."

The object of this exhausted discussion gazed curiously up at her rescuer. "Why don't you sell me? I'm nothing to you. I'm nothing to anyone except myself. Don't think I'm being ungrateful. I wouldn't have lived another month on that ship. I want to help you. I can't think of any other way to repay you for your kindnesses." She threw a warning glance the otter's way. Wisely, Mudge said nothing.

"All I have, though, is myself. If you need money so badly, selling me should solve your problem. I'm worth something." She turned away, unable to meet his eyes. "Even after the way I've been used."

He tried hard not to be angry with her. "Where I come from, Folly, we don't sell people."

"You don't?" She looked genuinely puzzled. "Then what do you do with people who have nothing else to do?"

"We put 'em on welfare, social security."

She shook her head. "Those words mean nothing to me."

He tried to explain. "We see to it that everyone is guaranteed some sort of minimum income, some kind of sustenance."

"Even if they're no good at anything?"

"Even if they're no good at anything."

"That doesn't seem very efficient."

"Maybe it's not efficient, but it's human."

"Brock's blocks, now there you 'ave it, luv. That explains it all. Sounds like the sort o' bizarre scheme a bunch o' 'umans would dream up.''

"Nobody gets sold," Jon-Tom announced with finality.

"Right then, mate. Wot do you propose we do for funds?" He indicated the rows of buildings lining the harborfront. "We need food and a place to sleep and supplies."

Jon-Tom glanced up at the heretofore silent Roseroar. "You wouldn't sell her, would you?"

The tigress turned away. "It ain't fo me to say." She sniffed toward the girl. "Perhaps she's just tryin' to tell yo she wants to go her own way."

Jon-Tom posed the question. "Is that true, Folly?"

"No. I have no place to go, but I don't want to cause trouble or be in the way, and I do want to help."

"Sensibly put," said Mudge brightly. "If you'll allow me, mate, I'll begin searchin' out the likely markets, and we can—"

"Wait a minute." Jon-Tom was nodding to himself. "We can sell the sloop."

"The magic boat?" Jalwar looked doubtful. "Is that wise?"

"Why not? From what Clothahump told me, Crancularn lies overland from Snarken. We've no further need for a boat, magic or not. As for returning home, I hope to be able to pay our way. I'm tired of sailing. I'd like to be a passenger for a while." He put a hand on Mudge's shoulder.

"You saw the way the wharfmaster jumped at the chance to get those two hammers. Think what some rich local would pay for the whole boat. There's nothing like it anywhere around here."

"I'd rather sell the girl," he murmured, "but the boat would fetch more. You're right about that, guv. I'm no yacht broker, but I'll do me best to strike us the best bargain obtainable."

"Mudge, with you doing the dealing, I know we'll come out well."

The otter concluded a sale that very afternoon. Payment was made in gold. They left behind a delighted trader in ships and a wharfmaster greedily counting out his commission. Jon-Tom had no regrets. He'd obtained the sloop for a song.

By nightfall they were established in a clean, moderately priced harborfront inn.

"Wot now, mate?" Mudge dug into his dinner and talked around mouthfuls of food. Jalwar displayed refined table manners, while Roseroar ate with precision and unexpected delicacy. Folly gobbled down everything set before her and still finished well ahead of the others. Confident she could take care of herself, Jon-Tom parceled out a pocketful of coin and sent her off in search of attire more suited to her new surroundings.

"We need to find out which way Crancularn lies," he told the otter as he sipped at his own tankard, "acquire sufficient supplies, and be on our way. Clothahump is waiting on us, and much as I'd like to, we can't linger here."

"Ah'm ready fo some clean countryside," agreed Roseroar. "Ah've had enough o' the ocean to last me fo a while."

"You're bound and determined to see this insanity through to the bitter end, aren't you, mate?"

"You know that I am, Mudge. I gave my word."

"I was afraid you'd say somethin' like that." He sighed, wiped gravy from his lips. "Wait 'ere."

The otter vanished into the main dining room of the inn, returned moments later. He was not alone. With him was a finely coiffed orangutan. This individual was dressed in old but well-cared-for clothing. Lace ruffles billowed from collar and sleeves. His orange beard was trimmed short and he puffed on a long, curved pipe. One earring of silver and garnet dangled from his left ear.

"So you weesh to traveel eenland?" There was an odd

lilt to his voice that reminded Jon-Tom of the other orang he'd met, the venerable Doctor Nilanthos of Lynchbany. That reminded him of the mugging victims the good doctor had worked on, and of the mugger, the flame-haired Talea. He forced his thoughts back to the present. Talea was far away.

"That's right. We need a certain medicine."

The primate nodded once. "Weel, you'll find no better place to seek eet than here een Snarken. Eet's the beegest city on the western shore of the Gleetergeist, and eef what you seek ees not to be found here, eet ees not to be found anywhere."

"You see, lad," said Mudge hopefully. "Wot did I tell you? Might as well start lookin' for 'is sorcerership's fix right 'ere."

"Sorry, Mudge."

"C'mon, mate. Couldn't we at least try a local chemist's shop?"

"What ees thee problem, stranger?" asked the orang. The aroma drifting from the bowl at the end of the thin pipe was fragrant and powerful. Jon-Tom suspected it contained more than merely tobacco. Evidently the orang noticed Jon-Tom's interest, because he turned the pipe about. "Care for a heet?"

Jon-Tom forced himself to decline. "Thanks, but not until we get this business straightened out."

"Hey guv, 'ow about me?" Mudge eyed the pipe hungrily.

"You were not offered," said the orang imperturbably.

"The medicine we seek," Jon-Tom said hastily, before Mudge could comment, "is available only from a certain shop. In the town of Crancularn."

The orang started ever so slightly, puffed furiously on his pipe. "Crancularn, ai?"

"In the Shop of the Aether and Neither."

"Weel now." The orang banged his pipe on the side of the table, knocking out the dottle while making certain not to stain his silk-and-satin attire. "I have neever been to Crancularn. But I have heard rumor of theese shop you seek. Some say eet ees no more than that, a device of the veelagers of theese town to breeng attention upon themselves. Others, they say more."

"But you've never been there," said Roseroar.

"No. I don't know anyone who's actually been there. But I do know where eet ees supposed to lie."

"Where?" Jon-Tom leaned forward anxiously.

The orang lifted a massive, muscular arm and pointed westward. "There. That way."

Mudge tugged irritably at his whiskers. "Precise directions, why can't any of these helpful blokes we run into ever give us precise directions?"

"Don't worry." The orang smiled. "Eef you want to find eet badly enough, you weel. People know where eet ees. They just don't go there, that's all."

"Why not?"

The orang shrugged, smacked thick lips around the stem of his pipe. "Beats mee, stranger. I've neever had the desire to go and find out. Thee fact that no one else goes there strikes mee as reeson enough not to go. Eef you are bound to go, I weesh you thee best of luck." He stepped back from the table. The main room of the inn's restaurant was jammed with diners now, and his table lay on the other side of the floor. He reached up, grabbed the nearest chandelier, and made his way across the ceiling gracefully, without disturbing any of the other customers.

"It doesn't make any sense," Jon-Tom was muttering. "If no one knows of any specific danger in Crancularn, why doesn't anyone go there?"

"I could think of several reasons," said Jalwar thoughtfully.

"Can you really, baggy-nose?" said Mudge. "Why don't you enlighten us then, guv'nor?"

"There may be dangers there that remain little known."

"He would have told us anything known," Jon-Tom argued. "No reason to keep it from us. What else, Jalwar?"

"There may be nothing there at all."

"I'll take Clothahump's word that there is. Go on."

The ferret spread his hands. "This shop you speak of so hopefully. It may be less than you wish for. Many such establishments never live up to their reputations."

"We'll find out," Jon-Tom said determinedly, "because no matter what anyone says, we're going there." His expression altered suddenly as he stared past the ferret.

"Wot is it, mate?" asked Mudge, abruptly alert. "Wot do you see?"

"Darkness. Nighttime. It's been night out for a long time. Too long. Folly should have returned by now." He whirled angrily on the otter. "Damn it, Mudge, did you . . . ?"

"Now 'old on a minim, mate." The otter raised both paws defensively. "I said my piece and you said you didn't want to sell 'er. I wouldn't do anythin' like that behind your back."

"If you were offered the right price you'd sell your own grandmother without *her* permission."

"I never knew me grandmum, mate, so I couldn't guess at 'er worth, but I swears on me works that as far as I know the girl's done only wot you said she could do: gone shoppin' for some respectable coverin' for that skinny naked body o' 'ers. Well, not all that skinny."

Jon-Tom had a sudden thought, turned on the largest member of their party. "Roseroar?"

The massive torso shaded the table as the tigress daintily set down half a roast lizard as big as the duar. She picked with maddening slowness at her teeth before replying.

"Ah will pretend ah didn't heah that insult, suh. Ah think it's obvious enough what has happened."

"What's obvious?" He frowned.

"Why, you gave her some gold. As she told yo herself, you owe her nothing and she owes you little, since you turned down her offah to sell herself. It's cleah enough to me that she's gone off to seek her own fortune. We've given her her freedom. She held no love fo us and ah must admit the feelin's mutual.''

"She wouldn't think of it like that," Jon-Tom muttered worriedly. "She isn't the type."

Mudge let out a sharp, barking laugh. "Now, wot would you know about 'er type, mate? I didn't know wot 'er 'type' was, and I've forgotten more about women of more species than you'll ever think on."

"She's just not the type, Mudge," Jon-Tom insisted. "This city's as new to her as it to us, and we're the only friends or security she's got."

"A type like that," said Roseroar disdainfully, "can find friends wherevah she goes."

"She just wouldn't run off like that, without saying anything. Maybe you're right, Mudge. Maybe she does want to strike off on her own, but she'd have told us first."

"Wot for?" wondered Mudge sarcastically. "To spare you from worryin' about 'er? Maybe she don't like long good-byes. Not that it matters. You've seen 'ow big this town is. Wot can we do about it?"

"Wait until morning," Jon-Tom said decisively. "We can't do much without sleep, and it'll be good to sleep on something that doesn't roll and pitch."

"Me sentiments exactly, mate."

"In the morning we'll make some inquiries. You're good at making inquries, Mudge. Like finding that orang to tell us the way to Crancularn."

"Cor, some 'elp 'e was." He pointed wildly backward. "That way! 'Ow 'elpful! That may be the most I can find out about the girl. I don't know why you bother, mate. I thought the main thing was gettin' that dope back to Clothy-wothy."

"Check on the girl first. She may be in some kind of trouble. I'll let her go her own way, but I want to make sure that's what she wants. I want her to say it to me."

Mudge looked disgusted. "It's your funeral, mate. Just don't make it mine, too."

They slept soundly. In the morning they began checking the clothing stores in the area. Yes, a girl of that description had been into several of the shops and then had moved on. The trail halted abruptly at the eighth shop. Beyond it, Folly had not been seen.

"Face it, mate, she's gone off on 'er lonesome."

"One last try." Jon-Tom nodded toward the corner, where a pair of uniformed skunks were lounging. Civil patrol, just as in Lynchbany, where their particular anatomical capabilities made them the logical candidates for the police service. It was simple for them to control an angry mob or recalcitrant prisoner through nonviolent means. Jon-Tom would much rather be beaten up.

The cops turned as he approached, taking particular note of the heavily armed Roseroar.

"Trouble, strangers?" one of the police inquired.

"No trouble." Both striped tails relaxed, for which Jon-Tom was grateful. "We're looking for someone. A companion, human female of about mid-to-late adolescence. Attractive, blonde fur. She was shopping in this area last night."

The cops looked at each other. Then the one on the left raised a hand over his head, palm facing the ground. "About so tall?"

"Yes!" Jon-Tom said excitedly.

"Wearing funny sort of clothes, dark blue pants?"

"That's her!" Suddenly he remembered who he was talking to. "What happened to her?"

"Not much, as far as I know. We were just coming on duty." He turned to gesture up a steep street. "Was about four blocks up that way, two to the left. She was out cold when we stumbled over her. Friend of yours, you say?"

Jon-Tom nodded.

"Well, we tried to bring her around and didn't have much luck. It was pretty plain what had happened to her.

The pockets of her pants and blouse had been ripped open and she had a lump here,'' he touched his head near his left ear, ''about the size of a lemon.''

''Somebody rolled 'er,'' said Mudge knowledgeably.

''My fault,'' said Jon-Tom. ''I thought she'd be okay.'' He stared at Mudge.

''Hey, don't be mad at me, mate. I didn't slug 'er.''

''She kept saying she could take care of herself.''

''I thought 'er mouth was bigger than 'er brain,'' the otter commented sourly. ''Take care o' 'erself, wot? Not by 'alf.'' He turned to the cop. ''Wot 'appened to 'er, then?''

''We relayed it in.'' He glanced at his partner. ''Do you know what headquarters did with her afterwards?'' The other skunk shrugged and the first looked thoughtful. ''Let me think.''

''Hospital,'' Jon-Tom suggested. ''Did they send her to a hospital?''

''Not that bad a bump, stranger. She was half-conscious by the time we got her into the station. Kept moaning about her mother or something. She didn't have a scrap of identification on her, I remember that. Also kept mumbling for someone named—'' he fought to recall, ''Pom-pom?''

''Jon-Tom. That's me.''

''She couldn't tell us where you were . . . that sock on the head rattled her pretty good, I'd think . . . and the name meant nothing to us. Weird as it was, we thought she was still off her nut. Mid-adolescent, you said?'' He nodded. ''I thought she looked underage for a human. Now I remember what happened to her. Social Services took her in. Several groups put in a claim and the Friends of the Street won.''

''Yeah, that's right,'' said his partner. ''I saw that on the report sheet.''

''Who are the Friends of the Street?'' Jon-Tom asked.

''Kind of like an orphanage, stranger,'' the cop explained.

He turned and pointed. "They're up on Pulletgut Hill there. Never been there myself. No reason. But that's where she was taken. I expect she'll be okay. From what I hear it's a well-run, sober, clean place."

Mudge put a consoling paw on Jon-Tom's arm. "See, mate? 'Tis all worked out for the best."

"Yes," growled Roseroar. "Let's get on with this quest of yours, Jon-Tom. The girl's in the kind of place best suited to helpin' her."

Jon-Tom listened to all of them, surprised Jalwar by asking for his opinion.

"Since you request the thoughts of a humble servant, I have to say that I agree with your friends. Undoubtedly the young woman is now among those her own age, being cared for by those whose business it is to succor such unfortunates. We should be about our business."

Jon-Tom nodded. "You're probably right, Jalwar." He looked at Mudge and Roseroar. "You're probably all right." He eyed the senior of the two cops. "You're sure this is a decent place?"

"The streets of Snarken are full of homeless youth. We bag 'em all the time. So there are many orphanages. Some are supported by taxes, others are private. If I remember aright, the Friends of the Street are among the private organizations."

"Okay, okay," Jon-Tom grumbled, out-reasoned as well as outvoted.

"So when do we leave, mate?"

"Tomorrow morning, I suppose, if you think you can lay in enough supplies by tonight."

"Cor, can a fish fry? Leave 'er to me, mate. You and the cat-mountain and the old bugger get yourselves back to the inn. Relax and suck in the last o' the sea air. Leave everythin' to ol' Mudge."

Jon-Tom did so, and was rewarded that evening by the sight of not one but two large, comfortable wagons tied up outside the inn. They were piled high with supplies and

yoked to two matched horned lizards apiece, the kind of
dray animals who could handle smooth roads or rough
trails with ease.

"You've done well," Jon-Tom complimented the otter.

Mudge appeared to be undergoing the most indescrib-
able torture as he reached into a pocket and handed over
three gold coins. "And 'ere's the change, mate."

Jon-Tom hardly knew what to say. "I didn't think
there'd be this much. You're changing, Mudge."

"Please don't say anythin', mate," said the tormented
otter. "I'm in pain enough as it is."

"Did you ever think of setting yourself up as a legiti-
mate merchant, Mudge."

"Wot, *me*?" The otter staggered. "Why, I'd lose me
self-respect, not to mention me card in the Lynchbany
Thieves' Guild! It'd break me poor mother's 'eart, it
would."

"Sorry," Jon-Tom murmured. "I won't mention it again.

Roseroar was giving the loads a professional inspection.
"Ah take back everything ah said about yo, ottah. Yo've
done a fine job o' requisitionin'." She turned to Jon-Tom.
"Theah's mo than enough heah to last us fo a journey of
many months. He spent the gold well."

Mudge executed a low bow. "Thanks, tall, luscious,
and unattainable. Now 'ow about a last decent meal before
we're back to eatin' outdoor cooking?" He headed for the
inn entrance.

Jon-Tom held back, spoke sheepishly. "Look, I understand how you all feel and I respect your opinions, and
you're probably all right as rain and I'm probably wrong.
I'll understand if you all want to go in and eat and go to
bed, but I'm not tired. I know it doesn't make any sense,
but I'm going up to this Friends of the Street place to
make a last check on Folly."

Mudge threw up his hands. "'Umans! Now, wot do you
want to go and waste your time with that for, mate? The
girl's a closed chapter, she is."

"A closed chapter," Jalwar agreed, "with a happy ending. Leave it be. Why aggravate yourself?"

"I won't aggravate myself. It'll just take a minute." He plucked one string of his duar. "I owe her a farewell song and I want to let her know that we'll probably be coming back this way, in case she wants to see us or anything."

"Pitiful," Mudge mumbled. "Plumb pitiful. Right then, mate, come on. Let's get it over with."

"You don't have to come," Jon-Tom reminded him. "What about your big supper?"

"It'll keep." He took the man's arm and urged him up the street. They climbed the first hill.

"Look at it, mate. The night's as black as the inside of a process-server's 'eart." He stared up the narrow, winding avenue. "You sure we can find this place?"

Jon-Tom nodded. "It's atop a hill. We can always ask directions. We're not helpless."

"No," said a new voice, startling them, "not now you're not."

"Roseroar . . . you're not hungry either?"

"Ah've got a bellyfull of thunder," she shot back, "but ah figured ah'd better come along to make sure you two don't end up in an alley somewheres. Those muggahs may still be working this area."

"We can take care of ourselves, luv," said Mudge.

"Ah'm sure you can, but you can take better care o' yourselves with me around."

Jon-Tom looked past her. She noticed the direction of his gaze. "Jalwah wanted to come, too, bless his heart, but there's climbing to do and he's more than a little worn out. He'll wait fo us and keep a watch on our supplies."

"Fine," said Jon-Tom, turning and starting to climb again. "We'll be back soon enough."

"Aye, right quick," Mudge agreed.

But they were both wrong.

X

The Friends of the Street occupied a complex of stone-and-mortar buildings atop a seaward-facing hillside. It was located in an area of comfortable individual homes and garden plots instead of the slum Jon-Tom expected.

"Whoever endowed this place," he told his companions as they approached the main entrance, "had money."

"And plenty o' it," Mudge added.

Several long, narrow, two-story structures were linked together by protective walls. Blue tile roofs gleamed in the moonlight. Dim illumination flickered behind a couple of windows, but for the most part the complex was dark. That wasn't surprising. It was late and the occupants should be in bed. Flowery wrought-iron trellises blocked the front doorway, but there was a cord to be pulled. Jon-Tom tugged on it, heard the faint echo of ringing from somewhere inside. Leaves shuffled in tall trees nearby. The thousand bright stars of Snarken electrified the shoreline far below.

The door opened and a curious lady squirrel peeked out at them. She was elderly and clad entirely in black. Black lace decorated the cuffs of her sleeves. Hanging from her

153

gray neck was a single golden medallion on a gold chain. Several letters had been engraved on it, but they were too small for Jon-Tom to make out.

"Yes, what is it?"

"Are you the master of this orphanage?" Jon-Tom asked.

"Me?" She did not smile. "No. What do you wish with the Headmaster?" She was watching Roseroar carefully.

"Just a couple of quick questions." He put on his most ingratiating grin.

"Office hours are from mid-morning to nightfall." She moved to shut the door.

Jon-Tom took a step forward, still wearing his grin. "We have reason to believe that an acquaintance of ours was recently—" he searched for the right word, "enrolled at the orphanage."

"You mean you don't know for certain?"

"No. It would have been within the last day."

"I see. Visiting hours are at nightfall only." Again the attempt to close the door, again Jon-Tom rushed to forestall her.

"Please, ma'am. We have to depart on a long difficult journey tomorrow. I just want a moment to assure myself that your institution is as admirable on the inside as it is from without."

"Well," she murmured uncertainly, "wait here. The Headmaster is at his late-eve devotions. I will ask if he can see you."

"Thanks."

The wait that ensued was long, and after a while he was afraid they'd been given a polite brushoff. He was about to use the bell-pull a second time when she reappeared trailing an elderly man.

As always, Jon-Tom was surprised to see another human in a position of authority, since they didn't seem to be among the more prolific groups here. In Clothahump's world mankind was just one of dozens of intelligent species.

The man was only a few inches shorter than Jon-Tom, which made him unusually tall for a local. With the exception of a radically different cut, his attire was identical with that of the much smaller squirrel: all black with lace cuffs and the same golden medallion. He held his hands clasped in front of his chest. His gray hair was combed neatly back at sides and forehead. A gray goatee protruded from his chin, and he wore thin wire glasses with narrow lenses. To Jon-Tom he resembled a cross between Colonel Sanders and a contrabassoon.

His smile and words both spoke of kindly concern, however. "Greetings. Welcome, strangers, to Friends of the Street." He gestured toward the squirrel. "Ishula tells me you have a friend among our flock?"

"We think so. Her name's Folly."

The Headmaster frowned. "Folly. I don't know that we have anyone staying with us by that . . . oh, yes! The young woman who was brought in the previous evening. She told us her terrible tale of being captured by pirates on the high seas. You are the ones she described as her rescuers, are you not?"

"That's right."

"To think that such awfulness is abroad in the world." The Headmaster shook his head regretfully. "The poor girl has endured more than any intelligent creature should suffer."

Jon-Tom had to admit that so far all of his concerns and fears looked unjustified. Still, he couldn't leave satisfied without at least a fast look at the facilities.

"I know it's late, and it's cold out here. We have to leave on a long trip tomorrow, as I told your assistant. Could we come in for a moment and have a look around? We just want to make sure that Folly's going to be well looked after. We place no claim on her and I'm sure she'll be much better off here than with us."

"Why, certainly, do come in," said the Headmaster. "My name is Chokas, by the way. Ishula, the gate."

The squirrel unlocked the iron grille as Jon-Tom made his own introductions.

"Delighted, ah am sure," said Roseroar as she ducked through the opening.

They found themselves in a long white hallway. Chokas led them down the tiled corridor, chatting effusively and not at all upset by their presence or the lateness of the hour. The squirrel trailed behind, occasionally pausing to dust a bench or vase with her tail.

Jon-Tom made polite responses to the Headmaster's conversation, but he was only paying partial attention. The rest of him searched for indications of subterfuge or concealed maleficence. He was not rewarded.

The corridor and the rooms branching off it were spotless. Decorative plants occupied eaves and niches or hung in planters from the beamed ceiling. There were skylights to admit the warmth of day. Without being asked, Chokas volunteered a further tour of the Friends of the Street. Beginning to relax, Jon-Tom accepted.

Padded benches paralleled clean tables in the dining room, and the kitchen was as shiny as the hallway.

"We pride ourselves on our hygiene here," the Headmaster informed him.

The larder was filled to overflowing with foodstuffs of every kind, suitable for sustaining the energetic offspring of many races. Beyond, the reason for the interlocking architecture became apparent. It circled to enclose a broad courtyard. Play areas were marked out beneath several bubbling fountains, and tall trees shaded the grounds.

Roseroar bent to whisper to him. "Come, haven't y'all seen enough? The girl will be well cared fo heah."

"I have to admit it's not the kind of place I expected," he confessed. "Hell, I'd be half-tempted to move in myself." He raised his voice as he spoke to the Headmaster. "Terrific-looking place you run here, Chokas."

The man nodded his thanks. "We are privileged to serve as guardians and protectors of the homeless and those who have lost their way at a tender age. We take our responsibilities seriously."

"What sort o' schooling do they get?" Roseroar asked.

"Histories, geographies, mathematics, training in the social verities, domestic subjects such as cooking and sewing. Physical education. Instruction in discipline and courtesy. A well-rounded curriculum, we believe."

"I've seen enough." Jon-Tom glanced toward the second-floor dormitories. "So long, Folly. It was interesting knowing you. Have a full and happy life and maybe we'll meet again someday." He turned back toward the entry hall. "Thanks again for the tour, Chokas."

"My pleasure. Please come visit us anytime, sir. The Friends of the Street encourages visitation."

The front door closed quietly behind them, leaving the trio standing on the cobblestone avenue outside. Roseroar started down the hill.

"That's done. Now we can get down to mo important business."

"I admit she's better off here than with us," Jon-Tom said. "Certainly it's a more stable environment than any alternative we could come up with."

"Hang on a minim, you two." Jon-Tom and Roseroar turned, to see Mudge inspecting the entrance.

"What's the matter, Mudge?" Come to think of it, Jon-Tom hadn't heard a single comment from the otter during the tour. "I'd think that you, of any of us, would be anxious to get back to the inn."

"That I am, mate."

"Come on, then, ottah," said Roseroar impatiently. "Don't tell me you miss the cub? You liked her no mo than did ah."

"True enough, mistress of massive hindquarters. I thought 'er obstinate, ignorant, and nothin' but trouble, for all that she went through. Life's tough and I ain't me sister's keeper. But I wouldn't leave a slick, slimy salamander who'd ooze all over me in a place like this."

"You saw something, Mudge?" Jon-Tom moved to stand next to him. "I thought it was neat, clean, and well-equipped."

"Bullocks," snapped the otter. "We saw what they wanted us to see, nothin' more. That Chokas chap's as slick as greased owl shit and I'd trust 'im about as far as I can piss." He turned to face them both. "I don't suppose either o' you sharp-eyed suckers 'appened to note that there are no windows on the first floor anywheres facin' the streets?"

Jon-Tom looked left, then right, and saw that the otter was correct. "So? I'm sure they have their reasons."

"I'll bet they do. Notice also that all the second-story windows are barred?"

"More decorative wrought iron," murmured Jon-Tom, his eyes roving over the upper floors.

"Decorative is it, mate?"

"This is a rough city," said Roseroar. "Orphans are vulnerable. Perhaps the bahs are to keep thieves from breakin' in and stealing youngsters to sell into slavery."

"If that's the case then the 'Friends' of the Street 'ave done a mighty professional job o' protectin' their charges from the outside. Observe that none of these trees over-hang any part of any of the buildin's."

That was true. A cleared expanse of street formed an open barrier between the nearest orchard and the outermost structures.

"But what does all of it prove?" Jon-Tom asked the otter.

"Not a bloody thing, mate. But I've been around a bit, and I'm tellin' you that my gut tells me somethin' 'ere ain't right. Me, I'd be curious to 'ave a little chat with one or two o' the occupants without that piranha-faced squirrel o' our charmin' guide Chokas about. I've 'eard descriptions o' orphanages, and this place makes the best o' them look like that dungeon we fled in Malderpotty. That's wot bothers me, mate.'' He gazed up at the silent walls. ''It's *too* sweet.''

''I'm not sure I follow you.''

''Look, guv. Cubs is dirty. They make filth the way I makes sweat. 'Tis natural. This place is supposed to be full o' cubs and it's as clean as milady's intimates.''

Roseroar spoke softly as she studied the barred upper windows. ''Ah did think it uncommon neat fo such an establishment. Almost like a doctah's office.''

''You too, Roseroar?'' Jon-Tom said in surprise.

''Me too what? What the ottah says makes sense. Ain't no secret ah've little love fo the cub, but ah'd sleep easier knowin' she's been properly cared fo.''

''If you both feel that way, then we need to talk with her before we go.'' Jon-Tom started back for the entrance. Mudge held him by an arm.

''Slow there, spellsinger. Ol' Chokas were friendly enough because we didn't ask no awkward questions or try to poke into places 'e didn't want us to see. If 'e'd wanted us to meet any o' 'is kids 'e'd 'ave brought 'em down to us. I don't think 'e'll be likely to accede to our little request.''

''He has a good reason. They're likely to all be asleep. It's late.''

''All of 'em?'' wondered Mudge. ''I doubt it. Wot about those offspring of the night-lifers? The gophers and the moles?''

''Maybe they have separate quarters so they can be active at night without disturbing the others,'' Jon-Tom suggested. ''If they're nocturnal, they wouldn't need lights in their rooms.''

''There'd still be some hint o' activity. Remember, mate, we're talkin' about a bunch o' young cubs.''

Jon-Tom chewed his lower lip. ''It was awfully quiet in there, wasn't it?''

''Like a tomb, mate. Tell you wot. Why don't you

spellsing the lot o' them to sleep the way you did that
bunch on the pirate ship?''

"Wouldn't work. On the ship, everyone was within
range of the duar and of my voice. Too many walls here.''

Mudge nodded. "Right then. My turn to perform a little
magic.''

"You?''

The otter grinned, his whiskers twitching. "You ain't
the only master o' strange arts around 'ere, mate.''

They followed him around the side, until they were far
from the entrance. As they walked Jon-Tom noted that no
other doors were visible in the complex. There was only
the single entrance. Still, there might be other doors
around the back. And the Friends of the Street were not
constrained by, say, the Los Angeles Fire Code.

Mudge halted near a tree that grew closer to the buildings than any of the others.

"Now then, my petite purr-box, I 'ave a little job for
you.'' He pointed up into the tree. "See that branch there?
The second one up?'' She nodded. "Can you climb up
there and then climb out along it?''

She frowned. "What foah? It won't hold mah weight.''

"That's precisely the idea, luv.''

Jon-Tom immediately divined the otter's intent. "It's no
good, Mudge. That branch'll throw you headfirst into the
wall. I'll end up with a furry Frisbee on my hands instead
of a valuable friend.''

"Don't worry about me, guv. I knows wot I'm about.
We otter folk are born acrobats. Most o' the time there's
nothin' more to it than play, but we can get serious with it
if we need too. Let me give 'er a try.''

"One try is all you'll get.'' He swing the duar around
until it rested against his chest. "Why don't I try spellsinging you onto the roof?''

Mudge looked unwilling. "That would work fine, wouldn't
it, mate? With you standin' 'ere below these barred windows caterwaulin' fit to shiver a bat's ears.''

"Ah resent the comparison, watah rat." Roseroar advanced up the tree trunk.

Mudge shrugged. "Don't matter 'ow you describe it. You'd wake the 'ole place."

"I could try singing quietly."

"Aye, and likely catapult . . . sorry again, Roseroar . . . me into the middle o' some far ocean. No offense, mate, but you know well as I that there be times when your spellsingin' don't quite strike the mark. So if it's all the same, I'd rather take me chances with the tree."

"Thanks for the vote of confidence," Jon-Tom muttered. A glance showed Roseroar already crawling carefully out onto the chosen limb. "Go ahead, but I think you're nuts."

"Why, guv, I didn't think me mental condition were a matter o' dispute anymore. An' the proof of it's that I'm standin' 'ere askin' you to let me catapult meself toward a stone wall instead o' lying in a soft bed somewhere back in the Bellwoods."

He moved aside as the thick branch began to bend toward the ground beneath Roseroar. She kept crawling along it until she couldn't advance any more, then swung beneath and continued advancing toward the end of the limb hand-over-hand. Seconds later the leaves were brushing the street.

Mudge nestled himself into a crook between two smaller branches near the end. "Wot's your opinion o' this, luv?"

Roseroar had to use all her weight to hold the branch down. She studied the distant roof speculatively. "A lot to miss and little to land on. Wheah do y'all wish the remains sent?"

"Two optimists I'm blessed with," the otter mumbled. "I thank the both o' you for your encouragin' words." He patted the wood behind him. "Wortyle wood. I thought she'd bend without breakin'. They make ship's ribs out o' this stuff." He glanced back at Roseroar. "Any time you're ready, lass."

"Yoah sure about this?"

"No, I'm not, but I ain't doin' no good sittin' 'ere on me arse talkin' about it."

"That ain't the part that's goin' to get smashed," she said as she stepped away from the quivering branch.

The wortyle wood whipped upward so fast the air vibrated in its wake. Mudge was thrown with tremendous force into the night sky. The otter did a single flip and described an elegant arc as he began to descend.

As it developed, his judgment was only slightly off. He didn't reach the roof, but neither did he smash into the side of the building. He fell only a little short.

At first it looked as if he was going to land hard on the cobblestones, but at the last instant he grabbed with his right hand. Short, powerful muscles broke his fall as his fingers locked onto the iron grating barring one window. He hung there for a long moment, catching his breath. Then he reached up with the other hand and pulled himself on to the iron.

His companions stood beneath the window, staring up at him. "Can you get in?" Jon-Tom asked softly.

Mudge responded with a snort of contempt, fiddled with the grate. Seconds later a metallic click reached Jon-Tom and Roseroar.

"He's very clevah, yo friend."

"He's had a lot of experience with locks," Jon-Tom informed her dryly. Another click from above signified the opening of the window.

They waited below, feeling exposed standing there on the otherwise empty, moonlit street. Minutes passed. A pink rope snaked down from the open window. Jon-Tom reached up to take hold of the chain of knotted bedsheets.

"They'll support me," he told Roseroar. "I don't think they'll hold you."

"Nevah mind. Y'all are just goin' to spend a few minutes talkin' to the girl-cub anyways." She nodded toward the nearby grove. "Ah'll wait foah y'all up in the same tree. Ain't nobody goin' to spot me up theah. If I see

anyone comin' this way and it looks tricky, I'll whistle
y'all a warnin'."

As she stood there in the pale light Jon-Tom was
conscious of her strength and power, but her words struck
him as odd. "I didn't know tigers could whistle."

"Well, ah'll let ya'all know somehow." She turned and
loped toward the trees.

Jon-Tom braced his feet against the wall and pulled
himself up. Mudge was waiting to help him inside.

Jon-Tom found himself standing in near blackness. "Where
are we?" he whispered.

"Some sort o' storage closet, mate." Mudge's night
vision was several cuts above his friend's.

But as they moved cautiously through the darkness
Jon-Tom's eyes adjusted to the weak illumination, and he
was able to make out buckets, pails, piles of dust rags,
curry combs, and other cleaning supplies. Mudge stopped
at the door and tried the handle.

"Locked from the other side." The otter hunted through
the darkness, came back holding something that looked
like an awl. He inserted it into the door lock and jiggled
delicately. Though Jon-Tom heard nothing, the otter was
apparently satisfied by some sound. He put the awl aside
and pushed.

The door opened silently. Mudge peered into a dark
dormitory. Against opposite walls stood beds, cots, mats,
and diverse sleeping stations for children of different
species. On the far wall windows looked down into the
courtyard with the trees and fountains. Unlike those on the
outside, these were not barred.

They tiptoed out of the closet and found themselves
walking between rows of silent youngsters. All of them
appeared to be neatly groomed and squeaky clean. There
wasn't a hair or patch of fur out of place. The dormitory
itself was comfortably cool and as spotless as the dining
room and entry hall had been.

"I don't see any indications of abuse here," Jon-Tom whispered as they went from bed to bed.

Mudge was shaking his head doubtfully. "Too neat, mate. Too perfect." They reached the end of the long chamber without finding Folly. The door at the end was also locked from the outside. "And another thing, mate. Too many locks 'ere." He used the tool to pick it.

Beyond was a short hall. A stairway led downward off the the left. Mudge picked the lock on the door across the hall and they entered a second dorm.

Grunts and whistles and snores covered their footsteps as they commenced an inspection of the new group of beds. Halfway down the line they found Folly. Jon-Tom shook her gently awake. She rolled over, woke up.

She was gasping with fright. There was no mistaking the look in her eyes, the tenseness of her body, the expression on her face. It reminded Jon-Tom a little of the look she'd display on the pirate ship whenever Corroboc appeared.

As soon as she recognized him she threw her arms around him and started sobbing.

"Jon-Tom, Jon-Tom. And Mudge too. I thought you'd forgotten me. I thought you'd go off and leave me here!"

"I didn't forget you, Folly." Acutely conscious of her curves beneath the thin black nightdress, he gently pushed her away. "What's wrong?"

She looked around wildly. "You've got to get me out of here! Quickly, before the night patrol shows up."

"Night patrol? You mean, someone looks in on you?"

"No, I mean *patrol*. No one's allowed out of bed after dark. If they catch you, they beat you. Bad. Not like Corroboc, but bad enough."

"But we were here earlier, and we didn't see any indications of—"

"Don't be a fool, mate," said Mudge tightly. "D'you think these servants o' the downtrodden would be stupid enough to hit their charges where it'd show?"

"No, I guess not. They beat you here?"

Folly spat on the floor. "Only out of love, of course. Every time they beat you it's out of love. They beat you if you don't learn your lessons, they beat you if you don't hold your knife right at mealtime, they beat you for not saying yes sir and no ma'am, and sometimes I think they beat you for the fun of it, to remind you how bad the world outside is." Her nails dug into his arms.

"You've got to get me out of here, Jon-Tom!" How much truth there was to her accusations, he couldn't tell, but the desperation in her voice was genuine enough.

Mudge kept a paw on the hilt of his short sword. "Let's make up our feeble minds, mate. Some o' these cubs are startin' to move around."

"I'm awake." Jon-Tom turned to the bed next to Folly's. It was occupied by a young margay. She sat up rubbing at her eyes. She wore the same black nightdress.

"Is what Folly says true?" he asked the young cat.

"Who . . . who are you?" asked the now wide-awake youngster. Folly hastened to reassure her.

"It's okay. They're friends of mine."

"Who're you?" Jon-Tom countered.

"My name's Myealn." To his surprise she began to sniffle. He'd never seen a feline cry before. "Pu-please, sir, can you help me get away from this place, too?"

Then he was being assailed by a volley of anxious whispers.

"Me too, sir . . . and me . . . me also . . . !"

The whole dorm was awake and crowding around Folly's bed, pawing at the adults, pleading in a dozen dialects for help. Tails twitched nervously from the backsides of dozens of nightclothes, all black.

"I don't understand," he muttered. "This looks like such a nice place. But it's not right if they beat you all the time."

"That's not all they do," said Folly. "Haven't you noticed how perfect this place is?"

"You mean, clean?"

She shook her head. "It's not just clean. It's sterile. Woe unto any of us caught with a dirt smudge or piece of lint on us. We're supposed to be perfect at mealtime, perfect at study, and perfect at devotions, so we can be perfect citizens when we're old enough to be turned out on the street again.

"A bunch of the supervisors here were raised here and this is the only home they know. They're the worst. We wear only black because a perfect person can't have any distractions and color is distracting. There're no distractions of any kind. No dancing, no singing, no merriment at all. Maybe all the jokes the pirates told were brutal and crude, but at least they had a sense of humor. There's no humor in this place."

Myealn had slipped out of her bed. Now she leaned close to Folly. "The other thing," she whispered urgently. "Tell them about the other thing."

"I was getting to that." Nervously, Folly glanced at the doorway at the far end of the room. "Since a perfect person doesn't need silly things like merriment and pleasure, one of the first things they do here is make sure you're made perfect in that regard."

Mudge frowned. "Want to explain that one, luv?"

"I mean, they see to it that no pleasurable diversions of any kind remain to divert you from the task of becoming perfect." The otter gaped at her, then waved to take in the shuffling crowd of anxious, black-clad youngsters.

"Wot a bloody 'ouse o' devils we stumbled into! You mean every one o' these . . . ?"

Folly nodded vigorously. "Most of them, yes. The males are neutered and the females spayed. To preserve their perfection by preventing any sensual distractions. They're going to operate on me tomorrow."

"Against your will?" Jon-Tom struggled to come to grips with this new, coldly clinical horror.

"What could we do?" Myealn sobbed softly. "Who would object on our behalf? We're all orphans, none of us even have guardians. And the Friends of the Street have a wonderful reputation with the people who run the city government because there's never any trouble here.''

"And the Friends of the Street put model citizens back into the population,'' Folly added. "People who never give the city any trouble.

Jon-Tom was so furious he was shaking. "If you got out of this place,'' he asked the trembling, altered youngsters, "where would you go?''

Again a flurry of desperate pleas. "Anywhere . . anyplace . . . the waterfront, I want to be a sailor . . I can sew, be a steamstress . . . I'm good with paints . . . I want to be . . . !''

He shushed them all. "We'll get you out. Somehow. Mudge, what about the dorm we came through? Can we risk going back that way with all these kids?''

"Fuck the risk, mate.'' Jon-Tom had never seen the otter so mad. "Not only are we goin' back into the other dorm, we're goin' to break every cub out o' this pit o' abomination. Come on, you lot,'' he told them. "Quietlike.'' Jon-Tom followed behind, making sure no one was left and shepherding them along like a giraffe among a flock of sheep.

The hallway and the stairs were silent. Once in the other dorm those awake went from bed to bed waking their friends and explaining what was happening. When they were through, the center aisle was full of milling, anxious young faces.

Mudge opened the door to the supply closet. At the same time the door at the other end of the dorm burst open. Standing in the opening was the powerful figure of a five-foot-tall adult lynx. Green eyes flashed.

"What's going on in here?'' He started in. "By the Eight Levels of Purity, I will have the hide off whoever is responsible!'' Then he caught sight of Jon-Tom standing like a pale tower above the heads of the youngsters. "How did you get in here?''

Jon-Tom faced him with a broad, innocent smile. "Just

visiting. A little late, I know. Special dispensation from Chokas.''

''Just visiting be damned! Where's your pass? These are not visiting times.''

Jon-Tom kept smiling as the cubs crowded close around him. ''Like I said, friend, it's a special occasion.''

The monitor carried a short, ugly black whip which he now drew back threateningly. ''You're coming with me to see the Headmaster, whoever you are. I do not know how you got in here, or you either,'' he added as he espied Mudge, ''but you are not leaving without making proper explanation. The rest of you,'' he roared, ''back to your beds!''

The youngsters milled around uncertainly. Many of them were starting to bawl.

'' 'Ere now, guv'nor, there's no reason to get upset.'' Mudge toddled toward him, smiling broadly.

The whip cracked just in front of the otter's nose. The children started to scatter for their beds, whimpering loudly.

''Now, hold on there, friend.'' Jon-Tom put his ramwood staff in front of his chest. ''Let's be careful with that whip, shall we?''

''Cute little gimcrack, snake master,'' said Mudge, still grinning and walking toward the monitor. The lynx eyed his approach warily.

''That is far enough, trespasser. Take another step toward me and I'll have one of your eyes out.''

Mudge halted, threw up both hands and gaped at the lynx in mock horror. ''Wot, and mar me perfection? Crikey, why would you want to muss up me perfect self?'' He started to turn, abruptly leaped at the monitor.

The lynx wasn't slow, but Mudge was a brown blur in the dim light. The whip snapped down and cut across the back of the otter's neck. Mudge's sword was faster still, slicing through the whip handle just above the big cat's fingers.

The monitor bolted for the open door. ''Mudge, no!''

Jon-Tom yelled, but Mudge didn't hear him in time. Or perhaps he did. The short sword spun end over end. It was the hilt that struck the lynx in the back of the head with a gratifyingly loud *thump*. The monitor dropped as if poleaxed.

Jon-Tom breathed a sigh of relief. "Smart throw, Mudge. We don't need a murder complicating our departure."

Mudge retrieved his sword. "That's right, mate, but I can't take the credit. I was *tryin'* to separate 'is 'ead from 'is shoulders."

"Quick now!" Jon-Tom instructed the youngsters as he headed for the storage closet. "Everyone out, before someone else shows up to check on you." He led them through the storage closet. "Don't push, everyone's going to get out ... don't shove in the back. . . ."

Roseroar strained to see better as shadows moved against the open window. So far no one had appeared to spot the dangling rope of pastel linen, but it would take only one passing pedestrian to give the alarm.

She expected to see Jon-Tom or Mudge or even the girl. What she did not expect to see was the silent column of cubs who began descending the sheets. Some species were built for climbing and climbed down quickly and gracefully, while others had a more difficult time with the descent, but all made it safely. She dropped clear of the tree and rushed toward the building. The cubs largely ignored her as they ran off in different directions, small dark shapes swallowed by the shadows.

The prepubescent exodus continued for some time. Finally Jon-Tom, Mudge, and Folly appeared at the open window.

At the same time, lights began to wink on throughout the orphanage complex.

XI

So the otter's suspicions had been well founded, she decided. That was the only possible explanation for the mass escape in progress. She waited anxiously as Mudge slipped down the rope. Folly followed closely.

Jon-Tom had just stepped through the window opening and was climbing over the iron grate when something whizzed past his head. It struck the street below. Roseroar picked it up, found herself inspecting a small club. The knobbed end was studded with nails. Not the kind of disciplinary device one would expect a dormitory supervisor or teacher to carry.

The last fleeing cub vanished down a narrow alleyway. Within the orphanage, bells were clanging violently. Mudge reached the bottom of the rope and jumped clear. Folly slipped, fell the last five feet, and almost broke an ankle. The reason for her fall was clear; a pile of pink linen spiraled down on top of her.

"Bloody 'ell!" The otter looked upward and cursed. "I 'ad the other end tied to a bedpost. Someone must 'ave cut it." He could see Jon-Tom hanging on to the grating with one hand while trying to defend himself with his staff.

From within the storage closet outraged shouts were clearly audible down on the street. The grating creaked loudly
as it bent on its hinges.

"They'll 'ave 'im in a minute," the otter muttered
helplessly, "if that old iron doesn't break free first."

Neither happened. Someone inside the supply room
jabbed outward with a spear. Jon-Tom leaned back to
dodge the deadly point, lost his grip, and fell. The staff
dropped from his fingers as he tumbled head over heels,
wrapped up in his lizard skin cape. Folly screamed. Lesser
wails came from dark shadows nearby as those few children who'd paused to catch their breath saw their benefac-
tor fall.

But there was no sickening thud of flesh meeting stone.
Roseroar grunted softly. It was the only hint of any strain
as she easily caught the plunging Jon-Tom in both arms.
He pushed away the cape which had become wrapped
around his head and stared up at her.

"Thanks, Roseroar." She grinned, set him down gently.
He adjusted his attire and recovered his staff. The duar,
still slung across his back, had survived the fall unscathed.

" 'Ell of a catch, luv!" Mudge gave the tigress a
complimentary whack on the rump, darted out of reach
before her paw could knock him silly. There were several
faces staring down at them from the open window, yelling
and issuing dire promises. Jon-Tom ignored them.

"Y'all okay?" Roseroar inquired solicitously.

"Fine." He slung the cape back over his shoulders,
brushed at his face. "If you hadn't caught me, Clothahump
would have a longer wait for his medicine."

"And y'all brought out the girl, ah see."

Folly stepped toward her. "I am *not* a girl! I'm as
grown-up as you are."

Roseroar lifted her eyebrows as she regarded the skimp
of a human. "Mah deah, no one is as grown-up as ah
am."

"Depends on whether someone prefers quality to quantity."

" 'Ere now, wot's all this?'' Mudge stepped between the ladies. ''Not that I mind if you two want to 'ave a go at each other. Just give me a ten-minute 'ead start before the fireworks commence, yes?'' He gestured to his right. ''I don't think now's the time for private digressions, though.''

At least a dozen black-clad adult shapes had appeared near the main entrance. Jon-Tom couldn't see if Chokas was among them, but he had no intention of hanging around to find out.

They headed off in the opposite direction, and Jon-Tom saw they needn't worry about pursuit. The black-clad gestapo maintained by the Friends of the Street wasn't after them. They were fanning out toward the alleys and side streets in search of their escaped flock.

Jon-Tom considered intercepting them. It was difficult not to, but he had to tell himself that they'd done everything possible for the children. Most, if not all, of them ought to make it to the safety of the crowded city below, and he suspected they were wise enough to discard their incriminating black-and-lace night clothes at the first opportunity.

One of their own was faced with the same dilemma. ''You've got to get out of that nightdress, Folly,'' he told her. Obediently, she started to pull it over her head, and he hastened to restrain her. ''No, no, not yet!''

They were racing down a steep street that led back toward the harbor area. It had begun to drizzle. He was grateful for the rain. It should aid the fleeing children in their escape.

''Why not yet?'' Folly eyed him curiously. Curiosity gave way rapidly to a coy smile. ''When you first saw me on Corroboc's boat I wasn't wearing anything but an iron collar. Why should my nakedness bother you now?''

''It doesn't bother me,'' he lied. ''It's raining and I don't want you contracting pneumonia.'' Citizens of Snarken out for an evening stroll watched the flight with interest.

"I don't mind if you see me naked," she said innocently. "You like me a little, don't you, Jon-Tom?"

"Of course I like you."

"No. I mean you *like* me."

"Don't be silly. You're still a child, Folly."

"You don't look at me the way you'd look at a child."

"She ain't built like no cub, mate."

Jon-Tom glared over at the otter. "Stay out of this, Mudge."

"Excuse me, guv'nor. None o' me business, right?" He skittered along next to Roseroar, running fluidly on his stubby legs and trying to hide a grin.

"I'm concerned for your welfare, Folly." Jon-Tom struggled to explain. "I don't like to see anyone taken advantage of. You noticed that we freed everyone from the orphanage and not just you."

"I know, but you didn't come to free everyone. You came because I was there."

"Of course. You're a friend, Folly. A good friend."

"Is that all?" As she ran there was a lot of movement beneath the damp nightdress. Jon-Tom was having a difficult time concentrating on the street ahead. "Just a good friend?"

Roseroar listened with one ear to the infantile dialogue while trying her best to ignore it. Idiot humans! She made certain to inspect every side street they passed. Surely, as soon as the Friends of the Street finished rounding up as many escapees as they could, they'd contact the police about the break-in.

Besides worrying about that new problem, she had to endure the banalities mouthed by the adolescent human female who was flirting shamelessly with Jon-Tom.

So what? She considered her discomfiture carefully. Why, she asked herself, should she find such harmless chatter so aggravating? Admirable the spellsinger might be, but he wasn't even a member of a related species. Any relationship besides mutual respect and strong friendship was clearly out of the question. The very thought was absurd! The man was a skinny, furless thing less than half her size. It made no sense for her to concern herself with his personal business.

She assured herself her interest was only natural. Jon-Tom was a friend, a companion now. It was just as he'd said to the girl: it hurt to see anyone taken advantage of. Roseroar wasn't about to let this scheming adolescent take advantage of him. And take advantage of him Folly would, if given half a chance. Roseroar was sure of that much. She shook her head as Jon-Tom allowed himself to be smothered with verbal pap, astonished at the naiveté displayed during courtship by the human species. She'd thought better of him.

She ignored it for as long as she could, until she was unable to stand the veiled remarks and coy queries any longer.

"Ah think we can slow down some now." Jon-Tom and Mudge agreed with her. Everyone slowed to a fast walk. Roseroar moved close to the girl. "And ah also think it would be a good ideah if we all kept quiet foah a while. We don't want to attract any undue attention. In addition to which, if ah'm forced to listen to any moah o' yoah simperin', girl, ah may vomit."

Folly eyed the tigress. "Something bothering you?"

"Nothin' much, little female. It's just that ah have a great respect foah the language. Hearin' it used so foolishly always upsets mah digestion."

Folly turned to Jon-Tom. She flashed blue eyes and blonde hair in the reflected light from storefronts and street lamps. Her skin, wet with drizzle, sparkled.

"Do you think I'm talking foolish, Jon-Tom?"

"Maybe just a little, yes."

She responded with a much practiced and perfectly formed pout. Roseroar sighed and turned away, wondering why she went to the trouble. The spellsinger had shown himself to be a man of intelligence and insight. It distressed her to see him so blatantly manipulated. She increased her stride so she wouldn't have to listen to any more of it.

"You don't like me," Folly murmured to Jon-Tom.

"Of course I like you."

"I knew you did!" She turned and threw her arms around him, making him stagger. "I knew you liked me!"

"Please, Folly." Jon-Tom reluctantly worked to disengage himself. Roseroar would have been happy to help, though she might have broken both of the girl's arms in the process. "Folly, I already have a woman." Her expression fell abruptly. She moved away from him, once more concentrating on the street ahead.

"You never told me that."

"It was never necessary to tell you. Her name's Talea. She lives near a town called Lynchbany, which lies far across the Glittergeist."

Otter ears overheard and Mudge fell back to join them. "O' course, she ain't really 'is woman," he said conversationally, thoroughly delighting in Jon-Tom's discomfort. "They're just friends is all."

Folly's delight returned upon hearing this disclosure. "Oh, that's all right, then!"

"Besides, you're much too young for what you're thinking," Jon-Tom told her, impaling Mudge with a stare promising slow death.

"Too young for what?"

"Just too young." Strange. The right words had been there on his lips just a moment earlier. Odd how they vanished the instant you needed them.

"Bet I could convince you otherwise," she said coquettishly.

"Here's the right cross street," he said hastily, lengthening his stride. "We'll be back at the inn in a couple of minutes."

A short furry shape jumped from an alcove ahead of

him. Roseroar reached for her swords. Folly hid behind
Jon-Tom as Mudge put a hand to his bow.

They relaxed when the shape identified itself.

"Jalwar!" Jon-Tom couldn't conceal his surprise. "What
are you doing out here?" He tried to see past the ferret.

The oldster put a finger to his lips and beckoned for
them to follow. They crept along behind him, turned down
a long narrow alley. It was ripe with moldering garbage.
Jalwar pointed to the main street beyond.

Both of their heavily laden wagons were still hitched to
the rails outside the inn. Idling around the wagons were at
least two dozen uniformed skunks and civet cats from
Snarken's olfactory constabulary. Several well-dressed ci-
vilians lounged next to the front wagon and chatted amia-
bly with the officer in charge of the cops.

Jalwar drew back into the shadows. "I saw them arrive," he whispered. "Many have stayed outside with our
wagons. Others went upstairs searching for us. I was
drinking and overheard in time to sneak away. I listened
when they came back down and talked to others and to the
innkeeper." The ferret's gaze shifted from Jon-Tom to
Mudge. "They were talking about you."

"Me?" Mudge squeaked, suddenly sounding defensive.
"Now, why would they be talkin' about me?"

"Because," Jalwar replied accusingly, "it seems you
spent some time playing at dice with several of them."

"So wot's wrong with a friendly little game o' dice.
Blimey, you'd think one o' them caught me in the sack
with 'is bleedin' daughter."

It came to Jon-Tom in a rush: the finely fashioned
wagons, the handsome dray animals, the new harnesses,
the mountainous stock of supplies.

"Mudge . . ." he said dangerously.

The otter retreated. There was little room to maneuver
in the alley, a fact he was acutely conscious of.

"Now, mate, take it easy. We needed them supplies,
now, didn't we? 'Tis in a good cause, ain't it? Think o' 'is

poor sickly wizardship lyin' and waitin' for us way back in
Lynchbany and all the folks who need 'im well and 'ealthy
again.''

"How did you manage it, Mudge? How did you cheat
so many of them at the same time?"

"Well, we otter folk are known for our quickness, and
I've always been quick as any.''

"Y'all must've been a little too quick this time.''
Roseroar peered toward the inn. "Judgin' from the number
o' police about, ah'd say you defrauded moah than a few
idle sailors.''

"Wouldn't be much point in defrauding poor folks,
now, would there, luv? Wot we got from sellin' the ship
weren't near enough to buy supplies an' equipment for a
proper expedition, but 'twere plenty to buy me into a
handsome game o' chance with a few leadin' citizens.''

"Fat lot of good those supplies do us now," Jon-Tom
muttered.

Jalwar was rummaging through a pile of broken crates.
"Here." He dragged out their backpacks. "I was able to
throw these from our rooms while they were still searching
for us below. It was all I had time to save.''

Jon-Tom wiped grime from his own pack. "Jalwar,
you're a wonder. Thanks.''

"A small service, sir." Jon-Tom didn't bother to correct
the ferret anymore. Let him say "sir" if it pleased him. "I
only wish I could have informed you sooner, but I could
not follow your path quickly enough." He smiled apologetically. "These aged legs of mine.''

"It wouldn't have mattered. We were occupied with
saving Folly.''

"What now?" Roseroar wondered as she hefted her
own massive pack.

Jon-Tom considered. "We can't hang around here. Now
the cops have two reasons for picking us up. They might
go easy on us over the Friends of the Street business, but
not about this. For one thing, that officer in charge is a

little too chummy with the citizens Mudge cheated. I'm not anxious to tour the inside of Snarken's prison."

"Give me a break, mate," whined the otter. "If you 'adn't been so set on goin' after 'er"—he pointed toward Folly—"we'd 'ave cleared this dump 'ours ago." He glared disgustedly at the girl. "I blame meself for it, though. Should've kept me concerns to meself." He added hopefully, "We could still sell 'er."

"No." Jon-Tom put an arm around her shoulders. "Folly stays with us until we can find her a safe haven."

"I could suggest something," she murmured softly. He moved his arm.

"Right then," he said briskly. "No point in hanging around here waiting for the cops to find us." He started back the way they'd come. Mudge followed, kicking at the garbage.

"Suits me, mate. Looks now like we're goin' to 'ave to walk all the way to this bleedin' Crancularn. Might as well get going. Only don't let's go spend the 'ole trip blamin' poor ol' Mudge for the fact that we ain't ridin' in comfort."

"Fair enough. And you don't blame me for this." So saying, he booted the otter in the rump so hard it took Roseroar's strength to extract him from the pile of barrels where he landed.

They slunk out of Snarken on foot—tired, anxious, and broke. Mudge grumbled every step of the way but acknowledged his mistake (sort of) by assuming the lead. It was also a matter of self-defense, since it kept him well out of range of Jon-Tom's boot.

Mudge also partly redeemed himself by returning from one short disappearance with an armful of female clothing, a bit of doubtful scavenging which Jon-Tom forced himself to rationalize.

"Lifted it from a drunken serval," the otter explained as Folly delightedly traded her black nightdress for the frilly if somewhat too-small attire. "The doxy I took it off won't miss it, and we've need of it."

They moved steadily through the city's outskirts. By the time the sun rose over the horizon to illuminate the now distant harbor, they were crossing the highest hill westward. There they traded some goods from Jon-Tom's pack for breakfast at a small inn, as he wanted to try and hold on to their three remaining gold pieces for an emergency. Midday saw them far from the city, hiking between rows of well-tended fruit trees.

Mudge was rubbing his belly. "Not bad for foreign cookin', mate."

"No, but we're going to have to eat lightly to conserve what money we have left."

"We could sell the girl's favors."

"Not a bad idea," Jon-Tom said thoughtfully.

Mudge looked at him in surprise. "Wot's that? You agrees?"

"Sure, if it's okay with her." He called ahead. "Hey, Roseroar! Mudge here has a suggestion about how you can help us raise some cash."

"No, no, no, mate!" said the suddenly panicky otter. "I meant the girl, the *girl*."

Jon-Tom shrugged. "Big girl, little girl, what's the difference?" He started to call out to the tigress a second time. Mudge slammed a muffling paw over Jon-Tom's mouth, having to stand on tiptoes to manage it.

"Okay, guv'nor. I get your point. I'll keep me ideas to meself."

"See that you do, or I'll repeat your suggestion to Roseroar."

"I'd deny 'avin' anything to do with it."

"Sure you will, but who do you think she'll believe, me or you?"

"That'd be a foul subterfuge, mate."

"In which inventions I have an excellent teacher."

Mudge wasn't flattered by the backhanded compliment.

They marched steadily westward. As the days passed the character of the country grew increasingly rural. Houses were fewer and far between. Semitropical flora made way for coniferous forest that reminded Mudge of his beloved Bellwoods. The palms and thin-barked trees of the coast fell behind them.

They asked directions of the isolated travelers they encountered. All inquiries were met with expressions of disbelief or confessions of ignorance. Everyone seemed to know that Crancularn lay to the west. Exactly where to the west, none were able to say with certainty.

Besides, there was naught to be found in Crancularn but trouble, and the country folk had no need of more of that. They were busy enough avoiding the attentions of Snarken's predatory tax collectors.

In short, Crancularn was well-known, by reputation if not by sight, and that reputation was not enticing to potential visitors.

Two days after the road had become a mere trail, they settled down to enjoy the bright sunshine. A clear stream followed the track, tumbling glassily on its course down to the now distant Glittergeist. An octet of commune spiders were busy building a six-foot-square web between two trees. They would share equally in any catch.

Jon-Tom studied the pinecone that had fallen near his feet. It was long and slim, and the scales shone like bronze. Mudge had slipped out of his boots and was wading the stream, wishing it were deep enough for him to have a swim, while Jalwar had wandered into the woods in search of berries and edible roots to supplement their meager diet. Roseroar catnapped beneath an evergreen whose trunk grew almost parallel to the ground, while Folly, as always, stayed as close to Jon-Tom as he would allow.

"Don't look so discouraged," she said. "We'll get there."

Jon-Tom was picking at the cone, tossing the pieces into the stream and watching the little triangular brown boats until they disappeared over slick stones.

"How can we get there if nobody can give us directions? 'West' isn't good enough. I thought it would be easy once we got out of Snarken. I thought at least a few of the country folk would know the way to Crancularn. From what Clothahump told me, this store of the Aether and Neither is supposed to be pretty famous."

"Famous enough to avoid," Folly murmured.

"Some of them must be lying. They *must* be. I can't believe not a soul knows the way. Why won't they tell us?"

Folly looked thoughtful. "Maybe they're concerned and want to protect us from ourselves. Or maybe none of them really do know the way."

"Mebbee they don't know the way, boy, because it moves around."

"What?" Jon-Tom looked back to see an old chipmunk standing next to a botherbark bush. He pressed against the small of his back with his left paw and gripped the end of a curved cane with the other. Narrow glasses rested on the nose, and an ancient floppy hat nearly covered his head down to the eyes. A gray shirt hung open to the waist, and below he wore brown dungarees held up by suspenders. He also had very few teeth left.

"What do you mean, it moves around?" Roseroar looked up interestedly and moved to join them. The chipmunk's eyes went wide at the sight and Jon-Tom hurried to reassure him.

"That's Roseroar. She's a friend."

"That's good," said the chipmunk prosaically. Mudge turned to listen but was reluctant to abandon the cool water.

The oldster leaned against the tree for support and waved his cane. "I mean, it moves around, sonny. It never stays in the same place for very long."

"That's crazy," said Folly. "It's just another town."

"Oh, it's a town, all right, but not like any other, lass. Not Crancularn." He peered out from beneath the brim of his hat at Jon-Tom. "Why thee want to go there, tall man?"

"We need something from there. From a store."

The chipmunk nodded. "Aye, the Shop of the Aether and Neither."

"Then you've heard of it!" Jon-Tom said excitedly. "We need something, a certain medicine, that can only be purchased in that store."

The oldster grunted, though it came out as more of a rusty squeak. "Well, that's thy business."

"Please, we've come a long way. From across the Glittergeist. We need directions. *Specific* directions."

Another grunt-squeak. "Long way to come to make fools of thyselves."

"It's not for us. A friend of mine, a teacher and a great wizard, is very sick and badly needs this medicine. If you can tell us how to get to Crancularn, we'll pay you, somehow."

The oldster shook his head sadly. "I'd tell thee if I could, boy, but I can't help you. I don't know where Crancularn is." Jon-Tom slumped. "But there's them that do. Only, I wouldn't be the one to go asking them."

"Let us worry about that," said Jon-Tom eagerly. "Who are they?"

"Why, the enchanted ones, of course. Who else?"

"Enchanted ones?"

"Aye, the little people of the magic. The fairy folk. You know."

Folly's eyes were wide with childlike wonder. "When I was a little girl, I used to hear stories of the fairy folk. My mother used to tell me." She went very quiet and Jon-Tom tried to rush the conversation to take her thoughts off more recent memories.

"Where would we find these fairy folk?" The thought of meeting real honest-to-Tinker Bell fairies was enough to motivate him. Getting directions to Crancularn would be a bonus.

"I wouldn't advise anyone to risk such an encounter, sonny, but I can see that thee art determined." He indicated the steep slope behind them. "They hide in the wet ravines and steep canyons of these hills, keeping to themselves. Don't much care for normal folk such as us. But thee art human, and it is said that they take human form. Perhaps thee will have better luck than most. Seek the places where the water runs deep and clear and the rocks are colored so dark they are almost black, where the moss grows thick above the creeks and..."

" 'Ere now, grandpa." Mudge spoke from his rocky seat out in the stream. "This 'ere moss, it don't 'ave no mental problems now, do it?"

The chipmunk frowned at him. "How could mere moss have mental problems?"

Mudge relaxed. Their near-disastrous experience in the Muddletup Moors was still fresh in his mind. "Never mind."

The chipmunk gave him an odd look, turned back to Jon-Tom. "Those are the places where thee might encounter the fairy folk. If thee must seek them out."

"It seems we've no choice." Rising, Jon-Tom turned to inspect the tree-fringed hillside.

The elderly chipmunk resumed his walk. "I wish thee luck, then. I wish thee luck. Thee will need it to locate the enchanted ones, and thee will need it even more if thee do."

The ridge above gave way to a heavily wooded slope on the far side that grew progressively steeper. Soon they were fighting to maintain their balance as they slipped and slid down the dangerous grade.

At least, Jon-Tom and Roseroar were. With their inherent agility and lower centers of gravity, Jalwar and Mudge had no difficulty at all with the awkward descent, and Folly proved lithe as a gibbon.

A stream ran along the bottom of the narrow gorge. It was broader than the one they'd left behind, but not deep enough to qualify as a river. Moss and many kinds of ferns clung to logs and boulders. Insects hummed in the cool, damp air while dark granite and schist soaked up the rays of the sun.

They spent most of the day searching along the creek before deciding to move on. An insurmountable waterfall forced them to climb up the far side of the gorge. They topped the next ridge, climbed down still another slope where they camped for the night.

By the afternoon of the following day they were exploring their fourth such canyon. Jon-Ton was beginning to think that the fairy folk were a myth invented by an especially garulous old rodent to amuse himself at the expense of some gullible travelers.

They were finishing up a late meal when Mudge suddenly erupted from his seat on a thick patch of buttery yellow flowers. His bark of surprised pain echoed down the creek.

Everyone jumped. Roseroar automatically reached for her swords. Folly crouched ready to run while Jalwar's fur bristled on his neck. Jon-Tom, who was more familiar with the otter's overreactions, left his staff alone.

"What the hell bit you?"

Mudge was trying to inspect his backside. "Somethin' sure as 'ell did. 'Ere, Folly, be a good girl and see if I'm bleedin'?" He turned to her and bent slightly.

She examined the area dominated by the short, stubby tail and protected by leather shorts. "I don't see anything."

" 'Ave a close look."

"You fuzzy pervert." She gave him a look of disgust as she moved away.

"No, really. Not that I deny the accusation, luv, but somethin' took a chunk out o' me backside for sure."

"Liar! What would I do with a chunk of you?"

The voice was high but firm and came from the vicinity of the flowerbed. Jon-Tom crawled over for a close look, searching for the source of the denial.

Tiny hands parted the stalks, which were as yellow as the thick-petaled flowers, and he found himself staring at something small, winged, feminine, and drastically overweight.

"I'll be damned," he murmured. "A fat fairy."

"Watch your mouth, buster," she said as she sort of lumbered out lightly until she was standing on a broken log. The log was brown with red longitudinal stripes running through the bark. "I know I've got a small personal problem, and I don't need some big-mouthed human reminding me of the fact."

"Sorry." Jon-Tom tried to sound contrite. "You are a fairy, aren't you? One of the enchanted folk?"

"Nah," she snapped back, "I'm a stevedore from Snarken."

Jon-Tom studied her closely. Her clothing resembled wisps of spun gossamer lavender candy. A miniature tiara gleamed on her head. Long hair trailed below her waist. The tiara had been knocked askew and covered one eye. She grunted as she struggled to straighten it. In her right hand she clutched a tiny gold wand. Her wings were shards of cellophane mottled with thin red stripes.

"We were told," Folly said breathlessly, "that you could help us."

"Now, why would I want to do that? We've got enough problems of our own." She stared at Jon-Tom. "That's a nice duar. You a musician, bright boy?"

" 'e's a spellsinger, and a right powerful one, too," Mudge informed her. "Come all the way from across the Glittergeist to fetch back medicine for a sick sorcerer."

"He's a right powerful fool," she snapped. She sat down heavily on the log, her legs spread wide in a most casual and unladylike manner. Jon-Tom estimated her to be about four inches high and almost as wide.

"I'm called Jon-Tom." He introduced his companions. An uneasy silence ensued and he finally asked, "What's your name?"

"None of your business."

"Come on," he said coaxingly. "Whether you help us

or not is up to you, but can't we at least be polite to one another?''

"What's this? A polite human? That doesn't make any sense, bald-body.'' She shrugged. "What the hell. My name's Grelgen. Want to make something of it?''

"Uh, no.'' Jon-Tom decided he was going to have to tread very carefully with this pint-size package of enchanted belligerence.

"Smart answer. You got anything to eat?''

Jalwar started to rummage through his pack. "I think we have some snake jerky, and there are a few hard rolls.''

"Ptui!'' She spat to her right. "I mean *real* food. Fruit tarts, cream cups, nectar custard, whipped honey rolls.''

Jon-Tom said carefully, "I think I am beginning to see what your problem is.''

"Oh, you are, are you, fungus-foot? You think everything's cut and dried, don't you? It's all so obvious to you.'' She was pacing now, back and forth atop the log, waving her tiny hands to punctuate her words.

"Say, you can't fly, can you?''

She turned to face him. "Of course I can fly, dumbutt.'' She wiggled her diaphanous wings. "What do you think these are for? Air-conditioning?''

"All right, then let's see you fly. Come on, fly.''

"Feh! You'd think I didn't have anything better to do than put on a show for a bunch of pituitary freaks.''

"You can't fly!'' Jon-Tom said triumphantly. "*That's* your big problem. You've gotten so . . .''

"Watch it, jack,'' she said warningly.

". . . so healthy that you can't lift off anymore. I wouldn't think it would make a difference. A bumblebee's too heavy for flight, but it manages, and without enchantment.''

"I'm a fairy, one of the enchanted folk,'' Grelgen informed him, speaking as one would to an idiot child. "Not a bumblebee. There are structural, aerodynamic, and metabolic differences you wouldn't understand. As for problems, you're the ones who are stuck with the biggie.''

She stabbed the wand at Mudge. "That turkey tried to assassinate me!"

Mudge gaped in surprise. "Wot, me? I did nothin' o' the kind, your shortness."

"You sat on me, rat-breath."

"Like 'ell I did! You crawled underneath me. Anyways, 'ow was I supposed to see you or anything else under all them flowers?"

Grelgen crossed her arm. "I was sitting there minding my own business, having a little afternoon snack of nectar and pollen, and you deliberately dropped your rat-butt right on top of me."

"You expect me to inspect every patch o' ground I sit down on?"

"In our lands, yes."

"We didn't know it were your lands." Mudge was fast losing patience with this infinitesimal harridan.

"Ah-*ha*! So, a casual assassin. The worst kind." She put two fingers to her lips and let out a sharp, piercing whistle. Jon-Tom listened admiringly. The sound was loud enough to attract an empty cab from two blocks down a Manhattan street.

What it did attract, from beneath mushrooms and flowers, from behind moss beds and tree roots, was a swarm of enchanted folk, several hundred of them. A few carried wands resembling Grelgen's, but most hefted miniature bows and arrows, crossbows, and spears. Jon-Tom put a hand out to restrain Roseroar from picking up her swords, even though the tigress weighed more than all the enchanted folk combined.

"Magic," he whispered warningly.

Roseroar yielded, but not to his admonition. "Magic or no, the tips of their weapons are moistened. I suspect poison. An ungallant way to fight."

"I guess if you're four inches tall you have to use every advantage you can think of."

Jalwar moved close, whispered to him. "Move carefully

here, spellsinger, or we may vanish in an arrogant conjuration. These folk have a deserved reputation for powerful magic.''

''That's how I figure it,'' he replied. ''Maybe they're not all as obnoxious or combative as our friend there.''

''What's that, what did you say?''

''I said,'' he told Grelgen, ''that it's nice of you to invite us to meet all your friends and relatives.''

''When one of us is threatened, buster, all spring to the rescue.''

Jon-Tom noted that none of the fairies surrounding them were in any condition to fly. Every one of them waddled about with obvious difficulty, and the slimmest was a candidate for the enchanted branch of Weight Watchers.

''You're our prisoners,'' she finished.

''I see,'' said Mudge. ''And wot if we decide not to be your prisoners?''

''Then you'll be dead,'' she assured him unpleasantly.

Mudge studied the array of glistening little weapons. '' 'Ospitable folk, wot?''

''Watch 'em,'' said Grelgen to her relations. She turned and sauntered to the end of the branch, hopped off, and landed with a wheeze in the grass below. There she entered into a mumbling conversation with several other wand-bearers. Most of them were clad only in rags and tatters.

Mudge *would* have to sit on someone of importance, thought Jon-Tom angrily. The conference broke up moments later.

''This way,'' said one of the other armed fairies, gesturing upstream. Surrounded by miniuscule guards, they were marched off up the creek.

''You sure you didn't see her, Mudge?'' Jon-Tom asked the otter.

''Would I 'ave been stupid enough to sit on 'er if I 'ad, mate? Use your 'ead. It were those bloody flowers.''

''You weren't looking, then,'' Jon-Tom said accusingly.

''So I weren't lookin'. Should I 'ave been lookin'?''

''No, I guess not. It's nobody's fault.''

"Pity I didn't flatten 'er," the otter murmured, careful to keep his voice down.

"It might not have mattered, sir," Jalwar murmured. "The fairy folk are known for their resilience."

"I can see that," said Mudge, studying their obese escort. "The one with the mouth looks like she could bounce."

"Be quiet," said Jon-Tom. "We're in enough trouble already. She'll hear you."

"Damned if I care if she does, guv." The otter had his hands shoved in his pockets and kicked disgustedly at pebbles as they walked along the side of the creek. "If she ain't got common sense to see that—"

A paw the size of his head covered his mouth and, incidently, most of his face. "Watch yo mouth, ottah," Roseroar told him. "Yo heard Jon-Tom. Let's not irritate these enchanted folk any moah than we already have."

"I'd like to irritate 'em," said the otter when she'd removed her paw. But his voice had become a whisper.

The stream narrowed. Canyon walls closed in tight around the marchers, all but shutting out the sun. Trees and bushes grew into one another, forming a dense, hard-to-penetrate tangle. The captives had to fight their way through the thickening undergrowth.

Dusk brought them to the outskirts of the enchanted folk's village. In appearance it was anything but enchanted. Tiny huts and homes were scattered around a natural amphitheater. Evidence of disrepair and neglect abounded. Some of the buildings were falling down, and even those cut into massive tree roots had piles of trash mounded up against the doorways. To Jon-Tom all this was clear proof of a loss of pride among the inhabitants.

Tiny lights flickered to life behind many of the miniature windows, and smoke started to curl from minute chimneys. Off to one side of the community a circular area was surrounded by a stone wall pierced by foot-high archways.

The six-inch high wall ended at both ends against a sheer cliff of gray granite.

The four captives filled this arena. Once they were inside the insignificant walls, Grelgen and two other fairies stood within the archways waving their wands and murmuring importantly. When the invocation was finished, she stepped back and retreated toward the village with her cronies.

Folly took a step toward the minuscule barrier and tried to step over. She gasped and drew back as if bitten, holding her right hand.

"What is it?" Jon-Tom asked anxiously.

"It's *hot*. The air's hot."

Experimentally, Jon-Tom waved at the emptiness above the tiny stone wall. An invisible wall of flame now enclosed them. He shook his hand and blew on his fingers to cool them, deciding they weren't going to blister. Escape wouldn't be easy.

Roseroar sighed and settled herself on the hard ground. "An ironic conclusion to yoah expedition, Jon-Tom. Captured and imprisoned by a bunch of disgruntled, not to mention uncouth, enchanted folk."

"Don't be so quick to give up. They may decide to let us go yet. Besides," he swung his duar around, "we have magic of our own."

Mudge looked imploringly heavenward. "Why me, wot?"

"I do not know that spellsinging will work against the fairy folk, sir," said Jalwar. "In my travels I have heard that they are immune to all forms of magic except their own. It may be that yours will have no effect on them, and may even be turned against you."

"You don't say." Jon-Tom's fingers fell from the duar's strings, together with what remained of his confidence. "I didn't know that."

"It may not be so, but it is what I have heard many times."

"We'll hold it as a last resort, then."

"Wot difference does it make, mate? 'Alf the time it

backfires on you anyhows. If it doubles back on us I wouldn't want it to 'appen while I'm stuck in this clearin'."

"Neither would I, Mudge." He looked out toward the winking lights of the village. "We may not have any choice. They don't seem much inclined to listen to reason."

"I think they're all crazy," commented Folly.

In the fading light she looked healthy and beautiful. The impermanent bruises and scars Corroboc had inflicted on her were healing fast. She was resilient, tough, and growing more feminine by the day. She was also making Jon-Tom increasingly uneasy.

He turned to Mudge, saw the otter standing as close as possible to the invisible barrier enclosing them.

"What's up, Mudge?"

The otter screwed up his face, his whiskers twitching. "Can't you smell it, too, mate? Garbage." He nodded toward the town. "It's everywhere. Maybe they're enchanted, but that's not the word I'd use to describe their sewage system."

"Ah saw their gardens when we came in," said Roseroar thoughtfully. "They appeahed to be untended."

"So fairy town's gone to hell," Jon-Tom murmured. "Something's very wrong here."

"Wot difference do it make to us, mate? We 'ave our own problems. Dealin' with 'Er Grossness, for one thing."

"If we could figure out what's wrong here," Jon-Tom argued, "maybe we could ingratiate ourselves with our captors."

"You ingratiate yourself, mate. Me, I'm for some sleep."

Jon-Tom didn't doubt that the otter could sleep on the bare rock. If Mudge were tossed out of a plane at twenty thousand feet, the otter could catch twenty winks before awakening to open his parachute. It was a talent he often envied.

"Sleeping won't solve our problem."

"It'll solve me immediate one, mate. I'm pooped."

"Perhaps yoah magic will work against the enchanted folk," Roseroar said hopefully.

"I don't know." Jon-Tom tapped the wood of the duar, was rewarded with a melodious thumping sound. The moon was shining down into the narrow defile, illuminating the dense woods surrounding them. "I'm going to hold off till the last possible moment to find out."

The tigress was slipping out of her armor and using it to make a crude pillow. "Ah don't know." She rested her massive head on black and white paws. "It seems to me that we're already theah."

Grelgen and the rest of the fairy council came for them in the morning. Their principal nemesis had changed into a flowing gown of orange chiffon. The bright pastel attire had not softened her disposition, however.

"We've been considering what to do with you bums most of the night," she informed them brusquely.

Jon-Tom stretched, pushed at his lower back, and wished he'd had the sense to use Roseroar for a cushion. He was stiff and sore from spending the night on the hard ground.

"All I can tell you is that we're innocent of any charges you discussed. So what are you going to do now?"

"Eat," she informed him. "Talk more later."

"Well now, I could do with a spot o' breakfast!" Mudge tried to muster some enthusiasm. Maybe Jon-Tom was right after all, and these cute little enchanted bastards were finally going to act in a civilized manner. "Where do we eat?"

"Wrong pronoun," Grelgen said. She turned to point with her wand.

Jon-Tom followed it into the brush. What the poor light of evening had kept hidden from view was now revealed by the bright light of day. Up the creek beyond the town, thick peeled branches spanned a shallow excavation. The firepit showed signs of recent use.

Mudge saw it, too, and his initial enthusiasm vanished. "Uh, wot's on the menu, luv?"

"Fricasseed water rat," she told him, with relish.

"Wot, *me*?" Mudge squeaked.

"Give the main course a bottle of elf dust. What better end for a guilty assassin?"

Up till now Jon-Tom had considered their predicament as nothing more than a matter of bad communication. This new vision of a bunch of carnivorous fairies feasting on Mudge's well-done carcass shoved everything over the edge into the realm of the surreal.

"Listen, you can't eat any of us."

Grelgen rested pudgy hands on soft hips. "Why not?

Jon-Tom struggled for a sensible reply. "Well, for one thing, it just doesn't fit your image."

She squinted sideways at him. "You," she said decisively, "are nuts. I'm going to have to consult with the Elders to make sure it's okay to eat crazy people."

"I mean, it just doesn't seem right. What about your honey rolls and custards and like that?"

Grelgen hesitated. When she spoke again, she sounded slightly embarrassed.

"Actually, you're right. It's only that every once in a while we get this craving, see? Whoever's unlucky enough to be in the neighborhood at the time ends up on the village menu." She glanced over at Folly and tried to regain some of her former arrogance. "We also find it helpful now and then to bathe in the blood of a virgin."

Folly digested this and collapsed, rolling about on the ground while laughing hysterically. Grelgen saw the tears pouring down the helpless girl's cheeks, grunted, and looked back over a shoulder. Jon-Tom followed her gaze.

On the far side of fairy town a bunch of muscular, overweight enchanted folk were sliding an oversized wooden bowl down a slope. At the sound of Grelgen's voice they halted.

"Right! Cancel the bathing ceremony!"

Cursing under their breath, the disappointed bowl movers reversed their efforts and began pushing their burden back into the bushes.

"So you think it's funny, do you? Right then, you're first on the fire instead of the water rat."

That put a clamp on Folly's laughter.

"Why her?" Jon-Tom demanded to know.

"Why not her? For one thing she's already depelted."

"Oh, no you don't." Folly braced herself against the bare granite wall, as far from Grelgen as she could get. "You just try and touch me! I'll squash you like a bug."

Grelgen looked disgusted, waved her wand almost indifferently, and whispered something under her breath. Folly leaped away from the wall, clutching her backside. The stone had become red-hot.

"Might as well resign yourself to it, girl," said Grelgen. "You're on this morning's menu and that's all there is to it. If there's anything that gets my gall it's an uncooperative breakfast."

"Please," Jon-Tom pleaded with her, dropping to his knees to be nearer eye level with their tormentor. "We mean you no harm. We only came into your lands to ask you for some information."

"Sorry. Like I said, we've got the craving, and when it comes upon us we've got to have meat."

"But why us?" Mudge asked her. "These woods must be full o' lizards and snakes enough to supply your 'ole village."

"Food doesn't wander into our custody," she snapped at him. "We don't like hunting. And the forest creatures don't stage unprovoked assaults on our person."

"Blimey," Mudge muttered. "'Ow can such small 'eads be so bloomin' dense? I told you that were an accident!"

Grelgen stared silently at him as she tapped one tiny glass slipper with her wand. Jon-Tom absently noted that the slipper was three sizes too small for her not-so-tiny foot.

"Don't give me any trouble. I'm in a disagreeable mood as it is." She whistled up a group of helpers and they started through one archway toward Folly. Her initial defiance burned out of her, she hid behind Roseroar. Jon-Tom knew that wouldn't save her.

"Look," he said desperately, trying to stall for time as he swung the duar into playing position and tried to think of something to sing, "you said that meat isn't usually what you eat, that you only have this craving for it occasionally?"

"What about it?" Grelgen snapped impatiently.

"What do you eat normally? Besides what you told me earlier."

"Milk and honey, nectar and ambrosia, pollen and sugar sap. What else would fairy folk eat?"

"So *that's* it. I had a hunch." A surge of hope rushed through him.

"What's it?" she asked, frowning at him.

He sat down and crossed his legs, set the duar aside. "I don't suppose there are any professional dieticians in the village?"

"Any what?"

"No, of course not. See, all your problems are diet-related. It not only explains your unnatural craving for protein, it also explains your, uh, unusually rotound figures. Milk's okay, but the rest of that stuff is nothing but pure sugar. I mean, I can't even *imagine* how many calories there are in a daily dose of ambrosia. You probably use a lot of glucose when you're flying, but when you stop flying, well, the problem only compounds itself."

One of the Elder fairies waiting impatiently behind Grelgen now stepped forward. "What is this human raving about?"

Grelgen pushed him back. "It doesn't matter." She turned back to Jon-Tom. "What you say makes no sense, and it wouldn't matter if it did, because we still have our craving." She started to aim her wand at the trembling Folly. "No use in trying to hide, girl. Step out here where I can see you."

Jon-Tom leaned sideways to block her aim. "Wait! You've got to listen to me. Don't you see? If you'd only change your eating habits you'd lose this craving for protein."

"We're not interested in changing our eating habits," said another of the Elders. "We *like* nectar and honey and ambrosia."

"All right, all right!" Jon-Tom said frantically. "Then there's only one way out. The only other way to reduce your craving for protein is for you to start burning off all these extra ounces you've been accumulating. You've got to break the cycle." He picked up the duar.

"At least give me a chance to help you. Maybe I can't do it with spellsinging, but there are all kinds of magic."

"Consider carefully, man," Grelgen warned him. "Don't you think we're aware that we have a little problem? Don't you think we've tried to use our own magic to solve it?"

"But none of you is a spellsinger."

"No. That's not our kind of magic. But we've tried *everything*. We're stuck with what we are. Your spellsinging can't help us. Nothing can help us. We've experimented with every type of magic known to the enchanted folk, as well as that employed by the magic-workers of the greater world. We're trapped by our own metabolisms." She rolled up her sleeves. "Now let's get on with this without any more bullshitting, okay?" She raised the wand again.

"Just one chance, just give me one chance!" he pleaded.

She swung the wand around to point it at him, and he flinched. "I'm warning you, buster, if this is some sort of trick, you'll cook before her."

"There's one kind of magic I don't think you've tried."

She made a rude noise. "Worm dung! We've tried it all."

"Even aerobics?"

Grelgen opened her mouth, then closed it. She turned to conference with the Elders. Jon-Tom waited nervously.

Finally she stuck her head out of the pile and inquired almost reluctantly, "What strange sort of magic is this?"

Jon-Tom took a deep breath and rose. Putting aside the duar, he began stripping to the waist.

Roseroar came over to whisper in his ear. "Suh, are yo preparin' some trick ah should know about? Should ah be ready with mah swords?"

"No, Roseroar. No tricks."

She shrugged and moved away, shaking her head.

Jon-Tom started windmilling his arms, loosening up. Grelgen immediately retreated several steps and raised the wand threateningly. "All you need is to learn this magic," he said brightly. "A regular program of aerobics. Not only will it reduce your unnatural craving for protein, it should bring back your old aerodynamic figures."

"What does that mean?" asked one of the younger fairies.

"It means we'll be able to fly again, stupid," replied one of the Elders as he jabbed the questioner in the ribs.

"Fly again." The refrain was taken up by the rest of the crowd.

"It's a trick!" snapped Grelgen, but the weight of opinion (so to speak) was against her.

"All right." She tucked her wand under one arm and glared up at Jon-Tom. "You get your chance, man. If this is a trick to buy time, it better be good, because it's going to be your last one."

"It's no trick," Jon-Tom assured her, feeling the sweat starting to trickle from beneath his arms. And he hadn't even begun yet.

"Look, I'm no Richard Simmons, but I can see we need to start with the basics." He was aware he had the undivided attention of several hundred sets of eyes. He took a deep breath, thankful for the morning runs which kept him in decent condition. "We're going to start with some deep knee-bends. Hands on hips . . . watch those wings, that's it. Ready." He hesitated. "This would work better if we had some music."

Grelgen grunted, turned, and barked a command. There was a brief delay. Several small figures made their way through the enchanted mob and took up positions atop the stone wall. Each carried a delicate instrument. There were a couple of flutes, a set of drums, and something that resembled a xylophone which had been in a bad traffic accident.

"What should we play?" piped one of the minuscule musicians.

"Something lively."

"A dance or roundelet?" They discussed the matter among themselves, then launched into a lively tune with faintly oriental overtones. Jon-Tom waited until he was sure of the rhythm, then smiled at his attentive if uncertain audience.

"Ready? Let's begin! Imitate me." He dipped. "Come on, it's not hard. One, two, three, and bend; one, two, three, and *bend*; . . . that's it!"

While Jon-Tom's companions looked on, several hundred fairy folk struggled to duplicate the human's movements. Before too long, groans and moans all out of proportion to the size of the throats they came from filled the air.

Grelgen was gasping and sweating. Her orange chiffon gown was soaked. "You're sure that you're not actually trying to murder us?"

"Oh, no." Jon-Tom was breathing a little hard himself. "See, this isn't an instantaneous kind of magic. It takes time." He sat down and put his hands behind his neck, wondering how far he could go before Grelgen gave up. "Now, this kind of magic is called situps. Up, down, up, down . . . you in the back there, no slacking, now : . . up, down . . ."

He worried constantly that Grelgen and her colleagues would become impatient before the new exercise regimen had time to do its work. He needn't have worried. The enchanted folk took weight off as rapidly as they put it on. By the seeond day the most porcine of the villagers could boast of shrunken waistlines. By the third the effects were being felt by all, and by the fourth even Grelgen could stay airborne for short flights.

"I don't understand, mate," said Mudge. "You said it 'tweren't magic, yet see 'ow quick-like they're shrinkin' down!"

"It's their metabolic rate. They burn calories much faster than we do, and as soon as they get down to where they can fly again, the burning accelerates."

The results were reflected in Grelgen's changing attitude. As the exercises did their work, her belligerence softened. Not that she became all sweetness and light, but her gratitude was evident.

"A most wondrous gift you have given us, man. A new kind of magic." It was the morning of the fifth day of their captivity and a long time since any of the enchanted folk had suggested having one of their guests for supper.

"I have a confession to make. It's not magic. It's only exercise."

"Call it by whatever name you wish," she replied, "it is magic to us. We are starting to look like the enchanted folk once more. Even I," she finished proudly. She did a deep knee-bend to prove it, something she couldn't have imagined doing five days earlier. Of course, she did it while hovering in midair, which made it somewhat easier. Still, the accomplishment was undeniable.

"You are free to go," she told them.

Roseroar stepped forward and cautiously thrust out a paw. The invisible wall of fire which had kept them imprisoned had vanished, leaving behind only a little lingering heat. The tigress stepped easily over the tiny stone wall.

"Our gratitude is boundless," Grelgen went on. "You said you came to us for help." She executed a neat little

pirouette in the air, delighting in her rediscovered mobility.
"What is it you wish to know?"

"We need directions to a certain town," he told her. "A
place called Crancularn."

"Ah. An ambiguous destination. Not mine to wonder
why. Wait here." She flew toward the village, droning like
a wasp, and returned several minutes later with four newly
slimmed Elders. They settled on the wall. Between them,
the four Elders held a piece of parchment six inches
square. It was the biggest piece of writing material the
village could produce.

"Crancularn, you said?" Jon-Tom nodded at her.

She rolled up the sleeves of her burgundy-and-lime
dress, waved the wand over the parchment as she spoke.
The parchment twisted like a leaf in the wind. It continued
to quiver as a line of gold appeared on its surface, tracing
the outlines of mountains and rivers, trails, and paths.
None of them led directly toward the golden diamond that
shone brightly in the upper-lefthand corner of the parchment.

Grelgen finished the incantation. The parchment ceased
its shaking, allowing the concentrating Elders to relax their
grip. Jon-Tom picked the freshly inscribed map off the
grass. It was warm to the touch. One tiny spot not far from
a minor trail fluoresced brightly.

"The glow shows you where you are at any time,"
Grelgen informed him. "It will travel as you travel. Hold
fast to the map and you will never be lost." She rose on
diaphanous wings to hover near his shoulder and trace over
the map with her wand. "See? No easy journey from here
and no trails directly to the place."

"We're told Crancularn moves about."

"So it does. It has that characteristic. But the map will
take you there, never fear. This is the cartography of what
will be as well as of what is. A useful skill which we
rarely employ. We like it where we are."

Jon-Tom thanked her as he folded the map and slipped it
carefully into a pocket of his indigo shirt.

Grelgen hovered nearby. "Tell me, man. Why do you go to Crancularn?"

"To shop for something in the Shop of the Aether and Neither." She nodded, a grave expression on her tiny face. "We've heard many rumors," he went on. "Is there something dangerous about the shop?"

"Indeed there is, man. Included among its usual inventory is a large supply of the Truth. That is something most travelers seek to avoid, not to find. Beware what purchases you make. There are bonuses and discounts to be had in that place you may not find to your liking."

"We'll watch our step," he assured her.

She nodded solemnly. "Watch your hearts and souls as well. Good luck to you, man, and to your companions. Perhaps if you return by a similar route we can show you the Cloud Dance." She looked wistful. "I may even participate myself."

"Dancing in the air isn't as difficult as dancing on the ground," said Folly.

Grelgen grinned at her. "That depends on what you're doing in the air, infant." With great dignity she pivoted and led the four Elders back to the village.

They were free, Jon-Tom knew, and so again were the enchanted folk.

XII

The map led them out of the narrow defile that was the enchanted canyon. Music and rhythmic grunts followed them as they left behind a village full of fairies aerobicizing like mad. Grelgen had a long way to go before she looked like Jane Fonda but she was determined to out perform her subjects, and Jon-Tom didn't doubt she had the willpower to do so.

Several days' march through game-filled country brought them over the highest mountain pass and down onto the western slopes. Despite Grelgen's insistence that the journey the rest of the way to Crancularn would not be easy, they were beginning to relax. Since leaving behind the enchanted village they had encountered no dangerous animals or sapients, and food was plentiful.

Ahead lay the desert. Jon-Tom felt certain they could cross it in a couple of days. All was well.

No more bad dreams bothered him, and he awoke refreshed and at ease. Fallen leaves had made a comfortable, springy bed. They were now back into deciduous forest, having left most of the evergreen woods behind.

He pushed his cape aside. A few wisps of smoke still

rose from the remains of last night's fire. Roseroar snored softly on the far side of the embers while Mudge dozed nearby. That in itself was unusual. Normally the otter woke first.

Jon-Tom scanned the rest of the camp and sat up fast. "Jalwar? Folly!"

The woods did not answer, nor did anyone else.

He climbed to his feet, called again. His shouts roused Mudge and Roseroar.

"Wot's amiss, mate?"

Jon-Tom gestured at the campsite. "See for yourself."

Mudge inspected the places where the missing pair had slept. "They aren't off 'untin' for breakfast berries. All their gear's gone."

"Could they have been carried off?" Jon-Tom muttered.

"Why would anybody bother to sneak in softly and steal that pair away while leavin' us snug and in dreamland?" Roseroar said. "Makes no sense."

"You're right, it doesn't. So they left on their own, and with a stealthiness that implies premeditation."

"What?" she growled in confusion.

"Sorry. My legal training talking. It means they planned to sneak out. Don't ask me why."

"Which way would they go?"

"Maybe there's a town nearby. I'll check the map." He reached into his pocket, grasped air. A frantic, brief search proved that the map was well and truly gone.

"Mudge, did you . . . ?"

The otter shook his head, his whiskers bristling in anger. "You never gave it to me, guv'nor. I saw you put it up yourself." He sighed, sat down on a rock, and adjusted his cap, leaning the feather down at its usual rakish angle. "Can't say as 'ow I'm surprised. That Corroboc might 'ave been a class-one bastard, but 'e knew wot 'e were about when 'e named that girl."

"Ah've been suspicious of her motives from the beginning," Roseroar added. "We should have sold the little bitch in Snarken, when we had the chance."

Jon-Tom found himself staring northwestward, through the thinning forest toward the distant desert. "It doesn't make sense. And what about Jalwar? He's gone, too, and that makes even less sense. How can he get anywhere without our help and protection?"

Mudge came and stood next to his friend, put a comforting paw on his shoulder. "Ah, lad. 'Ave you learned so little o' life since you've been in this world? Who knows wot old Jalwar promised the girl? 'E's a trader, a merchant. Obviously 'e made 'er a better offer than anything we 'ave. Maybe 'e were bein' marooned on that beach by 'onest folk 'e'd cheated. This ain't no world for takin' folks on faith, me friend. For all we know Jalwar's a rich old bugger in 'is 'ome town."

"If he wanted Folly to help him, why would they take the map? They wouldn't need it to retrace the trail back to Snarken."

"Then it's pretty clear they ain't 'eadin' for Snarken, mate." He turned and stared down the barely visible path. "And we ought to be able to prove it."

Sure enough, in the dew-moistened earth beyond the campsite the two sets of footprints stood out clearly, the small, almost dainty marks of Jalwar sharp beside Folly's sandalprints. They led downslope toward the desert.

" 'Tis plain wot they're about, mate. They're 'eading for Crancularn. That's why they stole the map."

"But why? Why not go theah with the rest of us?" Roseroar was shaking her head in puzzlement.

"You're as dense as 'e is, luv. Ain't it plain enough yet to both of you? Jalwar's a *trader*. They're goin' to try and buy up the 'ole supply o' this medicine 'is sorcerership needs so badly and 'old it for ransom." He stared at Jon-Tom. "We told the old fart too much, mate, and now 'e's bent on doin' us dirty."

"Jalwar, maybe . . ." Jon-Tom mumbled unhappily, "but I can't believe that Folly . . ."

"Why not, mate? Or did you think she were in love with you? After wot she went through, she's just lookin' out after 'erself. Can't blame 'er for that, wot?"

"But we were taking care of her, good care."

Mudge shrugged. "Not good enough, it seems. Like I said, no tellin' wot old Jalwar promised 'er in return for 'elpin' 'im."

"What now, Jon-Tom?" asked Roseroar gently.

"We can't turn back. Map or no map. I suppose we could go back to the village of the enchanted folk and get another one, but that would put us weeks behind them. We can't lose that much time if Mudge's suspicions are correct. They'd beat us to the medicine easily. I studied that map pretty intensively after Grelgen gave it to us. I can remember some of it."

"That ain't the 'ole of it, mate." Mudge bent and put his nose close to the ground. When he stood straight again, his whiskers were twitching. "An otter can follow a scent on land or through water if there's just enough personal perfume left to tickle 'is nostrils. This track's fresh as a new whore. Until it rains we've got a trail to follow, and there's desert ahead. Maybe if we pee on the run we can overtake the bloody double-crossers."

"Ah second the motion, suh. Let's not give up, Jon-Tom."

"I wasn't thinking of giving up, Roseroar. I was thinking about what we're going to do when we do catch up with them."

"That's the spirit!" She leaned close. "Leave the details to me." Her teeth were very white.

"I'm not sure that would be the civilized thing to do, Roseroar." Despite the deception, the thought of Folly in Roseroar's paws was not a pleasant one.

"All mah actions are dictated by mah society's code of honah, Jon-Tom," she said stiffly. She frowned at a sudden thought. "Don't tell me that after what's happened heah yo still feel fo the little bitch?"

He was shouldering his backpack. "We still don't know that she went with Jalwar voluntarily. Maybe he forced her."

Mudge was waiting at the edge of the campsite, anxious to get moving. "Come on now, mate. Even if you exclude age as a consideration, the girl was bigger and stronger than that old ferret. And she could always have screamed."

"Not necessarily. Not if Jalwar had a knife at her throat. Look, I admit it looks like she went with him voluntarily, but I won't condemn her until we know for sure. She's innocent until proven guilty."

Mudge spat on the ground. "Another o' your other-worldly misconceptions."

"It's not otherworldly. It's a universal truism," Jon-Tom argued.

"Not in this universe it ain't."

Roseroar let them argue while she assumed the lead, glancing occasionally at the ground to make sure they were still on the trail, scanning the woods for signs of ambush. For the moment she preferred to ignore both of her argumentative companions.

From time to time Mudge would move up alongside her to dip his nose to the earth. Sometimes the footprints of their quarry would disappear under standing water or mix with the tracks of other creatures. Mudge always regained the trail.

"Must 'ave took off right after the last o' us fell asleep," the otter commented that afternoon. "I guess them to be at least six hours ahead of us, probably more."

"We'll catch them." Jon-Tom was covering the ground easily with long, practiced strides.

"Maybe that ferret weren't so old as 'e made 'imself out to be," Mudge suggested.

"We'll still catch them."

But the day went with no sign of girl and ferret. They

let Roseroar lead them on through the darkness, until accumulating bumps and bruises forced Jon-Tom to call a halt for the night. They slept fitfully and were up again before the dawn.

By afternoon the last trees had surrendered to scrub brush and bare rock. Ahead of them a broad, hilly plain of yellow and brown mixed with the pure white of gypsum stretched from horizon to horizon. It was high desert, and as such, the heat was not as oppressive as it might have been. It was merely dauntingly hot. The air was still and windless, and the shallow sand clearly showed the tracks of Jalwar and Folly.

It was a good thing, because the sand did not hold their quarry's spoor as well as damp soil, and Mudge had increasing difficulty distinguishing it from the tracks of desert dwellers as they started out across the plain.

"I 'ope you remember that map well, mate."

"This is the Timeful Desert, as I remember it."

Mudge frowned. "I thought deserts were supposed to be timeless, not timeful."

"Don't look at me. I didn't name it." He pointed toward a low dune. "The only sure source of water is a town in the middle of the desert called Redrock. The desert's not extensive, but it's plenty big enough to kill us if we lose our way."

"That's a comfortin' thought to be settin' out with." The otter looked up at Roseroar. "Any sign o' our friends, tall tail?"

Roseroar's extraordinary eyesight scanned the horizon. "Nothing but sand. Nothing moves."

"Can't say as 'ow I blame it." He kicked sand from his boots.

By the morning of the next day the mountains had receded far behind them. Jon-Tom busied himself by searching for a suggestion of green, a hint of moisture. It seemed impossible that the land could be utterly barren.

Even a stubby, tired cactus would have been a welcome
sight.

They saw nothing, which did not mean nothing existed
in the Timeful Desert. Only that if any life did survive, it
did not make itself known to the trio of travelers.

He felt sure they would overtake Jalwar and Folly, but
they did not. Not all that day nor the next.

It was on that third day that Mudge had them halt while
he knelt in the sand.

" 'Ere now, 'ave either of you two noticed this?''

"Noticed what?'' The sweat was pouring down Jon-
Tom's face, as much in frustration at finding no sign of
their quarry as from the heat.

Mudge put a paw flat on the ground. "This 'ere sand.
'Ave a close look.''

Jon-Tom knelt and stared. At first he saw nothing. Then
one grain crept from beneath Mudge's fingers. A second, a
third, moving from west to east. Mudge's paw hadn't
moved them, nor had the wind. There was no wind.

At the same time as loose grains were shifting from
beneath the otter's paw, a small rampart of sand was
building up against the other side of his thumb. The sand
was moving, without aid of wind, from east to west.

Jon-Tom put his own hand against the hot sand, watched
as the phenomenon repeated itself. All around them, the
sand was shifting from east to west. He felt the small hairs
on the back of his neck stiffen.

" 'Tis bloody creepy,'' the otter muttered as he rose and
brushed sand from his paws.

"Some underground disturbance,'' Jon-Tom suggested.
"Or something alive under the surface.'' That was not a
pleasant thought, and he hastened to discard it. They had
no proof that anything lived in this land, anyway.

"That's not all.'' Mudge gestured back the way they'd
come. "There's somethin' else mighty funny. See that 'ill
we passed the other day?'' Jon-Tom and Mudge strained to

see the distant relative of a Serengeti kopje. '' 'Tis lower than it were.''

"Nothing unnatural about that, Mudge. It's just shrinking into the distance as we walk."

The otter shook his head insistently. '' 'Tis shrinkin' too bloomin' fast, mate." He shouldered his pack and resumed the march. "One more thing. Don't it seem to either o' you that we're walkin' downhill?''

Jon-Tom didn't try to hide his confusion. He gestured at the western horizon. "We're on level ground. What are you talking about?"

"I dunno." The otter strained to put his feelings into words. '' 'Tis just that somethin' don't feel right 'ere, mate. It just don't feel right.''

That night the otter's nose proved of more help than his sense of balance. They dug a hole through a dark stain in the sand and were rewarded with a trickle of surprisingly clear water. Patience enabled them to top off their water skins and relieve their major anxiety. It was decided unanimously to spend the night by the moisture seep.

Jon-Tom felt someone shaking him awake, peered sleepily into still solid darkness. Mudge stared anxiously down at him.

"Got somethin' for you to 'ave a looksee at, mate."

"At this hour? Are you nuts?"

"I 'ope so, mate," the otter whispered. "I sincerely 'ope so.''

Jon-Tom sighed and unrolled himself. As he did so he found himself spitting out sand. The full moon gleamed brightly on their campsite, to reveal packs, weapons, and Roseroar's feet partially buried in sand.

"The wind came up during the night, that's all." He found he was whispering, too, though there seemed no reason for it.

"Feel any wind now, mate?"

Jon-Tom wet a finger, stuck it into the air. "No. Not a breeze."

"Then 'ave a look at your own feet, mate."

Jon-Tom did so. As he stared he saw sand flowing over his toes. There was no wind at all, and now the sand was moving much faster. He drew his feet up as if the pulverized silica might bite him.

"Look all around, lad."

The sand was crawling westward at an ever more rapid pace. It seemed to accelerate even as he watched. In addition to the steady movement there came the first murmurs of a dry, slithery, rasping sound as grains tumbled over one another.

The discussion finally woke Roseroar. "What's goin' on heah?"

"I don't know," Jon-Tom muttered, eyeing the crawling ground. "The sand is moving, and much faster now than it was yesterday. I'm not sure I want to know what's making it move."

"Should we go back?" The tigress was slipping on her sandals, shaking the grains from the leather.

"We can't go back." He pulled on his boots. "If we go back now, we lose Jalwar, Folly, and likely as not, Clothahump's medicine. But I won't force either of you to stay with me. Roseroar, are you listening to me?"

She wasn't. Instead, she was pointing southward. "Ah think we might get ourselves a second opinion. We have company, y'all."

The line of camels the tigress had spotted was slightly behind them but moving in the same direction. Hastily gathering their equipment, the trio hurried to intercept the column of dromedaries. As they ran the sun began to rise, bringing with it welcome light and unwelcome heat. And all around them, the sand continued to crawl inexorably westward.

Mounted on the backs of the camels was an irregular assortment of robed rodents—pack rats, kangaroo rats, field mice, and other desert dwellers of related species. They looked to Jon-Tom like a bunch of midget bewhis-

kered bedouins. He loped alongside the lead camel, tried
to bow slightly, and nearly tripped over his own feet.

"Where are you headed in such a hurry?" The pack rat
did not reply. The camel did.

"We go to Redrock. Everyone goes now to Redrock,
man. Everyone who lives in the desert." The camel's
manner was imperious and wholly typical of his kind. He
spat a glob of foul-smelling sputum to his left, making
Jon-Tom dodge.

"Who are you people?" inquired the pack rat in the
front. There was room on the camel's back for several.

"Strangers in this land."

"That is obvious enough," commented the camel.

"Why is everyone going to Redrock?" Jon-Tom asked.

The camel glanced back up at its lead rider and shook its
head sadly. The rat spoke. "You really don't know?"

"If we did, would we be askin' you, mate?" said
Mudge.

The rat gestured with both paws, spreading his arms
wide. "It is the Conjunction. The time when the threads of
magic that bind together this land reach their apogee. The
time of the time inversion."

"What does that mean?"

The rat shrugged. "Do not ask me to explain it. I am no
magician. This I do know. If you do not reach the safety of
Redrock by the time the next moon begins to rise, you
never will." He slapped the camel on the side of its neck.
The animal turned to gaze back up at him.

"Let's have none of that, Bartim, or you will find
yourself walking. I am measuring my pace, as are the rest
of the brethren."

"The time is upon us!"

"No less so upon me than thee," said the camel with a
pained expression. He turned to glance back to where
Jon-Tom was beginning to fall behind. "We will see you
in Redrock, strangers, or we will drink the long drink to
your memory."

Panting hard in the rising light, Jon-Tom slowed to a walk, unable to maintain the pace. On firm ground he might have kept up, but not in the soft sand. Roseroar and Mudge were equally winded.

"What was that all about, Jon-Tom?" asked Roseroar.

"I'm not sure. It didn't make much sense."

"Ah you not a spellsingah?"

"I know my songs, but not other magic. If Clothahump were here . . ."

"If 'is wizardship were 'ere we wouldn't be, mate."

"What do you think of their warning?"

Sand was building up around the otter's feet, and he kicked angrily at it. "They were both scared. Wot of I couldn't say, but scared they were. I think we'd better listen to 'em and get a move on. Make Redrock by nightfall, they said. If they can do it, so can we. Let's get to it."

They began to jog, keeping up a steady pace and taking turns in the lead. They barely paused to eat and made lavish use of their water. The more they drank, the less there was to carry, and if the warning was as significant as it had seemed, they would have to drink in Redrock that night or not drink at all.

As for the nature of the menace, that began to manifest itself as they ran.

It was evening, and still no sign of the city, nor of the caravan, which had far outdistanced them. The sand was moving rapidly now, threatening to engulf their feet every time they paused to catch their breath.

At first he thought he was sinking. A quick glance revealed the truth. The ground behind them was rising. It was as if they were running inland from a beach and the beach was pursuing, a steadily mounting tidal wave of sand. He thought about turning and trying to scramble to the crest of the granular wave. What stopped him was the possibility that on the other side they might find only another, even higher surge.

So they ran on, their lungs heaving, legs aching. Once Mudge stumbled and they had to pull him to his feet while the sand clutched eagerly at his legs.

When he fell a second time, he tried to wave them off. It was as if his seemingly inexhaustible energy had finally given out.

" 'Tis no use, lad. I can't go on anymore. Save your-selves." He fluttered weakly with a paw.

Jon-Tom used the pause to catch his wind. "You're right, Mudge," he finally declared. "That's the practical thing to do. I'll always remember how nobly you died." He turned to go on. Roseroar gave him a questioning look but decided not to comment.

A handful of sand struck Jon-Tom on the back of the neck. "Noble, me arse! You *would've* left me 'ere, wouldn't you? Left poor old Mudge to die in the sand!"

Jon-Tom grinned, took care to conceal it from the apoplectic otter. "Look, *mate*. I'm tired, too, and I'm damned if I'm going to carry you."

The otter staggered after his companions. "I suppose you think it's funny, don't you, you 'ypocritical, angular bastard?"

Jon-Tom fought not to laugh. For one thing, he couldn't spare the wind. "Come off it, Mudge. You know we wouldn't have left you."

"Oh, wouldn't you, now? Suppose I 'adn't gotten up to follow you, eh? Wot then? 'Ow do I knows you would've come back for me?"

"It's a moot point, Mudge. You were just trying to hitch a ride."

"I admit nothin'." The otter pushed past him, taking the lead, his short, stubby legs moving like pistons.

"A strange one, yoah fuzzy little friend," Roseroar whispered to Jon-Tom. She matched her pace to his.

"Oh, Mudge is okay. He's a lazy, lying little cheat, but other than that he's a prince."

Roseroar considered this. "Ah believes the standards o' yoah world must be somewhat different from mine."

"Depends on what part of my culture you come from. Mudge, for example, would be right at home in a place called Hollywood. Or Washington, D.C. His talents would be much in demand."

Roseroar shook her head. "Those names have no meanin' fo me."

"That's okay. They don't for a lot of my contemporaries, either."

The sand continued to rise behind them, mounting toward the darkening sky. At any moment the wave might crest, to send tons of sand tumbling over them, swallowing them up. He tried not to think of that, tried to think of anything except lifting his legs and setting one foot down ahead of the other. When the angle of the dune rising in their wake became sharper than forty-five degrees the sand would be rushing at them so rapidly they would be hard put to keep free of its grasp.

All around them, in both directions as far as they could see, the desert was climbing for the stars. He could only wonder at the cause. The Conjunction, the pack rat had said. The moon was up now, reaching silvery tendrils toward the panting, desperate refugees. At moonrise, the rat told him. But when would the critical moment come? Now, in minutes, or at midnight? How much time did they have left?

Then Roseroar was shouting, and a cluster of hills became visible ahead of them. As they ran on, the outlines of the hills sharpened, grew regular and familiar: Redrock, so named for the red sandstone of which its multistoried towers and buildings had been constructed. In the first moonlight and the last rays of the sun the city looked as if it were on fire.

Now they found themselves among other stragglers— some on foot, others living in free association with camels and burros. Some snapped frantic whips over the heads of dray lizards.

Several ostrich families raced past, heavy backpacks

strapped to their useless wings. They carried no passengers. Nor did the family of cougars that came loping in from the north, running on hind legs like Roseroar. Bleating and barking, honking and complaining, these streams of divergent life came together in pushing, shoving lines that struggled to enter the city.

"We're going to make it!" he shouted to his companions as they merged with the rear of the mob. He was afraid to look back lest an avalanche of brown-and-yellow particles prove him a fatal liar. His throat felt like the underside of the hood of a new Corvette after a day of drag-racing, but he didn't dare stop for a drink until they were safely inside the city walls.

Then the ground fell away beneath him.

They were on a bridge, and looking down he could see through the cracks in the wood. The lumber to build it must have come from distant mountains. There was no bottom to the moat, a black ring encircling the city.

His first thought was that Redrock had been built on a hill in the center of some ancient volcanic crater. A glance at the walls of the moat proved otherwise. They were too regular, too smooth, and too vertical to have been fashioned by hand. *Something* had dug the awesome ring. Who or what, he could not imagine.

Thick smells and heavy musk filled the air around him. The bridge seemed endless, the gaps between the heavy timbers dangerously wide. If he missed a step and put a leg through, he wouldn't fall, but he would be trampled by the anxious mass of life crowding about him.

Once within the safety of the city walls, the panic dissipated. Lines of tall guards clad in yellow shepherded the exhausted flow of refugees into the vast courtyard beyond the gate. There were no buildings within several hundred yards of the wall and the moat just beyond. A great open space had been provided for all who sought shelter from the rising sands. How often did this phenomenon take place? The camel and the pack rat hadn't said, but it was obviously a regular and predictable occurrence.

"I have to see what's going on outside," he told Roseroar. She nodded, towering above most of the crowd.

Tents had been set up in expectation of the flood of refugees. Jon-Tom and his companions were among the last to enter, but they had interests other than shelter.

"This way," the tigress told him. She took his hand and pulled him bodily through the milling, swarming crowd, a striped iceberg breasting a sea of fur. Somehow Mudge managed to keep up.

Then they found themselves by the city wall, followed it until they came to stone stairs leading upward. Jon-Tom let loose of Roseroar's paw and led the way.

Would the sand wave fill the moat? If so, what would happen afterward?

A few others already stood watching atop the wall. They were calm and relaxed, so Jon-Tom assumed there was no danger. Everyone in the city was handling the situation too well for there to be any danger.

One blasé guard, a tall serval wearing a high turban to protect his delicate ears, stood aside to let them pass. "Mind the vibration, visitors," he warned them

They reached the top and stared out over the desert. Beyond the moat, the world was turning upside down.

There was no sign of the far mountains they had left many days ago. No sign of any landmark. Not a rock protruded from the ground. There was only the sand sea rising and rushing toward the city in a single wave two hundred feet high, roaring like a billion pans of frying bacon. Jon-Tom wanted to reach back and put his hand on the guard, to ask what was going to happen next. Since none of the other onlookers did so, he held his peace and like them, simply stood and gaped.

The massive wave did not fall forward to smash against the puny city walls. It began to slide into the dark moat, pouring in a seemingly endless waterfall into the unbelievable excavation. The wave was endless, too. As they watched it seemed to grow even higher, climbing toward the clouds as its base disappeared into the moat.

The thunder was all around him, and he could feel the sandstone blocks quivering underfoot. Jon-Tom turned. Across the roofs of the city, in all directions, he could see the wave. The city was surrounded by rushing sand hundreds of feet high and inestimable in volume, all of it cascading down into the depths which surrounded Redrock.

Thirty minutes passed. The wave began to shrink. Uncountable tons of sand continued to pour into the moat, which still showed no sign of filling up. Another thirty minutes and the torrent had slowed to a trickle. A few minutes more and the last grains tumbled into the abyss.

Beyond, the moon illuminated the skeleton of the desert. Bare rock stood revealed, as naked as the surface of the moon. Between the city and the mountains, nothing lived, nothing moved. A few hollows showed darkly in the rock, ancient depressions now emptied of sand and gravel.

A soft murmur rose from the onlookers as they turned away from the moat and the naked desert to face the center of the city. Jon-Tom and his companions turned with them.

In the exact center of Redrock a peculiar glassy tower stood apart from the sandstone buildings. All eyes focused on the slim spire. There was a feeling of expectation.

He was about to give in to curiosity and ask the guard what was going to happen when he heard something rumble. The stone under his feet commenced quivering. It was a different tremor this time, as though the planet itself were in motion. The rumbling deepened, became a roaring, then a constant thunder. Something was happening deep inside the earth.

"What is it, what's going on?" Roseroar yelled at him. He did not reply and could not have made himself heard had he tried.

Sudden, violent wind blew hats from heads and veils from faces. Jon-Tom's cape stretched out straight behind him like an iridescent flag. He staggered, leaned into the unexpected hurricane as he tried to see the tower.

The sands of the Timeful Desert erupted skyward from the open mouth of the glass pillar, climbing thousands of feet toward the moon. Reaching some predetermined height, the silica geyser started to spread out beneath the clouds. Jon-Tom instinctively turned to seek shelter, but stopped when he saw that none of the other pilgrims had moved.

As though sliding down an invisible roof, the sand did not fall anywhere within the city walls. Instead, it spread out like a cloud, to fall as yellow rain across the desert. It continued to fall for hours as the tower blasted it into the sky. Only when the moon was well past its zenith and had begun to set again did the volume decrease and finally peter out.

Then the geyser fell silent. The chatter of the refugees and the cityfolk filled the air, replacing the roar of the tower. A glance revealed that the bottomless moat was empty once again.

Beyond the wall, beyond the moat, the Timeful Desert once more was as it had been. All was still. The absence of life there despite the presence of water was now explained.

"Great magic," said Roseroar solemnly.

"Lethal magic." Mudge twitched his nose. "If we'd been a few minutes longer we'd be out there somewhere with our 'earts stopped and our guts full o' sand."

Jon-Tom stopped a passing fox. "Is it over? What happens now?"

"What happens now, man," said the fox, "is that we sleep, and we celebrate the end of another Conjunction. Tomorrow we return to our homes." She pushed past him and started down the stairs.

Jon-Tom resorted to questioning one of the guards. The muskrat was barely four feet tall and wore his fur cut fashionably short.

"Please, we're strangers here." He nodded toward the desert. "Does this happen every year?"

"Twice a year," the guard informed him, bored. "A grand sight the first time, I suppose."

"What's it for? Why does it happen?"

The muskrat scratched under his chin. "It is said that these are the sands of time. All time. When they have run their course, they must be turned to run again. Who turns them, or why, no one knows. Gods, spirits, some great being somewhere else who is bored with the task, who knows? I am no sorcerer or scholar, visitor." He turned to leave.

"Let 'im go, mate," said Mudge. "I don't care wot it's about. Runnin' for me life always tires me out. Me for a spot o' sleep and somethin' to drink." He started down the stairs. Jon-Tom and Roseroar followed.

"What do yo think happens heah?" the tigress asked him.

"I imagine it's as the guard told us. The desert is some kind of hourglass, holding all time within it." He gazed thoughtfully at the sky. "I wonder: if you could stop the mechanism somehow, could you stop time?" He turned toward the glassy tower. "I'd sure like to have a look inside that."

"Best not to," she told him. "Yo might find something. Yo might find your own time."

He nodded. "Anyway, we have other fish to fry."

"Ah beg yo pahdon?"

"Jalwar and Folly. If everyone else is forced to seek sanctuary here from the Conjunction, they would also. If they weren't caught by the sand, they should be somewhere here in the city."

"Ah declah, Jon-Tom, ah hadn't thought o' that!" She scanned the courtyard below.

"Unless," he went on, "they were far enough ahead of us to have already crossed the desert."

"Oh." She looked downcast, then straightened. "No

mattah. We'll find them." She began looking for an empty place among the crowds. Probably the few city inns were already full to overflowing with the wealthy among the refugees. The city gates were open and some were already filing back out into the desert.

"Yo know, somethin' just occurred to me, Jon-Tom. This old Jalwah, ah'm thinkin' we've been underestimatin' him all along. Do yo suppose he deliberately led us out heah into this desert knowin' we didn't know about this comin' Conjunction thing, and hopin' we might get oahselves killed?"

Jon-Tom considered only a moment. "Roseroar, I think that's a very good possibility, just as I think that the next time we meet up with our ferret friend, we'd better watch our step very carefully indeed."

XIII

Inquiries in the marketplace finally unearthed mention of Folly and Jalwar's passing. They were indeed several days ahead of their pursuers, and yet they had rented no riding animals. Apparently Jalwar was not only smarter than they'd given him credit for, he was also considerably stronger. The merchant who provided the information did not know which way the ferret and the girl had gone, but Jon-Tom remembered enough of the map to guess.

The desert reaches were much more extensive to north and south. There was no way back to Snarken except via Redrock. Therefore their earlier suppositions still held true. Jalwar was making for Cranculam as fast as possible.

Roseroar's search for nighttime lodging was terminated. There was no time to waste. Jon-Tom reluctantly allowed Mudge to scavenge for supplies, and the travelers then beat a hasty retreat from Redrock before their unwilling victualers could awaken to the discovery of their absent inventory.

"Of course, we'll pay for these supplies on our way back," Jon-Tom said.

"And 'ow do you propose we do that?" Mudge labored

under his restocked pack. The desert was oddly cool
underfoot, the sand stable and motionless once again. It
was as though the grains had never been displaced, had
never moved.

"I don't know, but we have to do something about this
repeated steali—"

"Watch it, mate."

"About this repeated foraging of yours. Why do you
insist on maintaining the euphemisms, Mudge?"

The otter grinned at him. "For appearances' sakes,
mate."

"It troubles me as well," Roseroar murmured, "but we
must make use of any means that we can to see this thing
through."

"I know, but I'll feel better about it if we can pay for
what we've 'borrowed' on our way back."

Mudge sighed, shook his head resignedly. " 'Umans,"
he muttered.

Despite Jon-Tom's expectations, they did not catch up
to their quarry. They did encounter occasional groups of
nomads returning to their campsites, sometimes sharing
their camps for the night. All expressed ignorance when
asked if they had seen any travelers fitting Jalwar's or
Folly's description.

On the third day they had their first glimpse of the
foothills which lay beyond the western edge of the Timeful
Desert. On the fourth they found themselves hiking among
green grass, cool woodlands, and thick scrub. Mudge
luxuriated in the aroma and presence of running water,
while Roseroar was able to enjoy fresh meat once more.

On their first day in the forest she brought down a
monitor lizard the size of a cow with one swordthrust.
Mudge joined her in butchering the carcass and setting the
steaks to cook over a blaze of thin, white-barked logs.

"Smells mighty good," commented a strange voice.

Roseroar rose to a sitting position. Mudge peered around

the cookfire while Jon-Tom put aside the duar he'd been strumming.

Standing at the edge of their little clearing in the trees was a five-foot-tall cuscus, a bland expression on his pale face. He was dressed in overlapping leather strips and braids, snakeskin boots of azure hue, and short brown pants. A single throwing knife was slung on each hip, and he was scratching himself under the chin with his furless, prehensile tail. As he scratched he leaned on the short staff he carried. Jon-Tom wondered if, like his own, the visitor's also concealed a short, deadly length of steel in the unknobbed end. The visitor's fur was pale beige mottled with brown.

He was also extraordinarily ugly, a characteristic of the species, though perhaps a female cuscus might have thought otherwise of the newcomer. He made no threatening gestures and waited patiently.

"Come on in and have a seat." Jon-Tom extended the invitation only after Roseroar had climbed to her feet and Mudge had moved close to his bow.

"That is right kind of you, sir. I am Hathcar." Jon-Tom performed introductions all around.

Roseroar was sniffing the air, glanced accusingly down at the visitor. "You are not alone."

"No, large she, I am not. Did I forget to mention it? I am sorry and will now remedy my absentmindedness." He put his lips together and emitted a sharp, high-pitched whistle.

With much rustling of bushes a substantial number of creatures stepped out into clear view, forming a line behind the cuscus. They were an odd assortment, from the more familiar rats and mice to bandicoots and phalangers. There was even a nocturnal aye-aye, who wore large, dark sunglasses and carried a short, sickle-shaped weapon.

Their clothes were on the ragged side, and their boots and sandals showed signs of much usage. Altogether not a prosperous-looking bunch, Jon-Tom decided. The presence

of so many weapons was not reassuring. These were not
kindly villagers out for a daily stroll.

Still, if all they wanted was something to eat. . . .

"You're welcome to join us," he told Hathcar. "There's
plenty for all."

Hathcar looked past him, to where Mudge was laboring
with the cooking. His tongue licked black lips.

"You are kind. Those of us who prefer meat haven't
made such a grand catch in many a day." He smiled as
best he could.

Jon-Tom gestured toward Roseroar. "Yes, she's quite
the huntress."

"She sizes the part. Still, there is but one of her and
many of us. How is it that she has been so successful and
we have not?"

"Skill is more important than numbers." One huge paw
caressed the hilt of a long sword.

Hathcar did not seem impressed. "Sometimes that can
be so, unless you are a hundred against one lizard."

"Sometimes," she agreed coolly, "but not always."

The cuscus changed the subject. "What seek you strangers in this remote land?"

"We're on a mission of importance for a great and
powerful wizard," Jon-Tom told him. "We go to the
village of Crancularn."

"Crancularn." Hathcar looked back at his colleagues,
who were hard-pressed to restrain their amusement. "That's
a fool's errand."

Jon-Tom casually let his fingers stray to his staff. He'd
had just about enough of this questioning, enigmatic visitor. Either they wanted something to eat or they didn't,
and double-talk wasn't on the menu.

"Maybe you think we look like fools," Hathcar said.
All hints of laughter fled from the gang standing behind
him. Jon-Tom didn't reply, waited for what might come.

The cuscus's smile returned, and he moved toward the
fire. "Well, you have offered us a meal. That's a wise

decision. Certainly not one to be made by fools.'' He pulled a throwing knife. "If I might try a bite? It looks well done. My compliments to the cook." Mudge said nothing.

Jon-Tom watched the visitor closely. Was he going to cut meat with it . . . or throw it? He couldn't decide.

Something came flying through the air toward him. He ducked and rolled, ending up on his feet holding the ramwood staff protectively in front of him. Mudge picked up his bow and notched an arrow into the string. Roseroar's longswords flashed as they were drawn. All within a couple of seconds.

Hathcar was careful not to raise the knife he now held. Behind him, his colleagues gripped their own weapons threateningly. But the cuscus was not glaring at Jon-Tom. His gaze was on the creature who had come flying through the air to land heavily next to the tall human.

The mongoose was clad entirely in black. It lay on its belly, moaning. Strange marks showed on its narrow backside.

"Faset," Hathcar hissed, "what happened?" The mongoose rolled to look at him, yelped when its bruised pelvis made contact with the ground.

"I happened." Everyone turned toward the voice.

The unicorn strolled casually into the clearing. It was gold. Not the light gold of a palomino but a pure metallic gold like the color of a coin or ring, except for white patches on its forehead and haunches. It might have risen from a vat of liquid gold except that Jon-Tom could clearly see that the color was true, down to the shortest hair.

In its mouth it carried a small crossbow. This it dropped at Jon-Tom's feet. Then it nodded meaningfully toward the still groaning mongoose. Jon-Tom now recognized the marks on the mongoose's pants. They were hoofprints.

Hathcar was beside himself as he glared furiously at the unicorn. "Who the hell are you, four-foot? And who asked you to interfere? This is none of your business."

The unicorn gazed at him out of lapis eyes, said coolly,

"I am making it my business." He smiled at Jon-Tom. "My name's Drom. I was grazing back in the woods when I heard the talk. Ordinarily I would have ignored it, as I ignored your presence." He nodded toward the mongoose, who was trying to crawl back to its comrades while avoiding Hathcar.

"However, I happened to chance upon this ebon worm as he was aiming his little toy at your back." Drom raised a hoof, brought it down on the crossbow. There was a splintering sound. "The unpleasant one there," and he nodded toward Hathcar, "was right. This was none of my business. I don't trouble to involve myself in the affairs of you social types. But I can't stand to see anyone backshot." He turned his magnificent head, the thin golden goatee fluttering, and glared back at Hathcar.

"Yo ah a true gentlemale, suh," said Roseroar approvingly.

"You should have stayed out of this, fool." Hathcar moved quickly to join his gang. "Anyway, he lies. No doubt this insect," and he kicked at the miserable Faset, "was trying to put a bolt through you. But that has nothing to do with me."

"You called him by name," Jon-Tom said accusingly.

"A casual acquaintance." Hathcar continued to retreat. His backers muttered uneasily.

"Glad you don't know 'im, friend." Mudge's arrow followed the cuscus's backpedaling. "I'd 'ate to think you 'ad anything to do with 'is little ambushcade."

"What about your invitation?" Hathcar wanted to know.

"I think we'd rather dine alone." Jon-Tom smiled thinly. "At least until we can sort things out."

"That's not very friendly of you. It's not polite to withdraw an invitation once extended."

"My back," the mongoose blubbered. "I think my back is broken."

"Shut up, asshole." Hathcar kicked him in the mouth and blood squirted. The cuscus tried to grin at the tall man. "Really, this thing has nothing to do with me." His band was beginning to melt into the forest. "Always hanging around, looking for sympathy. Sorry our visit upset you. I understand." Then he too was gone, swallowed by the vegetation.

Roseroar's ears were cocked forward. "They're still movin' about," she murmured warily.

"Where?" Jon-Tom asked her.

"Back among the trees."

"They are spreading out in an attempt to encircle you," said the one-horned stallion.

"Permit me to congratulate you on your timely arrival, mate." Mudge's eyes searched the woods as he spoke. "I never sensed 'im."

"Nor did I," said Roseroar, sparing a glance for the remains of the crossbow.

"I don't understand," Jon-Tom murmured. "We offered them all the food they could eat."

"It wasn't just your food they were after." Drom kicked the crossbow fragments aside. "I know that bunch by reputation. They were after your weapons and armor, your fine clothes and your money."

Mudge let out a barking laugh. "Our money! Now that's amusin'. We haven't a copper to our names," he lied.

"Ah, but they thought you did." The unicorn nodded toward the forest. "Small comfort that would have been to you if they had learned that afterwards."

"You're right there."

Roseroar was turning a slow circle, keeping the roasting carcass at her back as much as possible. "They're still out theah. Probably they think we can't heah them, but ah can." She growled deep in her throat, a blood chilling sound. "Our friend here is right. They're trying to get behind us."

"And to surprise you. Hathcar did not show his full

strength. Many more of his band remained concealed while he spoke to you.''

Jon-Tom eyed the silent trees in alarm. "How many more?"

"A large number, though, of course, I am only guessing based on what I could observe during my approach."

"We appreciate your help. You might as well take off now. Our problems aren't yours."

"They are now," the unicorn told him. "These are indifferent murderers, full of false pride. I have embarrassed their leader in front of his band. Now he must kill me or lose face and possibly his status as leader."

Roseroar strode toward the back of the clearing. "Move in heah, where theah's some covah."

The unicorn shook his head, the mane of gold rippling in the filtered light. "It will not be good enough, tigress. I can see that you are powerful as well as well-versed in war, but there are too many of them, and you will be fighting in very close quarters. If they come at you from all directions simultaneously you won't have a chance. You require a more defensible position."

"You know of one?" Jon-Tom asked him.

"It is not far from here. I think if we can get there we will be able to stand them off."

"Then let's get the hell out of here," he muttered as he shouldered his pack.

Mudge held back, torn between common sense and the effort he'd put into their supper. Roseroar saw his hesitation.

"A full belly's small consolation to someone with his guts hangin' out. Ah declah, short-whiskahs, sometimes ah wondah about yo priorities."

"Sometimes I wonder meself, lass." He looked longingly back at the lost roast as they hurried through the woods, following the stallion's lead.

Drom maintained a steady but slow pace to enable his newfound friends to keep up with him. Everyone watched the surrounding woods. But it was Roseroar's ears they relied on most.

"Stayin' carefully upwind of us, but I can heah them movin' faster. They're still behind us, though. Must think we're still in the camp."

"Wait a minute!" Jon-Tom called a halt. "Where's Mudge?"

Roseroar cursed under her breath. "Damn that ottah! Ah knew ah should've kept a closer watch on him. He's gone back fo some of that meat. Yoah friend is a creature of base instincts."

"Yes, but he's not stupid. Here he comes."

Mudge appeared, laboring beneath a section of roast nearly as big as himself. "Sorry, mates. I worked all day on this bloody banquet, and I'm damned if I was goin' to leave it all for those bastards."

"You're damned anyway," snapped Jon-Tom. "How are you going to keep up, hauling that on your back?"

The otter swung the heavy, pungent load off his shoulders. "Roseroar?"

"Not me, ottah. Yo stew in yoah own stew."

"We're wasting time," said Drom. "Here." He dipped his head forward. "Hold it still."

A quick jab and the roast was impaled on the spiral horn. "Now let's be away from here before they discover our flight." He turned and resumed his walk. "Disgusting."

"What is?" Jon-Tom asked as he jogged alongside.

"The smell of cooked flesh, the odiferous thought of consuming the body of another living creature, the miasma of carbonized protein, what else?"

Suddenly Jon-Tom wasn't so hungry anymore.

Creepers and vines strangled the entrance to the ancient structure. Roseroar was reluctant to enter. The strangely slitted windows and triangular doorways bespoke a time and people who had ruled the world long before the warmblooded.

"Sulolk used this place," murmured Drom as he trotted inside.

Distant shouts of outrage came from behind them, deciding the tigress. She bent beneath the low portal and squeezed in.

The single chamber beyond had a vaulted ceiling that enabled her to stand easily. There was more than enough room for all of them. Mudge was admiring the narrow windows, fashioned by a forgotten people for reasons of unknown aesthetics but admirably suited to the refugees' present needs. He notched an arrow into his bow and settled himself behind one thin gap.

Jon-Tom took up a stance to the left of the opening, ready to use his steel-tipped staff on anyone who tried to enter. A moment later he was able to move to a second window as Roseroar jammed a massive stone weighing at least three hundred pounds into the doorway, blocking it completely.

"This is a good place to fight from." Drom used a hoof to shove the cooling roast from his horn onto clean rock. "A small spring flows from the floor of a back room. Cracks in the ceiling allow fresh air to circulate. I have often slept here in safety." He indicated the damp grass growing from the floor. "There is food as well."

"For you," admitted Jon-Tom, watching the woods for signs of their pursuers. "Well, we have what's in our packs and the roast we saved." He glanced to his right, toward the other guarded window. "You shouldn't have done that, Mudge."

"Cor, it ain't no fun fightin' on an empty stomach, mate." He leaned forward; his black nose twitched as he sampled the air. "If they try chargin' us, I can pick 'em off easy. Our 'orny friend's right. This is a damn good place."

Rosewar was eyeing the wall carvings uneasily. "This is a very old place. I smell ancient feahs." She had drawn both longswords.

There was a thump as Drom settled down to wait. "I smell only clean grass and water."

Threatening shouts began to emanate from the trees. Mudge responded with some choice comments about Hathcar's mother, whom he had never met but whom thousands of others undoubtedly had. This inspired a rain of arrows which splintered harmlessly against the thick stone walls. One flew through Jon-Tom's window to stick in the earth behind him.

"Here they come!" he warned his companions.

There was nothing subtle about the bandits' strategy. While archers tried to pin down the defenders, an assortment of raccoons, foxes, and cats rushed at the entrance, carrying a big log between them. But Roseroar braced her massive shoulders against the boulder from behind and kept it from being pushed inward, while Mudge put arrows in the log wielders as fast as they could be replaced.

"Another bugger down!" the otter would yell each time an arrow struck home.

This continued for several minutes while Mudge reduced the number of Hathcar's band and Roseroar kept the boulder from moving so much as an inch inward. No martyrs to futility, those hefting the battering ram finally gave up and fled for the safety of the woods with the otter's deadly shafts urging them on.

No one had approached Jon-Tom's window during the fight. Mudge and Roseroar had done all the work and he felt pretty useless.

"What now? I don't think they'll try that again."

"No, but they'll bloody well try somethin' else," murmured the otter. "Say, mate, why don't you 'ave a go at 'em with your duar?"

Jon-Tom blinked. "I hadn't thought of that. Well, I had, but it's hard to think and sing when you're running."

"Why make music? To aggravate them?" asked Drom interestedly.

"Nope. 'E's a spellsinger, 'e is," said Mudge, "and a

right good one, too. When 'e can control it,'' he added by
way of afterthought.

"A spellsinger. I am impressed,'' said the unicorn.
Jon-Tom felt a little better, though he wished the golden
stallion would quit staring at him so intensely.

"What do you think they'll try next?'' Jon-Tom asked
the otter.

Mudge eyed the trees. "This bunch bein' about as
imaginative as a pile o' cow flop, I'd expect them to try
smokin' us out. If four legs there is right about the cracks
in the roof lettin' air in, they'll be wastin' their time.''

"Are yo certain theah's no back way in?''

"None that I was ever able to discover,'' Drom told the
tigress.

"Not that you'd fit places where some o' the rest of us
might,'' observed Mudge thoughtfully. He handed his bow
and quiver to Jon-Tom. "I'd better check out the nooks
and crannies, mate. We don't want some nasty surprises to
show up and stick us in the behind when we ain't lookin'.''
He headed for the crumbling back wall.

Jon-Tom eyed the bow uncertainly. "Mudge, I'm not
good at this.''

"Just give a shout if they come at us again. It ain't 'ard,
mate. Just shove an arrow through the window there. *They*
don't know you can't shoot.'' He bent, crawled under a
lopsided stone and disappeared.

Jon-Tom awkwardly notched an arrow, rested it on the
window sill as Roseroar took up a position behind the one
the otter had vacated.

"Ah don't understand,'' she murmured, squinting at the
forest. "We all ain't worth the trouble we're causin' this
Hathcar. That ottah brought down five or six o' them. If ah
was this fella ah'd give up and go in search of less deadly
prey.''

"That would be the reasonable thing to do,'' said
Drom, nodding, "except that as chief he has lost face
already before his band. He will not give up, though if he

suffers many more losses his own fighters may force him to quit." The unicorn climbed to his feet and strolled over to Roseroar's window. She made room for him.

"Hathcar!" he shouted.

A reluctant voice finally replied. "Who calls? Is that you, meddler with a spike in his brain?"

"It is I." Drom was unperturbed by the bandit leader's tone. "Listen to me! These travelers are poor. They have no money."

Cuscus laughter rang through the trees. "You expect me to believe that?"

"It's true. In any case, you cannot defeat them."

"Don't bet on that."

"You cannot break in here."

"Maybe not, but we'll force you out. It may take time, but we'll do it."

"If you do, then I will only lead them to another place of safety, one even harder to assault than this one. I know these woods, and you know I speak the truth. So why not depart now before suffering any more senseless losses? It's a stupid leader who sacrifices his people for no gain."

Muttering came from different places in the trees, proof that Drom's last words had hit home. Hathcar hastened to respond.

"No matter if you lead them elsewhere. We'll track you down no matter where you go."

"Perhaps you will. Or perhaps you'll find yourselves led into a trap. We of the forest have ways of defending ourselves against you lovers of civilization. There are hidden pits and tree-mounted weapons scattered throughout my territory. Follow me and find them at your peril."

This time the woods were silent. Drom nodded to himself. "Good. They're thinking it over, probably arguing about it. If they come to their senses, we may be able to get out of here without any more violence."

Jon-Tom peered through the narrow slit in the stone. "You think they'll really react that sensibly?"

"I don't know, but he knows I'm talking truth," said the unicorn softly. "I know this section of forest better than he does, and he knows that I know that."

"But how could we slip out of here and get past them?"

Drom chuckled. "I did fudge on that one a bit. Yet for all he knows there are a dozen secret passages out of here."

"If there are, they're bloody well still secret." Mudge emerged from the crawlspace he'd entered and wiped limestone dust from his shirt and whiskers. "Tight as a teenage whore. Nothin' bigger than a snake could get out the back way. We're safe enough here, all right." Jon-Tom gladly handed back the otter's bow and found himself a soft place on the floor.

"Then I guess we wait until they attack again or give up and leave us alone. I suppose we ought to stand watch tonight."

"Allow me, suh," said Roseroar. "Ah'm as comfortable with the night as ah am with the day."

"While we wait to see what they'll do," said Drom, "perhaps now you'll tell me what you people are doing in this country, so far from civilization."

Jon-Tom sighed. "It's a long story," he told the unicorn, and proceeded to relate it yet again. As he spoke, the sun set and the trees blended into a shadowy curtain outside. An occasional arrow plunked against the stone, more for nuisance value than out of any hope of hitting any of the defenders inside.

Hathcar had indeed lost too many in the futile attack to try it again. He knew that if he continued to fling his followers uselessly against an impregnable position they would melt quietly away into the woods. That night he moved away from the main campfire and sought counsel from an elderly rat and wolf, the two wisest of his band.

"So how do we pry those stinking bastards out of there?"

The rat's hair was tinged with white and his face and

arms were scarred. He picked at the dirt with one hand. "Why bother? Why not let them rot in there if they so desire? There are easier pickin's elsewhere."

Hathcar leaned toward him, glaring in the moonlight. "Do you know what happened today? Do you? They made a fool of me. Me, Hathcar! Nobody makes a fool of Hathcar and walks away to boast of it, nobody! Not on their own legs, they don't."

"It was just a thought," the rat mumbled. "It had to be said."

"Right. It's been said. It's also been forgotten." The rat said nothing.

"How about smoking them out?" suggested the wolf.

The cuscus let out a derisive snort. "Don't you think they've already thought of that? If they haven't tried to break out, it means they aren't worried about smoke; and if they aren't worried about it, it probably means it won't work if we try it."

"Could we," suggested the rat, "maybe force our way in through the roof?"

Hathcar sighed. "You're all looking at the obvious, all of you. I'm the only one who can see beyond the self-evident. That cursed four-legs led them straight here, so he's probably telling the truth when he says he knows it well. He wouldn't box himself into a situation he wasn't comfortable with. He says they can slip out anytime and hide somewhere else twice as strong. Maybe he's lying, but we can't take that chance. We have to take them here, while we know what we're up against. That means our first priority is to get rid of that horned meddler."

"How about moving a couple of archers in close? Those with good night vision. If they can sneak up against the wall they might get a clear shot inside."

Hathcar considered. "Not bad, except that if they don't snuff the unicorn right away that fucking water rat's likely to get 'em both. I've never seen anybody shoot like that." He shook his head.

"No, it's not good enough, Parsh. I'm sure they've got a guard up, and I won't send any more of the boys against that otter's bow. No, we have to bring the unicorn out somehow, far enough so we can get a clear shot at him. By himself, if possible."

The rat spat on the ground. "That's likely, isn't it?"

"You know, there may be a way."

Hathcar frowned at the wolf. "I was only half-serious, Brungunt."

"I'm wholly serious. All we need is the right kind of bait."

"That blow you took in Ollorory village has addled your brains," said Parsh. "Nothing's going to bring that unicorn out where we can get at him."

"Go on, Brungunt," said the thoughtful Hathcar.

The wolf leaned close. "It should be done when most of them sleep. We must watch and smell for when the stallion takes his turn as sentry. If they post only the one guard, we may have a chance. Great care must be taken, for it will be a near thing, a delicate business. Bait or no bait, if the meddler senses our presence, I do not think he can be drawn out. So after we set the bait we must retreat well out of range. It will work, you'll see. So powerful is the bait, it will draw our quarry well out where we can cut off his retreat. Then it won't matter if he bolts into the woods. The important thing is that we'll be rid of him, and the ones we really want will be deprived of his advice and aid."

"No," said Hathcar, his eyes gleaming, "no. I want that four-legs, too. I want him dead. Or better yet, we'll just hamstring him." He grinned viciously in the dark. "Yes, hamstring him. That's better still." He forced himself from contemplation of pleasures to come. "This bait? Where do we get it?"

Brungunt scratched an ear and even the skeptical Parsh looked interested. "First we must find a village or farm that numbers humans among its occupants." He was nodding to himself as he spoke. "This is an old, old magic we will work tonight, but you don't have to be a sorcerer to work it. It works itself. It is said by those who may know that a unicorn may not be taken by force, but only by stealth and guile."

"Get to the point," said Hathcar impatiently.

The wolf hurried his words. "We don't have to sneak up on him. He'll come to us. He'll follow a maiden fair and true. It is said."

Hathcar looked doubtful. "What kind of maiden? A coltish mare?"

"No, no. It must be a human maiden."

Parsh the rat was thoroughly shocked. "You expect to find a virgin around here? Species notwithstanding."

"There is a town not far from this place."

"Crestleware." Hathcar nodded.

"We can but try," said the wolf, spreading his paws.

"A virgin. Are you certain about this, Brungunt?"

"The bond is supposed to be most powerful. The girl need only lead him far enough for us to get behind him before he picks up our scent. Do not ask me to explain this thing. I only relate what I have heard told."

"Wouldn't cost us a one. You'd better be right about this, Brungunt, or I'll see your ears decorating my spear."

"That's not fair!" protested the wolf. "I am only relating a legend."

"Look to your ears, wolf." Hathcar rose. "And tell the others to look to theirs. Parsh, you come with me." He glared at Brungunt. "We will return as quickly as possible. This magic sounds to me like it works better in the dark, and I don't want to give that four legs another day to think of a better place." He glanced through the trees toward the moonlit ruins. "Hamstring him, yes. I'll see that damned meddler crawling to me on his knees, and then we'll break those as well."

XIV

Hathcar crouched low as he pointed toward the clearing in front of the silent fortress. The slim girl who stood next to him watched closely, her eyes wide. She had been awakened in the middle of the night by her mother and sent off in the company of this ugly stranger. She hadn't wanted to go, but her mother had insisted, assuring her it would only be until sunrise and that everything was all right, everything had been arranged. Then she would be brought home and allowed to sleep all day. And they had promised her candy.

"There is the place, little one."

"Don't call me little," she snapped. "I'm as grown up as you are! And my name's Silky."

"Sorry," Hathcar growled softly, restraining himself. He wasn't very fond of cubs, but he needed this one's cooperation.

"You're going to pay my daddy two gold pieces for luring out this unicorn to you. What makes you think he'll come out and follow me?"

"He'll come," Hathcar assured her. "Just be nice to him, tell him how strong and beautiful he is."

She stared warily at the cuscus and his two companions out of eyes that were not as innocent as her parents insisted they were. "You're sure this is a unicorn you're sending me after?"

"Are you sure you're a virgin?"

"Yes, I'm sure," she said tiredly. She'd heard this stranger discussing the matter with her mother.

Hathcar turned and pointed back through the woods. "Back this way there's a pool in a little hollow. Bring him there. We'll be waiting."

"What happens when we get there?" she asked curiously.

"None of your business, lit . . . Silky. Your daddy's being paid for your services. You do what I want you to and you don't ask questions."

"Okay." She hesitated. "You're not going to hurt him, are you? I've never seen a unicorn, but I've been told they're real pretty."

"Oh, no, no, we won't hurt him," said Hathcar smoothly. "We just want to surprise him. We're his friends, and we want to surprise him, and you won't tell him about us because that would ruin the surprise, wouldn't it?"

"I guess so." She smiled brightly. "I like surprises, too. Can I watch when you surprise him?"

"Sure you can," Hathcar assured her innocently. "I think you'll be surprised, too." He turned to leave her, Brungunt and Parsh following.

"It's dark," she said uncertainly.

"You'll be okay," Brungunt told her. "Didn't you say you were a big girl?"

"That's right, I am."

"Fine. Just bring the four-legs down to the pool."

"Why didn't we just abduct the little bitch?" Parsh wanted to know as they made their way through the woods to rejoin the rest of the waiting band.

"Big village," Hathcar told him. "A good place to buy supplies. The price hurts, but it'll be worth it. Besides,

Brungunt here said the girl had to act voluntarily or the
magic wouldn't work.''

"That's so," the wolf agreed, nodding. "It is so told."

"So it's better all around this way," Hathcar finished.

Silky stood waiting, counting away the minutes to allow
the unicorn's friends time to ready their surprise. Then she
strolled out into the small clearing in front of the broken
old building. She was wearing her best dress. It clung to
her budding figure as she moved. Her mother had spent
fifteen minutes combing out the long auburn hair to make
certain her daughter looked her best. The old wolf had
insisted on it.

Two gold pieces. That would buy a lot of things for the
family, including candy. She determined to do exactly as
the cuscus ordered, even if he'd been lying to her about
the surprise he was planning. After all, the horned one was
nothing to her.

Still, she was trembling slightly at the prospect of
actually meeting a unicorn as she stepped out into the
silvery moonlight. There were many stories told about the
shy, solitary four-legs. They kept to themselves in the deep
forest, shunning civilization and intelligent company.

The ancient stones before her were silent. Should she
cry out? If she did, what could she say? "Here, unicorn"?
There was no one to advise her, since Hathcar had joined
the rest of his friends far back in the trees, out of sight and
scent. The old wolf had assured her she had only to
approach the ruins and the unicorn would come to her.
Would come and would follow back to the pool. And the
surprise waiting there.

She stood before the ruins and waited.

Within, there was movement she could not see. Drom's
head lifted, his nostrils twitching. He blinked at the bodies
sleeping soundly around him. It was his turn on watch.

Trotting silently so as not to disturb his newfound
friends, he moved to one window slit and peered out.
Standing alone in the moonlight was a small, slim figure.

A human figure, young and pure. Ancient emotions began to pluck at him.

Nodding at no one in particular, he quietly began pushing at the boulder which blocked the entryway. He worked with care, wanting to make positive identification of the beckoning shape outside without waking his companions.

When the stone had been edged to one side he walked through the opening and stepped out onto the grass, sniffing at the air, which was heavy with the girl's clean, sweet-smelling scent. She was alone. The night was still, and there was no wind to mask concealed odors.

He walked over to the girl, who eyed him nervously and took a step backward.

"Hello. You're . . . awfully pretty." She licked her lips, glanced over a shoulder once, then said confidently, "Won't you come and walk with me? It's a nice night in the forest."

"In a minute, little one. There's something I have to do first." Turning, he moved back to the ruins and stuck his head inside, let out a soft whinny. "Wake up."

There were stirrings on the floor. Lightest of sleepers, Roseroar sat up fast when she saw that the boulder defending them had been moved.

"Now what?" She stared at the unicorn. "Explain yoself, suh." She was on her feet and heading for the boulder. Drom cut her off. "If they come at us now . . ." she began warningly.

"Relax, cat-a-mountain. They're not coming. They're not even watching us." Behind them, Jon-Tom and Mudge were also awakening.

"How do yo know?" Roseroar was peering cautiously out. She saw and smelled the girl immediately, but no one else.

"Because they've decided to try something else." He let out a soft, whinnying laugh. "By the time they realize this latest ploy has failed, it will be too late. We'll be long gone from this place and beyond their reach. Who among you is the fleetest of foot?''

''Roseroar over the long distance, me over the short. I think,'' Jon-Tom told him sleepily, still not sure just what was going on.

''Good. You and the otter climb onto my back and ride.''

A sweet but anxious voice sounded from outside. ''Who are you talking to? Why don't you come out and talk with me?''

''Who the 'ell is *that*?'' Mudge rushed to a window. ''Blimey, 'tis a girl!''

''What?'' Jon-Tom joined him, gaped at the figure standing in the clearing. ''What's she doing here?''

''Tempting me.'' Drom chuckled again. ''Hathcar and his curs have moved out of scent range, no doubt to lie in wait to ambush me as I am drawn helplessly to them by this irresistibly pure young female.''

''I'm not sure I follow you.''

''It's part of an ancient legend, a very old magic.''

''Lousy magic,'' said Jon-Tom.

''Oh, no, it's very good magic, and very true. Only not in my case. We're wasting time.'' He turned his flank to Jon-Tom, tilted his head low. ''Can you mount by yourself? Use my mane for a grip if you need one.''

Jon-Tom climbed onto the broad, strong back easily, pulled Mudge up behind him.

''Leave some room,'' Drom instructed him. ''We're not leaving the girl here for Hathcar.'' He trotted outside, Roseroar pacing him easily while restlessly searching the woods for signs of their enemies.

Silky watched them approach. Hathcar and the old wolf hadn't said anything about the unicorn's companions. She stared worriedly at the big cat loping alongside the four legs. The tigress could swallow her in one gulp.

Then the unicorn was standing close and smiling down

at her over his goatee. "Do not be afraid, little one. All is well. How came you into this business?"

She hesitated before replying. "They paid my mother and father. They paid them two gold pieces for me to come with them for the night and help them surprise you."

"Surprise me. I see," murmured Drom, nodding knowingly.

"You were supposed to follow me." She turned and pointed. "That way, to a hollow full of water so your friends could surprise you."

"And a fine surprise that would've been, wot?" growled Mudge softly.

"There's been a change in plans," Drom informed her. "Get onto my back, in front of this handsome gentleman. We're taking you back to your parents. You did as requested and drew me out of my refuge. We're just going to take a little detour, that's all. So you've fulfilled your end of the contract, at least in part, and your parents should be entitled to keep whatever payment they've already received for your service."

"I don't know." She scuffed the ground with one foot. "I didn't bring you to the pool."

"Is that your fault?" Drom leaned close. "You don't really like those people out there, do you?"

"No," she said suddenly. "No, I don't. But I had to do it. I had to."

"You are a true innocent, as you would have to be. You have done all you could."

"What about my candy?" she asked petulantly.

Jon-Tom reached down a hand. The girl took it reluctantly and he swung her up in front of him. Her nearness reminded him uncomfortably of Folly.

Drom turned and exploded into a wild gallop, restraining himself only enough to allow Roseroar to keep pace. Jon-Tom felt confident the unicorn could carry three fully grown men with ease. He, the girl, and Mudge were no burden at all.

After they'd covered several kilometers, the stallion slowed. Roseroar was panting hard and they had made a clean escape from the ruins.

"Wish I could see those bastards' faces when they come lookin' for us," Mudge commented.

"They'll be looking for this one, too." Jon-Tom smiled down at the other passenger. "Where's your village, little girl?"

"I am *not* a little girl!"

"Sorry, young lady. Where do you live?"

She stared into the woods. Her sense of direction was superb. A hand gestured to the north. "That way."

Drom nodded and changed direction as he headed down a gentle slope. He called back to Jon-Tom. "Will you continue on to Crancularn in search of your medicine, now that you have escaped the attentions of Hathcar's band?"

"We must," Jon-Tom told him. "You're welcome to accompany us if you like."

"Aye, mate," said Mudge. "We'd be glad of your help."

"I have never been to Crancularn, though I know of it. I would be delighted to accompany you."

"It's settled, then," said a pleased Jon-Tom. Not only was the unicorn a welcome addition to their trio, it had to be admitted that riding was more fun than walking.

By morning they were at the outskirts of the girl's village. Cultivated fields surrounded the town. Jon-Tom let her down gently.

"I didn't do all I was supposed to do," she muttered uneasily.

"You did all you could. It's not your fault that their plan didn't work."

The town was enclosed by a strong wooden palisade and looked more than capable of withstanding an attack by any angry bunch of bandits. He didn't think Hathcar would try to take revenge for his failure against the girl or her parents.

"I still think you're pretty," the girl said to Drom. "Can I kiss you good-bye? That's supposed to be good luck."

Drom smacked his lips with evident distaste. "I'd prefer you didn't, but if you must." He dropped his head, stood still for a buss just below the right eye.

"Geh!" he muttered as she pulled away. "Now be on your way, human, and count yourself fortunate this night."

"Good-bye, unicorn. Good-bye, strangers." She was still waving at them as they disappeared back into the forest.

No armed mob of angry, frustrated bandits materialized to interrupt their progress as they swung back to the west. With luck it would be midday before Hathcar finally realized his plans had fallen through and ventured to check on the ruins.

"I think I understand what was going on," Jon-Tom murmured. "The girl was a virgin."

"'Ere now, mate," Mudge protested, "I've been around meself, but even I can't tell for certain just by lookin'."

"She'd have to have been for it to fit." He glanced down at their mount. "She was a virgin, wasn't she, Drom?" Roseroar looked on curiously.

"The sight and scent of her suggested so," the stallion replied.

"I read something somewhere about the attentions of a virgin girl being irresistible to a unicorn."

"An ancient and more-or-less accurate notion, which Hathcar was counting on to draw me out. They would have succeeded with their plan except for ignorance of one fact."

"Wot fact, mate?" Mudge asked.

Drom turned to look back at the otter. "I'm gay." He increased his pace.

"Uh, 'ere now, mate, maybe we'd all be better off walkin' after all."

"Nonsense. We are still not far enough away from Hathcar's troop to chance slowing down."

"That's debatable. Besides, there's no need for you to keep on carryin' us about like this. Don't want to make you uncomfortable or nothin'."

"It sounds to me as though you are the one who is feeling uneasy, otter."

"Wot, me? Not me, guv'nor. It's just that I—"

"What's wrong with you, Mudge?" Jon-Tom asked him. "I thought you'd be glad of the chance to rest your precious feet."

"Relax, otter," the stallion said. "You are not my type. Now if you happened to be a Percheron, or a Clydesdale, or maybe a shire . . ." He let the images trail off.

"If you have to worry about something, think about Hathcar," Jon-Tom instructed the otter.

Mudge did so, though he still kept a wary eye on their mount. Later, his confusion was broken by the sound of distant thunder. Or perhaps it was only a bellow of outrage.

Silky's parents kept the money already paid to them by Hathcar, and as Jon-Tom surmised, the cuscus did not try to take it back by force from the heavily defended town. There seemed no way for him to vent his rage and frustration until it occurred to him that since the girl had truly done her best, if anything she actually deserved a bonus.

So it was that while Silky did not get her much-desired candy, she was the only girl in the village who could look forward to the coming winter confidently, clad as she was in her brand-new wolfskin coat.

The travelers stopped in late afternoon. The roast that Mudge had risked his life to salvage was almost gone, but Roseroar soon brought in enough fresh food for all. Drom nibbled contentedly at a nearby field of petal pedals. Each blue-and-pink flower produced a different musical note when it was munched.

Mudge ate close to Jon-Tom. "Don't it bother you, mate?"

"Don't . . . doesn't what bother me?"

The otter nodded toward the unicorn. " 'Im."

Jon-Tom bit into his steak. The meat was succulent and rich with flavor. "He saved us once and might save us again. As for his personal sexual preferences, I could care less. He'd be downright inconspicuous on Hollywood Boulevard."

"Well, maybe you're right. Now, me, I knew it from the first. The way 'e minced out of the woods toward us."

Drom overheard, lifted his muzzle, and said with dignity, "I do not mince, otter. I prance." He looked at Jon-Tom. "You really believe your former acquaintances will beat you to Cranularn and to the medicine you have come for?"

"I hope not, but I fear it. They stole our only map."

"That is a small loss. Do not regret it." The unicorn crunched a clump of purple *ormods* with petals the shade of enameled amethyst. The flowers hummed as they were consumed. "I can guide you there."

"We were told it moves around."

"Only in one's imagination. There are those who stumble through it without seeing it, or circle 'round it as if blind. So they say it has moved. It does not move, but to find it you must wish to. I know. I was told by those who could know. I will lead you to Cranularn."

"That's bleedin' wonderful," Mudge confessed aloud. He was mad at himself. There was no reason for him to be nervous or wary in the unicorn's presence. Drom was a likable chap, wasn't he, and Mudge didn't look in the least like a shire horse, did he? And hadn't he always been told never to look a gift unicorn in the mouth? He was upset with himself.

Hadn't the four-legs carried himself and Jon-Tom all this way from Hathcar's territory without complaining? Why, with him galloping along and the rest of them taking turns

riding him, they might yet overtake that prick Jalwar and
his whore of a helpmate Folly.

They made rapid progress westward, but still there was
no sign of their former friends.

When they finally found themselves on the outskirts of
Crancularn itself, Jon-Tom found it hard to believe. He'd
half come to think of the town as existing only in
Clothahump's imagination. Yet there it was.

Yes, there it was, and after too many close calls with
death, after crossing the Muddletup Moors and the Glittergeist
Sea and innumerable hills and vales, he was more than a
little discouraged by the sight of it.

The setting was impressive enough: a heavily forested
slope that climbed the flank of a slowly smoking volcano.
The town itself, however, was about as awe-inspiring as
dirty, homey Lynchbany. Tumble-down shacks and ram-
shackle two-and three-story buildings of wood and mud
crowded close to one another as if fearful of encountering the
sunlight. A dirty fog clung to the streets and the angular,
slate-roofed structures. As they headed toward the town, a
familiar odor made his nostrils contract: the thick musk of
the unwashed of many species mixed with the stink of an
open sewer system. His initial excitement was rapidly
fading.

Massive oaks and sycamores grew within the town
itself, providing more shade where none was required and
sometimes even shouldering buildings aside. Jon-Tom was
about to ask Drom if perhaps they might have come to the
wrong place when the unicorn reared back on its hind
hooves and nearly dumped him and Mudge to the ground.
Roseroar snarled as she assumed a defensive posture.

Coming straight at them, belching smoke and bellowing
raggedly, was a three-footed demon. A rabbit rode the
demon's back. This individual wore a wide-brimmed felt
hat; a long-sleeved shirt of muslin, open halfway; and a
short mauve skirt similar to the kilts favored by the

intelligent arboreals of this world. His enormous feet were unshod.

The demon slowed as it approached. Jon-Tom drew in a deep breath as it stopped in front of him and hastened to reassure his companions. "It's all right. It can't harm you."

"How do yo know, Jon-Tom?" Roseroar kept her hands on her sword hilts.

"Because I know what it is. It's a Honda ATC Offroad Three-wheeler." He admired the red-painted demon. "Automatic too. I didn't know Honda made an ATC with automatic."

"Funny name for a demon," Mudge was muttering.

"Hiya," said the rabbit cheerfully, revving the engine. "Can I help you folks?"

"You sure can." Jon-Tom pointed at the ATC. "Where'd you get that?"

The rider raced the motor and Drom shied away. "From the Shop of the Aether and Neither. Where else?"

Jon-Tom felt a burst of excitement. Maybe Clothahump was right. The inexplicable presence of the ATC in this world was proof enough that powerful magic was at work here.

"That's where we want to go."

"Figures," said the rabbit. "Nice of you to drop in. We don't get a lot of visitors here in Crancularn. For some reason, travelers avoid us."

"Might be your wonderful reputation," Mudge told him.

The rabbit eyed them appraisingly. "Strangers. Don't know if Snooth will serve you. She don't get much business from outsiders." He shrugged. "Ain't none of my business, your business."

"Who's Snooth?" Jon-Tom asked him.

"The proprietress. Of the Shop of the Aether and Neither." He looked back over his shoulder, pointed. "Go through town and stay on the north trail that winds around

the base of the mountain. Snooth's place is around the side
a ways.'' He turned back to inspect them a last time.

"You're a weird-looking bunch. I don't know what
you've come to buy, but you'll need all the luck you can
muster to pry anything out of Snooth's stock. And no, you
can't have one of my feet to help you." He put the
all-terrain vehicle in gear and roared off into the woods,
the ATC popping and growling.

"I still say it were a demon," Mudge muttered.

"No demon, just a machine. From my world."

"Ah'd dislike being a resident o' yoah world, then, Jon-
Tom." Roseroar made a face. "Such noise. And that
smell!''

It had to have been conjured, Jon-Tom knew. Conjured
by a magic even more powerful than Clothahump's. His
heart raced. If this Snooth could bring something as solid
as the ATC into this world, something lifted from a
dealership in Kyoto or L.A. or Toronto, then perhaps she
could also send things back to such places.

Things like himself.

He didn't dare dwell on that possibility as they made
their way through town. For the most part, the busy, bored
citizenry ignored them. Many of them were using or
playing with otherworldly devices. Jon-Tom began to have
second thoughts about his chances of being sent home.
Maybe this Snooth was no sorceress but just some local
shopkeeper who happened to have stumbled onto some
kind of one-way transdimensional gate or something.

Mudge pointed out a traveling minstrel. The diminutive
musical mouse was plinking out a very respectable polka
not on a duar or handlebar lyre or bark flute but on a
Casiotone 8500 electronic keyboard. Jon-Tom wondered
what the mouse was using for batteries.

Not all the devices in use were recognizably from his
own world. The sign over a fishmonger's stall was a
rotating globe of red and white lambent light that spelled
out the shop's name and alternated it with that of the

owner. There appeared to be nothing supporting the globe. As they stared, the globe twisted into the shape of a fish, then into the outlines of females of various species in provocative poses. Sex sells, Jon-Tom reminded himself. Even fish. He walked over to stand directly underneath the globe. There was no source of support or power, much less a visible explanation for its photonic malleability. One thing he was sure of: it hadn't come from his own world.

Neither had the device they saw an old mandrill using to cut wood. It had a handle similar to that of a normal metal saw, but instead of a length of serrated steel the handle was attached to a shiny bar no more than a quarter-inch in diameter. The baboon would hitch up his gloves, choose a piece of wood, put both hands on the handle and touch the thin bar to the log. It would cut through like butter.

There were other worlds, then, and this Snooth apparently had access to goods from many of them. As they made their way through the town, he thought back to his companion's reaction to the ATC. To someone unfamiliar with internal combustion devices on a world where magic held sway, it certainly must have looked and sounded like a demon. Crancularn was full of such alien machines. No wonder it had acquired an unwholesome reputation.

But the townsfolk themselves were open and friendly enough. In that they were no different from the inhabitants of the other cities and villages Jon-Tom had visited. As for their blasé acceptance of otherworldly devices, there was nothing very extraordinary about that. People, no matter their shape or size or species, were infinitely adaptable. Only a hundred years ago in his own world, a hand-held television or calculator watch would have seemed like magic even to sophisticated citizens, who nonetheless would have made use of them enthusiastically.

For that matter, how many of his contemporaries actually understood what made a computer tick or instant replay possible? People had a way of just accepting the workings of

everyday machinery they didn't understand, whether it was
powered by alkaline batteries or arcane spells.

Then they were leaving the town again, fog drifting lazily
around them. They had attracted no more than an occasional cursory glance from the villagers. Huge trees hugged
the fertile lower slopes of the volcano, which simmered
quietly and unthreateningly above them.

Inquiries in town had produced no mention of visitors
resembling Jalwar or Folly. Either the two had lost their
way or else with Drom's aid they had already passed the
renegade pair in the woods. Jon-Tom experienced a pang of
regret. He still wasn't completely convinced of Folly's
complicity in the theft of the map.

No time for that now. The rabbit on the ATC implied
they might have trouble purchasing what they wanted from
this Snooth. Jon-Tom struggled to compose a suitably effective speech. All they needed was a little bit of medicine.
Nothing so complex as a malleable globe or toothless saw.
His hand went to the tiny vial dangling from the chain
around his neck. Inside was the formula for the desperately
needed medicine. He hadn't brought it this far to be turned
away empty-handed.

There was no sign, no posted proclamations to advertise
the shop's presence. They turned around a cluster of oaks,
and there it was, a simple wooden building, one story
high. It was built up against the rocks. A single wooden
door was set square in the center of the storefront, which
was shaded by a broad, covered porch.

A couple of high-backed rocking chairs sat on the
porch, unoccupied. Wooden shingles in need of repair
covered the sloping roof that likewise ran up into the
rocks. Jon-Tom estimated the entire building enclosed no
more than a thousand square feet of space. Hardly large
enough for store and home combined.

As they drew close, a figure emerged from inside and
settled into the farther rocking chair. The chair creaked as
it rocked. The tall kangaroo wore a red satin vest which

blended with her own natural rust color and, below, a kilt similar in style to the rabbit's. There were pockets and a particularly wide one directly in front to permit the owner access to her pouch. Jon-Tom stared at the lower belly but was unable to tell if the female was carrying a joey, though once he thought he saw something move. But he couldn't be sure, and since he was ignorant of macropodian etiquette, he thought it best not to inquire.

She also wore thick hexagonal granny glasses and a heavy necklace of turquoise, black onyx, and malachite. A matching bracelet decorated her right wrist, and she puffed slowly on a corncob pipe which was switched periodically from one side of her mouth to the other.

He halted at the bottom of the porch steps. "Are you the one they call Snooth?"

"I expect I am," the kangaroo replied, "since I'm the only one around here by that name." She took her pipe from her lips and regarded them thoughtfully. "You folks aren't from around here. What can I do for you?"

"We've undertaken one hell of a shopping trip," Jon-Tom told her.

She sighed. "I was afraid of that. Just when I got myself all nice and comfortable. Well, that's par for the course."

Jon-Tom's eyes grew wide. "That's an expression of my world."

"Is it? I traffic with so many I sometimes get confused. Sure as the gleebs are on the fondike."

Jon-Tom decided to tread as lightly as possible, bearing the rabbit's admonition in mind. "We don't want to disturb you. We could come back tomorrow." He tried to see past her, into the store. "You haven't by any chance had a couple of other out-of-town customers in recently, have you? An old ferret, maybe accompanied by a human female?" He held his breath.

The kangaroo scratched under her chin with her free hand. "Nope. No one of that description. In fact, I haven't had any local out-of-town customers stop by in some time.''

Forbearing to inquire into the nature of a local out-of-towner, which seemed to Jon-Tom to be a contradiction in terms, he permitted himself a moment of silent exultation. They'd done it! With Drom's help they'd succeeded in beating Jalwar to Cruncularn. Now he could relax. The object of their long, arduous journey was almost in his grasp.

He turned to leave. "We don't want to upset your siesta. We'll come back tomorrow."

A small brown shape pushed past him. Mudge took up an aggressive stance on the lowest step. "Now let's 'old on a minim 'ere, guv'nor.'' The otter fixed the proprietress with a jaundiced eye. "This 'ere dump is the place I've been 'earin' about for weeks? This cobbled-together wreck is the marvelous, the wondrous, the magnificent Shop o' the Aether and Neither? And you're the owner?''

The kangaroo nodded.

"Well," announced Mudge in disgust, "it sure as 'ell don't look like much to me.''

"Mudge!" Jon-Tom angrily grabbed the otter by his shoulder.

The kangaroo, however, did not appear upset. "Appearances can be deceiving, my fuzzy little cousin." She turned to face Jon-Tom as she stood on enormous, powerful feet. She was as tall as he was. The rickety porch boards squeaked under her weight.

"I can tell just by looking at you that you've come a long ways to do your shopping. Except for the Cruncularni-ans, most of my customers travel far to buy from me, some by means most devious. Some I sell to, others I do not." She turned and pointed toward a thin scrawl on a worn piece of wood that was nailed over the doorway. The sign said:

WE RESERVE THE RIGHT TO REFUSE SERVICE TO ANYTHING

"It's not for ourselves that we come seeking your help," Jon-Tom told her. "We're here at the behest of a great wizard who lives in the forest of the Bellwoods, far across the Glittergeist Sea. His name's Clothahump."

"Clothahump." Eyes squinted in reflection behind the granny glasses. She put out a hand, palm facing downward, and positioned it some four feet above the porch. "Turtle, old gentleman, about yea high?"

Jon-Tom nodded vigorously. "That's him. You've met him?"

"Nope. But I know of him by reputation. As wizard's go, he's up near the top." This revelation impressed even the skeptical Mudge, who'd always thought of Clothahump as no better than a talented fakir verging on senility who just happened to get lucky once in a while. "What's wrong with him?"

Jon-Tom fumbled with the vial around his neck, removed the small piece of paper from within. "He says he's dying, and he's in terrible pain. He says this can cure him."

Snooth took the fragment, adjusted her glasses, and read. Her lips moved as she digested the paper's information. "Yes, yes...I believe I have this in stock." She glanced back at Jon-Tom. "Your devotion to your mentor does you credit."

Which made him feel more than a little guilty, since the main reason he'd undertaken the journey was to protect his only chance of returning home by ensuring Clothahump's continued good health.

"You overpraise my altruism."

"I think not." She stared at him in the most peculiar fashion. "You are better than you give yourself credit for. That is why you would make a good adjudicator. Your good instincts outweigh your common sense."

For the second time since arriving at the store Jon-Tom's eyes widened. "How did you know that I was studying to be a lawyer?"

"Lucky guess," said Snooth absently, dismissing the matter despite Jon-Tom's desire to pursue it further. She held out the paper with the formula written on it. "May I hold on to this?"

Jon-Tom shrugged. "Why not? It's the medicine we need."

Snooth tucked the paper neatly into her pouch. Again Jon-Tom thought he saw something moving about within. If Snooth was carrying a joey, it was evidently either too immature or too shy to show itself.

"Come on in." She turned and pushed wide the door.

Her visitors mounted the steps and crossed the porch. The front room of the building was furnished in simple kaleidoscopic style. To one side was another rocking chair, only instead of being fashioned of wood it was composed of transparent soap bubbles clinging to a thin metal frame. The bubbles were moving in slow motion and looked fragile and ready to burst.

"Surely you don't sit in that?" Roseroar said.

"Wouldn't be much use for anything else. Like to try it?"

"Ah couldn't," the tigress protested. "Ah'd bust it as well as mah tail end."

"Maybe not," said the kangaroo with quiet confidence.

Reluctantly, Roseroar accepted the challenge, turning to set herself gently into the chair. The soap bubbles gave under her weight but did not break, nor did the thin metal frame. And the bubbles kept moving, massaging the chair's new occupant with a gentle sliding motion. A rich throbbing purr filled the room.

"How much?" Roseroar inquired.

"Sorry. That's a demo model. Not for sale."

"Come on, Roseroar," Jon-Tom told her. "That's not what we came for." She abandoned the caressing chair sadly.

As they crossed the room, Jon-Tom had time to notice a circular recording device, a heatless stove, and a number of utterly alien machines scattered among the familiar. Snooth led them through another doorway barred by opaque ceramic strips that hung in midair and into a back store room filled with broken, jumbled goods. A bathroom was visible off to the left.

A second suspended curtain admitted them to the store.

Jon-Tom's brain went blank. He heard Roseroar hiss next to him and even the always voluble Mudge was at a loss for words. Drom inhaled sharply in surprise.

As near as they could tell, the shop filled the whole inside of the mountain.

XV

Ahead of them was an aisle flanked by long metal shelves. The multiple shelving rose halfway to the forty-foot-high ceiling and was crammed with boxed, crated, and clear-packaged goods. Jon-Tom saw only a few empty slots. The shelving and the aisle between ran away into the distance until all three seemed to meet at some distant vanishing point.

He turned and stared to his left. Shelves and aisles marched off into the distance as far as he could see. He looked right and saw a mirror image of the view on his left.

"I never dreamed . . ." he began, only to be interrupted by the proprietress.

"Oh, but you have dreamed, shopper. Everyone dreams." She gestured with a negligent wave. "There are a lot of worlds in the plenum. Some produce a lot of goods for sale, others only a few. I try to keep up with what the major dimensions are doing. It isn't an easy job, being a shopkeeper. There's one place where time runs backwards. Plays hell with my inventory."

Jon-Tom continued to gape at the endless rows. "How

do you know what you've got here, let alone where it's located?''

''Oh, we're very up-to-date in the store.'' From a side pocket she extracted a length of bright blue metal six inches long and two and half an inches thick. A transparent facing ran the length of it. There were no buttons or switches visible.

''Pocket computer.'' She showed it to Jon-Tom. As he watched, words scrolled rapidly across the face. Languages and script changed as he stared. Twice Snooth turned it vertically and the words scrolled from top to bottom. Several times they reversed and traveled from right to left. Once there were no letters at all, only colors changing in sequence. Once there was only music.

''Thought-activated. Handy little gadget. Bought it from a place whose location can't be determined, only inferred. Very talented folks there. See?''

A chemical formula appeared on the transparent facing and froze in position. A long numerical sequence appeared below it.

''Down this way.'' Snooth hopped off to her left, eventually turned down an aisle.

Roseroar stared at the endless ranks of goods. ''How many shelves do y'all have down heah?''

''Can't really say,'' the kangaroo replied. ''It changes all the time.''

''You run this whole place by yourself?'' Jon-Tom asked her.

She nodded. ''You get used to it. I like stockwork, and the perks are good.''

''How far is the medicine?''

''Not far. Only about half a day's hop. Any longer and I'd have paused to pack us a meal or dig out a scooter.''

''Is that anything like the Honda ATC we saw one of your customers riding around outside of town?''

''That'd be Foharfa's toy. He's going to break his neck on that thing one of these days. No, a scooter's just an inertialess disc. You guide it by sensing your relationship to the local planetary magnetic field.''

Jon-Tom swallowed. "I'm afraid I don't have a license to drive anything like that.''

"No matter. I'm enjoying the walk.''

"Can we buy one to get us 'ome, maybe?'' Mudge asked hopefully.

"Sorry. I've none in general stock. Besides, I make it a rule not to let certain goods travel beyond Crancularn. The world's a complicated enough place as it is. You can overtechnologize magic if you're not careful.''

"Looks like your business is rather slow,'' observed Drom.

Snooth shrugged in mid-hop. "I'm not looking to get rich, unicorn. I just like the business, that's all. Besides, it's a good way to keep up with what's going on in the greater cosmos. Goods are better than gossip and more honest reflections of what's happening elsewhere than official news pronouncements and zeeways.''

"Must be 'ard on profits,'' Mudge commented.

"That depends on what kind of profit you're trying to make, otter.''

Jon-Tom eyed the kangaroo uneasily. "That's a funny thing for a shopkeeper to say. Are you sure you aren't some kind of sorceress yourself?''

"Who, me?'' Snooth appeared genuinely shocked. "Not I, sir. Too many responsibilities, too many regulations attached to the profession. I prefer my present employment, thank you. And the cost-of-living in Crancularn is low.'' A pause, then, "What about this ferret and girl you referred to earlier?''

"They were traveling with us,'' Jon-Tom explained. "We had an unfortunate parting of the ways.''

"Unfortunate, 'ell!'' Mudge rumbled. "The dirty buggers stole our map, they did, and it were only by dint o' good luck and this spellsinger's determination and this one-horn's knowledge o' the lay o' the land that we. .!''

Snooth interrupted him, smiling at Jon-Tom. "So you are a spellsinger? I noticed the duar you carry right off, but I imagined you to be no more than a traveling musician."

"I'm still an amateur," Jon-Tom confessed. "I'm still learning how to control my abilities."

"I think one day you will, though I sense you still have a long way to go."

"It's just that it's so new to me. The magic, not the music. Everything's so new to me. I'm not of this world."

"I know. You smell of elsewhere. Do not let your transposition faze you. Newness is life's greatest pleasure and delight." She indicated the shelves walling them in. "Every new product I encounter is a source of wonderment to me."

"I wish I could share your enthusiasm. But I can't help my homesickness. You can't, by any chance, send me home by the same means you use to stock your goods?" he asked hopefully.

"I am truly sorry," Snooth told him softly, and it struck him that she was. "This is only a receive-and-disperse operation. I can only ship products, not people."

Jon-Tom slumped. "Well, it's no more than what I expected. Clothahump said as much."

"You must tell me about your travels. Oddly, I know more about many other worlds than about this one. The result of being tied to my business."

So partly to please her and partly to help relieve his own disappointment, Jon-Tom regaled her with a recitation of the adventures they had experienced during their long journey. It took at least the half day Snooth had claimed before she finally called the march to a halt. Jon-Tom looked down the aisle. They still were not in sight of its end.

Strange medications filled bottles and jars and containers of unfamiliar material. The twenty-foot-high shelves they had halted before represented a cosmological pharmacopia. Jon-Tom made out pills and drops, salves and unguents, bandages and bindings, scattered among less recognizable items.

Snooth regarded the shelving for a moment, consulted her blue metal bar, and hopped a few yards farther down the aisle. Then she climbed one of the motorized ladders that ran from the topmost shelf to tracks cut in the stone floor and ascended the shelving halfway.

"Here we are," she said, sounding gratified. She opened an ordinary cardboard box and removed a small plastic container. "Only one. I'll have to restock this item. I don't have the room to keep more than one of any item on the shelves. There are instructions on the side which I presume your wizard will know how to interpret."

"I'm sure he will," Jon-Tom said, reaching relievedly for the container.

"Stop right there, please."

Jon-Tom whirled. Roseroar growled and reached for her swords as Mudge tried to ready his longbow.

"Don't!"

A figure emerged from behind a translucent crate containing frozen flowers and came toward them. In his hands Jalwar held something resembling a multiple crossbow. At least three dozen lethal-looking little darts were clustered in concentric circles at the tip of the weapon.

"Poison. Enough to kill all of you at once. Even you, mistress of long teeth." Roseroar continued to glower at the new arrival, but let her paws fall slowly from the hilts of her swords.

"A wise decision," Jalwar told her.

Jon-Tom was staring past him. "Folly. Where's Folly?" When the ferret did not immediately reply, Jon-Tom felt a surge of excitement despite the precariousness of the situation. "So she *didn't* go with you voluntarily, did she!"

"No." Jalwar made the admission indifferently. "But she came, and that was all I required. I needed assistance in hauling rudimentary supplies, and she struck me as the easiest of all of you to manipulate. As a beast of burden she proved adequate.'' He smiled thinly, enjoying himself. ''Then, too, the destruction of innocence has always appealed to me, and she still had a little left.''

Jon-Tom struggled to restrain himself. He didn't for a second doubt the lethality of those multiple darts or Jalwar's willingness to employ them.

''Where is she? What have you done with her?''

''In good time I will tell you, my impetuous blind friend.'' The ferret cocked an eye toward Snooth. ''So that is the precious medicine our friend Clothahump requires so desperately. How interesting. I suddenly feel the need for some medication myself. You, proprietress! I'll take that container, if you don't mind.''

''Take a 'elluva lot more than that to cure wot ails you, mate,'' said Mudge insultingly.

''You think so, do you? Yet I am not so sick that I have failed to outwit you all. I did not think you would make it here without the map, and in my confidence I slowed my approach. I thought in any event that with the aid of my help I would always know your location. Indeed, without that help I would not have been able to rush in close on your heels and track your progress within this place from two aisles over.''

''What help?'' Jon-Tom asked warily.

''Now, be that the right tone with which to greet an old comrade, man?'' said a voice Jon-Tom had hoped never to hear again. He turned to his right.

''Corroboc.''

The parrot executed a half bow. ''It be right good of you to remember me name. That singing magic you worked on me ship, that be my fault for not guessing you had more than entertainment for old Corroboc in mind. But I'm not the one to dwell on old regrets. No, not I, even though me worthless crew chose a new captain and set me adrift barely within flying range o' the mainland.

''There I found your strange boat and picked up your

trail. I knew o' your aims and thought somehow to follow until I found a way o' repayin' you all for your kindnesses to me. In the forest I saw two of you leave from the rest.'' He nodded toward Jalwar.

"When I saw the respect with which he were treatin' me old friend Folly, I thought to meself, now here be one after me own heart. So I settled down for a chat, and after an exchange of pleasantries me and the good ferret here, we came to an understandin', har.''

"That bird will cut out our hearts and dance on them,'' Roseroar whispered to Jon-Tom. "We might as well rush them now.''

"Steady on, you oversized bit o' fluff,'' Mudge warned her. "All the cards 'aven't been dealt yet, wot?''

"Whisper all you want,'' snapped Jalwar. "It will avail you naught.''

Corroboc pulled a short, thin sword from the flying scabbard slung at his waist. Holes in the blade made it light and strong. He caressed the flat side of the blade lovingly.

"Many days have I had to anticipate the pleasures of our reunion. I beg you not to provoke me new friend lest he put an end to you all too quick. I want our meeting to be a memorable experience for all. Aye, memorable! You see, I've no ship, no crew anymore. All I have left to me be this moment, which I don't want to hurry.''

Realization rushed in on Jon-Tom as he turned on Jalwar. "You work for Zancresta, don't you? You've been working for Zancresta from the first! Running into you on the northern shore of the Glittergeist was no coincidence. Those brigands weren't attacking you. It was all a ploy to let you worm yourself into our company.''

"An apt metaphor, Jon-Tom,'' said Roseroar.

"Tell me something,'' Jon-Tom went on quietly. "How much is Zancresta paying you to keep this medicine from Clothahump?''

The ferret burst out laughing, though the business end of

the strange weapon he held did not waver. "Paying me? You idiots! Spellsinger? Pah! *I* am Zancresta! Wizard of Malderpot, supreme master of the arcane arts, diviner of the unknown and parter of the shrouds! Fools, beggars of a humble knowledge, you are blinder than the troglodytes of Tatrath and dumber than the molds that grub out an existence in the cracks between the stones."

The ferret seemed to swell in their eyes as they stared, though neither his size nor shape actually changed. But the curved spine stiffened, the voice was no longer shaky, and an inner unholy light emanated from suddenly bottomless eyes while a barely perceptible dark aura sprang to malevolent life around him.

"I didn't think you'd get this far, none of you! But where a spellsinger, however inept, is involved, there are never any assurances. So when you escaped from Malderpot and my servants lost you in the woods, I determined to find you myself. Your bold and unforeseen move into the Muddletup Moors confused me, I must admit. But only for a time, and I was just able to intercept you on the shores of the Glittergeist and execute my little charade.

"I did not think I would be with you long, but luck and false fortune seemed to follow you wherever you went. Across the ocean, on this kindred spirit's vessel, even into the land of the bellicose enchanted folk. When you not only managed your release from their hands but induced them to assist you with a map, I determined to press on ahead on my own to seek out this Shop of the Aether and Neither and buy up all the necessary medicine before you could arrive.

"And again you surprised me, not out of cleverness or insight, but through blind luck. So Corroboc and I paralleled your progress through this bloated emporium of useless goods, he flying above to check periodically on your position, until you kindly located the object of the quest for me. Which I will now take possession of." He glanced up at Snooth.

"I do not think she has in hand a device or medicine that can save her from the fast-acting effects of hruth venom. Once that container has been handed over I will relieve you of your weapons and leave you to the tender attentions of my patient friend. Perhaps he will grow bored before all of you are dead." Corroboc made neat, thin slices in one of his own feathers with the razor-sharp sword while Zancresta looked suddenly wistful.

"Ah, the day that I stand at that fat fraud's bedside, holding the precious medicine he so desperately requires just beyond his feeble reach, making him plead and beg for it, that will be a day of triumph indeed."

"What have you done with Folly!"

Zancresta came back from his private reverie. "Ah, my pack animal and my insurance. I have never feared you, spellsinger, but your talents act in ways wayward and unpredictable. Sometimes it is awkward to deal with such implausibilities, and I do worry some on the impetuous nature of your companions.

"Knowing of your insipidly tender nature, I took care to keep the girl tightly under my control, lest she foolishly try to run to you for misguided salvation."

"You hypnotized her?"

"I am unfamiliar with the term, but if you mean did I blur her simple mind in order to make her compliant, yes. I no longer have need of her as crude labor or as insurance against your actions, however." He pointed down the aisle.

"These shelves reach far back into the mountain, which you may have noticed is of volcanic origin. I would presume that each aisle ends in a fairly hot place. Perhaps the proprietress stores goods back there that require constant heat. Being of a warm nature myself, I dismissed the girl and bid her wander down to the end of the aisle. She acquired on Corroboc's ship a dark coloration which I venture to say will change rapidly to red as she stumbles into the hot center of this mountain."

Jon-Tom took a step backward and Zancresta raised his peculiar multiple dart-thrower. "Let her go. She is nothing."

There was a flash of gold from behind Roseroar. Again Zancresta raised the weapon, but a feathery hand came down on his arm.

"Nay, let the horned one go," snarled Corroboc. "I've no real quarrel with him. He won't be in time to save the girl and I want these three left alive and conscious." He started toward the ladder, sword in one hand, the other outstretched toward Snooth. "The medicine, if you please, hag."

"As you wish."

"No!" Jon-Tom shouted. "Don't give it to him!"

The kangaroo's reply was firm. "I am not a party to what is a private quarrel. This is between you and him." She handed over the precious container. "Here, catch." At the last instant she tossed it toward the pirate captain.

Corroboc grabbed for the small plastic cylinder and missed. It struck the floor, vaporizing instantly and spitting out a thick cloud of black smoke.

Jon-Tom threw himself sideways and down. The dart-thrower twanged and something struck his boot while others thunked harmlessly into the back of his thick snake-skin cape. He heard no screams of pain and prayed that his friends had also managed to dodge Zancresta's weapon. He started to rise, preparing to do battle with his staff, when it occurred to him that in a hand-to-hand fight Roseroar's swords and Mudge's bow would be more effective, and that, in any case, they had a sorcerer to deal with now. So he put the ramwood aside and fumbled with the duar. An old Moody Blues tune came to mind, suitable for combating evil. He played and sang.

It had its intended effect. As the smoke began to dissipate he could hear the ferret moan, see him staggering backwards clutching at his head.

But Zancresta was not to be so simply vanquished.

Gathering his strength, he glared at Jon-Tom and began to recite:

> "Nails of rails and coils of toil,
> Come to me now, rise to a boil,
> Become with strength my herpetological foil!"

The sorcerer's fingers stretched, elongated, became powerful constrictors that writhed and curled toward Jon-Tom.

Whether it was out of fear for Folly or for himself or sheer anger, he couldn't say, but now the music flowed easily through him. Without missing a bar he segued straight into a slithering song by Jefferson Airplane. The snakes shriveled and shrank to become ferret fingers once more.

A second time Zancresta threw out his hands toward Jon-Tom.

> "Xyleum, phylum, cellulose constrained,
> Hypoblastic hardwood rise up now unrestrained.
> Chlorophyllic transformation make thyself known.
> Long and strong and sharp and straight
> And solid as a stone!"

The wooden stake that materialized to leap at Jon-Tom's chest was the size of a small tree. A few branches erupted from its trunk, and it continued to grow even as it flew toward him, sending out roots and leaves. He barely had time enough to switch to a throaty rendition of Def Lepard's "Pyromania."

The huge, growing spear blew up in a ball of fire. The force of it knocked Zancresta backward to the floor.

It gave Jon-Tom a moment to check on his companions. They were unhurt, but there was plenty of blood on the floor of the aisle. It all came from the same source, and was sticky with green and blue feathers. A beaked skull lay sightless in one place, a leg elsewhere, a pair of wings on a half-empty shelf. More blood stained Roseroar's muzzle and claws. Her swords were still sheathed and clean. She hadn't needed to use them, having dismembered Corroboc as neatly as Jon-Tom would have a fried chicken.

Mudge stepped forward to fire a single arrow at Zancresta. The sorcerer raised a hand, uttered one contemptuous word. The arrow turned rotten before it crumpled against the ferret's hip. Meanwhile Jon-Tom wondered and worried about Folly. If only Drom had time enough to reach her before . . . !

Sensing his opponent's lapse of concentration, Zancresta waved a hand over his head and declaimed stentoriously. A small black cloud appeared in the air between them. Thunder rolled ominously.

Jon-Tom barely had the presence of mind to shout the right words from Procol Harum's "In Held I Was" and hold up the duar in front of him in time to intercept the single bolt of lightning that emerged from the cloud. The instrument absorbed the bolt, though the impact sent him stumbling. The cloud disintegrated.

Now, for the first time, there was a hint of fear in Zancresta's eyes. Fear, but not surrender. Not yet. He stood staring at his opponent, making no effort to draw his torn and ragged clothes tighter about him.

"Not accident, then," he muttered as he stood there. "Not just luck. I worried about that, but in the end gave it little credence. Now I see that I was wrong. You think you've won, don't you? You think you've beaten me?" He looked up at the ladder. Snooth stood on it holding the original container of medicine. Zancresta had been so busy watching Jon-Tom that he hadn't seen the proprietress switch it for the smoke bomb.

"You all think you've beaten me. Well, you haven't. Not Zancresta, you haven't. Because you see, I came prepared to deal with every possibility, no matter how remote or unlikely. Yes, I even came prepared to deal with the chance that this stripling spellsinger might possess some small smidgen of talent "

"Go ahead and try something." Jon-Tom felt ten feet tall. He could feel the power surging inside him, could feel the music fighting to get out. His fingers tingled and the duar was like a third arm. He was riding high, on the same kind of high the stars got when they sang in front of thousands in the big halls and arenas. He stopped just short of levitating.

"Come on, Zancresta," he taunted the sorcerer, "trot out anything you can think of, bring forth all your nastiness! I've got a song for every one of 'em, and when you're finished"—he was already humming silently the last song he planned to sing this day—"when you're finished, Jalwar-Zancresta, I've got a final riff for you."

The ferret pursed his lips and shook his head sadly. "You poor, simple, unwilling immigrant, do you think I'm so easily beaten? I know a hundred powerful conjurations to throw at you, remember a thousand curses. But you are correct. I know that your music could counter them." Something was wrong, Jon-Tom thought. Zancresta ought to have been begging for mercy. Instead, he sounded as confident as ever.

"Your music is strong, spellsinger, but you are feeble here." He tapped his head. "You see, as I said, I came prepared to deal with anything." He looked to his right.

"Charrok, I need you now."

From behind a partly vacant shelf, a new shape appeared. Jon-Tom braced himself for anything, his fingers ready on the duar, his mind full of countering songs. The figure that emerged did not inspire any fear in him, however. In fact, it was singularly unimpressive.

The mockingbird stood barely three feet tall, shorter even than Corroboc. He wore an unusually plain kilt of black on beige and yellow, a single matching yellow vest devoid of adornment, and a single yellow cap.

Zancresta gestured at Jon-Tom. "That's the one I told you about. Do what I paid you to do!"

The mockingbird carefully shook out his wings, then the

rest of his feathers, put flexible wingtips on his hips and cocked his head sideways to eye Jon-Tom.

"I hear tell from Zancresta here that you're the best."

"The best what?"

The mockingbird reached back over a shoulder. Roseroar and Mudge tensed, but the bird produced not an arrow or spear but a thin wooden box overlaid with three sets of strings.

"A syreed," murmured Roseroar.

Charrok nestled the peculiar instrument under one wing and flexed the strong feathers of the other. "Now we're going to learn who's really the best."

"Bugger me for a mayor's mother!" Mudge gasped. "The bloody bastard's a spellsinger 'imself!"

XVI

"That," said the mockingbird with obvious pride, "is just what I am."

"Now, look," said Jon-Tom even as he made sure the duar was resting comfortably against his ribs, "I don't know you and I've no reason to fight you. If you've been listening to what's been going on you know who's on the side of right here and who on the side of evil."

"Evil-schmieval," said the mockingbird. "I'm just a country spellsinger. I don't go around making moral judgments. I just make music. The other I leave to solicitors and judges." Feathers dipped toward multiple strings. "Let's get to it, man."

The voice that emerged from that feathered throat was as sweet and sugary as Jon-Tom's was harsh and uneven, and it covered a range of octaves no human could hope to match.

Well then, Jon-Tom decided grimly as he saw the smile that had appeared on the ferret's face, it was up to him to respond with musical inventiveness, sharper lyrics, and better playing. If nothing else, he could at least match the mockingbird in enthusiasm and sheer volume.

The mountain rattled and the shelving shook. The floor quivered underfoot and stone powder fell from the ceiling as the two spellsingers threw incisive phrases and devastating rhymes at each other. Charrok sang of acid tongues and broken hearts, of mental anguish and crumbling self-esteem. Jon-Tom countered with appropriate verses by Queen and the Stones, by Pat Benatar and Fleetwood Mac. Charrok's clashing chords smashed violently against Jon-Tom's chords by the Clash. The mockingbird even resorted to calling up the defeated warriors of the Plated Folk, and Jon-Tom had to think fast to fight back with the pounding, sensual New Wave of Adam Ant.

As the two singers did battle, Mudge struggled to get a clear shot at Zancresta. The wizard had witnessed several demonstrations of the otter's prowess with the longbow, however, and was careful not to provide him with a decent target.

Jon-Tom was finally forced to pause, no matter the consequences. He was panting hard and his fingers were numb and bloody from nonstop strumming. Worse, his throat stung like cracked suede and he feared creeping hoarseness.

But the arduous duel had taken its toll on his opponent as well. Charrok no longer fluffed out his feathers proudly between songs, nor did he appear quite as confident as he had when the battle had begun.

At which point Jon-Tom thought to try another line of attack entirely.

"That last tune, the one about the drunken elephant with the knife? That was pretty sharp. You got some good riffs in there. I couldn't do that."

"Sometimes," Charrok croaked, "it's harder with fingers than with feathers." He held up his right wing and wiggled the flexible tips for emphasis. "You're not doing too badly yourself, though. What was that bit about dirty deeds done dirt cheap?"

"AC/DC," Jon-Tom replied tiredly. "I thought it might conjure me up a few berserk assassins. No such luck."

"Good try, though," Charrok complimented him. "I could almost feel the knife at my throat."

Zancresta stepped forward, careful to keep the body of his hired instrument between himself and Mudge.

"What is this? I am not paying you to indulge in casual conversation with this man. I am paying you to kill him!"

Charrok turned. His gaze narrowed as he stared up at the sorceror. "You hold on a minute there, Mr. Zancresta, sir. You hired my spellsinging, not my soul."

"Don't get existential with me, you warbling bumpkin! You'll do as you're told!"

Charrok was unperturbed by the sorcerer's outburst. "That's what I've been doing." He nodded toward Jon-Tom. "This fella's mighty damn good. He might, just might, be better than me."

"I don't know who's best and I don't care," Jon-Tom said hastily, "but you sing like a storm and you play like a fiend. I'd appreciate it a lot if you could show me that last song." He strummed an empty chord on the duar. "Maybe I've only got five fingers here, but I'd damn sure like to give it a try."

"I don't know . . . a duar only has two sets of strings and my syreed three. Still, if you dropped a note here and there. . . ." He started to walk over. "Let's have a looksee."

"No fraternizing with the enemy," Zancresta snapped, putting a restraining paw on the mockingbird's shoulder. Charrok shook it off.

"Maybe he ain't my enemy."

"Of course I'm not," said Jon-Tom encouragingly, moving forward himself. "A gig's a gig, but that shouldn't come between a couple of professionals." When Charrok was near enough, Jon-Tom put a comradely arm around the bird's shoulders, having to bend over to do so. "This isn't your fight, singer. Two musician-magicians of our caliber shouldn't be trying to destroy each other. We should be collaborating. Imagine the wizardry we could work! This shouldn't be a duel, it should be a jam session.''

"I'd like that," said Charrok. He searched the aisle beyond. "Where are the berries?"

"Not that kind of jam. I mean we should play together, make music and magic together."

A hand reached out and clutched in frustration at the mockingbird's vest. "I won't have this!" The ferret was jumping up and down on short legs. "I tell you, I won't have it! I've paid you well to serve me in this matter. We have a contract! There is too much at stake here."

"Yea, including my reputation," Charrok told him frostily. "But," he glanced up at Jon-Tom, "that can always be settled between friends. As for your money, you can have it back. I've decided I don't want . . ."

"Look out, mate!" Mudge yelled. The otter threw himself forward, hit Zancresta just in time to make the subtle knife thrust the ferret had been aiming at Jon-Tom beneath Charrok's wing miss. The two went rolling over together on the floor.

"Hold him, suh!" Roseroar thundered as she advanced, ready to remove Zancresta's head from his neck as easily as she would a stopper from a bottle.

But the ferret was scrambling to his feet, leaving a bleeding Mudge lying on the floor. Displaying incredible agility, the sorcerer dodged under Roseroar's wild rush and started climbing up the nearest shelf. Boxes and cartons came flying down at the tigress, who batted the missiles aside impatiently as she tried to locate her quarry. Then she was climbing after him, slowly but relentlessly.

Jon-Tom was bending over Mudge, whose paws were clasped over the knife wound. The otter's eyes were half-closed as he stared up at his companion.

"This is it, guv'nor. I'm on me way out. I'm dyin'. I knew it would come someday, but I never thought it'd be like this, wot? Not in some bloody store 'alfway across the

world. I was meant to die in bed, I was." The limpid
brown eyes were full of sadness and regret. "We 'ad some
good times, though. A few laughs 'ere, narrow escape
there. Cor, 'twere much to be sung of." The eyes closed,
reopened weakly.

"Sorry it 'ad to end like this, mate. If you 'ave a song
left in you to sing you might sing one for old Mudge. Sing
me a song o' gold, spellsinger. If I can't die in bed maybe
I can die under a pile o' gold. Bury me in the damn stuff
and I'll slip away 'appily."

Jon-Tom knelt alongside the limp otter, holding his head
up with one hand. "Mudge," he said quietly, "that knife
didn't go in more than half an inch, and you're not
bleeding that bad. If you want to get gold out of me you're
going to have to do better than that."

The otter fixed him with pleading eyes. "Gold? Why, I
wouldn't try to trick you into conjurin' up me some gold at
a time like this, mate. Would I?" Jon-Tom didn't reply.

Mudge moved his hands, and his eyes went wide with
surprise. "Crikey, would you 'ave a look at this! It's
'ealin' right over, it 'tis! Thanks be to your magic, mate.
I'll never forget this, guv, never!"

"I'll bet you won't," said the disgusted Jon-Tom. He
stood, and Mudge's head bounced off the floor.

"Ow! Damnit, you bloody smart-arsed, know-it-all,
over-sized, shallow-voiced son of a . . . !"

Jon-Tom didn't hear the rest. He'd turned to look down
the aisle. It was full of smoke from conjured lightning and
dust fallen from the ceiling. There was no sign of Zancresta
or the vengeful Roseroar. The fight had moved to another
aisle, another row of shelving. Snooth had also vanished,
which was understandable. The proprietress had retreated
to a place of safety to await the outcome of the fight,
exactly as Jon-Tom would have done had their positions
been reversed.

"Get up, Mudge," Jon-Tom said impatiently. "We've
got to help Roseroar."

The otter rose, still holding a paw over the light wound. "That she-massif doesn't need any 'elp, mate. I'll 'elp you look for 'er, but odds'll get you she finds that bastard Zancresta first." He winced, inspected his knife cut. "Ruined a good vest, 'e did."

"Wait." Jon-Tom squinted into the haze that filled the aisle. "I think she's coming."

But it wasn't Roseroar. It moved on four legs and its golden coat glowed even in the weak light. Clinging to the broad back was the naked form of a young woman toasted pink as a boiled lobster.

Drom trotted to a halt beside them. He was foaming at the mouth and soaked with lather.

"Hot," he told them unnecessarily. "Excruciatingly hot." Folly slid off the unicorn's back into Jon-Tom's arms, barely conscious. "She was walking blindly toward an open lava pit. I got there just in time."

"Jon-Tom." He held her carefully, acutely conscious of the first-degree burn that covered her whole body. "I . . . I didn't know what was happening, what I was doing. Jalwar . . . he made me feel so *strange*. I couldn't think my own thoughts anymore." She leaned against him.

"That morning when he woke me and made me follow him out of our camp, I wanted to cry out, to warn you, but I couldn't. He made me go with him, and he made me fetch and cook and carry for him, but it wasn't me, it wasn't me! It was like I was a prisoner in my own body and I couldn't get out." She was sobbing now, the tears wet against his chest. She leaned back and looked up at him in astonishment.

"I'm crying. I didn't think I could cry anymore."

"You were hypnotized," Jon-Tom told her. When she continued staring at him in puzzlement he explained further. "A kind of magic. You couldn't help yourself." He hugged her to him and when she moaned in pain he was quick to release her. "We'll have to do something about your burn. Maybe Snooth has something. We can buy

medicine for you, too. I still have the three gold pieces
that Mudge didn't lose in Snarken."

"It's all right," she whispered. "I'm all right now."
She turned to Drom. "I wouldn't have been if he hadn't
shown up. I didn't know what to think when he came
galloping down the corridor after me. Then he told me
who he was and that he was a friend of yours and you
were all here inside the mountain with him. That you were
fighting Jalwar-Zancresta." She ran to the unicorn and,
putting her arms around his neck, hugged him gratefully.

Drom tolerated the attention briefly before stepping back
and pulling free. "I am glad to have been of assistance,
madame, but leave us not get carried away with our
emotions."

"But I thought . . ." Folly looked hurt and Jon-Tom
hastened to reassure her.

"Drom's not being unfriendly, Folly. He's just being
himself. I'll explain later." He looked at the unicorn. "It
was a fine bit of rescue work, Drom."

"I try." The unicorn searched the aisle. "Where is the
evil one? And the great feline? Did you defeat him during
my absence?"

"No." Jon-Tom smiled at the mockingbird. "This is
Charrok. When Zancresta discovered that he couldn't defeat me with his own magic, he tried to do it with another
spellsinger. Charrok and I conjured up quite a musical
storm before we came to the conclusion that harmony is
better than dissonance. As for Roseroar, she's gone after
Zancresta."

"I should pity the ferret, then."

"That's the truth, mate," said Mudge. "That's some
broad. If she were only a fourth 'er size."

"You have to learn to think big, Mudge." Jon-Tom
became serious. "Zancresta's as fast on his feet as he is
with his mind. He might give her the slip in here."

" 'E can't get out, though, mate," Mudge commented.
"Unless there's another way in, and I'd bet me tool there's

only the one. I'd say the best we can do now is find that oversized she-rat who runs the place. She 'ad the medicine when the fight started, and I'd wager she's kept it with 'er."

It was a long hike back to the entryway, and Jon-Tom's appraisal of the ferret as being fleet of foot turned out to be accurate, for when they turned up the last aisle Zancresta was already there.

"Ah just missed him in a side aisle," Roseroar rumbled angrily, having rejoined them only moments earlier. "He won't get away this time."

Zancresta's clothes were shredded, and he looked very unwizardly as he stood panting heavily before the exit. A glance down the side aisle showed his tormentors approaching rapidly. There was nothing, however, to prevent his escaping to plot against them from the outside. Nothing except an old female kangaroo.

"Get out of my way, hag! My time is precious and I have none to waste in argument."

"I'm not here to argue with you." Snooth spoke calmly, the pipe dangling from her lips. Her right hand was extended, palm upward. "You owe me payment."

"Payment? Payment for what?" Zancresta snarled impatiently. His enemies were hurrying now, the ferocious tigress in the lead. He did not have much time.

"For damage done to stock and fixtures."

"I was trying to escape from that insane female who even now approaches. You can't hold me responsible for that."

"I hold you responsible for everything," she replied darkly. "You initiated conflict. You interrupted a sale. I forgive you all that, but you must pay for the damage you've caused. I'm not running a philanthropic organization here. This is a business." She gestured with the palm. "Pay up."

"Fool! I said I've no time to argue with you. This little store you have here is a very clever piece of work, I'll admit that. But I am Zancresta of Malderpot and I am not impressed. I give you one chance to get out of my way.''

Snooth did not move. The wizard's paw dipped into an intact pocket and he flung something small and round at her as the kangaroo's hands went to her belly. There was a *crump*! as the small round thing exploded, filling the portal with angry red smoke. Jon-Tom had tried to shout a warning. It came too late.

''Now I will leave over you, hag!''

But there was something else in the doorway now, something besides the uninjured and glowering Snooth. It rose from her pouch, the pouch where Jon-Tom thought he had detected hints of movement before. It rose and grew and it was immediately clear it was no joey, no infant kangaroo. It was far larger, and it expanded as Jon-Tom and his companions slowed to a halt.

Zancresta backed slowly away from the apparition. It enlarged until it reached the roof forty feet overhead, and still it grew, until it could only fit in the cavern by bending low against the rock ceiling.

It had the shape of a red kangaroo, but its face was not the face of a gentle vegetarian like Snooth. The ears were immense, sharply pointed, and hung with thick gold rings. The long snout was full of scimitarlike teeth, and sulfurous eyes centered on tiny black pupils glared downward. Gray smoke encircled and obscured the behemoth's waist, rising lazily from Snooth's pouch. Gorillalike arms hung to the floor, where backturned knuckles rested on the smooth stone.

A bright crimson band encircled the huge forehead. It was inscribed with glowing symbols drawn from an ancient place and time. A thin silken vest flapped in an unfelt wind against the mountainous chest.

And there was the voice. Not gentle and matronly like Snooth's, but awesome in its depth and richness. The apparition spoke, and the earth trembled.

''BEHOLD, ODIOUS IMP, TOILER IN OBSCURITY, MED-

DLER IN INEFFECTUALITY: I AM HARUN AL-ROOJINN, MASTER OF ALL THE SPIRITS OF TIME PAST AND TIME FUTURE WHERE MARSUPIALS RULE AND ALL OTHERS ARE BUT TINY SCURRYING THINGS THAT HIDE IN ROCKS AND FEED ON WORMS! BEHOLD, AND BE AFRAID!" A hand big enough to sail the Glittergeist if fitted out with sails and rigging reached for Zancresta.

The sorcerer cowered back against the shelving. His expression was desperate as he sought refuge and found none. He dropped to his knees and begged.

"Forgive me, forgive me, I did not know!"

"IGNORANCE IS THE EXCUSE OF THE CONTEMPTUOUS," bellowed the djinn. "ABUSERS OF KNOWLEDGE RARELY SEEK ENLIGHTENMENT FROM OTHERS. THOSE WHO TRAMPLE CONVENTION DESERVE NO PITY. THOSE WHO DO NOT PAY WHAT THEY OWE DESERVE TO PERISH."

"I'm sorry!" Zancresta screamed, utterly frantic now. "I was blinded by anger."

"YOU WERE BLINDED BY EGO, WHICH IS FAR WORSE."

"It is a terrible thing to feel inferior to another. I can't stand it. I was overcome with the need to redeem myself, to restore my standing as the greatest practitioner of the mystic arts. All I have done was only for love of my profession." He prostrated himself, arms extended. "I throw myself on your mercy."

"YOU LOVE ONLY YOURSELF, WORM. MERCY? YOU WOULD HAVE SLAIN MY MORTAL TO SAVE A FEW COINS, TO SHOW YOUR DOMINANCE. MERCY? YEA, I WILL GRANT YOU MERCY." The ferret's head lifted, and there was a hopeful look on his tormented face.

"THIS IS MY MERCY: THAT YOU SHALL DIE QUICKLY INSTEAD OF SLOWLY!"

Zancresta shrieked and dodged to his left, but he wasn't fast enough to escape that immense descending hand. The fingers contracted once, and the shriek was not repeated. There was only a quick echo of bones crunching. Jon-Tom and his companions stared numbly.

The hand opened and dropped the jellied smear that had been Jalwar-Zancresta, Wizard of Malderpot.

"I ask you," the djinn muttered in slightly less deafening tones, "you try to run a little business down through the ages and you find eternity full of welchers. Speaking of which"—the massive toothy skull and burning yellow eyes lifted to regard Jon-Tom— "there is more yet to do."

"Hey, wait a minute," said Jon-Tom, starting to back away, "we're ready to pay for what we want. We didn't come here to stiff anybody." He glanced toward Snooth, who only shrugged helplessly. Apparently now that the djinn had been called, she was powerless to control it.

"Pay for your goods you may, but now I have been called forth, and I must also be paid. How will you do that, pale worm? I have no need of your money. Perhaps you will sing me a song so that I may let you leave?" Volcanic laughter filled the Shop of the Aether and Neither.

Jon-Tom felt a hand pushing at him. "Well come on, then, mate," Mudge whispered urgently, "go to it. I'm right 'ere behind you if you need me 'elp."

"You're such a comfort." Still, the otter was right. It was up to him to somehow placate this djinn and get them out of there. But he was exhausted from his duel with Charrok and Zancresta, and worn out from thinking up song after song. He was also more than a little irritated. Not the most sensible attitude to take, perhaps, but he was too tired to care.

"You listen to me, Hargood ali rooge."

The djinn glowered. "I don't like mortals who get my name wrong."

"Okay, I can go with that," Jon-Tom replied, "but you'll have to excuse me. I've had a helluva couple of weeks. We came here to get some medicine for a sick friend. If that old fart hadn't intruded," and he gestured at the smear on the floor, "we'd be out of here and on our way by now. We didn't have a damn thing to do with his actions."

"TRULY YOU WOULD HAVE BEEN ON YOUR WAY, BUT WHICH WAY IS RIGHT AND PROPER FOR YOU TO GO, LITTLE MORTAL?"

"Do you still have the medicine, Snooth?" The kangaroo nodded, opened a fist to show the precious container. A hand the size of a bus lowered to block her from Jon-Tom's sight.

"THE MEDICINE YOU MAY TAKE. IF YOU CAN SATISFY ME. AND YOU HAVE SEEN WHAT HAPPENS TO MERE MORTALS WHO DISPLEASE ME."

Jon-Tom was beginning to understand why Crancularn had acquired a less than favorable reputation among travelers in this part of the world, in spite of the miracles it offered for sale.

"YOU THINK LONG, MORTAL. DO NOT THINK TO TRICK ME BY SOME FOOLISHNESS SUCH AS ASKING ME TO SHRINK MYSELF INTO A BOTTLE." A hand hovered above them and Folly flinched. "I DON'T NEED TO CHANGE MY SIZE TO SHOW MY POWER. ALL I NEED TO DO IS PUT MY THUMB ON YOUR HEAD."

"Whatever happened to the customer's always right?" Jon-Tom shot back.

The djinn hesitated. "WHAT OTHERWORLDLY IDIOCY IS THAT?"

"Just good business practice."

"A MORTAL WITH A KNACK FOR BUSINESS." The djinn looked interested. "I WILL LET YOU PAY WITH YOUR BUSINESS, THEN, AND PERHAPS YOU AND YOUR FRIENDS WILL LEAVE HERE WITH YOUR BONES INTACT. YOU ARE A SPELLSINGER. I HAVE HEARD MANY SPELLSINGERS, BUT NONE THAT PLEASED ME. I DO NOT THINK I KNOW OF ONE FROM YOUR WORLD. SING ME A SPELLSONG OF YOUR WORLD, WORM. SING ME A SONG THAT WILL AMUSE ME, INTRIGUE ME. SING ME SOMETHING DIFFERENT. THEN, AND ONLY THEN, WILL I LET YOU TAKE THE MEDICINE

AND GO!'' The djinn folded arms with thick muscles like
the trunks of great trees.

"THINK CAREFULLY ON WHAT YOU WILL SING. I GROW
IMPATIENT QUICKLY AND WILL NOT ALLOW YOU A SEC-
OND CHANCE.''

Jon-Tom stood sweating and thinking furiously. What
song could he possible sing that would interest this offspring of magic, who had access to the goods of thousands
of worlds? What did he know that might be offbeat and
just weird enough to have some effect on a djinn?

Off to his left Roseroar stood watching him quietly.
Mudge was muttering something like a prayer. Folly paced
anxiously behind him while Drom pawed at the floor and
wished he were outside where he'd at least have a running
chance.

Feathers caressed his neck. "You can do it, colleague.''
Charrok was smiling confidently at him.

Mystical. It had to be overtly mystical, yet not so
specific as to anger the djinn into thinking Jon-Tom was
trying to trick him. What did he know that fit that
description? He was just a hard rocker when he wasn't
studying law. All he knew were the hits, the platinum
songs.

There was only one possibility, one choice. A song full
of implications instead of accusations, mysterious and not
readily comprehended. Something to make the djinn think.

He let his fingers slide over the duar's strings. His throat
was dry but his hoarseness was gone.

"Watch it, mate,'' Mudge warned him.

To his surprise Jon-Tom found he could smile down at
the otter. "No sweat, Mudge.''

"Wot can you sing for 'im 'e don't already 'ave,
guv'nor?'' The otter waved at hand at the endless shelves
crammed with goods from dimensions unknown. "Wot
can you give 'im in song 'e don't already own?''

"A different state of mind,'' Jon-Tom told him softly,
and he began to sing.

He was concerned that the duar would not reproduce the eerie chords correctly. He need not have worried. That endlessly responsive, marvelously versatile instrument duplicated the sounds he drew from memory with perfect fidelity, amplifying them so that they filled the chamber around him. It was a strange, quavering moan, a galvanizing cross between an alien bass fiddle being played by something with twelve hands and the snore of a sleeping brontosaurus. Only one man had ever made sounds quite like that before, and Jon-Tom strained hands and lips to reproduce them.

"If you can just get your mind together," he crooned to the djinn, "and come over to me, we'll watch the sunrise together, from the bottom of the sea."

The words and sounds made no sense to Roseroar, but she could sense they were special. Bits and pieces of broken light began to illuminate the chamber around her. Gneechees, harbingers of magic, had appeared and were swarming around Jon-Tom in all their unseeable beauty.

It was a sign the song was working, and it inspired Jon-Tom to sing harder still. Harun al-Roojinn leaned forward as if to protest, to question, and hesitated. Behind the fiery yellow eyes was a first flicker of uncertainty. Jon-Tom sang on.

"First, have you ever been experienced? Have you ever been experienced?" The djinn drifted back on nonexistent heels. His great burning eyes began to glaze over slightly, as if someone were drawing wax paper across them.

"Well, I have," Jon-Tom murmured. The notes bounced off the walls, rang off the ears of the djinn, who seemed to have acquired a pleasant indifference to those around him.

Jon-Tom's own expression began to drift as he continued to sing, remembering the words, remembering the chords. A brief eternity passed. It was Mudge who reached up to break the trance.

"That's it, mate," he whispered. He shook Jon-Tom hard. "C'mon, guv, snap out o' it." Jon-Tom continued to play on, a beatific expression on his face. The djinn hovered before him like some vast rusty blimp, hands folded over his chest, great claws interlocked, whispering.

"BEAUTIFUL . . . Beautiful . . . beautiful . . ."

"Come *on*, mate!" The otter turned to Roseroar, who was swaying slowly in time to the music, her eyes blank. A thin trickle of drool fell from her mouth. Mudge tried to kick her in the rump, but his foot wouldn't reach that high. So he settled for slapping Folly.

"What . . . what's happening?" She blinked. "Stop hitting me." She focused on the drifting djinn. "What's happened to him? He looks so strange."

" 'E ain't the only one," Mudge snapped. " 'Elp me wake the rest of 'em up."

They managed to revive Drom and Charrok and Roseroar, but Jon-Tom stubbornly refused to return to reality. He was as locked into the deceptively langorous state of mind he'd conjured up as was the target of his song.

"Wake *up*!" Roseroar demanded as she shook him. He turned to her, still playing, and smiled broadly.

"Wake up? But why? Everything's so beautiful." He looked half through her. "Did I ever tell you how beautiful you are?"

Roseroar was taken aback by that one, but only for a moment. "Tell me later, suh." She threw him over her left shoulder and started for the door, keeping a wary eye on the stoned djinn.

"Just a second." Drom paused at the portal and snatched the container of medicine from Snooth's fingers.

"Hey, what about my payment, sonny?"

"You've already been paid, madame." The unicorn used his horn to point at Harun al-Roojinn. "Collect from him." Drom trotted out, through the storeroom of broken devices, through the living area, and out the front door to join his friends.

Snooth watched him go, hands on hips, her expression grim.

"Tourists! I should've known they'd be more trouble than they're worth." She stomped out onto the porch and watched until they'd vanished into the woods. Then she reached inside, found the sign she wanted, hung it on the door, and slammed it shut. The message on the sign was clear enough.

OUT TO LUNCH
BACK IN TEN THOUSAND YEARS

Jon-Tom bounced along on Roseroar's powerful shoulder. Mudge kept pace easily alongside, Folly rode atop the reluctant but soft-hearted Drom, and Charrok scouted their progress from above.

As the Shop of the Aether and Neither receded behind them, Jon-Tom gradually began to emerge from the mental miasma into which he'd plunged both himself and Harun al-Roojinn. Fingers moved less steadily over the duar's strings, and his voice fell to a whisper. He blinked.

" 'E's comin' round," Mudge observed.

"It's about time," said Folly. "What did he do to himself?"

"Some wondrous magic," muttered Drom. "Some powerful otherworldly conjuration."

Mudge snorted and grinned. "Right, mate. What 'e did to the monster was waste 'im. Unfortunately, 'e did 'imself right proud in the process."

Jon-Tom's hand went to his head. "Ooooo." Shifting outlines resolved themselves into the running figure of Mudge.

" 'Angover, mate?"

"No. No, I feel okay." He looked up suddenly, back toward the smoking mountain. "Al-Roojinn?"

"Zonked, skunked, blown-away. A fine a piece o' spellsingin' as was ever done, mate."

"It was the song," Jon-Tom murmured dazedly. "A

good song. A special song. Jimi's best. If anything could dazzle a djinn, I knew it would be that. You can put me down now, Roseroar.'' The tigress set him down gently.

"Come on, mate. We'd best keep movin' fast before your spellsong wears off.''

"It's all right, I think." He looked back through the forest toward the mountain. "It's not a restraining song. It's a happy song, a relaxing song. Al-Roojinn didn't seem either happy or relaxed. Maybe he's happy now.''

They followed the winding trail back toward Cranculam and discovered a ghost town populated by slow-moving, nebulous inhabitants who smiled wickedly at them, grinning wraiths that floated in and out of reality. "It's there but some don't see it," Drom had said. Now Jon-Tom understood the unicorn's meaning. The real Cranculam was as insubstantial as smoke, as solid as a dream.

They forced themselves not to run as they left the town behind, heading for the familiar woods and the long walk back to far-distant Lynchbany. Somewhere off to the right came the grind of the ATC, but this time the helpful rabbit, be he real or wraith, did not put in an appearance. Once Jon-Tom glanced back to reassure himself that he'd actually been in Cranculam, but instead of a crumbling old town, he thought he saw a vast bubbling cauldron alive with dancing, laughing demons. He shuddered and didn't look back again.

By evening they were all too exhausted to care if Al-Roojinn and a dozen vengeful cousins were hot on their trail or not. Mudge and Roseroar built a fire while the others collapsed.

"I think we're safe now," Jon-Tom told them. He ran both hands through his long hair, suddenly sat up sharply. "The medicine! What about the—!''

"Easy, mate." Mudge extracted the container from a pocket. " 'Ere she be, nice and tidy.''

Jon-Tom examined the bottle. It was such a small thing on which to have expended so much effort, barely an inch

high and half again as wide. It was fashioned of plain
white plastic with a screw-on cap of unfamiliar design.

"I wonder what it is." He started to unscrew the top.

"Just a minim, mate," said Mudge sharply, nodding at
the container. "Do you think that's wise? I know you're a
spellsinger and all that, but maybe there's a special reason
for that little bottle bein' tight-sealed the way it is."

"Any container of medicine would be sealed," Jon-Tom
responded. "If there was any danger, Clothahump would
have warned me not to open it." Another twist and the cap
was off, rendering further argument futile.

He stared at the contents, then held the bottle under his
nose and sniffed.

"Well," asked Drom curiously, "do you have any idea
what it is?"

Jon-Tom ignored the unicorn. Frowning, he turned the
bottle upside down and dumped one of several tablets into
his palm. He eyed it uncertainly, and before anyone could
stop him, licked it. He sat and smacked his lips thoughtfully.

Abruptly his face contorted and his expression under-
went a horrible, dramatic change. His eyes bugged and a
hateful grimace twisted his mouth. As he rose his hands
were trembling visibly and he clutched the bottle so hard
his fingers whitened.

"It's got him!" Folly stumbled back toward the bushes.
"Something's got him!"

"Roseroar!" Mudge shouted. "Get 'im down! I'll find
some vines to tie 'im with!" He rushed toward the trees.

"No," Jon-Tom growled tightly. "No." His face fell as
he stared at the bottle. Then he drew back his hand and
made as if to fling the plastic container and its priceless
contents into the deep woods. At the last instant he
stopped himself. Now he was smiling malevolently at the
tablet in his hand.

"No. We're going to take it back. Take it back so that
Clothahump can see it. Can see what we crossed half a
world and nearly died a dozen times to bring him." He

stared at his uneasy companions. "This is the medicine. This will cure him. I'm sure it will. Then, when the pain has left his body and he is whole and healthy again, I'll strangle him with my bare hands!"

"Ah don't understand yo, Jon-Tom. What's wrong if that's the right medicine?"

"What's wrong? I'll tell you what's wrong." He shook the bottle at her. "It's acetylsalicylic acid, that's what's wrong!" Suddenly the anger went out of him, and he sat back down heavily on a fallen tree. "Why didn't I think that might be it? Why?"

Mudge fought to pronounce the peculiar, otherworldly word, failed miserably. "You mean you know wot the bloody stuff is?"

"Know it?" Jon-Tom lifted tired eyes to the otter. "You remember when I arrived in this world, Mudge?"

"Now, that would be a 'ard day to forget, mate. I nearly spilled your guts all over a field o' flowers."

"Do you remember what I was wearing?"

Mudge's face screwed up in remembrance. "That funny tight shirt and them odd pants."

"Jeans, Mudge, jeans. I had a few things with me when Clothahump accidently brought me over. My watch, which doesn't work anymore because the batteries are dead."

"Spell's worn out, you mean."

"Let's don't get into that now, okay? My watch, a lighter, a few keys in a small metal box, and another small box about this big." He traced an outline in the air in front of him.

"The second box held a few little items I always carried with me for unexpected emergencies. Some Pepto-Bismol tablets for an upset stomach, a couple of Band-Aids, a few blue tablets whose purpose we won't discuss in mixed company, and some white tablets. Do you remember the white tablets, Mudge?"

The otter shook his head. "I wouldn't 'ave a looksee

through your personal things, mate.'' Besides, he'd been interrupted before he could get the two boxes opened.

"Those tablets were just like these, Mudge. Just like these.'' He stared dumbly at the bottle he held. "Acetylsalicylic acid. Aspirin, plain old ordinary everyday aspirin."

"Ah guess it ain't so ordinary hereabouts," said Roseroar.

"Now, mate," said Mudge soothingly, "'is wizardship couldn't 'ave known you 'ad some in your back pocket all along, now could 'e? It were a sad mistake, but an 'onest one."

"You think so? Clothahump knows *everything*."

"Then why send us across 'alf the world to find somethin' 'e already 'ad in 'is 'ouse?"

"To test me. To test my loyalty. He's grooming me to take his place someday if he can't send me home, and he has to make sure I'm up to the reputation he's going to leave behind. So he keeps testing me."

"Are you tellin' me, mate," muttered Mudge carefully, "that this 'ole damn dangerous trip was unnecessary from the beginnin'? That this 'ere glorious quest could've been left undone and we could've stayed comfy an' warm back in the Bellwoods, doin' civilized work like gettin' laid an' drunk?"

Jon-Tom nodded sadly. "I'm afraid so."

Mudge's reaction was not what Jon-Tom expected. He anticipated a replay of his own sudden fury, at least. Instead, the otter clasped his hands to his belly, bent over, and fell to the ground, where he commenced to roll wildly about while laughing uncontrollably. A moment later Drom's own amused, high-pitched whinny filled the woods, while Roseroar was unable to restrain her own more dignified but just as heartfelt hysteria.

"What are you laughing about? You idiots, we nearly got killed half a dozen times on this journey! So what are you laughing about?" For some reason this only made his companions laugh all the harder.

Except for one. Soft hands were around his neck and still softer flesh in his lap as Folly sat down on his thighs.

"I understand, Jon-Tom. I feel sorry for you. I'll always understand and I'll never laugh at you."

He struggled to squirm free of her grasp. This was difficult since she was seated squarely in his lap and had locked her hands tightly behind his neck.

"Folly," he said as he wrestled with her, "I've told you before that there can't be anything between us! For one thing, I already have a lady, and for another, you're too young."

She grinned winsomely. "But she's half a world away from here, and I'm getting older every day. If you'll give me half a chance, I'll catch up to you." By now the unicorn was lying on his back kicking weakly at the air, and Mudge was laughing hard enough to cry. Jon-Tom fought to free himself and failed each time he tried, because his hands kept contacting disconcerting objects.

Mudge looked up at his friend. Tears ran down his face and formed droplets on the ends of his whiskers. "'Ow are you going to magic your way out o' *this* one, spellslinger?" Something nudged him from behind, and he saw that the unicorn had crawled over close to him.

"Small you may be, otter, but you are most admirable in so many ways. I look forward to joining you on your homeward journey. It will give us the chance to get to know each other better. And it is said that where there is a will, there is a way." He nuzzled the wide-eyed otter's haunches.

Then it was Jon-Tom's turn to laugh. . . .

ALIEN³

novelization by
Alan Dean Foster

based on a screenplay by
David Gler & Walter Hill and *Larry Ferguson*

Story by
Vincent Ward

Here, even the wind screams. Abandoned hulks of machinery rust in the colourless landscape. Dark, oily seas beat against a jagged black shore. And the remnants of a re-entry space vehicle crash into the rough waves.

In it sleeps Ripley, a woman who has battled the Enemy twice. It killed her whole crew the first time. The second time, it slaughtered a spaceload of death-dealing Marines. Now on this prison planet that houses only a horde of defiant, captive men, she will have to fight the ultimate alien horror one more time.

Before it rips apart a whole world . . .

FICTION

☐	Alien	Alan Dean Foster	£4.50
☐	Aliens	Alan Dean Foster	£4.50
☐	Alien³	Alan Dean Foster	£4.50
☐	Spellsinger	Alan Dean Foster	£4.99
☐	Spellsinger 2	Alan Dean Foster	£4.99
☐	Spellsinger 3	Alan Dean Foster	£3.99
☐	Spellsinger 4	Alan Dean Foster	£4.50
☐	Spellsinger 5	Alan Dean Foster	£4.50
☐	Spellsinger 6	Alan Dean Foster	£4.50
☐	Cyber Way	Alan Dean Foster	£4.99
☐	Cat-a-Lyst	Alan Dean Foster	£4.99
☐	Codgerspace	Alan Dean Foster	£4.99

Orbit now offers an exciting range of quality titles by both established and new authors. All of the books in this series are available from:

Little, Brown and Company (UK) Limited,
P.O. Box 11,
Falmouth,
Cornwall TR10 9EN.

Alternatively you may fax your order to the above address. Fax No. 0326 376423.

Payments can be made as follows: cheque, postal order (payable to Little, Brown and Company) or by credit cards, Visa/Access. Do not send cash or currency. UK customers and B.F.P.O. please allow £1.00 for postage and packing for the first book, plus 50p for the second book, plus 30p for each additional book up to a maximum charge of £3.00 (7 books plus).

Overseas customers including Ireland, please allow £2.00 for the first book plus £1.00 for the second book, plus 50p for each additional book.

NAME (Block Letters) ....

....

ADDRESS ....

....

....

☐ I enclose my remittance for _____

☐ I wish to pay by Access/Visa Card

Number ☐☐☐☐☐☐☐☐☐☐☐☐☐☐☐☐

Card Expiry Date ☐☐☐☐